YOU WERE

NEVER NOT

MINE

ALSO BY MONICA MURPHY

YOU WERE
NEVER NOT
MINE

NEW YORK TIMES BESTSELLING AUTHOR
MONICA MURPHY

Entangled Publishing, LLC
644 Shrewsbury Commons Ave., STE 181
Shrewsbury, PA 17361
rights@entangledpublishing.com

Amara is an imprint of Entangled Publishing, LLC.

Visit our website at www.entangledpublishing.com.

Edited by Rebecca Barney
Cover design by LJ Anderson, Mayhem Cover Creations
Edge design by Bree Archer
Stock art by bounward/GettyImages,
Larysa Oblovatna/GettyImages, and saemilee/GettyImages
Interior design by Britt Marczak

ISBN 978-1-64937-887-3

Manufactured in the United States of America

First Edition June 2025

10 9 8 7 6 5 4 3 2 1

To the Whit Lancaster lovers out there - this one is for you

PLAYLIST

"Home to Another One" - Madison Beer

"Conceited" - Lola Young

"every day is a game" - Night Tapes

"Unrequited Love" - Ella Walton

"Super Sonic" - Alex Amor

"Please Please Please" - Sabrina Carpenter

"Designer" - Tokyo Tea Room

"Let Go" - Emily Rowed

"Disillusioned (with serpentwithfeet)" - Daniel Caesar, serpentwithfeet

Find the rest of the *You Were Never Not Mine* playlist here: https://spoti.fi/42mOHc3

Or scan the QR code below:

PROLOGUE

SINCLAIR

THE PAST

I can feel their eyes on us before I can even make out their faces. The row of boys leaning against the brick half-wall that surrounds the campus. Their body language gives off complete boredom, but I can feel the anticipation ripple in the air, and they're a part of it. Giving off vibes that can't be denied—what a privilege it is, to be on this campus. It's the first day of school at Lancaster Prep on a crisp, faux fall day, despite it being early September on the East Coast. The heat wave that's come over the region makes the mornings pleasant, with a faint chill in the air, but the afternoons can be brutal.

No one out here cares about the weather though, least of all me. Despite the apprehension currently flowing through my veins, I'm eager to see the boys. We've been warned of this ritual before we even came to the campus in the group text that was formed soon after our admission into the most prestigious boarding school in the country.

Every year on the first day of school, the senior boys of Lancaster Prep lie in wait, judging the incoming freshman girls on their beauty and personality, ultimately deeming which ones are worthy of popularity and which ones...

Aren't.

The moment I heard about this, I was disgusted—and intrigued. It's an archaic, despicable tradition that has only recently been brought back to life. Demeaning and classless. Sexist and misogynistic, yet here we all are. The entirety of the freshman class—well, the girls—giddy and nervous, our blood pumping and our heads buzzing. Our hair perfect and our makeup probably layered on too thick because we're all trying to appear older than we are, desperate to impress the senior boys. Despite our awkward bodies and itchy uniforms with the too-long skirts, we still think we look grown-up. This is a big deal. We're in high school now and finally, *finally* on our way to adulthood.

Glancing at the other girls clustered around me, my gaze zeroes in on their waists. I can see where the material is bunched up around their middles, the hem of the normally modest skirts hitting about mid-thigh. Some are even shorter and I realize my misstep.

Panicked, I hitch up my skirt too, wincing when I feel my long-sleeved button-up shirt gather around my waist along with the excess fabric of the skirt. I already have long legs, which causes anything short to look even shorter on me, but I don't care. Maybe the boys will like my legs. Anyway, I want to be accepted.

I want to belong.

"Oh my God, there *he* is." They say he as if we should all know who it is, and we do. This particular boy doesn't need a name because we understand exactly who she's referring to.

August Lancaster.

The Lancasters rule the school, which is fitting because their family has owned it for generations. When there's a Lancaster on campus, they are undeniably the most popular student in attendance. And August Lancaster rules above all. He comes from the most powerful family within the Lancaster enclave. He's the eldest son of Whit and Summer Lancaster, the oldest of three and by far the most well-known member of his generation of the family. No one messes with August. Everyone wants to be in his favor, and to defy him, to earn his disgust or worse—his disdain—is social suicide.

"Get in good with the Lancasters," my mother told me on move-in day when my parents dropped me off—it's been a mantra on repeat throughout the summer from my mom—that gleam in her eyes a reminder that she is always scheming. Trying to up her social status. The Lancasters equal money in her eyes and she is always down for that. Money has lately become her favorite thing, especially considering my parents came into a bunch of it.

"Ugh, he's gorgeous. I hate him," says another girl, her tone telling me she doesn't hate him at all. Her face is familiar—they all are—but I don't remember her name. It's been nothing but a flurry of welcome meetings since I arrived on campus, and while I remember the girl who just uttered that sentence went on vacation this summer in Turks and Caicos and has a nice tan to prove it that makes her blue eyes pop, I can't for the life of me recall her name.

"What I'm experiencing whenever I see him doesn't feel like hate. Not even close," another girl says and I can't help it. I'm too curious to let that one go.

"What are you feeling then?" I ask her.

The group of girls I'm with goes silent. Every single one of them. I slow my steps and scan their faces, hating what I see because I recognize it. I've seen this sort of expression before. Barely contained amusement, all at my expense.

A sigh leaves me and I brace myself for what's about to come.

"How old are you again?" one of them asks, her gaze narrowing as she stares at me.

"I'm a freshman like the rest of you." I lift my chin, hoping I don't sound as embarrassed as I feel.

"Right, but what are you, like...twelve?"

The other girls titter nervously and I take a step back from the one who's currently watching me with a faint sneer curling her upper lip.

"I'm fourteen." The two words leave my throat on a rasp and I swallow hard, averting my head, my gaze landing on the line of boys slouching against the bridge ledge, their expressions turning impatient.

Oh. The realization hits me the longer I watch them. These are not boys. They look more like men. They're all tall and broad and devastatingly handsome. Like every single one of them. They fill out their uniform suits as if they were custom tailored to drape their frames perfectly. Their faces are chiseled from stone and their hair is longish on top and artfully messy, the strands blowing around in the gentle breeze.

There's one who stands the tallest out of all of them though. He's in the dead center of the group, his dark blond hair fluttering across his forehead and getting in his eyes. He angrily swipes it away with long, elegant fingers, his icy cold glare landing directly on me.

I recoil automatically, taking such a big step back that I run into one of the girls who not so gently pushes me out of her way the moment our bodies collide. Laughter rings in the air and I send her a questioning look, trying to ignore the way they're all ridiculing me.

The disappointment fills me as I turn my back on them. I don't fit in here. At all. And I have no idea why. Can they see it on me that I'm not actually like them? My family has never been what anyone would call wealthy until the last few months.

"Come on, girls!" one of the boys suddenly yells, clapping his hands together three times and startling all of us into action. "Show us what you've got!"

I follow along with the other girls, grateful they've forgotten about me. We're standing in a row in front of the seniors, most of the girls flicking their hair over their shoulders, thrusting their chests out. Trying to look more...sultry? I think that's what they're aiming for, but they just look foolish because, come on. We're all fourteen, maybe fifteen tops, and we don't know anything about being sexy.

Well, save for the one girl in our class who's absolutely stunning. I remember her name. Raina. Her long dark hair with the perfect waves that cascade down her back and her perfect body with curves in all the right places. She's more developed than any of us, especially me. What's worse is she's nice so you can't even hate her for being so beautiful.

Not that I'd hate her for such a superficial reason but...maybe I would.

Yeah. I probably would.

We shuffle and shift positions, excited whispers sounding among us, and the boy who clapped the first time around does it again. We go silent and when I stare straight ahead, I see that I'm in the center of the line. Standing in front of the meanest looking one of the bunch, and the most handsome too. I feel a pointy elbow jab me in the side and when I jerk my gaze to the right, I find said owner of the pointy elbow inclining her head toward the mean boy.

"That's August," she whispers, her eyes wide.

I nod, the implication of what she's said sinking into my brain. This is the boy who my mother wants me to...what? Entice into a relationship so we can make a great marriage and Mom will have forever access to the Lancaster social status?

Please. This boy—excuse me, *man*—is going to dismiss me in an instant.

The boys launch into their assessment, all of them having something to say about us while we can only stand there and take it. The warning bell hasn't rung yet. We're all supposed to be in the assembly room for the first day of school speech and orientation. I'm feeling anxious, eager to get going because one thing I hate is being late, and I nearly jump out of my skin when I hear a harsh male voice.

"You. Come here."

My gaze finds August Lancaster's and I realize he's speaking to me.

Oh God. I can't move. I can't even speak. I'm completely frozen, staring at him as if he just sprouted two heads and he's about to attack me. The longer I just stand there speechless, the more pissed off he becomes.

"What the fuck? Are you *dumb?*" A few of the boys start to laugh and he sends them a menacing look, cutting off their laughter in an instant. When he turns his attention back to me, he squints, tilting his head to the side. My body faintly shakes as his gaze rakes over me from head to toe, making my skin tingle. And not in a bad way either, which leaves me even more confused. "I said, come here."

I take a step forward as if I have no control of myself, bowing my head for a moment, trying to gather my courage to face him. I hate how easily he commanded me. I did what he said like I'm a trained pet.

"Hmm." I glance up to find him considering me, tugging on his bottom lip with his thumb and index finger. His mouth is a flushed, deep red. His lips are lush and look soft, though I'm sure they're actually hard and demanding. A man like him would never kiss a girl softly. He'd kiss with pure intent, never letting up until he got what he wanted.

My heart flutters in my chest and my skin goes hot from the way he's studying me. His gaze meets mine once more and we stare at each other for a moment too long and I frown, confused. But then I can tell by the slight curl of his upper lip that suddenly appears—he doesn't like what he sees.

"Skinny legs," he announces, his deep voice ringing loud so that everyone can hear him. "Flat chested. Built like a boy and she's probably boring too." His gaze flickers away from me and

I'm dismissed, just like that. "Next."

My jaw drops and I'm gaping at him, the horror washing over me slowly as the girls laugh at me, their relief apparent because they're so glad I'm not them. All while I stand there with my head hanging down, staring at my flat chest and wishing I could run. I've never been more humiliated in my life. Did he really say I was built like a boy? And he called me boring? He doesn't even know me. How can he sum me up in a few choice words by looking at me for a couple of seconds?

I don't care if he's a Lancaster. This guy is a dick.

And this dick just lifted his hand into the air and snapped his fingers at...me?

"Did you hear me?" His tone is bored, as is the expression on his stupidly handsome face, and I snap my jaw shut, wishing I could come up with a proper insult. But I know better. To say something to him in return would be asking for trouble. "Get out of here. We're not interested in you."

"Not even close," says the one who's standing next to him. He's dark haired with eyes the color of obsidian and I physically recoil when our gazes lock. I can feel the bad vibes coming off of him even from this far.

Turning on my heel, I scurry away, my hurried steps taking me as far as I can possibly get. No cruel laughter trails after me, but I can hear him bark out a demand at another girl and I glance over my shoulder, coming to a stop when I realize he's looking at Raina.

Beautiful, perfect Raina who stands tall and proud before him, a barely-there smile curving her luscious lips.

August is quiet for a moment, scrutinizing her almost as thoroughly as he did to me.

"You'll do," he tells her, not impressed whatsoever, but she smiles broadly, pleased by his approval. She glances back at the rest of the girls, the triumph on her pretty face obvious and my heart sinks.

God, this school is ridiculous. And I'm supposed to endure the next four years here, dealing with this sort of horrific behavior and misogynistic attitudes? Not that I have much say at all here, but still. I hate this place. More than anything?

I hate August Lancaster.

CHAPTER ONE

SINCLAIR

FOUR YEARS LATER

PRESENT DAY

"**G**od, you're so slow. Come on, Sinclair. Pick it up!" My roommate and newest friend Elise comes to a complete stop in the middle of the sidewalk, her exasperation obvious as she gawks at me. "From the way you're acting, I'm starting to think you don't even want to go to this party."

"I don't." I've been telling her that since she first informed me that we were going. Like I didn't have a choice. "You already know this."

"Oh, come on." Elise's tone turns pleading, her eyes going wide. We've only been on campus for a month and while I did the boarding school thing throughout the entirety of high school, this is Elise's first time living away from home. And from the moment she arrived, it's like she's doing everything in her power to go wild during the first semester of university life. And going to a party thrown by a particular—and extremely exclusive but wildly popular—frat is top on her wish list. "We're going to have the best time! There are so many hot guys who are in this frat. We'll find boyfriends by the end of the night for sure!"

Her naivety is shocking—and concerning.

"They're all awful, Elise. Not a single one of them wants to be our boyfriend," I remind her for what feels like the hundredth time.

It's laughable, thinking any of them wants to be a boyfriend, especially to girls like us. I'm not knocking myself or Elise, but we're young. Barely eighteen and completely inexperienced. Maybe some of our fellow first years would be interested in us, but strictly for a hookup. And how do I know this?

I went to Lancaster Prep with almost all of them, including the one who shall not be named. He's the president of this brotherhood of assholes—no surprise considering he's king asshole of the world—and this means he basically rules the entire campus, because of course he does. I thought I would only have to suffer that one year at Lancaster dealing with him, but here we go again. I'd hoped to avoid him on campus too. This place is huge and there is no reason for us to interact whatsoever. So why am I willingly walking into the lion's den? "They're only interested in what you can do for them. To them."

"And what exactly can I do for them?" She falls into step beside me, curling her arm through mine and practically dragging me forward so we can keep up with the rest of our new friend group who are all chattering excitedly about the party we're going to. I have a surreal moment of déjà vu and shake my head, telling myself it won't end up like the last time I first encountered *him*. "I'm just little ol' me."

Please. She could do plenty. All of it involving sexual favors. I adore Elise. She's been a great friend and roommate from the moment we met during move-in day. But she's also incredibly naïve and adorably wholesome. She grew up in a very small town where she knew everyone and she has trust issues. Meaning, she trusts every single person she meets.

It's a problem. One that I hope won't eventually hurt her. And it won't, as long as I have anything to do with it.

"I'm sure one of the douchebags will approach you," I start.

She cuts me off by clapping her hands excitedly like she's a five-year-old who was just informed she's getting an ice cream cone for a job well done. "That's exactly what I want! Have you seen the guys in that frat? They're all *gorgeous*."

I swear there are literal stars in her eyes. And Elise isn't wrong. It's just that the gorgeous faces and stellar bodies mask their ugly souls and assholish ways.

"And then one—or maybe a few—of those asshats are going to ask you for a hand job. Or a blow job." Now I'm the one who's dragging Elise while she digs in her heels, trying to get me to stop.

"No way." She snakes her arm away from mine and throws her hands in the air, both of us coming to a stop again. We're going to lose sight of the rest of our group if we keep this up. "You think every guy on this campus is looking to hook up with us and nothing more."

I stare at her with a deadpan expression. "Because they are."

"They're not all that bad." Elise rolls her eyes.

"Yes, they are."

"No, they're not." She starts walking again and I trail after her. "Not every man thinks with his penis, Sinclair. I can't help it if you've had a few bad experiences over the years. I'm the eternal optimist."

I burst out laughing at her using the word penis. Elise rarely curses or uses crude slang words. She's a good girl and I love that for her. I really do. But I also can't always protect her from the scumbags of the earth, which means all of that good girl shine is going to get rubbed off here eventually and she'll end up jaded. Like me.

Not that I have extensive experience with guys. I graduated from high school a dateless wonder. I didn't go to any of the dances with a boy. I've never had a boyfriend. For a while there, I was the absolute laughingstock of the entire school thanks to August Lancaster.

Oh shit. I just thought of his name when I'm not supposed to.

But seriously. He made my first year of high school the most miserable experience of my life. I don't know why or how I became his target, but I was, and it was a nightmare. The things that boy—man—put me through...

A shudder moves through me at the memories.

The moment he graduated from Lancaster Prep, I breathed a sigh of relief. And while I was faintly terrorized at school the beginning of my sophomore year by the boys who were part of his friend group, they eventually left me alone and I was able to walk across campus unscathed. But what came out of my experience with August and his constant harassment for a solid year when I was basically a child?

I trust no one, especially of the male variety. They're the worst. I'm almost proud of my dateless status. I'd rather cruise through life unharmed and untouched than deal with some jackass who gets me to fall hopelessly in love, only for him to dump me hard and leave me a broken, sobbing mess. I saw it enough during high school with the friends I had, and I'm guessing I'm bound to see it happen with my roommate, AKA the eternal optimist.

"Hey." Elise grabs hold of my arm, causing me to stop and I turn to face her. Her expression is grave, her brown eyes wide and unblinking. "If you don't want to go, you don't have to. I just thought..."

Her voice drifts and she goes annoyingly silent.

"You just thought what?" I prompt when she remains quiet.

"That it could be a fun way to meet hot guys!" She rests her hands on her hips. "I mean, who cares about that one guy who ruined your life for a year?" Yes, I told her about him because I had to. "I know you hate him, and he deserves your hatred. He's a dick."

I blink at her, shocked she called him that.

"But there are going to be so many people there, I doubt you'll even run into him," she tacks on. "So...screw that guy! Let go of all of your resentment and have fun for once in your life."

I can't even take offense to what Elise said because she's probably right. The parties that this particular frat hosts are huge. The house will be packed with a variety of people and besides, I'm not even on August Lancaster's radar. I'm sure he hasn't thought about me in years. Like why would he? He dismissed me the moment he first set eyes on me.

Well. Sort of. I still don't understand his fascination with me back then. That's the word I use to describe it because why else would he torment me for so long?

"Though he is superhot." Elise giggles, covering her mouth with her fingertips.

My gaze sharpens the moment it lands on her. "When have you seen him?"

"I've seen photos of him. Everyone knows who he is." She shrugs and starts walking. All I can do is fall into step beside her.

And there's the problem. He's practically a celebrity on this campus, the same as he was back at Lancaster Prep. Everyone knew him and bowed down to him. It was annoying and made him incredibly obnoxious. He thought he was untouchable. Worse?

He was.

"By the way, you look gorgeous," Elise calls from over her shoulder, her steps getting faster. "He'll probably see you and fall instantly in love."

I grimace. "That's the last thing I want."

"Oh, whatever." She waves a dismissive hand. "Don't even worry about that guy. He's not going to know who you are."

CHAPTER TWO

AUGUST

It's another Friday night and there's a wild party currently taking place at the house.

Fucking great.

But what else is new? This is the grind we've been on since I showed up on campus three years ago. The AAO fraternity—Alpha Alpha Omega because of course we have alpha in there twice—has been around since the dawn of time. AKA our founding date, which is 1877. Only the richest, most elite families are allowed into the fraternity, and becoming a member is by invitation only.

Generations of Lancasters have been members, not that many Lancasters have gone to college these last twenty years or so. Not even my father, who had no real interest in going to a university. His interests were strictly in my mother, and that isn't even a joke. He admitted as much to me when I was a preteen and hormonal as fuck.

"Hopefully you'll meet a woman like your mother," he said to me, careful not to give me too many details because that is the last thing I want to know about. "And you'll never want to even look in another woman's direction again."

I adore my mother but that sounded like a death sentence

then and it still does now. Why would I tie myself down with one particular woman when I could have...many? Anybody I want?

"You look like someone pissed in your beer."

I tilt my head to the side, contemplating the glass I'm currently clutching. "First of all, I'm not drinking beer because it does, in fact, taste like what I imagine piss tastes like. And second, what the hell do you care how I look?"

I finally lift my gaze to find my best friend Cyrus Thornhill smiling at me, appearing amused at my expense, which is a normal look for him. He finds me funny, which is unusual because no one finds me amusing, least of all myself. But he's the only person I can tolerate in my presence for an extended period of time, so I allow it.

"You've been in a mood since the semester started." Cyrus settles heavily onto the couch I'm sitting on, jostling me, and I send him a dirty look, which he completely ignores. He comes from a family who made their fortune in biotech—which classifies him as coming from new money, but I don't hold that against him. "What's your problem?"

I say nothing. Just sip on the thirty-year-old scotch that is my personal stash and no one is allowed to drink it. If I catch anyone doing so without my permission, there is always hell to pay.

"You need to get laid." Cyrus's voice is tinged with amusement.

"I had sex last night." I yawn, which I didn't even mean to do, but that's how much it affected me.

"What was her name?"

"I couldn't tell you."

"Hair color?"

I squint as I try to conjure up her face and hair in my memory, but I come up with nothing. "Brown?"

Cyrus chuckles and swipes the glass right out of my hand, draining it in an instant, the motherfucker. "You're guessing."

A sigh leaves me. "I can't remember a thing about her."

Well, that's a lie. I remember how she squealed when she pretended to come. Like I imagine a stuck pig sounds and it filled me with such disgust, my dick deflated like a balloon and I told her to shut the fuck up. Which she did of course, and then proceeded to give me an adequate blow job. I came on her face and told her to leave.

"You're a callous asshole." He hands me back my empty glass then rises to his feet, heading toward the cabinet where I keep my scotch stash.

"Tell me something we don't know." We're in the sitting room at the back of the house and no one else is with us. They know when they see me sitting alone and glowering at everything that I want to be left alone, and they do exactly that. It's a pleasant feeling, knowing you have so much power. But it's also…

Lonely. Thank God for Cyrus.

"You need to find a cause." He grabs a fresh glass for himself and fills it with a generous pour, doing the same for my glass. Within seconds we're both sipping on the finest scotch that slides down my throat smoothly, Cyrus settling back on the couch next to me, his demeanor casual. Like he has all the time in the world and just wants to have a simple chat.

I call bullshit. More like I'm thrown by his approach and don't quite know what he means by using the word cause, not that I'll admit my confusion out loud.

"What the hell are you talking about?" My voice is gruff, my gaze going to the front of the house, which is currently filled to the absolute brim with people. None of them are familiar. Not even most of the guys, and I'm in the damn frat with them. No one interests me. No one matters, save for the man sitting next to me and my family. Everyone else can go to hell.

Why the hell am I here again? I should drop out. My parents wouldn't care. Well, my mom might fret over it for a moment and my father will question my decision-making but otherwise, they won't care. We have more money than we know what to do with.

It's been properly invested to carry us through multiple generations and maybe that's part of the problem.

I'm fucking bored.

Oh I know, poor pitiful me. Rich boy singing the blues. It's pathetic, I get it, but it's true. I'm lonely. Bored. I need some excitement in my life, and I'm wondering if continuing with my education, even though I'm so close to graduating, is a mistake.

"You sit idle in class. Here in the house. During a party for the love of God. You don't even drink to get drunk. It's because you think this shit tastes good." Cyrus takes a sip, making a disgusted face. "It's horrible."

"You have zero class, Copeland." He knows it, too. "It's the finest scotch you can buy."

"And it tastes like shit." He swigs it down like a heathen, finishing it in one gulp while I watch him, my lip curling in faint disgust. "What the fuck do you even stand for, Lancaster?"

I jerk my gaze away from his, watching the front of the house once more, my gaze snagging on the door, which is currently opening. A group of girls enters the house, wearing matching expressions of wide-eyed wonderment as they look around. They all look painfully young and I'm about to blast Cyrus with a scathing response when my gaze snags on one of the girls in particular.

And lingers.

It's the utter contempt that's on her face that catches my attention. All of the other women surrounding her are practically bouncing, they're so delighted to be here. Not her. She's got her arms curled in front of her in pure defensive mode and they're nestled just underneath her tits. They're the perfect size—her tits— not too large and not too flat either. Her hair is a rich, dark brown and flows just past her shoulders. I can't tell what color her eyes are, but it doesn't matter.

There's something about her that feels almost...familiar. Is it because she appears as irritated as I feel? Perhaps. Or is it something else?

"You're staring." Cyrus states the obvious and all I can do is grunt, annoyed that he caught me. "Want me to go get her for you?"

That sounds fucking awful. Like I'm a god and I expect to be served the tastiest morsel in the house—and right now, that would be her. "No."

"Oh, come on. It's the first time I've seen your eyes spark like that in a while."

"My eyes don't spark." I shake my head. Rattle the ice in my now empty glass. When did I finish that off anyway? "Spark. What the hell, Copeland? You sound like you're interested in me romantically."

His laughter is a booming, pleasant sound, but I refuse to smile. That'll only encourage him. "You wish, Lancaster. I could not give a shit what you do—sexually—and apparently you feel the same considering how you can't even remember who you fucked last night."

"They're all the same." I can't look away from her. They're moving as a group deeper into the house, a bunch of my fraternity brothers approaching them. I would guess these women are freshmen. Babies. Probably not even worthy of the word women because they're barely out of high school. I'm not interested.

Yet I am.

"Except for that one," Cyrus observes.

Except for that one.

CHAPTER THREE

SINCLAIR

This house is nothing like I thought it would be. I've watched enough movies and shows to get a general idea of what a frat house typically looks like. Older and a little run-down. Full of guys who are all slobs and can barely keep the place clean. Beer cans stacked everywhere and liquor bottles tipped over, spilling their contents onto the floor. There should be a couple sitting on top of the pool table, making out, and loud music playing and beer pong being played somewhere.

But there's none of that here at Alpha Alpha Omega—God, what a fitting name, right? The interior is immaculate, with plush, oversized midnight-blue velvet couches and glittering chandeliers hanging above us. Portraits of past members line the walls, some of them photographs and the older ones are actual paintings. There's not a single red Solo cup in sight. Everyone is clutching an actual glass and they look expensive, reminding me of my mother's Baccarat highball glasses she never let any of us touch when we were growing up. She was always too afraid we'd break them.

No one is afraid in this house, though. Everywhere I look, someone has a beautiful glass in their hand, filled with a brownish liquid that tells me they are definitely not drinking beer.

What the hell kind of frat party is this anyway?

"It's so quiet in here," I murmur close to Elise's ear.

She sends me a quick look before speaking in a hushed tone. "I feel like I'm in a library."

Huh. This party is a real rager.

"Well hello. What are your names?" We're greeted by a tragically beautiful, dark-haired woman who's watching us with the deepest brown eyes that immediately make me think of sadness, hence the tragic thought. She has a smile on her face, her lips slicked in the deepest ruby red lipstick shade I think I've ever seen. She's dressed in all black and there's not a single logo on display, but I can tell her clothes are expensive. She even smells like money—meaning her perfume is a deep, rich scent that I know is pricey.

"I'm Elise, and this is Sinclair." Elise points at me before flashing that disarming smile of hers at the woman, whose lips don't shift whatsoever.

"Were you invited?" the woman asks, her tone cool.

Elise lifts up on her tiptoes to try and look beyond the woman's shoulder, where the rest of our group is already mingling with the guys. "We're with them."

The woman doesn't even bother looking in the direction Elise is pointing. "You're underage."

Elise's expression turns crestfallen. "Well, ye—"

I nudge her in the ribs extra hard, which makes her stop talking, thank God. "I know practically every man in this room." I rattle off a few names, most of them obscure ones because why would I state the obvious ones? Everyone has heard about them and she'd think I was lying. "I went to school with them."

Her right eyebrow arches perfectly, her disbelief obvious. "And where exactly did you go to school?"

I tilt my chin up and say with as much pride as possible bleeding into my voice, "Lancaster Prep."

And with that answer, she appears duly impressed, which was my plan. "Ah. Well, then. Welcome. My name is Yolanda. I'm the housemother. Would you care for something to drink?"

Well, that was easier than I thought it would be. "Please. Whatever everyone else is having."

"Same," Elise offers weakly.

Yolanda's head inclines toward us. "Will do."

She turns on her heel and hurriedly walks away, off to fix our drinks, I suppose. Elise's shoulders sag the moment she's out of sight.

"You knew just what to say." Her voice is tinged with the faintest hint of awe. "I was panicking."

"You almost agreed with her about being underage and she would've kicked us out." I make a scoffing noise, shaking my head. "What frat cares about how old the partygoers are?"

"I guess this one is different." Elise tilts her head back, taking everything in. "This house is massive. And so clean."

"Here you go." Yolanda appears before us again like magic, a drink in each hand. We take them from her, the both of us murmuring our thank yous. "Enjoy yourselves."

She's gone before we can say anything else, and Elise and I share a look before we each take a sip from the glass.

"Oh God," I choke out once the liquor hits the back of my throat. It burns going down, settling warmly in my stomach. "That's strong."

Elise starts coughing, drawing the attention of pretty much everyone in this house, and all I can do is stand there, patting her on the back awkwardly, sending an apologetic smile at everyone staring, and they all look away from us. Some of them roll their eyes. A few of them even laugh. At Elise. At us.

I don't like any of them. This house—this fraternity—sucks.

"We should leave," I tell my friend once she's composed herself. "This isn't our type of party."

"No, see that's where you're wrong. I think it's definitely your type of party considering you know everyone here. I'm the sore thumb who stands out." Elise sets her glass on a nearby end table, wiping her hands together.

"I don't really know them. I just know *of* them. That's a big difference." I very much kept to myself at Lancaster Prep and never really felt like I belonged there. It doesn't help when the most popular, influential Lancaster calls you out for your flaws and harasses you for a solid year.

"Hey, are you okay?" A tall, golden-haired god is standing at Elise's side, his hand on her elbow, his voice full of concern as is his expression. His cheekbones are sharp and his jaw square and it appears he's been carved out of granite. "Do you need any help?"

I'm about to tell him to leave us alone but then I catch the starstruck look on Elise's face and the way her eyelashes flutter. "The drink—it was just—so strong."

"Ah, whiskey will do that to you. Would you like something else to drink?" His tone is gentle, as is the glow in his hazel eyes, and I press my lips together so I don't say anything to ruin the moment. I don't know him at all. His face isn't familiar, and I can tell Elise is struck dumb by his good looks and attentive ways. I get it, I do.

"Do you have any Trulys?" she asks as he steers her away from me and they both start to walk.

"No, but we'll find something you might like." He sounds amused at her Truly question. I watch them go, about to trail after them because I don't want to be left alone in this house and I know Elise wouldn't mind.

But then a strange feeling spreads over my skin, making every hair on my body stand on end. Someone's watching me. I can tell. And while it's the tiniest bit creepy, there's also something intriguing about it. Who's watching me? Is he as handsome as the man who just basically swept Elise off her feet?

Slowly I turn in the direction where I think the person watching me is standing, anticipation making my movements slow. I lift my head, my gaze searching, landing on the last face I expected to see.

August Lancaster.

Seriously?

We stare at each other from across the room. He's sitting on one of those plush couches, his curious gaze locked on me. He doesn't appear disgusted by my appearance, which throws me a little because I'm not used to him studying me with...God, what is that? Interest?

No freaking way.

His gaze shifts, raking over me slowly, taking me in and for the briefest, strangest moment, I...I like it. My skin tingles everywhere his gaze lands and when it finally returns to mine, I see it. A flicker in those familiar blue eyes that my body automatically responds to with an unfamiliar, clenching sensation between my thighs.

I'm captivated by his attention, my lips parting, my nipples actually hardening behind my bra and I stand a little taller, pushing my hair over my shoulder so it's trailing down my back. Drift my hand down my front like I'm...what? Some sort of seductress set out to entice August Lancaster? The bully of my high school life? The horrible boy who made my life absolute torture?

Clearly, I've lost my mind.

A huff leaves me as I turn on my heel and start walking. Fast. I'm disgusted by my response to him. I have no business thinking that way. He's horrible. A menace. A goddamn monster if I'm being truthful so what the hell was that reaction I had? Is there a secret part of me who wants to be accepted by him? Do I want him to find me attractive?

Maybe. And God, it kills me to even contemplate that thought.

I'm not even paying attention to where I'm going as I move through the cavernous house, my vision blurry. My thoughts hazy. All I can think about is that I need to leave. Get out of here and get away from this boy—man—who would most likely toy with me to get what he wanted and then leave me in the gutter somewhere out in the cold. All alone and crying over him yet again.

Ugh, my thoughts are dramatic and ridiculous. I can't help it.

I blindly push past a cluster of people, then another, ignoring the way one of the girls snaps, "Hey!" when I barely run into her.

"Sorry," I mutter, coming to a brief stop so I can polish off the rest of the liquor that's in the glass I'm still holding. I drink it all in one swallow, ignoring the burn in my throat and waiting for the warmth to coat my stomach, which happens in seconds. Giving me the comfort and the absolute strength that I need to get the hell out of this house and away from August.

I spot the front door that we just walked through only minutes before. It's heavy and darkly stained, with a small square window that's covered in two strips of hammered iron. Looks like something straight out of medieval times and I wonder just how old this stupid house is. I'm reaching for the door handle when I hear a voice. The voice.

His voice.

"In a hurry?"

It's deep and settles all over me like syrup poured on my skin, sweet and sticky and stopping my progress completely. Hanging my head, I take a deep breath, exhaling slowly before I turn to face him. My nemesis.

The most beautiful man I've ever seen.

CHAPTER FOUR

SINCLAIR

I steel my spine along with the spinning out of control emotions that are currently running through me like water when I finally face *the* August Lancaster, lifting my chin up. Trying my best to appear haughty. Completely unaffected by him and his electric proximity.

Because that's what it feels like, standing this close to him. Electric. As if there's a current running between us, drawing me closer to him despite my reluctance. And I'm definitely reluctant. I don't want to be anywhere near this guy. He's the freaking worst.

August tilts his head to the side as he studies me, his gaze still curious, though his face is mostly expressionless. He doesn't want to give away a thing, I'm sure, and I envy him in that moment. That he can appear so unaffected while I'm standing in front of him, rattled to my core.

"Why are you leaving?" His voice is much deeper than I remember and that makes sense, considering it was four years ago when he terrorized me. He's older now. More of a man than ever and God, I can see it in his frame. The impressive height and breadth of him and that look on his chiseled face. I called the guy who approached Elise earlier a golden god but I was mistaken.

The true golden god is August. The rest of the men in this house are mere mortals, while he is Zeus, the ruler of Mount Olympus. My thoughts are ridiculous but come on. *Look* at him. His face is constructed of pure marble. Hard and smooth and made up of clean, sharp lines. The only thing soft are his lips. They're a rich, deep pink, and I'm struck with the sudden urge to kiss them.

I shake my head once, pushing the thought out of my brain. I have clearly lost all sensibility being in this man's presence. I cling to my old hateful feelings, reminding myself that I don't like him. At all.

"Why do you care?" I finally toss out, my tone as snotty as can be. At least my voice isn't shaking, which is a miracle as I am currently trembling from head to toe.

His smile is faint. As if he likes the idea that I was rude to him. "You just got here."

"You were paying attention?"

"I keep watch on everything that happens in this house." He takes a step closer and I practically throw myself against the heavy wooden door, my fingers curling around the handle. "Who are you?"

"No one that matters." I shake my head over and over again, not about to say my name. It's not the most common name there is—Sinclair is my mother's maiden name and since she is one of three sisters, she felt bad that the family name wasn't going to be carried on so she did the next best thing and gave her first daughter her maiden name. I hated it growing up. I always wanted to be named Kylee or Casey or any type of "ee" name because I was surrounded by girls with cutsie names just like that.

His smile is a faint curling of his lush mouth and my heart trips over itself at the sight of it. "I doubt that." His gaze drops to the hand that is still holding the glass. "You want another drink?"

I would be a fool to accept his offer. I need to leave. Now. At this very second.

"Please," is what I say instead, mentally cursing my weakness. He reaches for me and I shrink back, which makes him pause, his brows drawing together. "Care to hand over the glass?"

"Oh." I push away from the door completely, coming closer to him, and I catch a whiff of his cologne. It's spicy and warm and I have the fleeting thought that I want to bathe in it, which is just... what? Oh, I know. Unsettling. "Here."

I hold the glass out to him and he takes it from me, his fingers purposely brushing against mine, sending a jolt of electricity straight up my arm. I contain my reaction to him as best as I can, pressing my lips together. Only for my mouth to fall open when he turns his back to me and starts walking without saying another word.

Go after him, the tiny voice inside my head whispers and I bolt into action, following August as he moves deeper into the house. Until he's in the massive room where I first spotted him, heading straight for the bar that's set up in the farthest corner. There is a variety of cut-glass decanters and containers sitting on the bar and not a single bottle of wine or alcohol with a label in sight. Everything is clean and elegant and absolutely beautiful. Impressive. My family would never—my dad proudly displays the expensive wine and liquor bottles in their home. Always flaunting their wealth once they came into it, while I was uncomfortable about it. I was twelve when my father's startup began amassing actual money. My parents immediately enrolled me in Lancaster Prep without me having any say in where I got to go to high school.

Talk about wealthy. I was surrounded by it my four years there. And while it was intimidating sometimes, no one has as much wealth as a Lancaster. Everyone knew this.

I keep my gaze fixed on the broad expanse of his back as he sets both of our glasses on the counter and refills them. He moves with controlled efficiency, as if he never wastes his time, and within seconds, he's turning to face me, holding the refreshed drink in my direction.

I take it from him without touching his fingers, and I'm secretly proud of this little fact. "Thank you."

"You're welcome." He keeps his gaze fixed on me as he takes a sip, his lips wet from the liquor and the urge to lick them nearly takes me out.

What is wrong with me? I'm not drunk. Well, maybe I'm a little buzzed because I guzzled that first glass of what tasted like very strong alcohol in a matter of minutes.

"I feel like I know you," he eventually says, after we stand there in silence together in front of the bar for what feels like five minutes but is probably only thirty seconds tops.

I slowly shake my head, my lips seemingly attached to the edge of the glass. I take another sip before I answer, the liquid is giving me courage. "Doubtful."

His brows draw together. "Why do you say that?"

"Because I have no idea who you are." The lie comes easy and I'm impressed with myself.

"Really?" His voice drips with doubt, and I get it. He's practically a celebrity on our campus.

I just won't give him the satisfaction that I know who he is. And I'm not about to reveal that we've encountered each other in the past, either. It's shocking how he doesn't recognize me, though I've changed quite a bit from the too-skinny girl with braces on her teeth and pimples on her face.

"Really." I smile and he does too and *oh*. He is devastatingly handsome.

I tear my gaze from his so I don't get too caught up in his good looks, taking another fumbling gulp from my drink. Praying it makes me drunker quicker so I can withstand this conversation that I have no business engaging in.

"Maybe I just recognize something in you that I'm feeling as well," he admits, his voice so low I swear I can feel it vibrating within me.

I jerk my gaze back to his, frowning. "What do you mean?"

"I watched you enter the house. You looked absolutely disgusted at being here. Maybe even a little bored." It's his turn to sip from his glass, never taking his gaze away from mine as he does so. "And my immediate thought when I saw you was, 'I feel the same way that she looks.'"

"Oh." I duck my head, hating that he could read my mood so well. My father always said I would make a terrible poker player and an even worse negotiator, which was a sin in his eyes. My father is the king of negotiators and can keep a straight face through anything. No one can ever read his moods and it's scary sometimes.

August leans in, his cheek almost pressed to mine when he whispers, "Busted."

My entire face heats up at his nearness and he backs away, a knowing smirk on his face.

"The house is beautiful." I look around, taking it all in yet again and the walls are so dark, it almost gives the place an ominous feel. "Nothing like what I thought a fraternity would look like."

"We're not your typical frat." He pauses with the glass directly in front of his lips. "Are you telling me this is the first frat party you've been to?"

I nod, not bothering to speak.

"We've been on campus for over a month. There are parties every week. Almost every day."

I shrug, then drain the last bit of my glass, shocked that it's already gone. "I've been busy."

"With what?"

"School. Studying." I take college seriously because I refuse to be like so many of the other girls my age who get into a prestigious university, party their asses off, get drunk on the daily and end up basically flunking out within the first year, if not the first semester. But it doesn't matter because they'll find some rich boy from a rich family who'll take care of them the rest of their lives as long as they give him babies and are the dutiful wife.

Like my mother. She pretends my father doesn't have affairs and it's fine because he buys her new jewelry whenever he feels guilty, which is often. It's a great arrangement and they don't seem to complain about it, ever.

That's not what I want. I want independence. My own career and my own life where I don't have to rely on a man to take care of me. Am I taking advantage of the fact that my father pays for my expensive college education? Yes. I would be a fool to try and do it on my own. But I'm not going to end up a boring little housewife like every other woman I know.

His smile returns, faint and almost evil looking. "Such a dutiful student."

"I have goals." That's all I say and I can tell he's intrigued.

"What type of goals?"

"I thought about going to medical school." Maybe. Maybe not. I'm focused on getting good grades no matter what I want to do but if I'm being real with myself?

I have no clue what I want to do as a career. How are we expected to know anyway? I'm barely out of high school and I'm supposed to have my entire life mapped out in front of me? Give me a break.

"Ambitious," he murmurs, his gaze dropping to my empty glass. "Want another refill?"

"I shouldn't," I protest as he takes the glass from my grip and turns to refill it, pouring himself more too. "Really. I should go," I tell the broad expanse of his back.

"But we're talking." He faces me once more, pressing the glass against my palm and I take it. "I want to hear more about your goals."

"They're boring." Why does he act interested? He doesn't care. He has no idea who I am. He hasn't even asked my name and I'm sure once I say it to him, he'll remember. And abandon me as quickly as he can.

"You think so?" His brows lift. "Then why are you doing it?"

"To make something of myself."

His gaze drops to the Alhambra sweet bracelet on my wrist. The matching pendant dangling from my neck. "You come from money."

I don't want to tell him how my father made his fortune because it's a tad embarrassing. "My family does well."

"Modest, too. Has anyone ever told you that you're stunning?"

I blink at him, shocked that he would compliment me. I even glance around, making sure no one is lurking in a corner filming our conversation so he can broadcast it on social media. I wouldn't doubt August would do something like that. At least, eighteen-year-old August wouldn't hesitate to humiliate me in that manner.

But there's no one lurking in any dark corners. It's just me and August and he seems…genuine.

"No," I finally say, my voice so soft I wonder if he can hear me. I clear my throat. "No one has ever used that particular word to describe me before."

"It's true," he says without hesitation. "Though I'm not sure if you believe me when I say it."

"I don't."

He appears taken aback by my blunt response, but his expression neutralizes in seconds. That knowing smile is curving his lips once more and yet again, he leans in close to me, his cheek practically pressed to mine when he whispers in my ear, "Guess I'll just have to work extra hard to convince you that I'm telling the truth then."

CHAPTER FIVE

AUGUST

We talk for hours. *Hours.* I have no idea what time it is, and I still don't know her name, but we keep drinking the good scotch that Cyrus hates, and I'm drunk. She is too. The more she drinks, the more animated she becomes. Her golden-brown eyes are sparkling and her cheeks are flushed and the longer I look at her, the more beautiful she becomes. We talk about everything and nothing at all and all I can think about as I watch her mouth move is what she might look like with my cock nestled between her lips and I'm instantly hard.

Aching.

This woman isn't interested in me that way though. I don't think she is, at least, so why am I talking to her again? She doesn't offer up any sultry glances or flirtatious remarks like every other woman at this party who's dying to do exactly that once she gets in my presence.

No, this woman is straightforward and earnest, yet also mysterious and coy. I want to know more. I want to know everything, including how she tastes and what color her nipples are. I imagine they match the shade of her perfectly pink lips, which aren't covered in lipstick or gloss, not even lip balm, which is jarring. Every woman who comes into this place slicks her mouth with an abundance of gloss, and then there's Yolanda. Her lipstick is so damn dark, I don't think I've ever seen her without it and I probably wouldn't recognize her if she showed up not wearing it. She keeps a tube of that stuff in every room possible in this house. I'm fairly certain there's one sitting on my dresser at this very moment that I found in the hallway a few days ago.

Glancing around, I immediately wish I could banish everyone from this house. It's not private enough here. The older I am, the more boundaries I mentally and physically establish. I get sick of my fellow fraternity brothers and their antics, despite the fact I'm supposed to be a good example and lead them. I'm the fraternity president, a position I didn't necessarily want but how could I turn it down when they offered it? If I had my choice, I'd fully move out of this house and never come back. I'm over it. I'm over pretty much everything in life lately, bored out of my skull...

Except for this woman sitting beside me on the velvet couch.

I stretch out my arm, desperate to touch her and I do, drifting my fingers along the inner crook of her elbow. She shivers, jerking her arm away from me and keeping it tucked firmly against her side.

"Can I ask you a question?"

"Sure." She sounds hesitant though and I second-guess myself for a split second before I speak.

"Are you not interested? In me?" I can't help but ask because I'm drunk as fuck and why else would she not respond to me touching her. I can feel the chemistry brewing between us. Swirling all around us. And I don't feel this sort of thing for just any woman.

Maybe I'm drunker than I realize. And I sound like an insecure little fuck which is borderline embarrassing, but again—I'm too inebriated to care.

She laughs and it's the sweetest fucking sound, unlike anything I've heard before. "Why would you ask me that?"

I decide to be honest with her, something I rarely do. "You didn't want me to touch you."

Her smile is demure and she even ducks her head for a moment, watching me through her thick eyelashes. "I'm not here for a hookup."

Well that's a damn shame. All I can think about is getting her naked in my bed. "That's why anyone is here tonight."

"Not me."

"Huh." I'm baffled. "That's too bad."

She lifts her head, her eyes flaring wide. "You *want* to hook up with me? Really?"

"Don't sound so shocked." I keep my voice level, like what she said doesn't bother me but fuck it. It bothers me. "Like I've already told you countless times. You're beautiful."

I clamp my lips shut, hating how forthcoming I'm being. I don't do this sort of thing. A woman has its purposes in my life and that's mostly for fucking. On occasion going to dinner, but damn. That always creates expectations that I can't and won't meet so I don't bother.

Conversing with a woman all night while at a party isn't something I normally do either but this woman is an exception. Have I just fallen for the "she's not like other girls" nonsense?

Apparently so.

She waves a hand as if she's sweeping away what I just said, a little hiccup escaping her. She immediately covers her mouth with said hand, her eyes widening all over again. "You're drunk," she murmurs from beneath her palm.

"No, I think you're the drunk one." I lean forward, carefully removing her hand from her face so I can stare at her unabashedly. "Tell me your name."

"Nope." She shakes her head again and again. To the point I worry she's going to make herself dizzy. "I'm not telling."

"That's unfair."

"Life is unfair." Her eyes narrow. "Someone said that to me once."

Lots of people say that sort of shit all the damn time. "Who told you that?"

"No one important."

"The person must've been somewhat important if you remember them saying that to you."

"Fine." She sighs, the sound almost sad. "My high school bully said it to me after one particular sadistic moment where he tortured me." It's her turn to lean in close and I catch the scent of her perfume. It's rich and sweet and makes my nose twitch in a good way. In a *I want to bury my face in her neck* way.

"Tortured you?" I can hear the anger in my voice. Does she notice? And who the hell would torture her? She's gorgeous. Interesting.

"Not literally, but he was awful. Made my life miserable for an entire year when I was in high school."

"Tell me his name and I'll ruin him," I practically growl. "Financially. Socially. Whatever you want. I'll destroy him."

She throws her head back and laughs and laughs, like I just told her the most hilarious joke. All I can do is watch her, mesmerized by her, and I can't even explain why. She's not impressed by me whatsoever, and I'm used to every person I meet being impressed by me just by hearing my last name. Every woman I encounter wants to get my dick inside her in the hopes that I'll fall madly in love with them and want to marry them. I can treat them like absolute garbage and they lap up my treatment like I'm spoiling them. It's so fucking bizarre. And disappointing.

Not this girl. She claims she doesn't know who I am and I tend to believe her. She doesn't mention anything about the Lancaster family and she's very much at ease with me, despite her reluctance to tell me anything.

There are diamonds in her ears and Van Cleef jewelry hanging from her neck and wrist, which means she definitely comes from money, but so many people who go to this school are wealthy. She's also classy. Her clothing isn't garish and her shoes look expensive, and when you've been around wealthy people your entire life, you can just tell. She has that rich girl air about her, but she's oblivious to who I am and I like it.

And I never thought I'd like that sort of thing. I revel in being August Lancaster. I act like a dick because everyone allows me the privilege. The only person I'm not a dick to is my mother. That woman is a saint. She has to be to stay with my father, because dear old Dad is a bigger dick than I ever could be. I aspire to be exactly like him one day and work hard to emulate Whit Lancaster in every way possible. To the point that it's become second nature. Most of the time, I do a damn good job of it too.

Not tonight though.

"I'm serious," I tell her when the laughter finally dies. "I'll take him out. I know people."

I sound like a mafioso, which is fucking ridiculous, but it's true. I do know people who can do all sorts of things for a price, like my uncle Spencer. When money is no object, you have access to people and their services that the common man wouldn't be able to fathom.

"I appreciate the offer." Her smile is blinding, it's so big. "But he's already dead to me."

CHAPTER SIX

SINCLAIR

The man is oblivious.

Gorgeous and sexy and drunk too, but also completely oblivious to my identity, and I thought he'd recognize me the instant he saw me. Not that I think he *should* remember me. I wasn't that memorable to him back in the day when I was a fourteen-year-old, painfully shy, brace-face with no boobs and awkward AF. Sometimes when I'm being real with myself, I can look back and recognize exactly why he made fun of me. I was ripe for the picking, as the old saying goes. Naïve and vulnerable and desperate to belong. I felt out of place, out of my league and scared out of my mind. He could probably smell the desperation emanating from me and honed right in.

"If you ever need me to take him down, I'm your man," he says with the utmost sincerity. Would he be angry if I started laughing again? Because I'm close to cracking. "But if you want my help, I do have some criteria that needs to be met first."

"Criteria? Such as?" I sound like I'm teasing. Flirting. Finally. I never feel comfortable enough to flirt with any guy—I get too in my head. But I guess all it took was a boatload of horribly strong scotch to loosen me up.

His expression turns deadly serious. "I need to know a few... facts about you first."

"Like what?" I ask warily.

"Your age, first of all."

"Eighteen," I answer without hesitation.

He makes a tsking noise. "You're a baby."

"A legal adult," I correct.

"Still a baby." He hesitates. "Don't you want to know how old I am?"

Oh right. I'm not supposed to know. "Tell me."

"Twenty-two." His smile is lethal. "A lecherous old man compared to you."

"Please." I roll my eyes and cross my arms, looking like—no doubt—a big old baby. "What's your other criteria?"

"Your name." His gaze locks with mine. "I need to know it. Now."

I blink at him, suddenly terrified. There's a lump in my throat I can't swallow past and the truth looms before me. Big and ugly and about to come crashing down upon me the moment I reveal who I am. "I thought you liked the mystery."

"I'm fucking over the mystery." He reaches for me, his fingers tangling with mine for the briefest moment and I don't try to jerk out of his hold. Which is like a small miracle because I don't necessarily like it when people touch me. "Tell me."

"Sinclair," I whisper, bracing myself for the moment he recognizes my name. "Sinclair Miller."

He studies me in silence while I sit in quaking fear, ready for him to burst out laughing when he figures out that I'm the very girl he used to taunt for being ugly. Pathetic. Dumb. "Sinclair."

I nod once, still trembling.

"Sin." His smile becomes pure sin as well. "I like that."

That's all he says and it hits me—he doesn't know who I am. He doesn't recognize my name. This man that has loomed large in my memories for so many years, doesn't recall me at all.

And that pisses me off.

"What's your name?" I toss at him, my tone hostile, which matches my new mood.

"Promise you won't freak out?"

Is he for real right now? "I promise."

A sigh leaves him and he runs his fingers through his golden-brown hair, messing it up in the most adorable way possible. God, he's gorgeous and it's infuriating. "August. August Lancaster."

"Ahhh." That's the only thing that comes out of my mouth and I can tell he hates it.

"That's it? That's all you've got?"

"What do you want me to do? Slobber all over you because you're a Lancaster?"

"Want the truth? That's what usually happens." He shrugs.

"Well, I'm not interested in you like that."

"Really."

"Really," I return, deadpan.

"Prove it."

I'm frowning. "Huh?"

"Prove it." He sprawls his big body across the couch, spreading his legs and patting his thigh. "Come here."

"What? No." I shake my head as he's reaching for my hand, tugging on it until I have no choice but to practically fall into him. He catches me at the last second, his gaze locking with mine.

"Sit on my lap, Sin." His smile is devilish. "See if I can tempt you."

Next thing I know I find myself perched carefully on his hard, muscular thigh, my heart racing, my head spinning. Being this close to him, I can smell his delectable scent. To the point that it's overwhelming me, and not in a bad way. I take in his incredibly smooth skin, the lush curve of his lips, the thick eyelashes that frame his intense, icy blue eyes. He is truly beautiful and the memories come back, one after the other, crowding my brain and reminding me why I hate him.

The taunting sound of his voice. The choice words he used to hurt me. It was like he knew all of my weaknesses and I never understood how he was able to get inside my head like he did.

Maybe he had some sort of sixth sense or something, but it was disconcerting how he left me in shambles every time we had an interaction.

I'm in shambles at this very moment but for different reasons. There's something bubbling between us that I don't recognize and it scares me. Far worse than his humiliating words and the way he used to laugh at me, always coaxing his friends to join in.

I hate him. Sitting on August Lancaster's lap is the opportunity that younger me would've wished for. It would take nothing for me to grab him by the balls and twist until he screamed in pain. Or I could kick him. That might be easier because I could run right after I did it, reveling in the sound of his agonizing groans the moment my foot made contact with his nuts.

I've never done anything like that in my life, but I can envision it and lord help me, it makes me smile.

"You should do that more often," he murmurs.

I jerk my gaze to his, startled. "Do what?"

"Smile." He leans in, mouth mere inches from mine. "Are you tempted yet?"

"N-no." Damn it, my shaky voice just gave me away, because I am tempted. Despite everything, the hate burning in the pit of my stomach, the unease slipping through my blood...

I want to touch him. Just once. Pretend that we don't have a shared past and just revel in him. Something I've never been tempted with before.

"Liar." The smirk that appears on his face is as infuriating as it is appealing. "I bet I could have you naked and screaming in my bed in the next twenty minutes."

The vision his words conjure up leaves me feeling sweaty. "Twenty?"

"Okay. Fifteen." His smile is as cocky as I've ever seen it.

"I would never."

"Oh, but you might." His hand settles on my cheek, angling my head just so. "It would be good between us."

I've never done anything that he's referring to so I have no idea if it would be good or not. Sex doesn't interest me because it involves feelings and feelings are messy. Watching my mother weep in despair after discovering another one of my father's affairs has turned me off of love completely. It doesn't exist. Why bother?

"You don't know that for sure," I whisper because it's like my voice has disappeared, and I don't know where it went. When he threads his fingers into my hair, slightly tugging on the strands, I close my eyes for a moment and enjoy the way he's touching me. Soft yet rough. The contradiction is alluring.

Tempting.

"I can just tell. Can't you?" His lips brush mine in the briefest of kisses. There and gone in an instant but leaving an imprint on my fucking soul if I'm being truthful. My entire body tingles at the short contact, leaving me a quivering mess.

As if he can sense my giving in, he quickly stands, grabbing hold of my hand and keeping me upright and I'm grateful I don't fall. He doesn't say a word to me as he yanks me through the crowds of people in the frat house. Just leads me toward the stairwell and practically runs up the stairs, me trailing behind him, our hands still linked, our fingers curled around each other's. I let him take me down the hall, anticipation buzzing through my veins as he whips out a key from his pants pocket when we stop in front of a closed door. He unlocks it and pulls me inside, shutting the door and pushing me against it.

Our mouths clash, a whimper leaving me when his tongue thrusts between my lips, curling around mine. The kiss is hungry and all-consuming and terrifying, and I rest my hands against his broad chest, desperate to stop him so I can escape.

Instead, it's like my hands have a mind of their own, my fingers curling into the fabric of his shirt, tugging him closer. The moan that ripples through the air startles me, even more so when I realize I'm the one who made the sound. His hands are everywhere, slipping beneath my shirt, his assured fingers drifting across my bare skin and oh God, I feel like I've died and gone to heaven.

Only to realize it's my tormentor who's making me feel this way.

The clarity hits me like someone punched me in the face. *What the hell am I doing, letting August touch me like this? Kiss me like this?*

I push him off of me with a strength I didn't know I had. He stumbles backward, glaring at me. His chest rises and falls at a rapid pace and his lips are damp and swollen from kissing me. I'm filled with the sudden urge to grab hold of him and beg him to do it again but I can't. I won't. I need to take control of this situation.

And get the hell out of here.

"Let's try this..." I clear my throat, trying to channel my inner seductress who's never come out to play before. "In your bed."

The irritation in his eyes clears and he's reaching for my hand again, which I give him willingly. "Best thing you've said all night, Sin."

No one has ever called me that in my life and I shouldn't like it, but I do.

August leads me to the massive bed that's covered in a thick black comforter and trepidation fills me. I've kissed a handful of boys, but I've never done anything else. What this boy did to me freshman year ruined me for the rest of my high school life. Any guy who remembered what I went through wasn't interested and any guy who didn't know or remember and approached me? I turned him down flat. Every single time. That fear always lingers in my head, reminding me that I'm not good enough, that they're all awful. Like him.

The very one who's trying to get me in his bed.

Deciding I need to turn the tables, I let go of his hand and get in front of him, shoving his chest as hard as I can. He has no choice but to fall backward onto the bed and he lies there for a moment with a startled look on his face before he rises up on his elbows, contemplating me with a satisfied smile on his face.

"I like a woman who takes charge."

"Really?" I find that hard to believe. I get the sense that he is a take-charge person at all times and I secretly like it.

No, you don't. He's an asshole who will use you and discard you as quickly as possible. You're doing him a service, putting him in his place.

His smile grows. "Nah. But I'll let you do whatever you want just so I can see you naked. Maybe on your knees with my dick in your mouth?"

My knees literally wobble at his proposition and I lock them, tilting my nose into the air. "I usually don't have dicks in my mouth on the first date."

August bursts out laughing and I swear it sounds rusty. Like he doesn't do it often, which isn't a surprise. I'm sure he sits around and plots people's demise on a regular basis, which doesn't call for much laughter, except for the evil kind. "You're funny, and I don't think anyone is funny."

"I should take that as a compliment?"

"Definitely." He collapses on the bed, staring at the ceiling and I watch as he closes his eyes for a moment. "The room is spinning."

I glance up at the slow-moving ceiling fan above him. "That's just the fan."

He ignores what I said. "I'm drunk as fuck."

"Me too." I shuffle my feet, nearly tripping over them, and I almost fall onto the bed, saving myself at the last second. "I should go."

"No. No way." He rises up like Dracula sitting up in his coffin, back from the dead. All he needs is a cape, his hair slicked back and some sharp canines—he'd make a great vampire. "You can't leave yet."

"It's late."

"I'm horny."

"Sounds like a personal problem."

"Fuck, it is." He flops back onto the bed, shocking me with how honest he's being. And how relaxed he seems. Maybe alcohol is some sort of truth serum? "I just had sex last night. Why do I want you so bad?"

My stomach curdles like I ate something past the expiration date and I take a step back. His confession is like a bucket of cold water poured over my head. "Last night."

"Yeah." He sounds miserable. "I can't even remember her name. Or her face."

Anger washes over me, leaving me cold. A tiny, flickering flame burns low in my belly and I recognize it. It's pure, unadulterated rage.

"Does that make me an asshole?" he asks after I haven't said anything. "I am. I know I am. Ninety-nine percent of the time, I'm okay with it."

"What about the other one percent?"

"Like right now? I hate myself for being so...callous." He props himself on his elbows once more, studying me with a dazed look on his handsome face. "I'm drunk. That's the only explanation for me feeling this way right now."

"Right." I nod. "Because normally, you don't have feelings."

He frowns.

"And you're cruel," I tack on.

His brows lower and I realize I've said too much.

Turning away from him, I scan the top of his dresser, which is immaculate. I take in the sleek, brown leather box sitting there, a watch discarded on top of it that is expensive. I recognize the brand because my father owns a few. I'm guessing that's why August keeps his bedroom door locked.

My gaze lands on the tube of lipstick that's sitting next to the leather box, and my stomach twists. I'm sure the last nameless, faceless girl he had sex with left it behind as some sort of memento, and without thought I stalk my way toward the dresser, swiping the lipstick off the top of it and taking off the lid. I twist the bottom of the lipstick, and the rich, dark red color has me so pissed, there might be steam coming out of my ears.

I would never wear lipstick like this. Would never allow myself to be used by a man like this ever again. It happened once before for an entire freaking school year, when I was young and stupid and defenseless, but not anymore. Tonight, I make a stand.

Emotion sweeps over me, possessing me as if a ghost entered my body, and I take a step closer to the dresser, pressing my stomach against the edge as I twist the lipstick to about halfway up, not wanting to break it off. I start writing with it on the mirror, my movements jerky, my breaths coming faster, and when I'm finished, I take a step back, admiring my handiwork.

"What are you doing?" August groans, rolling over on his side, and I chance a quick look at his face, noting that his skin has a pale green tinge to it.

"Leaving you a message." I cap the lipstick and unable to help myself, I toss it at him with all my might, but my aim is for shit. It hits his leg.

"*Ow.* What the hell was that for? Fuck, I think I'm going to puke." He doesn't even look at me. Just scrambles off the bed and runs into the connected bathroom, slamming the door behind him.

Ignoring the disappointment that threatens, I remind myself I did the right thing. A good thing. Studying the message I wrote on the mirror one last time, I turn and make my way out of August Lancaster's bedroom, knowing that I'll never see it—or him—again.

Good.

CHAPTER SEVEN

SINCLAIR

THE PAST

"**F**lat-chested little freak."

I hear the words despite his low-spoken tone and I lift my chin, trying to pretend I didn't. He wanted me to hear them though. I know he did.

God, I hate August Lancaster.

I'm walking along the path that winds through campus, headed for the dining hall. I've been at Lancaster Prep for two weeks and while I've made a friend—singular—I wish I knew more people. That they would accept me into their cliques. I thought this place would be a fresh start, that we would all be on equal footing, but that's not the case. Most everyone went to middle school together or their families move within the same social circles, while I'm new on the scene. Thanks to my parents coming into such a windfall, my mother wanted me to go to the best school I could possibly get into. Did my father buy my admission?

I think so, though the words have never been said.

Hearing heavy footsteps behind me, I pick up the pace, hurrying toward the dining hall. I can feel his presence looming, drawing nearer and suddenly feeling a flash of courage, I whirl on him, causing August to stop dead in his tracks.

"Leave me alone." The words are firm, despite the way I'm quaking inside and out. My knees are practically knocking against each other and I lock them, praying he doesn't see any sign of weakness.

"Ah, so she does speak." He tilts his head, his gaze running over me from the top of my head, all the way down to my loafered feet. Reminding me of how he looked at me on the first day of school. "You have freakishly long legs."

I know I have long legs, but his comment makes it sound like a bad thing. I hate how he examines me. The longer he stares, the more I want to squirm under his examination. "Why am I only the sum of my body parts?"

"What exactly are you trying to say? Are you—standing up for yourself?" He sneers the words like they're a curse, and oh God, I'm now irrationally angry.

"What's wrong with that? No one else defends me, so I need to learn how to take care of myself." I stand up straighter, hoping I look strong. Fake it till you make it, right? Guess that's what I'm doing.

"If you actually stood up for yourself, you'd tell me to fuck right off." His expression is amused, like I'm a plaything he enjoys toying with, and I curl my hands into fists, wishing I could hit him. Not that I could do much damage. He's tall and broad and could probably squash me like a bug. "See? Look at you. You're so mad, you can't even manage a single word now, can you?"

An infuriated noise leaves me and I turn away from him, marching like a soldier toward the dining hall, blinking away the tears. I refuse to cry in front of him. It's not that he hurt my feelings just now. More like I'm frustrated. He antagonizes me every chance he gets, usually in front of his friends.

Today though, he's solo. Why? Does he hate me that much? What did I ever do to him?

"Hey." He's caught up to me, grabbing hold of the crook of my elbow and turning me around so I have to face him. I jerk out of his hold, hating how my skin tingles. Burns from his touch. It means nothing. My body reacts because I hate him so damn much. "I shouldn't have called you a freak."

I go still, waiting for the apology that will follow.

"But you do have freakishly long legs." He grins, the sight of it stealing my breath and for a moment, I get lost in that smile.

Stupid.

Stupid, stupid, stupid.

"I hate you," I hiss at him through clenched teeth.

"I know." His grin doesn't falter. "It's kind of fun, right? This whole enemies thing we've got going on?"

Enemies? We're enemies? He's got to be kidding me.

"You're a dick." I turn and walk away, and this time he doesn't chase after me or call my name or even call me by a name. He remains eerily quiet and I'd never admit this out loud, but...

I'm disappointed.

CHAPTER EIGHT

AUGUST

My head is pounding when I crack open my eyes and I immediately close them, pissed that the curtains somehow got left open last night and now all of this fucking sunlight is spilling into the room. My eyelids ache as I try and keep my eyes shut, and with a groan I roll over on my side, everything from last night coming at me all at once.

The party. The scotch. The fucking girl. The puking.

Not my best moment.

I haven't lost control over myself like that in a long time, if ever. I blame the woman. She had me thinking crazy shit. Like she was the love of my life. Please. No more indulging in thirty-year-old scotch for me.

Eventually I pull myself out of bed and shuffle into the bathroom. Take a piss and then wash my hands, peering at my reflection in the mirror. I look like absolute shit. Bloodshot eyes, and scruff covering my cheeks and jaw. My hair is a nightmare and I push it away from my face, leaning over the counter to examine myself even closer. I swear my skin is a little green and I rub at my cheek. Slap it a little even but I remain as pale as a ghost. A ghost with a hint of green.

My stomach roils and I rest my hand over it, worried I might throw up again, but the moment passes. I strip off my clothes and take a long shower, standing under the hot spray of water for far too long. Once I'm dried off and I've brushed my teeth, I'm back in the bedroom, standing in front of my dresser about to grab a pair of boxer briefs when I realize there's a message written on my mirror in lipstick. Yolanda's lipstick.

FUCK RIGHT OFF, AUGUST LANCASTER!
YOU'RE A COMPLETE DICK!

XO,
SIN

I can't help it—I start to laugh. What kind of message is that? I thought she liked me? Though she did have a touch of hostility to her there at the end. Was she pissed because I was drunk? She had to be too.

Standing in my room naked, I swear I can still smell her. That sweet, rich scent of her perfume. I can see her too. Her beautiful face and that infuriated expression on it when she out of nowhere hurled that fucking lipstick straight at me. What if it had hit me in the face? She could've done some real damage because she threw that thing hard.

Once I'm dressed, I grab my phone and start a simple search, entering her name. I've got far more extensive programs and apps on my laptop that can dig up information on pretty much anyone in the entire world, but as Sin said last night, I do like the mystery of it all. The mystery of her.

The information pops up quickly, but it's not much. There is one thing that shocks me though, and it's the words, Sinclair Miller graduated Lancaster Prep...

What the hell?

I immediately call my sister who is the biggest gossip in the land and also two years younger than me and with a better memory. And it's not that I have a bad memory about high school. It's more that I choose to remember certain things and forget everything else because those things—people, moments, etc.— aren't worth storing in my memory banks for later.

"Augie! How are you?" Iris picks up on the fourth ring, right as I'm about to end the call and I can hear her baby screaming in the background.

"What the hell is wrong with that child?" I mutter, wincing at the piercing wails coming from my niece.

"She's hungry and you're interrupting us," Iris explains. The baby's crying gets louder and Iris is shushing her as she fumbles around with something—God, is she going to drop her own daughter? Until finally the baby goes completely silent and Iris sighs in relief. "Ah, now we can talk in peace."

"Are you feeding her with a bottle?" I ask hopefully. I don't like the thought of my sister with her tits out, nursing the monster known as Astrid because that is an image I don't ever need in my brain.

"No, silly. I'm doing it like the cavewomen did back in the Stone Age. It's free milk, why wouldn't I feed my baby with it?" Iris laughs, knowing just how to get under my skin and it works.

"Heathen."

"Puritan," she tosses back gleefully. "Why are you calling? I know it's not to check up on me."

"Are you implying I don't care?"

She remains quiet and I swear I can hear that child of hers sucking noisily and God damn, I cannot *take* it. I almost end the call right there, but I'm too curious about Sinclair Miller to do it.

"I wanted to ask you if you remembered someone from high school," I start and she interrupts me because truly, Iris is the most impatient person I know.

"I remember *everyone* from high school. You know this. Who are you asking about?"

"Her name is Sinclair Miller." The silence that greets me is ice cold. I don't even hear the baby feeding any longer and I feel like I just mentioned someone that is supposed to be dead. "Do you remember her?"

"Oh, I definitely do. Are you telling me that you don't?" She sounds shocked. Even…amused?

"No." I would remember a dark-haired beauty with golden eyes and a body that was meant to be worshiped like Sinclair. And that name. Sinclair. Sin. She is sin personified and how did I let her slip by me in the halls of Lancaster Prep without noticing? Was I that oblivious? "Was she in your class?"

No, of course she wasn't. Sinclair is only eighteen. Unless she was lying to me. But why would she lie and say she was younger than she is? That makes no sense.

"She wasn't. But August. She was…oh God, how do I say this? You know her."

"I do?"

"Yes, you heartless jackass, you do. She was the girl you tormented your senior year. The flat-chested girl with the braces." Iris makes a disapproving sound. "You were so awful to her. I tried to make you stop. I could see how much your words upset her, but you didn't even care. I don't know why you were so fixated on her. You were such a mean fucker back in high school."

"I'm still a mean fucker," I remind her.

A sigh leaves my sister and the baby makes a growling noise. That kid is savage. "I can't believe you don't remember her. You made it a point to torment her daily for the entirety of your senior year. Some of your shitty friends tried to keep it up after you graduated, but they eventually gave up because you were the true ringleader. Hopefully she had a more peaceful high school existence once that stopped."

It comes back to me slowly. At the words flat-chested and braces. Sinclair Miller. I never knew her name, or if I did, I promptly forgot. I remember the first day of school and how she stared at me. The slight fear on her face with the defiant curl to her upper lip. Pathetic.

Intriguing.

I singled her out and targeted her because it was fun and she always had such a visceral reaction to my taunts. All of my friends thought I was hilarious anytime I provoked her. I made her life miserable and enjoyed every single second of it. Looks-wise, she wasn't much then but I saw the potential. Sort of.

Things change. Flat-chested girls grow up and become gorgeous. Then get shitfaced with you and leave rude lipstick messages on your mirror.

"Did you run into her on campus? Did she want to lop your head off with a machete? Because that's what I'd want to do if I were her," Iris says with a laugh.

"I—yes. I ran into her." My gaze returns to the message written on my mirror with lipstick. Yolanda's lipstick. Our housemother is elegantly beautiful, but she's fucking forty. I have zero interest in her and wonder sometimes why she puts up with us. But I also like how level-headed and calm she is, and she's needed in this house. Her obsession with that damn lipstick she wears probably sent Sinclair into a fit when she saw it.

Didn't help that I rambled about the woman I fucked a couple of nights ago. The one who I can't remember? Just like I don't recall Sinclair either?

Hell. She must think I'm an absolute monster.

"And did she slap you? I'm sure she's been waiting for a moment like that for years." Iris's voice is full of relish. Like she can envision Sinclair slapping the shit out of me in public. I won't tell her about the lipstick throwing. My sister would eat that up.

"No, she didn't slap me." I sound dazed and confused. I *am* dazed and confused. Seriously, how could she go from being an awkward, flat-chested freshman in high school to the beautiful woman that she is now? And how could she stand being in my presence knowing what I'd done to her?

"Where did you run into her anyway? Was it at a party? God, sometimes I feel like I've missed out on everything." She starts cooing and I can tell she's not talking to me anymore. She's speaking to the nightmare that is Astrid. And she's only a nightmare because she's a defenseless little being who cries and eats and shits all the time. "But then I wouldn't have you my little sunshine dollop of deliciousness now, would I? And how could I ever let go of your father and his magical dick?"

"Jesus, Iris." I close my eyes, holding my phone in a death grip, pissed that she'd say something like that. "I don't need to hear about Brooks and his dick."

"It's a good one though, Augie. I needed that reminder because every once in a while, I get a little itch. Like maybe I'm missing out on something better in life. But what's better than a man who loves you and making a family with him?"

"It would've been better if you waited about ten years," I tell her, but she just laughs.

"No regrets, August. That's my motto and I stand by it. Don't I, baby? Oh yes, I do. Yes, I do."

I hear cooing noises and can tell they're coming from my niece. Anyone else would think it's sweet. I find it a complete distraction.

"Iris. Focus. Tell me everything you know about Sinclair."

A long-suffering sigh leaves my sister. "Like I told you, I don't know much beyond how you made her life a living hell your entire senior year for whatever reason, I'm still not sure. After you and your bully ass friends left, some of the younger guys tried to keep it up, but she'd lost the braces by then and got boobs. Eventually they became bored and left her alone."

"What happened next?" I sound eager for any morsel of information and I clear my throat, reminding myself that I don't care that much.

"I don't know. She kind of faded into the background. I didn't have any classes with her."

"What about Rowan? Did he have classes with her?" I mention our cousin who also attended Lancaster Prep around the same time.

"I'm not sure. You should ask him."

I end the call before she can say anything else and immediately call my cousin. He answers on the first ring.

"What the hell do you want on a Saturday morning?" He sounds grumpy but I'm guessing he's not. He's just being a typical Lancaster male.

"Greetings to you too, cousin." I sound like a formal prick, but he wouldn't expect anything less. "I have a question for you."

"Hopefully I have an answer."

I don't bother with niceties or asking how he is. Rowan and I are cut from the same cloth and he wouldn't expect me to ask those questions anyway. "Do you remember a girl at Lancaster Prep named Sinclair Miller? She'd be in the class before you, I think. You would've graduated a year after she did."

"Sinclair Miller? Sounds vaguely familiar."

"Have any classes with her? Any sort of interaction at all?"

"I don't know...wait a minute. Bells is shouting." The sound is muffled because I assume Row put his hand over the phone. "You knew her? Yeah?" His voice comes through crystal clear. "Bells remembers her. Wait—hold on."

Arabella is on the phone in seconds, her sweet voice with the faint British accent making me smile despite my raging hangover and insane curiosity. "Sinclair Miller is a delightful girl who graduated the year before we did. I had her in a few classes. She's very...determined."

"Determined? How?"

"Intense. Smart. Has goals. I aspired to be her for about a minute my junior year and then realized it was a waste of my time. I'm not built like her. Not even close." She pauses for only a moment. "Why are you asking anyway? Don't tell me you're interested in her."

"Why do you say it like that?" I'm not interested. Not at all. Just curious. Puzzled by her willingly spending time with me last night. Even telling me about her bully who she said was dead to her—and it was me all along.

That makes no damn sense.

"Oh I know all about your 'relationship' with her. She would tell anyone willing to listen how August Lancaster made her freshman year a living hell." Arabella makes a disgusted noise that has my heart shriveling. "You were cruel, August. I'm disappointed in you."

Fuck. There's probably no going back from this.

CHAPTER NINE

SINCLAIR

Monday morning and I'm walking along the campus trails with determined steps, eager to get to my first class early so I can take a few minutes to go over my notes one more time before our test. The first few weeks of college were fairly easy. A sort of easing into the swing of things, I suppose, and now it's getting harder. There are more tests, more papers due, more group projects coming together.

I hate group projects. I much prefer working alone so I don't have to depend on anyone else for my grade. I trust no one and with reason—I've been disappointed countless times over the years by various people. Some random person I don't know that I'm forced to work with will undoubtedly let me down. It's inevitable.

I pushed all thoughts of August Lancaster out of my mind and focused on studying throughout the weekend. Well, after I slept most of Saturday away because the hangover that I woke up with was horrible. I barely remember getting back to my dorm room, though I know I found Elise with her golden god after I came downstairs from August's room. I was a raging, drunk mess and dragged her away from the boy who was still hanging on to her hand. He didn't want her to leave and we played tug of war with

Elise for a second, before she finally jerked her hand out of his and told him to text her.

Ugh, and she tried her best to get information out of me about Friday night all weekend, but I wouldn't say a word. The entire night feels like a secret that will die with me. Fuck August Lancaster and his tempting ways. He's the devil.

Despite his Lucifer tendencies, I dreamed about him Friday night. What might've happened if I'd let him take it further. If I'd rolled around with him on that big bed of his, our mouths fused and our tongues twisting. His fingers between my legs, stroking roughly. Harder. Stoking the fire that burned inside me. I was so hot. Hotter than I've ever been in my life and when I woke up from the dream, it was to find my own hand between my thighs, fingers beneath my panties rubbing my soaked skin.

Elise was snoring—a sure sign she was also drunk—while I touched myself to thoughts of August's wicked grin and naughty words and perfect, kissable lips.

I hate myself for falling under his spell. He's not a nice person. And he proved that by admitting he didn't remember the name of the girl he had sex with approximately twenty-four hours before he dragged me into his bedroom. And then he had that lipstick there. Like it belonged to that poor girl who probably left it behind so he wouldn't forget her.

It didn't help. He forgot everything while her memory lives on in my mind. What was her name? What did he do to her? Did he kiss her like he kissed me? Tell her she was stunning like he complimented me? I'm sure he uses the same lines on women over and over again because it works. All he has to say is his name—again, he admitted that to me as well—and women fall at his feet.

We are pathetic, silly creatures who fall for a man just because of his looks, money and power. It's horrible.

I get through the test—it was easy, I aced it—and go to my second class, which is English 101. The standard first year class we're all forced to take to ensure we have the writing skills to get through the rest of college. One of my strongest skill sets is researching and writing papers so this class is easy for me. The guy who sits next to me every single day and tries to get my attention on a constant basis, though? He's struggling.

Our professor hands back the most recent papers we turned in and I smile when I see the bold A circled at the top, along with the comment "So insightful!" written below it.

"You kick ass in here," the guy says, sounding miserable.

I glance over at him, noting the C- written on top of his paper. "Thank you?"

He takes the paper and crumples it in his hand before shoving it in his backpack. "I need to focus."

"Why can't you?" I probably shouldn't engage in conversation with him, but I can't help myself. I'm curious.

"You're a complete distraction." He grins at me.

I roll my eyes at him. "Come on, now. I'm not going to take responsibility for you failing this class."

"I'm not failing." He rests a hand against his chest like I offended him. "I've got a solid C in here."

"That's kind of bad." I wrinkle my nose.

"Says the star student."

"I don't know about that—"

"Didn't I see you at the Alpha Squared house Friday night?"

His quick change of subject leaves me dumbstruck for a moment.

He nods, his dark brown hair flopping across his forehead and he swipes it out of his eyes. "I did. You were talking to the prez in his inner sanctum."

"His inner sanctum?" I frown.

"Yeah. No one is allowed in that section of the house. You have to be invited in. He has—criteria, is what he calls it."

I remember him telling me about criteria, but it was all specific to me. "We were just talking." I shrug, trying to play it off.

"Yeah?" He sounds hopeful, and I nod my answer. "Good. Because if you're with him, I know I don't have a chance."

"I am definitely not with him." The words spill out of me rapidly and now it's his turn to frown. "Seriously. I don't think he dates anyone."

"I know. That's why I was shocked to see him talking to you for like…hours. I was also jealous." He's smiling again and I wonder how he's so at ease with confessing all to me. I would never. "I've been trying to get you to talk to me for weeks."

"We've been in school for a little over a month," I remind him.

"Right. And I've been trying to talk to you every day we're in this class and you act like I don't exist."

I immediately feel bad. It's not like I was ignoring him on purpose. I just get too into my own head sometimes and tend to ignore everything—and everyone—around me. "I'm sorry. I didn't mean to treat you like that."

"It's cool." He leans back, sprawling in his desk chair, and I take him in. He seems tall—it's hard to tell since he's sitting down—and he has dark hair and eyes. He dresses decently—today he's in a black hoodie and jeans. Black and white Nike Dunks on his feet, which Elise would call a red flag because she doesn't trust any guy who wears Dunks—weird, I know—but I'm going to let that one tiny fault pass.

"What's your name?" I ask because it's the least I can do after ignoring him for the past five weeks.

"Tim."

"I'm Sinclair."

"I know." His smile widens. "I like your name."

"Thank you."

"Want to grab a coffee sometime? Like after class?"

He's wasted no time and I suppose I should appreciate that, but I'm still a little uneasy. Is this some sort of setup? He knows August and was at the frat house. Is he a part of it? "Are you in that frat?"

"Alpha Squared? Yeah. I just rushed and got in." He's grinning, and I wonder if he expects me to congratulate him.

I don't.

"Do you know August well?" I ask.

"Not at all. That guy hardly speaks to anyone. Only his best friend Cyrus. That dude though? He's cool."

"Uh huh." I have no idea who Cyrus is and I don't care to find out either. "I have a class after this one."

"Right after?"

Well, technically no. I have an hour between my second and third class, but he doesn't know that. "Sort of."

"We can hang out for like, twenty minutes. Come on. I want to convince you I'm a good guy despite my shitty writing skills."

A tiny laugh leaves me and he looks pleased. "Maybe."

"I'm buying."

"Oh, well then. I can't resist."

He's nodding. "Soon you won't be able to resist anything I say or do."

I don't know why his statement fills me with the faintest sense of apprehension but...

It does.

. . .

We're at the campus coffee shop after class and it's swarming with students and faculty. Supposedly it's the best coffee around, not that I would know. I've never come here. And when I admit that to Tim, he's flabbergasted.

"Seriously? What the hell, Sinclair? You've been missing out on the best coffee in the entire city." He says this with the utmost sincerity, his expression full of shock. I'm sure he's exaggerating. "Are you from around here?"

I slowly shake my head as I scan the menu. I don't even know what to order. "I'm not a big coffee drinker."

"Damn, girl. You are blowing my mind left and right today," he mumbles, glancing around the café. "Hey, there's a table over there.

You should snag it before someone else does. I'll order for you."

"Make sure it's sweet and not too loaded with caffeine, okay?" I tell him as I start to head for the table.

"It's a coffee place. All of the drinks are loaded with caffeine," he calls after me and I smile to myself.

I don't know why I felt apprehensive earlier. Tim is nice. Extremely friendly and open. Not an arrogant ass like some people I know.

One person I know.

August.

And I don't even know him, I think as I settle in at the tiny table that's right by the window. A few hours of conversation at a frat party is not necessarily getting to know someone. Besides, I have zero desire to spend time with him again. He's a horrible, unlikable person.

So why can't I stop thinking about him?

Frustration ripples through me and I check my phone to see I have a text from my roommate.

Elise: *GG asked me to go to dinner with him tonight!*

Oh no.

Me: *You told him no, right?*

I mean, she barely knows the guy, but here I am having coffee with a stranger so maybe I shouldn't have said that.

Elise: *Why would I tell him no? You saw him, didn't you? He's gorgeous! And really sweet.*

Sweet. Ha.

But then I glance over at Tim, who's animatedly making our coffee order and even pointing at some pastries behind the glass display, and I realize he's kind of sweet too.

For now.

Me: *You said yes?*

Elise: *I definitely said yes and I hope you'll come back to our room around four because I'm going to need help figuring out what to wear.*

Me: *I'll be there.*

I slip my phone back into my pocket and glance out the massive window by my side, watching people walk past. The campus is packed. Thornhill is a private university and considered an Ivy League school. The competition at this university is fierce and if I want to do well, I'm going to have to work my ass off, which I can do. But that means no distractions. Like Tim.

I check my phone again, cruising through social media quickly, getting antsy as Tim waits patiently for our drinks. I look out the window again, my gaze snagging on a familiar face and I gasp in horror when I see him staring back at me.

It's August.

CHAPTER TEN

AUGUST

I'm hallucinating. Seeing her face everywhere, even in coffee shop windows like I'm some lovesick fool who can't think of anything else but *her*. I've become the ultimate cliché and I even shake my head once. Close my eyes and count to three before I open them again, fully expecting her to be a mirage that dissolves into nothingness.

But no. Sinclair Miller is sitting at a small table by herself at the campus coffee shop where everyone and their goddamn mother go to grab a drink like their lives depend on it. I rarely go. Caffeine has never appealed to me and sometimes I wonder if I'm the fucked-up one who's missing out.

Clearly, I am because my goddamn dream girl is sitting inside the café I never go to, those big golden eyes locked on mine. She looks like she's just seen a ghost.

I can relate.

Without hesitation I veer toward the door and enter the coffee shop, grimacing at the wave of heat and noise that greets me. Music is blaring over hidden speakers and I can hear the grinding of espresso beans. The hiss of steam from the massive coffee machines. The line to purchase a too-expensive drink is long, winding its way throughout the shop, and I don't know what the fuck I'm doing here.

My gaze lands on the back of Sinclair's head and I'm about to approach her table—and say what, I have no fucking idea—when I hear someone call my name.

I come to a stop and turn to my right to see one of our eager pledges waving at me like he's a toddler who just spotted his mother and is about to piss his pants, he's so excited. Irritated, I go to him because at least it gives me purpose and I'm still trying to come up with what I want to say to Sin.

"Hey, prez. Good to see you. You come here often?" The newest member of our fraternity asks me, a giant smile on his goofy face. He seems like a too friendly fucker and I never trust those types. Meaning, I immediately hate him.

"I come here never," I tell him, and he rears back as if I offended him.

"Weird. That's what Sinclair said too."

Anger simmers in my gut, threatening to overflow, and I take a deep breath, reminding myself I need to remain calm. This guy—Troy, Ty? He's done nothing wrong. "You know Sinclair?"

Realization dawns and he takes a step backward. "Yo, bro. I'm not trying to get with her, if that's what you're thinking. Is she your girl? I don't want to step on any toes. I saw you two talking Friday night and I asked her about it—"

I interrupt him. "What did she say?"

"That it was nothing. That you don't have a girlfriend." He frowns, his thick brows lowering over his eyes and giving him a Neanderthal appearance. I expect him to swing his arms and start grunting at any second. "You don't have one, do you? As in, Sinclair?"

Swallowing hard, I'm fully prepared to blast this ingrate and tell him to go straight to hell. That she belongs to me. But that's bullshit and we both know it. "She's not my girlfriend."

I spit the words out, one after the other, and he blinks with every single one. Dumbass. "Right. Cool. I was hoping you would say that."

My hands curl into fists as if I have no control over them. "Are you two on a—date?"

"She's in my English class and yeah. I asked her to coffee and she said yes." He rubs his hands together, that stupid smile still on his face. "I've been trying to catch her attention since the first day of school and finally today, she noticed me."

Hmm. Her timing is questionable.

"Tim! Your order is ready!" the barista screams, making me wince. Jesus, it's so loud in this establishment.

"Hey, I gotta go but it was great seeing you." Tim—not Troy or Ty—grabs my hand without my permission and pumps it twice in the most overenthusiastic shake I've ever been given. "Wish me luck that I don't blow this."

Before I can wish him luck, which I would never do because I want him to fail spectacularly, he strides away and grabs the two drinks and a pastry bag from the barista, smiling and winking at her as if he doesn't have a care in the world. I stand there and watch him head over to the table where Sinclair is sitting. Watch her tilt her head back when he pauses beside her and sets a cup on the table in front of her, and how she smiles at him.

My heart fucking pangs and I rub at my chest absently, surprised that the vital organ still exists.

Tim settles into the chair across from her and gleefully tears into the paper bag, pulling out a massive Danish that is cherry-filled and looks messy.

I would never eat anything like that and from the faintly disgusted look on Sinclair's face, I'm thinking she never would either. That gives me the slightest hint of satisfaction.

She pushes her chair back and stands and I freeze, my gaze tracking her every movement as she approaches the counter and grabs some extra napkins and a plastic knife, along with a couple of forks. The moment she turns away from the counter, she spots me.

Sin doesn't look happy to see me either.

I brace myself as she marches right up to me, her body practically vibrating with defiance and anger. I don't even flinch when she thrusts her index finger in my face, fully prepared for her wrath, and holy shit, is that my dick twitching?

A pissed-off Sinclair is a hot Sinclair, apparently.

"Are you *stalking* me?" Her accusatory tone is sexy as fuck.

"No." I scoff like what she's suggesting is absurd. "I don't stalk anyone, least of all you."

"Then why are you in this coffee shop?"

"Why are *you* in this coffee shop? Everyone comes here. I'm in here all the time." The lie spills smoothly from my lips.

She pauses, leaning back a little as if she needs to assess me. "You are?"

"Yes." I bend down and lean in close, my face in hers. "And I *never* see you. So who are you to tell me that I'm stalking you? Maybe you're stalking me."

Her mouth twists into a little pout that is positively delectable just before she exhales loudly. "Stay away from me or I might sic my new boyfriend on you."

I chuckle. "Tim? He's about as intimidating as a puppy. You sic him on me and he'll end up licking my face, not biting my ass."

An aggravated noise leaves her and she turns on her heel, leaving me where I stand so she can go rejoin her "new boyfriend."

Please. That's never going to happen. Not if I have anything to say about it.

CHAPTER ELEVEN

SINCLAIR

An entire blissful week passes without a single August Lancaster sighting and I feel like I can finally breathe again. And sleep again too because I'm tired of dreaming about him every single night. He doesn't haunt my thoughts throughout the day as much as he used to—thank goodness—and I actually dreamed of giving a presentation in front of my ethics class in just my underwear last night. Instead of the usual dream consisting of August going down on me with his hot tongue and sucking lips, only to wake up with my fingers in my panties yet again.

I call that progress.

Maybe he got the hint when I called him a stalker?

Doubtful.

Perhaps he realized I meant it when I called Tim my new boyfriend.

Probably not.

Whatever happened to keep August away from me, it doesn't matter. I haven't seen him for a full five days and I'm grateful. I feel normal again. Somewhat. Sort of.

Okay not really because he's left such an impression on me that it's become difficult to get him completely out of my thoughts. And then there's Tim. Sweet, adorable, overeager Tim who has taken me to coffee three times this past week and I keep going despite the aftereffects of all that caffeine. I'm left jittery every time and I can't think straight for what feels like hours. But when I asked Tim for a decaf latte the last time we went there, he scoffed like I asked him to poison me.

I don't fully understand his obsession with caffeine, but I don't question it. He's nice and he appreciates the help that I give him with his English papers. He's a terrible writer and can't concentrate for too long and I hate to break it to him, but I'm going to guess it has something to do with all that coffee he consumes.

It's Saturday afternoon and I'm locked up in my dorm room writing a paper for my ethics class—it's why I had the nightmare about giving a presentation in my undies, I'm sure of it—when the door swings open so fast, it slams against the wall. Elise darts into the room, the door banging closed behind her, and she starts twirling around with her head tilted back, a giant smile on her face.

"Are you okay?" I ask carefully, wondering if she's having a seizure.

"I am fantastic!" She throws her body on the end of my bed, jostling me, and I grip the sides of my laptop so it doesn't fall onto the floor. "I just had SEX and it was amazing!"

"Wait a minute." I close my laptop and set it aside, studying her. Searching for signs that she's been ravished, but I see none beyond her cheeks being a little pinker than normal. It's cold outside so maybe that's why. "You had sex? With who?"

"GG!" That's what we call her golden god, aka Rafael. His family is Italian and his mother is a blonde from Sicily and that's where the golden comes from, Elise explained to me a few nights ago when she wouldn't fall asleep and kept talking about her new man, as she calls him. She kept me up for hours, rattling on and on about GG and at one point I wanted to tell her about August, but I kept my mouth shut. How can I explain my interaction with him when I don't fully understand what happened? "Oh my God, it was so good."

"Really?" I always hear horror stories about the first time and how bad it is. And I know for a freaking fact Elise is—was—a virgin. "It didn't hurt?"

"Noooooo." She draws the word out like I'm an idiot for even asking. Or maybe that's my own insecurities making me feel that way. "It helps that he ate me out for like an hour and I came so many times I could barely feel it when he finally was inside me."

Hmm. Or does that mean GG has a tiny dick? I'm not about to ask.

"Anyway, it was great and my thighs are sore and so is my jaw and I want to do it again. Immediately."

"With GG or with someone else?"

"With GG of course!" She rolls around on my bed and I wrinkle my nose, wondering if she took a shower after having sex with Rafael or if she is rubbing her post-sex sweat all over my comforter. "He invited us to go to the football game tonight."

"Us?"

"Yes. He said Tim wants to go too but he didn't know how to ask you." Elise rolls off my bed and stands beside it, resting her hands on her hips. "You need to work on not being so stiff all the time, Sinclair. Tim told GG that you intimidate him."

"Stiff? I'm not stiff. I've hung out with Tim all week." And I'm not going to change my behavior to make Tim feel better. That's just not my way of doing things. He should accept me for who I am—and I thought he did. But maybe not? "We're getting to know each other and maybe I'm...shy? I'm definitely not intimidating."

"You so are. Even GG thinks you're scary. I told him that you throw up walls as a defense mechanism, but he didn't seem to get what I was saying." She shrugs and I'm starting to think GG not only has a small penis, but he's also stupid.

A sigh leaves me and I lean over to set my laptop on top of the mini fridge that sits between our beds and acts like a bedside table. "I don't know if I want to go to the football game."

Elise's face falls like I just crushed all of her hopes and dreams. "Oh, come on. It'll be fun!"

I hate football. I don't really care about any sports, if I'm being real with myself. So going to a football game on a Saturday night sounds like my idea of torture. "It'll be cold," is my lame response.

"Not that bad! It's only September. The games will get really cold in October." Elise nods with an authoritative air as if she knows exactly what she's talking about, even though this is her first year here.

"Why can't Tim ask me to go?" What I really want to say is, doesn't he have the balls to ask me?

"Like I said, he's intimidated by you." Elise speaks slowly, as if I'm having trouble comprehending what she's saying. I do my best to battle the frustration that's currently filling me, but I finally give in to it.

"I think that's just an excuse." Elise tries to interrupt me but I keep talking. "Like I said, we've been hanging out all week, getting to know each other. And he's still intimidated by me and can't ask me to the football game?"

Elise shrugs helplessly. "That's what he told me."

"You tell Tim if he wants me to go with him, he needs to ask me." I cross my arms and lean against the rickety headboard, ignoring the way it pokes against my back and makes it ache.

"Fine." She pulls her phone out of her pocket and starts typing. "I'm texting Rafael and telling him to tell Tim."

"Perfect." This is dumb. Like we're playing the telephone game as if we're in kindergarten, yet we're in college.

"Okay done." I hear the swoosh of a text being sent and she heads over to her tiny dresser. "I need to take a shower."

I knew she was still covered with sex sweat. I need to wash my comforter, but the laundry facility we use is subpar. It'll take like twenty dollars and hours of my time monitoring the machines to make sure it's washed and dried properly.

Gross.

The moment Elise leaves our room to go shower, I grab my laptop and attempt to finish my ethics paper, but I'm too distracted.

I keep thinking about what she said. What Tim and Rafael think of me and I…

I hate it.

I don't mean to be intimidating. I would've never described myself with that word at all. I'm the one who's intimidated by others and have been since I was a kid. Especially with bullies who do their best to torment me and make my life miserable.

Not able to shake my frustration, I grab my phone and send a text to Tim, deciding to be upfront with him. There's no point in playing games. He needs to know how I feel.

Me: *You shouldn't be so intimidated by me that you can't ask me to the game.*

The moment the text is sent, I'm filled with regret. I was probably way too pushy, saying that. He might think I'm a complete bitch. Maybe I am a complete bitch.

Closing my eyes, I thunk the back of my head against the headboard once. Twice. I am an utter failure when it comes to this dating stuff.

My phone vibrates in my hand and I nearly drop it in my eagerness to see if it's from Tim. And it is.

Tim: *I didn't want Elise to tell you that.*

Hmm. I take his response as a good sign.

Me: *Well she did and I hate that you feel that way.*

Tim: *I don't feel that way all the time. Just…*

Me: *Most of the time?*

Tim: *Yeah.*

Me: *Now's your chance to ask me. So ask me.*

He doesn't respond for what feels like hours. I'm gnawing on my lower lip, stressed the hell out while waiting for him to say something. Anything. And finally, he does.

Tim: *Hey, Sinclair. Want to go to the game with me tonight?*

Smiling, I tap out my answer.

Me: *I would love to.*

CHAPTER TWELVE

AUGUST

I'm minding my business in the front living room of the frat house on a late Saturday afternoon, quietly mulling over my life decisions and wondering if I've completely lost my mind. Why do I feel this way? Maybe it's because I'm currently spying on two idiot freshmen talking about their date plans for the night when normally I wouldn't give a damn what these fools are doing.

"She called you out on your shit, huh? I told you Elise would tell her." The one guy with the light blond hair is a bit of a dunce, but not as bad as Tim.

"Elise promised she wouldn't!" Poor Timmy. He sounds completely butt hurt.

"They're roommates and that chick is Elise's best friend. She tells her everything."

Tim groans. "Great. You think they talk about me?"

In his fucking dreams they talk about him.

"They definitely talk about you. I'm sure Elise told her everything that happened between us today too." Oh that guy now sounds incredibly smug.

"What happened?"

"You know what happened." I get the sense that they're both watching me, looking for some kind of reaction, but I keep my gaze focused on the book that is currently sitting open in my lap. The very book that I'm not reading and have no idea what it's about. I just pulled it straight off the bookcase and cracked it open.

"Oh right." Tim drawls the two words out. "You fucked her."

His voice dropped about ten octaves when he said that last sentence, but I could still make it out because it's quiet this afternoon in the frat house. I'd guarantee about ninety percent of the guys who stay here are still sleeping right now because they all got shit-faced last night, and I'm jealous.

But I'm too curious to leave. What if they say something about Sinclair and I miss it?

Fuck, I'm pathetic. Almost as bad as these two imbeciles.

"Was she any good?" Tim asks.

"Does she need to be any good? As long as they've got a tight pussy, that's all that counts, right?" They both laugh and even high-five each other, and while I would normally agree with his assessment, I sort of feel bad for the girl they're talking about. Elise? I have no idea who she is, but what they're saying about her is pretty fucking awful.

Again, I've lost my mind. Since when do I care about some unknown woman's feelings? Never. Until now.

Wait. I do know who she is because they just said it only moments ago. She's Sinclair's roommate. At least, that's who I assume they're talking about because who else is Tim going to the game with tonight? God, like we're still in high school and holding hands while watching a football game and shit. Talk about boring.

I abhor football. It's a ridiculous sport. I don't care that my cousin used to play it once upon a time and that his sister is going to marry some big quarterback star who comes from a football legacy family. It still bores me. I can respect the hustle and the determination it takes to get there, but do I want to watch a bunch of men run into each other on a field while throwing a ball?

No.

"Think I've got a chance getting into Sinclair's panties?" Tim asks his friend.

I see red. Burning, flaming hot red.

"At the rate you're going?" I'm hanging on his friend's every word, unable to breathe as I wait for him to finish his response. "No."

I exhale, pressing my head against the back of the chair.

"We'll see." Tim sounds abnormally confident. Who knew he had it in him? "I got her begging me to take her to the game tonight. I think she wants me."

Imagining Sinclair wanting this fool is laughable.

"In your dreams, bro." His friend laughs, though it's more of a braying sound and reminds me of a donkey.

"I bet I'll be able to get her on her knees in front of me by the end of the night," Tim starts, and I can't take it anymore.

Slamming my book shut, I leap to my feet and turn to face them. "Are you taking them to the suite?"

They both go deadly silent, sharing a look before Tim speaks first. "What suite?"

"The box suite that the frat has." I keep my voice calm. Measured. Inside, I'm raging. Furious. Ready to pull this guy apart. But I refuse to react. "Best seats in the stadium."

They share another look, his friend shrugging before Tim turns to me once again. "We didn't know about it. And we already bought tickets."

"In the student section for ten dollars?" When they both nod, I wonder how these two got into our frat in the first place. We do have certain criteria. Meaning we don't let just any dickhead into our club. "Those are terrible seats."

"It's where all the action is," his friend protests.

"What's your name?" I ask him.

"Rafe."

"Well, Rafe, you're fucking wrong. All of the action happens in the suite. Free food and booze. Excellent view of the field."

Their eyes light up and Tim starts nodding enthusiastically, which is what he usually does. "How do we get tickets?"

"I control all of them." That's a lie. I just happen to know the person who doles them out and he always gives me however many tickets I want—which is usually none since I never go to the games. But I do go to concerts and other events at the stadium. "And first-year members rarely get a chance at them."

They both drop their heads, their sadness eminent.

"But I've decided to make an exception for you two," I add.

Their heads jerk up in unison, the two of them wearing matching grins. God, they're easy to please.

"No way," Tim breathes.

"Are you serious?" Rafe asks.

I hold up my hand. "Don't say another word and the tickets are yours."

They both press their lips together, nodding. Solemn and quiet—just the way I like them.

"I'll make sure they're available at the will call office. Don't even bother sitting in the student section. You'll impress your—" I choke on the word a little "—*dates* by taking them to the suite."

I can tell Tim is dying to say something. Probably thank me profusely and slobber all over me like the annoying golden retriever that he is, and I point at him, holding my index finger out as a warning. He gets it, remaining silent, and a trickle of satisfaction runs through me.

I've got them where I want them for the night.

CHAPTER THIRTEEN

SINCLAIR

THE PAST

I got invited to go to a football game with some of the girls from my English class and I'm so excited I could almost burst. This is what I've wanted since I started at this stupid school—friends. Acceptance. It's been hard infiltrating their groups, but I think finally I've made some progress.

I'm meeting them at the front gates of the football field and I wasted so much time trying to figure out what to wear—it's rough to come up with something when you're so used to wearing the uniform all the time and never have to make that decision—now I'm running late. Jogging across campus with a Lancaster Lions T-shirt on along with my favorite jeans that fit me right and make my butt look good when a familiar voice stops me dead in my tracks.

"Jesus, watch where you're going."

I skid to a stop, nearly running into the one person I hate the most on this campus. "Oh. I didn't see you."

He sneers at me like I'm a disgusting rodent who dared to run across his shoes, which would be gross, but yeah. I hate how he looks at me like that all the time. "If you'd look up for once, then maybe you wouldn't run into people."

I've never run into someone before on this campus and I definitely didn't actually run into him either. And though it's my automatic response for just about everything, I'm not going to say I'm sorry to him. August Lancaster can fuck right off, which is what he told me to say to him a few weeks ago.

"Are you going to the football game?" he asks when I still haven't spoken.

I nod.

The sneer gets bigger if that's possible. "It's the stupidest sport ever invented."

"You don't like football?"

"It's boring." He yawns for good measure.

"You're not going?" Why oh why am I making conversation with him? I can't stand him.

"Of course not. We're leaving campus and going into town." He runs his gaze over me as usual. "Want to come with?"

"Absolutely not" is my automatic response. I'm not stupid. To go off campus with August is asking for trouble. He hates me.

And the feeling is mutual.

He laughs, the sound mocking. "Figures. A scared little girl like you wouldn't know what to do anyway."

I take a deep breath, ready to blast him with an insult, but he walks away, whistling like he's cheerful and everyone knows— *everyone* knows he's not a cheerful person. It wouldn't surprise me at all if someone discovered he had devil horns sprouting out of the top of his head.

I keep walking until I'm at the gates of the football stadium, smiling when my new friends greet me with enthusiasm. Maybe it won't be so bad here once I have good friends I can count on. They'll make up for how I've been treated by stupid August.

The problem is, for the rest of the night, I kept thinking about him and how he asked me if I wanted to come with him. I still stand by my decision, but there's the tiniest part of me that wishes I would've said yes.

Just to know what might've happened.

CHAPTER FOURTEEN

SINCLAIR

Tim and Rafael pick us up outside of our dorm hall. And when I say pick up, I mean they walked over from the frat house and met us on campus so we could all go to the stadium together. It's a crisp night, with a chill in the air brought on by a gentle breeze, and I grabbed a sweatshirt just in case. Tim takes one look at me carrying it around and shakes his head.

"You won't need that."

"Why not?" I frown, glancing over at Rafael and Elise to find him nuzzling his face into her neck, and she can't stop giggling. I'm guessing those two are going to maul each other all night.

Great.

"It's a surprise." Tim's voice is smug, his expression not giving anything away, and I decide not to press. I'm not a big fan of surprises, but I don't think the one he's planning is going to be bad.

At least, I hope it's not.

Mr. Golden God finally stops trying to grope Elise and we all chat as we make our way to the stadium. The closer we get, the more crowded the area becomes and the line to get into the stadium is long. Tim doesn't lead us to the line though. Instead, he goes over to the ticket box office, stopping in front of the window that says Will Call.

"We have tickets waiting for us," Tim says with utter confidence.

"You bought tickets in the student section, right?" Elise asks.

"Nope. Somewhere better," Tim answers, just before he starts talking to the woman sitting behind the glass.

"I love the student section." Elise mock pouts. "Everyone buys you beer and you can get really drunk with no judgment."

"We have great seats, babe." Rafael winds his arm around Elise's waist and starts groping her again, which she allows freely. "Trust me."

Never trust a man who says *trust me* is my immediate thought, but I keep it to myself.

"Okay." Tim approaches us, holding up four actual tickets. "Let's go."

We follow him into the stadium, going up the stairs that lead to the top. Elise is complaining the entire time, bitching about nosebleed seats and how she'd rather sit with people our age than with a bunch of old fogey alumni who'll get mad at her for yelling too loudly.

"We're not sitting in the nosebleeds." Her Golden God sounds irritated. "We're in the suite, okay?"

"Damn it, Rafe. I didn't want you to spoil the surprise." Tim almost stomps his foot, he's so mad. "The frat has a box suite and we got tickets to it." He says this directly to me, ignoring Elise.

"Wait, a box suite?" Elise grabs hold of Tim and hugs him. "That's amazing!"

"I got the tickets too, babe," Rafael whines.

I'm starting to think I really don't like that guy.

"Oh, and you did a good job, baby." Elise wraps her arms around him and holds him close. "I can't wait to see this suite!"

We walk along the corridor that wraps around the upper level of the stadium and are on the other side before Tim finally turns to the aisle and shows our tickets to the employee who's checking. The older man nods and hands them back to Tim. "Have a great time."

Within seconds, we're in the suite, and it's nice. Tim and Rafael seem awestruck by the entire situation but considering the frat they're in, I'd assume they come from money. Pretty much everyone on this campus either comes from tremendous wealth or they're extra smart and got in on a scholarship. Neither Tim nor Rafe strike me as particularly intelligent, so I have to go with their family's wealth is what got them into this school.

"Look at all the TVs!" Tim is bounding around the suite like an overexuberant puppy. "And the food. What a spread!"

The other people milling about the suite are watching the boys—because that's what they're acting like, complete boys—with barely concealed contempt. Elise is already standing in front of the table that's basically a giant charcuterie board, a plate clutched in her hand as she's loading up on a variety of meats and cheeses.

I offer an apologetic smile in the direction of an older couple who are wearing matching concerned expressions. I can tell they're loaded. She has on so much jewelry I'm nearly blinded by all the diamonds winking at me. I have no idea who they are, but they look important. Everyone in this suite looks important, save for us.

How did Tim and Rafael get tickets to this again?

After I load my plate with mostly crackers and fruit, I go over to the bar and get a Coke, not in the mood to drink tonight. Elise joins me in seconds, requesting a Tito's and soda with a twist of lime and the moment the bartender hands the drink over, she slams it back.

"You should probably slow down—" I start, but she whirls on me, her expression serious.

"Don't start. I'm letting loose and having fun tonight." She leans in close to me and practically shouts in my ear. "Free alcohol, Sinclair! We have to take advantage."

Oh dear.

Tim and Rafe join us at the bar, Tim chewing with his mouth open as he orders a beer for both of them. He grins at me and I swear I see bits of yellow cheese between his teeth and I shouldn't judge. He's nice and he's funny and he's harmless. I can't help but recoil inside though, faintly disgusted at the fact that he's eating like a slob and acting like he has no class.

Maybe Elise and Tim and everyone else are right. Maybe I am intimidating and I come off snotty. And Elise is definitely right when she says I throw up walls to protect myself from getting too close to anyone. There's no one I want to get close with. Not even Elise at the moment, because she's acting so different around her "new man," ugh.

Is it because they just had sex and now she's worried about keeping him interested? I think it's a good sign that he's taking her out tonight. But then again, I don't like how possessive he acts around her. Always grabbing at her and trying to kiss her, even when she's squealing and trying to get away from him. The way he keeps calling her babe too. I find that annoying. They've gone on a couple of dates, if you can call it that, and they've had sex once. Now they're acting like they're already a couple? It's odd.

My gaze shifts to Tim to find he's still watching me, his brows furrowed and the expression on his face makes me think he can't figure me out. Which is fine. I can't figure me out either.

"You okay?" He slides closer to me, his hand coming close to mine, and I jerk away before he can touch me, grabbing a grape from my plate and popping it into my mouth.

"I'm great!" My voice is overly bright and terribly fake and I realize I am talking with my mouth full just like him. "Why do you ask?" I say only after I've chewed and swallowed the grape. Hoping he gets the hint.

"You seem almost like you're...embarrassed by us. All of us." He points at Rafe and Elise, who are currently cuddling together in front of the bar, Elise hand-feeding Rafael a piece of salami while the bartender watches them with amusement.

"I'm not embarrassed." I paste a smile on and grab my Coke, taking a sip of it.

"What are you drinking? Jack and Coke? Oh, maybe rum and Coke. Am I right?"

I nod. "Yep." I have a feeling they'll think I'm weird for not drinking and I don't want to make myself stand out any more than I already do.

"Cool. You need a refill?" He turns toward the bartender like he's going to make a request and I rest my hand on his arm, stopping him.

"I'm fine. Really." I send him a soft smile, which works. He softens too. I can even feel the tension leave his arm beneath my hand and I wonder if he was nervous. If he was trying to impress me.

Probably.

"Want to go sit and watch the game?" he asks.

"Sure."

We take our plates and drinks and head over to the stadium seating that's right in front of the window that overlooks the stadium. The first quarter has already started and we settle into seats that are far from where the rest of the people are sitting.

"Don't really know them so..." Tim shrugs as he settles into the seat next to mine, his elbow jabbing into me and nearly sending my plate to the ground. A little yelp leaves me and I save some of the food, but most of it is on the floor. "Shit, Sinclair. I'm sorry. Want me to get another plate for you?"

"No, it's o—" I start, but he's already gone, leaving me alone.

Sipping from the skinny straw in my glass, I keep my gaze fixed on the field below, watching the teams scramble around. I have zero concept of what happens during a football game and I sit forward, wishing I understood at least a little bit. My dad wasn't much of a football fan and never watched it when he was home, which was a rare occurrence.

My father was always working, always trying to come up with a business idea that would make him millions—direct quote. When I was in middle school, he did. And once the business took off, he was never around. My older brother had graduated and went off to college and Mom was always either with my dad or her friends. Meaning I spent a lot of time alone.

That's sad. I'm sad. A sad little, lost, rich girl who doesn't have any feelings and will most likely die a virgin because not even the overly-friendly Tim knows quite how to handle me.

"Jesus, that guy is a wreck."

All the hairs on the back of my neck rise and I swear my heart settles itself in my throat, making it hard to speak. I'd recognize that voice anywhere. It haunts my dreams. And my nightmares.

I'm hearing things. I have to be. He's not here. He would have zero reason to be here. Last I recall, he hated football and I'm sure he still does. Right?

"Are you dating him, Sin? Really? You know you could do much better," August drawls as he settles into the chair right next to mine.

Right.

Next

To.

Mine.

"What the hell are you doing here?" I whisper, trying not to look at him. Oh God, I can smell him though. And I can feel him too. His thigh is pressed next to mine and it's just as firm and as thick as I remember it. His body heat radiates, making me want to cozy up to him, and that is the most insane thought I think I've ever had in my life.

"It's the frat's suite. I come to the occasional game or two." He slouches in his chair, resting his elbow on the arm rest, right next to mine, and I don't move. It's like I can't.

It's like I don't want to.

"For some reason I didn't think you'd like football," I murmur.

"My cousin is marrying the top pick for the upcoming NFL draft. I've learned to love football."

I finally turn my head to look in his direction, finding it hard to believe he *loves* football, as he claims. It was a huge mistake, looking at him. My gaze meets his, drowning in those pretty blue eyes, hating the amusement I see there. All of it at my expense.

"Are you impressed with the suite?" he asks. "That's all Tim wanted—was to impress you."

Realization dawns. He did this on purpose. "You gave Tim the tickets?"

"They were going to waste tonight." He shrugs. "I thought I'd make his weekend with the offer."

"You don't give a shit if tickets go to waste or not." What was his ulterior motive? It wasn't to…see me, was it?

No. Impossible.

"Oh, but I do." His expression is serious, as is his voice.

I glance around, looking for a stray female around our age, but I don't see one. "Where's your girlfriend?"

He frowns. "My *girlfriend*? I don't have one."

"Then whose lipstick was that in your room?" I shouldn't care. Nope, I shouldn't, but I sound like a jealous cow and I'm so annoyed at myself. I wish I could take it all back.

August laughs, making me feel like a joke. "That's our housemother's lipstick. She keeps the frat in line. Yolanda has been there for years. She wears this really dark stuff and she owns about fifty tubes of it. Leaves them all over the house."

"Uh huh." I don't believe him. His housemother. Please.

"I'm serious." He looks pissed that I don't believe him and I kind of like it.

"Yo, Lancaster. Prez. What are you doing here?" Tim plops into the seat on the other side of me, handing over a fresh plate with a variety of picks from the charcuterie board. "I didn't think you'd show up."

"Of course I would. I love football." August grins at Tim while jabbing his elbow into my side. "Right, Sin?"

"Sin?" Tim's eyes go wide as he studies us. "I never put that together. That her name could be Sin."

"Of course you didn't." August keeps that smile on his face, but I see the glimmer of meanness in his gaze. I recognize it and a tiny flicker of fear lights within me. "You don't notice a lot of things, huh, Timmy?"

Tim laughs and chugs from the can of beer clutched in his hand. "I guess I don't. Oh, what the fuck!" He jumps to his feet as the rest of the people watching the game start shouting while August doesn't say a word. Neither do I.

He's staring at me, his attention not on the game and the bad call that was just made. He could not care less because this man doesn't care about football at all. He doesn't like it. I know he doesn't. I don't either. There's another reason he came to this game tonight—this suite.

And maybe this is my ego talking, but I think his reason has everything to do with me.

CHAPTER FIFTEEN

AUGUST

It's finally halftime and I'm afraid I might pluck my eyeballs straight out of my head, I'm so over being in this suite. Watching this game with these drunken fools that are actual members of my frat—still not sure how that happened—and Rafe's equally drunk girlfriend or hookup or whatever he wants to call her. Sin's roommate, which is probably the best thing I can label that girl who has zero qualms about letting the lecherous Rafe feel her up every chance he gets. In public. They're all so drunk, they don't care about the ruckus they're causing, and I've already gone to the various donors and alumni that are occupying the box with us tonight, promising donations and contributions to their various charities if they can pretend to ignore the little mess our first years are causing this evening.

They all nodded and murmured their thanks, telling me they understood, though they don't understand shit. I'm not doing this out of the graciousness of my heart or because I want these freshman idiots to have a good time. I'm suffering through this night for this certain woman who has been sitting next to me the entire time. Driving me out of my mind with fucking lust because of her scent and her soft hair and the thick white crewneck college sweatshirt she's currently wearing. She's pulled her hair into a ponytail and every time she swings that head—which is often—the ends slap me in the cheek and I think she's doing it on purpose.

It's fine. I like it. Far too much and I don't fucking understand why because I don't like this woman. Can I even call her a woman? More like she's a girl—barely eighteen, barely out of high school, probably doesn't have an ounce of experience, and if I made even a minor attempt at seducing her, she'd probably scream bloody murder and run like the devil himself was chasing her.

Maybe I am the devil. I probably am. I'm no better than the skeevy Rafael who is currently sitting on the other side of Tim with his precious Elise. His hand is up her shirt and I can see his fingers move beneath the fabric of her tight T-shirt as they work at her nipple.

Seriously, what the fuck?

"Hey." I lean forward, my gaze meeting Rafe's. His eyelids are at half-mast and I wonder if he's high as well as drunk. "Take that shit somewhere else."

Rafe removes his hand from beneath Elise's shirt and salutes me, making her giggle. "Yes, sir."

He stands, grabs hold of Elise's hand, and within seconds, they're gone.

"Where did they just go?" Sin glances up from her phone, of which she's paid attention to more than Tim tonight. I take that as a good sign. She nudges Tim, who's focused on the field and not paying attention to her. The stupid prick. "Where did your friend and Elise go?"

"What?" He glances around before returning his gaze to hers, his expression sheepish. "I didn't even notice they left."

"I told them to take it somewhere else," I drawl, sounding bored as fuck because guess what?

I'm bored as fuck. With the game, at least. Not with the woman sitting next to me. She will hardly look at me and I'm sure she's still pissed. She was not happy to see me and that's putting it mildly. I annoy her, which is fine. Perfect. She annoys me too. More than anything, my thoughts and—oh God I sound like a sap—my *feelings* about her annoy me.

"Ahh." That's all Tim says. He returns his attention to the game, completely unbothered. Guess my explanation was enough for him.

Sinclair's exasperated sigh goes right over Tim's head and she turns to glare at me. I smirk at her, unable to help myself, and her entire face reddens. "Take what somewhere else?" she asks, her voice vaguely shrill.

I have no patience for a shrill sounding woman, but I'll try my best. "They were sitting over there practically having sex. Or did you not notice?"

"Having sex?" Her voice rises and I send her a look. She lowers her tone, thank God. "What do you mean?"

"His hand was up her shirt and I'm pretty sure I saw a wet spot on the front of his pants." Jesus, do I need to give her a play-by-play? How did she not notice the two of them grinding on each other? "I told them to get out if they were going to keep that sort of thing up."

"Wow. You didn't have to be so rude to my friends by kicking them out," she mutters, her disgust obvious.

"You're saying you didn't have a problem with them going at it in here? They're representatives of our fraternity, you know. Have you seen everyone in here tonight?" I wave a hand in the general direction of the rest of the crowd. "There are some serious VIPs in this suite."

"Like Tim and Rafael?" She raises her brows, no doubt challenging me, and I have to admit to myself...

That thing she does with her brows and the way she tries to defy me? Maybe even tease me? Hot.

Hotter than hot.

"Right. Like your little buddies," I drawl.

"They're not my little buddies." She leans in closer, giving me an excuse to subtly sniff her hair. God, she's delicious. "Rafe and Elise had sex earlier today for the first time. And it was her first time ever."

"He's fucked," I tell her with a groan.

Sin frowns. "*He's* fucked? More like she is. He's been groping her all night."

So she did notice. "She hasn't complained from what I could tell."

"Because she's drunk."

"And why aren't you? I've seen you drinking your fair share of rum and Cokes all evening."

"There's no rum in here." She rattles the ice in her glass.

"Bullshit."

"Try it." She holds the glass out to me and I take a sip from the skinny straw. And no, I don't care that I saw her lips wrapped around it earlier. That doesn't matter whatsoever. She's right—it's just plain Coke in there. "See?"

I'm pleasantly surprised that she's not an actual drunken fool like the rest of them. I like to drink on occasion, but I do it in moderation for the most part—save for the time I took Sinclair back to my room. I was drunk off my ass that night and paid the price the next day. I haven't had a drop of alcohol since.

"I guess you weren't lying."

"I'm not a liar."

There's something about her fierce tone that has me thinking she's trying to send me some sort of unsaid message.

"Are you calling me one?"

"Are you?"

"I don't know." I glare at her. "Am I?"

A huff escapes her and she jerks her gaze from mine, watching the game like she cares. All while I watch her like I care. And there's the lie. I don't care about anyone else in this world except my family and myself. Oh, and Cyrus, who unfortunately couldn't make it tonight because he went on a date.

Such a shame. I think he would've found the first years' antics hilarious.

"You're staring at me," Sin whispers, her lips barely moving, her attention still on the game. Tim isn't paying attention to us. No one is. I decide to test her limits.

"Can't help it." I lean forward, brushing the hair that's resting against her cheek and tucking it behind her ear. She shivers—it's the tiniest of movements, but I notice and triumph floods me. A reaction. Finally. "You're in my line of vision."

"You're supposed to be watching the game."

"I could not give a fuck about the game."

She turns to face me, a smile on her face. "I knew you were lying! You hate football, don't you?"

Interesting how cheerful she sounds, asking me that question.

"You caught me." I barely react.

"See? You are a liar." She shakes her head.

"You don't like it either. You've barely watched the game all night." I point at the phone sitting in her lap. "You'd rather scroll social media than watch this stupid game."

She sinks her teeth into her lower lip, looking guilty as fuck and goddamn, seeing her bite her lip is making me hard, which is ridiculous. "Caught."

"Knew it." I lean in close to her, my mouth at her ear and I lower my voice to a rough whisper. "Let's get out of here."

Sinclair jerks away from me as if she needs the space. "Are you serious?"

I say nothing. Just stare at her for a while, my gaze dropping to her mouth. Her sexy as fuck, utterly kissable mouth. It's always formed in a pout and I realize that's its natural shape. "Deadly."

"No." Her gaze slides to the side, like she's considering Tim, who hasn't considered her for hours. "I'm on a date."

"And you're bored with him. He doesn't even pay attention to you." My smile is small and wicked, I'm sure. "I can make things a little more...interesting."

"What exactly are you suggesting?" She appears genuinely perplexed.

I lean back into her, my mouth at her ear once again. "Go to the bathroom and wait for me."

Her sharp inhalation of breath tells me she thinks that's either a terrible or wonderful idea. "Absolutely not."

I don't let her response faze me. "I'll make it worth your while."

"How?" She turns her head toward mine, our mouths so close I could kiss her. I remember what it was like when I did. How sweet she tasted.

"Once I get you alone, I'll make you come so hard, you'll see stars."

Her chest rises and falls. Rises and falls and I worry that I took it too far. What am I going to do, fingerfuck her in the bathroom and make her scream my name? Come on. I'm just as bad as Rafe.

"Is that a promise?"

Her words are spoken so softly that at first, I thought I was hearing things. But no. She said that.

She fucking said it.

"Yes," I reply without hesitation, giving her a gentle shove. "Go."

She jumps to her feet and stretches her arms above her head, causing her sweatshirt to rise and show off a slice of her bare stomach. I stare at the exposed skin, thinking of all the many, *many* deplorable things I want to do to her and I shift in my seat. Trying to ease the ache that's growing in my dick.

"I need to go to the bathroom," she says loud enough for the entire suite to hear. Not that anyone is paying attention to her. Not even Tim, though that's nothing new.

"Okay. There are bathrooms in the suite," Tim says, never looking away from the game.

She sends me an unreadable look and then walks away. I'm tempted to jump up and follow her right this second but I wait a few. Count to ten. Check my notifications. Pretend to watch the field.

Then I hightail it out of there and head for the bathrooms, trying not to look too eager. Desperate to control the frantic beating of my heart. This is the most exciting thing I've ever done since...I don't know when. If I'm being honest with myself, I've been bored not just tonight, but for days. Weeks. Months. Years.

Nothing stimulates me. Nothing interests me either, with the exception of her.

Sin.

I test the door handle and slip into the women's bathroom with ease, remembering that it's a single and no one else will be inside. Sinclair is standing at the sink, her hands braced against the counter, her head swiveling in my direction when she hears the distinct click of the lock sliding into place. She faces me fully, her mouth working, her eyes wide and I know she's going to tell me no. That we shouldn't do this.

"I don't think I can go through with this," she admits, her voice shaky. She won't look at me when she says it either and I know in that moment, I've won. This girl is going to let me do whatever I want to her.

And she's going to love every minute of it.

CHAPTER SIXTEEN

SINCLAIR

My entire body is shaking from nerves and excitement and I have a major moment of regret, doing what he said. Meeting him in this bathroom. I stare at myself in the mirror while I wait for him, running through all the reasons this is a terrible idea.

More than anything, it's a mistake, a massive mistake. He doesn't care about me. He's using me because there's probably some small part of him that gets off knowing that the guy who's actually interested in me is waiting for me outside while I'm in here with August. Alone.

The moment he slips into the bathroom, I freeze, my gaze catching his in the mirror. He appears completely unaffected, turning the lock into place while he continues to watch me and my heart is beating so frantically, I'm afraid he might be able to hear it.

This is bad. So so bad.

Despite knowing this entire situation is bad, anticipation flows slow as thick honey through my veins, leaving me languid instead of tense. I didn't have a sip of alcohol tonight, yet I feel drunk. Drunk on the emotions coursing through my blood and spinning in my head. What exactly does he want to do to me?

How is he going to do it? How is he going to make me come so hard I'll see stars?

I can't wait to find out—no. I can't find out. I need to walk out of here. Now.

"I don't think I can go through with this," I whisper.

He doesn't react whatsoever. Just watches me with that contemptuous expression on his face. Like he's disappointed by what I'm saying. I'm sure he is.

"I'm going to leave," I continue.

He chuckles and steps away from the door that he was blocking. "Go ahead."

I remain where I stand, my hands braced on the counter behind me, shivers slowly taking over my body. I don't move and he knows he's got me where he wants me, slowly approaching like a cat toying with a mouse, until he's standing so close to me, my chest brushes his every time I take a breath.

"You haven't left." He states the obvious.

"I'm going to." I take a deep breath. "Right now." My exhale is shaky, giving away my nerves.

August settles his hand on my waist, light enough that I could slip away from him if I wanted. He takes another step forward, our feet becoming tangled with each other, and when he dips his head, I close my eyes and tilt my head back, waiting for the sweet sensation of his mouth brushing mine.

It doesn't happen. Disappointment floods me and I open my eyes to find him watching me carefully. Close enough that I can make out every tiny pore on his face. The faint scar just at the corner of his lips. Those lips part, his gaze searching, and I'm enthralled with the fact that his face is perfectly smooth. Not a patch of skin was missed when he shaved and I want to touch him. See if his skin is as smooth as it looks.

"I shouldn't kiss you," he murmurs. "I should make you wait."

"Why?" I breathe, dismayed at what he's saying. That's what I was most looking forward to.

Oh God, I am seriously going to hell for what I'm doing right now. On a date with one boy and letting another one—I seriously cannot refer to August Lancaster as a *boy*, what is wrong with me—touch me. Wanting him to actually kiss me.

"You've tortured me all fucking night with your taunting words and the scent of your hair."

I blink at him, shocked by his words. "Wait, what?"

He ignores my question and presses his face against my neck, making me moan the moment his lips make contact with my sensitive skin. I keep my grip tight on the tiled edge of the bathroom counter, my eyes falling closed the moment I feel his tongue sneak out for a lick.

Oh. God. What is he doing to me?

"You're a bad girl, Sin," he whispers against my throat, his fingers sliding up, settling just under my chin and jaw, his entire hand wrapped around the front of my neck. "Sneaking into the bathroom with me while your date waits for you."

Guilt crashes over me and I'm about to pull away when he settles his other hand between my legs, cupping me there like he owns it and even through the thick denim of my jeans, I can feel him. My clit pulsates, eager to feel his bare fingers on my flesh, and I wonder if that's going to happen.

I hope so.

"Undo your jeans for me. Show me what you've got." His deep, rough voice seems to reach right inside me, making me quiver, and without hesitation, I release my hold on the counter and unsnap and unzip my jeans, my fingers fumbling with eagerness. He removes his hand from me to get out of my way and the fly of my jeans flops open, showing off my very basic, very boring black cotton panties.

August takes a step away from me, his gaze dropping to my crotch, his gaze going molten hot. There is no warning for what he does next. Just slides those long, thick fingers into the front of my jeans, cupping me there again, but this time there's only a thin cotton barrier between his hand and me.

I jerk against his palm with a gasp, my eyes falling closed, and he removes his hand, leaving me bereft. "Open your eyes, Sin. Watch me."

My eyelids are heavy, but I open them, ensnared by the darkness of his gaze, my lips falling open when those fingers slide back in. Beneath my panties now, touching my bare flesh. Tangling in my scant pubic hair. He pauses, a frown appearing on his stupidly beautiful face.

"You don't wax your pussy?"

I slowly shake my head, unable to form words. There is no point for me to wax or anything like that. No one has ventured down south save for me.

"Next time I see you, I want this cunt completely bare. Not a single hair left behind." He presses against my lower lips, spreading them open with two fingers and sinking into nothing but embarrassing wetness. "Look at you. Soaked, despite your hatred for me."

I hate him. I do. Calling my vagina a cunt and demanding I shave it bald for him. Who the hell does he think he is? I refuse to do anything that he asks again because this was a huge mistake. One I might never come back from because God, the guilt. The guilt swarms all around me, enveloping me completely, and I sway against him, my head falling back, tears stinging the corners of my eyes.

August removes his hand from inside my panties and drops to his knees in front of me, taking my jeans down with him. I almost scream, the move is so shocking and when I glance down at him, he grins the evilest smile that I've ever seen in my life as he slowly eases my underwear down. His focus returns to what he's revealing, my panties sliding down past my hips until they're about mid-thigh.

"Spread your legs," he demands and I comply like the weak, stupid girl I am, and oh God, his mouth is on me. On my pussy. His tongue and his lips and his teeth doing something to me that has my legs shaking and my hands settling on top of his head. I sink my fingers into his soft hair, holding him to me, and he doesn't seem to mind as he eats at me. Licks and sucks with such infinite precision, I'm already on the verge of orgasm.

His tongue flutters over my clit. Circling it. Sucking it between his lips while I pant like I've just run a thousand miles. The sounds of our breathing and the rustling of our clothing fills the room, as well as the scent of my pussy, and I open my eyes for a moment, watching his head move between my thighs.

I will never forget this. The time I snuck into a bathroom at a football game with August Lancaster and watched him go down on me. Never, ever, never.

As if he can sense me watching, he tilts his head back and pulls away from me slightly, his eyes gleaming with pure satisfaction and his lips covered with my juices. "Want to come?"

I nod.

"Ask nicely." He drifts his fingers down the inside of one thigh, making me quake. "Use your voice, Sin. Tell me what you want."

This asshole. He would make me ask. "I want to come."

He leans in closer, his lips literally brushing against the sensitive flesh between my thighs. "What was that?"

"I want to—" I clear my throat. "Make me come."

"You didn't ask nicely." He traces the very tip of his tongue over my clit, sending a jolt of electricity throughout my entire body. "Be polite, Sin. I know you've got it in you."

"Please," I choke out and he smiles. The rat bastard has me exactly where he wants me and good god, I'm enjoying it.

What's wrong with me?

"Beg, pretty girl. I want to hear you cry and sob for it." He slides his fingers up my thigh, drifting them back and forth along my slit before he presses deeper. Penetrating me with one finger, he keeps his movements slow. As if he's trying to be careful. When he adds another one and pumps them lightly inside my extremely tight, virginal pussy, I reach for the counter behind me, worried I might fall to the floor.

"Does that hurt?" he croons. "You're a virgin, right?"

I don't say anything and he stretches me wider by adding another finger, making me wince. "Can you take it like a big girl?"

A big girl? He sounds like he's mocking me and I hate it.

I hate him.

"Shut up," I say, my voice trembling, my eyes falling closed.

His fingers pause and oh God, he spreads them wider, stretching me fully until I'm crying out. "See? It hurts your little virginal cunt, doesn't it? And I'm going to keep doing it until you beg me to use my mouth. I want to hear you cry, Sin. I want you to say my name and beg for me to fuck you with my tongue. And only then will I stop."

He thrusts those fingers deeper inside me, as far as he can go, and suddenly, I'm crying. The tears are streaming down my face and my entire pussy aches but not in a terrible way. There's something pleasurable accompanying the pain and I'm starting to wonder if I'm in shock.

"Please, please, please." I'm begging. Sobbing, just like he wanted. "Please stop. Fuck me with your tongue, August. I'm begging you."

In an instant, he removes his fingers from inside me and his mouth is back on my flesh, using his tongue to search my folds. Licking and sucking them between his lips before focusing all of his attention on my clit. It doesn't take long for the orgasm to slam into me and I'm coming with a shout, crying out his name while my pussy convulses uncontrollably. Wave after wave slams into me, making it hard to speak. To see. To think and all the while he keeps his mouth on me, letting me ride out the climax on his tongue until I'm slumped against the counter, my knees threatening to give out on me.

August removes his mouth from my pussy and grips my hips, pinning me against the counter as if he knows I'm about to melt onto the floor. My harsh breaths are the only thing I can hear and I almost miss it when he leans in and drops the softest kiss to my thigh before he rises to his full height, towering over me.

"You're a mess." He sounds faintly disgusted and when I peer up at him, I realize he looks...annoyingly unruffled. Not a hair out of place. His clothes are neat and even his mouth, which was just all up in my business and should be covered in my juices, looks normal. "Get yourself cleaned up."

I blink at him, shocked he could be so rude after what he did to me, but I suppose I shouldn't be surprised. This is just so...August Lancaster of him. He's staying on brand and I wonder if I should be grateful because at least it means he's consistent.

Swallowing hard, I glare at him. "You won't help me?"

His expression turns smug. "Of course not. Who do you think I am? A saint?" He leans in close and that's when I smell it. The scent of me is all over him. "Next time, Sin, you're going to suck me off. And I'm going to come down your throat. Multiple times. Get ready for me."

Before I can respond, he's exited the bathroom, the door shutting softly behind him. I glance around the white-tiled room, my head spinning, my clit still throbbing and I wonder for a moment if that really happened.

Glancing down at myself, I see my stretched-out panties sagging around my knees, resting on top of my jeans, which are bunched around my calves and I know that yes. Yes, it happened.

And I don't know what to do about it.

CHAPTER SEVENTEEN

AUGUST

I head into the men's room after I leave Sinclair a trembling, almost incapable mess, desperate to get away from her before I do something stupid like, I don't know.

Help her out? Treat her tenderly? Like I would ever do that. But shit.

I was tempted.

I clean myself up a little more. Readjust my still-hard cock in my jeans, thinking of something boring like visiting my sister and her imbecile fiancé. Brooks Crosby drives me insane with his bumbling ways. I make him nervous as shit and I relish in it.

Realizing I'm on the right track, I think of my niece shitting her pants and yep, that deflates my dick considerably enough that I can return to the suite and no one would be the wiser.

I consider washing my face but the scent of her delicious cunt lingers and I decide not to. Jesus, she smells good. And is as tight as she can possibly be. Was I an asshole for stretching her with my fingers while I demanded she beg me to ease up? Yes.

Yes, I was.

But she liked it. She could've screamed at me to stop and I would've, but she wanted my mouth on her. She wanted my fingers inside her juicy pussy. She came so hard I thought she was going to pass out, but luckily enough, she didn't.

I reenter the suite like I haven't a care in the world, strolling into the room while nodding and smiling at everyone who glances in my direction. I'm even whistling and I don't fucking whistle ever. I'm not even the lucky one who got an orgasm out of that encounter so why am I so cheerful?

My gaze lands on the oblivious Tim and I realize that's why. I love that I got one over this idiot who has no idea that his date even left to meet with me. I can feel my upper lip curl in disgust, my gaze cutting to the left and I do a double take when I realize Sinclair is sitting there. Right next to Tim and watching the game like she actually cares.

Slowly I approach the stadium seats, noticing that they're now mostly empty. My gaze goes to the scoreboard and I see that we're losing by a rather large margin and that the majority of the people milling about the suite have left. This game is pretty much over.

Well. At least the one on the field.

I settle into the seat right next to Sinclair's but she won't even look at me, which allows me plenty of time to study her. There's a faint sheen of sweat along her hairline and her cheeks are a bright pink. Her eyes are sparkling, despite the frown currently curving her delectable mouth, and I have a moment of regret that I didn't kiss her there.

Oh well. Perhaps next time.

"We're losing," I announce loudly and Tim glances over at me, a faint smile on his doofus face when he realizes I'm back.

"Hey, there you are! You and Sinclair disappeared at the same time," he says.

"That's because I was eating her out in the women's bathroom," I say drolly.

Sinclair jabs me in the ribs with her pointy elbow but I barely glance in her direction. A nervous laugh leaves Tim and that's when I see it. The faint doubt shadowing his eyes. He doesn't know if he should believe me or not.

He should.

"I didn't know you were such a jokester," Tim says, still laughing.

"I'm not." I'm dead serious.

"Please." Sinclair waves a dismissive hand and turns so she's facing Tim, her back to me. "He's just messing with you. Ignore him."

I'm about to ask Tim if he has any gum so I can get the taste of his date's pussy out of my mouth, but Sinclair keeps talking.

"Are you ready to go? We should get out of here, don't you think?" She keeps her back to me and I let her, not bothering to interfere.

I slouch in my chair like I don't have a care in the world and blatantly watch them leave. Tim offers up an awkward wave in my direction while Sinclair practically runs to the door, she's so eager to get away from me.

I wonder if her cum still coats her thighs.

"Hey, thanks again for the tickets, prez," Tim says with a sheepish smile. "Bummer that we didn't win."

"Oh, someone *definitely* won tonight." I grin at him, enjoying myself. "Hope you have a shit evening, Timmy."

Tim frowns, slowly shaking his head. "Okayyy. See ya later."

They exit the suite and I swear I hear someone breathe a sigh of relief. When I glance over my shoulder, I see it's a recent graduate. He was a senior when I was a sophomore and a real egotistical asshole, even by my standards. He staggers toward me, a leer on his face, and I wait for his approach, already annoyed.

"What the hell were you thinking, letting those two first-year pledges have tickets to the suite tonight," he practically roars. I can smell the alcohol on his breath, my gaze sharpening as I examine him more closely.

It's obvious he misses the college life. He's got on a university hat and hoodie and he's three sheets to the wind, as my grandfather would say. I wonder if this pathetic little man is bored. I'd peg him at about twenty-five and if I remember correctly, he came into a massive trust fund when he turned twenty-one. Now he has nothing to do but show up at the alumni suite on a Saturday night and make a drunken fool of himself.

I recognize that look on his face though. The disappointment in his eyes and the way his mouth is formed into a permanent frown. His displeasure with his life permeates from his skin like cologne and I have a nasty little realization that if I don't watch out, this could be me.

Fuck that.

"Well?" he retorts when I haven't responded.

I shake my head, making a tsking sound and that seems to bother him even more. His face turns red and I swear he's going to stroke out.

"It was a hazing thing, you know? Invite the lowest pledges at the frat and see if I can fuck one of their dates." I shrug, like no big deal.

The man nods, his expression easing. I'm talking his language. He thoroughly enjoyed hazing everyone back in his day. "And did you?"

"Did I what?" I'm already done with this conversation.

"Fuck one of their dates?"

My smile is slow, the taste of Sinclair's pussy still lingering on my tongue. "Not quite. But I will."

CHAPTER EIGHTEEN

SINCLAIR

We walk back to the dorm buildings on campus, Tim and me. He can't stop talking about the game and the suite and how the food was great and he drank way too much beer, but he is so incredibly disappointed that our team lost, and honestly? I'm surprised I can keep up with his steady stream of conversation. That I can even comprehend it because all I can think about is August.

On his knees in front of me. His mouth on me, his tongue licking me everywhere. His fingers shoved so deep inside me it hurt and God, I wanted it. I wanted more and I wanted him and I begged for it. Sobbing like a little baby while I said please over and over and when he finally rocked my world and gave me my first orgasm brought on by someone else and not myself.

I'm not over it. Not even close.

Ugh.

"You okay, Sinclair? You're a little quiet," Tim says and I wonder if he asked me a question and I didn't respond.

"Just tired." I offer him a wan smile. "And sad our team didn't win."

That was the right thing to say because he launches into another tirade about how they should've won. All the right pieces were supposed to fall into place and it should've been an easy win.

Yada, yada, yada. I'm tuned out, August's face filling my brain. That smug smile. The way his eyes sparkled when he told Tim that he was *eating me out* in the women's bathroom.

Who says that? Who *does* that?

August. That's who.

A shiver moves through me as I think of the words *eating me out* again. He did it spectacularly. His tongue was everywhere, and the way he sucked on my clit. Oh my God. I had no idea it could be like that. Feel like that. The orgasm that swept over me was so intense. Made the ones I've experienced by myself seem like nothing.

"I wonder if we'll get to watch a game in the suite again," Tim says, interrupting my orgasmic thoughts.

I seriously hope not. "I'm thinking with what happened between your friend and mine, we won't be welcomed back."

"Right. Rafe was getting seriously freaky with Elise. You think they're into public sex or what?" Tim glances over at me and then immediately looks away. "I probably shouldn't have asked you that."

Here he is, being respectable while I'm remembering how August said he was going to come down my throat the next time he sees me. Multiple times.

My entire body quakes in anticipation.

"It's no big deal." I shrug, reveling in my newfound sexuality. Thank you, August, for that. "I barely know Elise, but I do know they, uh, had sex earlier."

"Yeah." Tim clears his throat, seemingly uncomfortable. "Rafael might've mentioned that to me."

Oh boy. If they're talking about Rafe and Elise having sex, then they've probably talked about me. "He got really drunk tonight."

"So did she." He sends me a curious look. "But you were calm—and pretty quiet. You must really know how to control your liquor."

"Yep." That's all I say because I'm not about to tell him I wasn't drinking.

And why not? Am I afraid Tim is going to judge me? That's silly. I told August I wasn't drinking without any hesitation.

But there's something about August that has me confessing everything all the time. Like he asks me a question and I dutifully answer it. He gives me a command and I do as he says without hesitation. It's weird.

My entire reaction to him is weird.

I slow down as we approach our building. "Guess I'm home."

Tim and I both come to a stop in front of the double doors of my dorm hall. He smiles at me, reaching out like he's going to grab my hand or something and I take a step back, not wanting him to touch me after I was touched so thoroughly by August. I ignore the flicker of hurt I see in Tim's eyes. "I had fun tonight."

"Me too."

"Maybe we could do this again." His voice is hopeful.

"Maybe." Mine is not.

"Well. Good night. See you in class." Tim waves and walks away. I stand in the middle of the pathway, watching him until he disappears completely before I dash into the building and run up the stairs versus waiting for the very old and very slow elevator to take me to the second floor.

I practically sprint down the hall and unlock my dorm room door, pushing it open so it bangs against the wall, disappointed to find the room empty. Elise isn't here.

Dang it. I wanted to tell her all about...

Wait. Tell her all about August? And what he did to me? And how much I liked it while my sweet, innocent date was watching the game without a care in the world? I look like a complete and total slut. A cheater, even though Tim and I aren't together. I'm a bad person.

Terrible.

Grateful that Elise isn't here, I gather up my things and go to the communal bathroom where I take a long, hot shower. Considering most everyone is probably out tonight, I'm taking advantage of there being enough hot water and no one else in the bathroom with me. The effect is kind of ruined though when I have to wear flip flops while taking a shower. I'm not about to get any bacterial infections or a fungus.

Ah, college dorm life.

Once I'm finished, I make my way back to the dorm room, hopeful Elise is back, but the room is still empty. Unable to help myself, I plop down on the edge of the bed still in my robe and wearing nothing underneath it while I send her a quick text.

Me: *Where are you?*

She responds almost immediately.

Elise: *With Rafe. We're in his room. I'm going to stay here all night as long as the RA doesn't catch us.*

Me: *Are you at the frat? Does Rafe have a room there?*

If he does, that means she might see August and oh God, what if he says something to her? He would never.

Would he?

Knowing him, he probably would.

Elise: *No we're at his dorm room. That he shares with Tim. Who just showed up.*

Me: *Please tell me you're not going to have sex in front of him.*

Elise: *I would never! I was literally a virgin like twelve hours ago. I'm not a ho.*

Me: *You were letting Rafe feel you up in the suite.*

Elise: *No one noticed.*

Everyone noticed.

Elise: *I have to go. Tim just revealed his secret stash of liquor bottles under his bed. We're going to get drunkkkkkkkkkk*

Me: *Have fun.*

I toss my phone on the bed and rise to my feet, shuffling over to the full-length mirror I have hanging on the wall. I undo the belt of my robe and shrug the heavy terrycloth fabric off my shoulders, standing naked in front of the mirror so I can study myself, searching for anything different.

But I don't look different. Not at all. I look like the same, boring girl I was when I first showed up on campus. I had no idea what was in store for me, and I can't believe what happened between August and me tonight. My bully is now the guy who gave me my first orgasm and that should kind of piss me off.

For whatever strange reason, it doesn't.

I take a step closer to the mirror, my gaze dropping to the spot between my thighs. It's not like I have a massive bush growing down there but he acted disgusted to discover I actually have—shocker—pubic hair. Didn't stop him from going down on me, now did it?

I should make a waxing appointment. And I should ask Elise to go with me. It'll be…fun.

At the very least, a true bonding experience.

I tilt my head to the side, my gaze wandering, my hands coming up to cup my breasts. They're not huge, but I'm not flat-chested like I used to be either. My body is okay. August didn't pay much attention to it. He was too focused on my pussy, and I sort of hated how he called it a cunt. That's a word I don't use and it's offensive.

Fine, I didn't hate it. Everything he said to me was hot and it feels like what happened between us earlier was a total fantasy. Unreal. But then I see it. The tiniest mark on the inside of my thigh. I rub at it, wincing at the sting of pain and I realize…August must've bitten me at some point. Or sucked my skin so hard, he gave me a hickey. On my thigh.

I touch it again, shivering the moment my finger makes contact. We've shared something incredibly intimate. But what does that mean? What's going to happen next? Will he ignore me the next time I see him?

A sigh escapes me and I shake my head. Yes, he probably will ignore me. Pretend it never happened because he's just that awful. Maybe I should make it my mission to torment him. Remind him of what he's missing out on. Will that make me seem like some kind of stalker? Maybe.

But I'm willing to take the chance.

CHAPTER NINETEEN

SINCLAIR

Elise never came back to our room that night. She didn't come back all of Sunday either. I texted her to make sure she was okay and she reassured me she was fine and she'd be home later.

I spent the entire day in bed. If I wasn't sleeping, I was reminiscing about my experience with August. Going over every moment again and again. To the point that I'm worried I've become fixated. Not that I'm at fault for feeling this way. I blame August. Who wouldn't become fixated after having the most earth-shattering orgasm of their life? He's ruined me.

Finally, around six, Elise bursts into our dorm room, leaning against the back of the door the second it slams shut. "Hi."

I'm still in bed but at least I have my laptop open and I'm trying to do homework. When I glance up and take her in, I'm immediately frowning. "Are you okay?"

She looks like she's been through a terrible storm and came out the other side, barely keeping it together. Her hair is windblown and her makeup is smudged. Black circles rim her eyes and her lips are red and swollen. She's in a weird combination of clothes—obviously wearing a pair of men's gray sweats that swim on her and a baby tee that I recognize as hers. There are black Adidas slides on her feet that are way too big and she kicks them off, her expression full of disgust.

"Not really," she says on a sigh as she goes to her bed and collapses on top of it. She's hugging her pillow, pressing her face against it so her voice is muffled. "I don't know how to tell you this."

I close my laptop and set it aside. "Tell me what?"

Elise remains quiet for an unnerving amount of time and my heart begins to thump. If she's hooked up with—oh God—August? I will be livid. More at him than her because he would do something like that to get under my skin. He's that much of an asshole.

And why am I thinking she'd get with August anyway? Of course she wouldn't. She's not interested in him like I am—and she doesn't even know I'm interested in him.

I hate that I'm interested in him. That I hooked up with him and he treated me so terribly. Said all of those awful things that I liked. What's wrong with me?

Why does he consume my thoughts?

"I stayed at Rafe and Tim's dorm room last night. All day today. I basically had to beg them to let me leave a few minutes ago," she starts, speaking into the pillow.

I'm frowning. "Okay."

"We drank all last night. All day today. We also..." She clears her throat and lifts her head, though she's facing the wall and not me. "Had sex."

I blink at the back of her head, which is snarled like a rat's nest. "You had sex in front of Tim?" I worried she would do that and she proved me right.

"Not just with Rafe." She's still facing the wall, like she can't look at me. "I had sex with...Tim. And then the two of them. Together."

What? WHAT?! Is she for real right now?

"Elise..."

"I know," she wails, finally turning to look at me. She's already crying, tears streaming down her reddened face, her mascara running black little rivers across her skin. "I'm a whore. I stole your man!"

Oh. I didn't even think that. I was too worried about the possibility she messed around with August. Not Tim. If she thinks she's horrible, then I am too.

"You're not a whore. And you definitely didn't steal my man." I crawl out of bed and go to her, pulling her into my arms. She starts sobbing into my sweatshirt, drenching it with her tears, and I just hold her, running my hand over her hair, trying to untangle it, but I give up because seriously. It's a mess. "Tim and I aren't together."

"I know. He said the same thing." Her shoulders shake and I wonder if she's so upset over the fact that she feels guilty in regards to me or does it have to do with the fact that she had sex with two guys this weekend. At the same time.

Like seriously? She goes from a virgin to having a threesome all in the span of approximately forty-eight hours.

Elise pulls away slightly, her tear-filled gaze meeting mine. "Do you hate me?"

"Of course, I don't hate you." I brush her hair away from her face, hating how torn up she looks. I'm not worth her stress, especially after what I did with August. "I only like Tim as a friend anyway."

She nods, her lower lip sticking out for a moment. "I had a feeling you'd say that. You didn't seem that interested in him last night."

I wasn't, and I was hoping I wasn't overly obvious, but it sounds like I was. "How was it?"

Elise frowns. "How was what?"

"Having sex with two guys at the same time?" I don't know if I want to understand the exact logistics but I am curious.

"Oh." She shifts away from me with a shrug. "It was all right."

"All right? They basically held you captive in their dorm room and you can only describe it as all right? You make it sound underwhelming."

"Well, at first, we were so drunk that I didn't even know it was happening until it was? I was kissing Rafe on his bed and he had his hands on my boobs and then...Tim got on the bed behind me and put his hands on my stomach and the next thing I knew they were all over me." Elise covers her face. "I'm embarrassed."

"I'm surprised you're not traumatized."

She drops her hands. "Why would you say that?"

"Because you were still a virgin Friday and now you're having full-blown threesomes," I point out.

Her laughter sounds uncomfortable. "Yeah. About that."

"About what?"

"I lied to you." Another sigh leaves her. "I wasn't a virgin. I've been having sex since I was fifteen."

My mouth hangs open for a moment and I snap it shut, irritated. I don't like it when people lie to me. It's why I gave August so much shit last night. It's a true trigger of mine. "Why would you lie about that?"

"I don't know! We were playing true confessions and when you said you were a virgin, it felt natural to say I was one too. I wanted to make you feel like you weren't a freak of nature," she explains.

"Gee thanks." My tone is heavy on the sarcasm because come on. That was kind of rude. She basically just called me a freak of nature.

"I didn't mean it like that. I'm sorry. More than anything, I didn't want to look like a total slut. My body count is...unusually high." She ducks her head, seemingly embarrassed.

I don't even want to know what her body count is but...

"How many guys have you been with?"

"I've been with girls too," she admits, her head still bent.

"Oh. Well, how many people have you been with?"

"Twenty-two." She lifts her head, her relief obvious. "It was twenty until this weekend."

"I guess you can play the Taylor Swift song in celebration."

Her face brightens. "That's a great idea!"

Elise taps at her phone and the song starts on the tiny speaker on our bedside table slash mini fridge. I didn't mean for her to play that song at this very moment, but too late now.

"What are you going to do?" I ask as I watch her move about our room. She's pulling clothes out of her dresser, those sweatpants she's got on slipping down, making it obvious she has no underwear on underneath. "And whose sweats are those?"

"Tim's. He's skinnier than GG so I thought they were the better option for me to wear."

"What happened to the rest of your clothes?"

The uneasy expression on her face makes me not want to know after all. "I'm not sure."

I leave it at that.

Once she's left the room to take a much-needed shower—thank God she didn't try to roll around on my bed like she did yesterday—I mull over what she told me. I know college is for experimenting and I secretly hoped I'd have a few experimental moments. Last night was the first one and I felt pretty much like a sex goddess after it happened.

Figures that my roommate would completely one-up me. I can't top a threesome in a dorm room. I don't know if I want to.

Yeah...I definitely don't want to.

· · ·

It's your typical Monday where every professor seems to dump some big project or test on us and by the time I'm entering my English class, already overwhelmed and it's only my second class. Plus, I'm nervous because this is the first time that I'm going to see Tim after Saturday night and I have no idea how he's going to act around me. He has to know that I know what happened between them all and I'm sure he'll be embarrassed. Right? I'd be mortified if I were him.

But no. I settle into my desk chair and he shows up within seconds of my arrival, that amiable smile on his face like usual as he sits next to me.

"How's it going?" he asks as he digs around in his backpack. "Have a good weekend?"

"Yeah. It was great," I drawl, trying to keep things casual. Maybe I'm being too casual? I'm not sure. Tim is acting like his usual self so I'm going along with him. "How about you?"

"Pretty boring." He plops his notebook on top of his desk and turns to smile at me. "Missed you."

Alarm bells are clanging in my head. How could he miss me when he was so busy having sex with Elise and Rafe?

"Seriously?" The word slips out of my mouth before I can stop myself but hashtag no regrets. He is acting completely out of pocket.

He nods, his expression serious, his mouth formed into the tiniest pout. I don't like it. The way he's looking at me right now and the way he's behaving. He's throwing me off. "I should've made a move on you Saturday night."

Tim would've been sorely disappointed if he did because I would've rejected him outright. "Nothing would've happened."

"Don't be so sure about that." His confidence is unbelievable.

"Right. So you ended up making a move on my roommate instead?" I arch a brow, waiting for his response.

He turns about fifty shades of red and turns away from me, obviously embarrassed. "Uh."

"Yeah. I heard *all* about it." I emphasize the word all because Elise didn't hold back. She was reserved at first with the details, but by the time we were in bed and it was late? Forget it—she couldn't stop talking about it. She told me everything, which I assume was easier for her in the darkness. It was easier for me too because then we didn't have to look at each other when she said phrases like, *double penetration* and *they jerked each other off.*

No judgment but I'm an eighteen-year-old prude who hasn't done shit yet. This is the sort of thing that I've only seen in porn. While Elise is living her best life and doing it for real.

"Damn." He swivels his head in my direction and I see the misery in his dark eyes. "Does that mean I lost my chance with you?"

Poor silly Tim. I can't believe he thought he still had a chance after he fucked my roommate and only friend on this entire campus.

"Definitely," I tell him and he hangs his head in defeat.

"I was hoping—"

"Yeah, no. I'm not interested. I can't imagine going out with you and Rafe and Elise on a double date. Next thing we know you're all going to try and convince me to join in during your sexual—escapades." I sound like an old lady, calling what they did escapades but my God, this is embarrassing.

"We wouldn't do that, I swear." His tone turns pleading. "Come on, Sinclair. It was—we were feeling wild that night. I don't know how to explain it, but we swore it would never happen again."

Elise never mentioned that part. Pretty sure she wants it to happen again.

"She knows how I feel about you. I didn't lie when I told Lancaster I've been trying to get your attention since day one of school."

I hate that he brought up August. I don't want to think about him.

I can't stop thinking about him.

"And now you're telling me the dream is over? I'll never get a chance to take you out again?" Tim rests both hands over his heart, like he's in pain. Or praying, I can't tell. "Come on, Sin. Give a guy a break."

"Okay, first of all, do not call me Sin." I hate it. At least, I hate hearing the nickname come from Tim's lips. That's August's thing, not his. "And second, no. Your dreams are dashed because we are definitely not going on another date."

Elise even told me she was hoping they could turn into a throuple, but maybe that's not Tim's plan. I'm so confused.

"That's too bad." Tim exhales loudly. "I could've rocked your world."

I almost laugh and thankfully I'm saved by our professor striding into the classroom. She immediately starts talking and I turn to face the front of the room, relieved I don't have to continue our conversation.

And did Tim really say he could've rocked my world? Please. I'll let his experimental ass stay with Elise. He can continue rocking her world because I don't want anything to do with him. He's a nice guy but really? We had no spark. Plus, there's the fact that he's literally been inside my roommate and came on her tits—a direct quote from Elise—so yeah.

No thank you.

Class is almost over when I feel my phone buzz in the pocket of my hoodie. I discreetly pull it out to see what it is—our professor hates to see us on our phones—and I frown when I see it's a number. One I don't recognize. The message says:

I can't stop thinking about you.

I glance over at Tim who is literally dozing. His eyes are closed and everything, so he definitely didn't send it. I can't imagine August admitting something like this either, and he doesn't even have my phone number.

Feeling brave because I've got nothing to lose, I respond to the mysterious text.

Me: *Who is this?*

But I get no reply. Probably a wrong number.

Figures.

CHAPTER TWENTY

AUGUST

We're at a bar on a Thursday night, Cyrus and me. One pretty far off campus so there aren't a lot of college students in here, thank Christ. I want to drink my bourbon in peace. Not surrounded by a bunch of rowdy frat boys and their overly made-up girlfriends whose tits are practically falling out of their shirts.

I sound like an old ass man. Cyrus tells me that too after I grumble about something minute, like the way the server winked at me after handing me my drink. She's practically my mother's age for the love of God.

"You need to ease up," Cyrus tells me once the server is gone. "You're tense as fuck."

I say nothing. Just sip from my glass and let the irritation simmer in my gut.

"When was the last time you got laid anyway? You've been acting like a complete dickhead for a week," Cyrus continues.

My mind goes to Sin in the bathroom. Me on my knees in front of her, my face in her cunt, her clit between my lips. Her fingers sliding into my hair, keeping me in place, like she was worried I might stop.

The moment lives on replay in my brain. Her alluring scent, her soft skin and musky taste. The way she called out my name when I made her come. How she took my fingers so well even though I stretched her out on purpose. I wanted to hurt her, like I'm some sadistic fuck.

She never really protested. Just begged me for more.

I can't stop thinking about her and it's aggravating as shit.

"I got laid last night." I think Cyrus is having a conversation with himself, since I'm not participating. "And it was a complete letdown."

"Why?" I can't help but ask.

"Terrible kisser."

"You usually don't care about that sort of thing." Cyrus doesn't like to kiss women. I'm not a fan of it either. Only because kissing leads to romantic thoughts and I'm not a romantic.

But Sinclair's perfect, puffy lips won't get out of my head, no matter how hard I try, and I'm dying to stuff my cock inside her mouth. Come down her throat, just like I promised.

"I liked her." Cyrus keeps his gaze fixed on his glass, which he is currently twirling in between his fingers. It's already empty and I glance down at mine to find it's empty as well. "She had a nice laugh."

"Had? What did you do, kill her in her sleep?"

Cyrus bursts out laughing. "Of course not. I would never let her sleep over. You know this."

I'm grinning. So is Cyrus.

"Tell me why you're so damn bitchy all the time."

"I take offense to that." I don't sound offended at all.

"No you don't because you know it's true. What's your problem? Is it a woman? That faceless one you can't remember fucking?"

"Who?" I am genuinely confused.

A long worn-out sigh escapes my best friend. "I guess it's not that particular woman. Who is it then?"

I don't want to admit anything to him, and he's my closest ally on this campus. In my entire life. I could never tell my siblings about her. Iris is too nosy, bossy and has a big mouth. Vaughn is too young and while he is most definitely a Lancaster, I would shock his virgin ears with my lustful thoughts about Sinclair Miller.

Iris would also find it infinitely amusing that I'm obsessed with the girl I used to bully. She'd tell me that's my ultimate karma, especially if Sinclair got back at me for my past actions. My sister would eat that shit up.

I also can't tell my parents anything. My mother doesn't need to hear about my illicit affairs and my father would give me unnecessary advice that I would never take. Not that I don't respect him, but the man has been obsessed with my mother since they were fourteen years old. He just *knew* as he's always told me, and I have no idea what that's like. To have that instant connection. Like a lightning strike. Boom, you're done for. Obsessed forever.

"You don't know her," is how I start and no joke, Cyrus rubs his hands together like a greedy villain.

"This ought to be good."

I launch into the story of how I supposedly bullied Sinclair when she was a freshman at Lancaster Prep. I don't quite remember all the details and I haven't had a chance to look at a yearbook yet because what's the point. I tell him about our recent interactions. End it with the one in the bathroom at the suite, giving him a few details but not all of them. Some things are sacred.

Sacred? Seriously, something is so fucking wrong with me, I don't know what to do about it.

"And now you want to see her again," Cyrus says once I'm finished talking.

I nod, miserable. Confused. Angry. "It makes zero sense."

He says nothing.

"She's eighteen. A baby. She'll probably run the moment I try and shove my dick in her face."

"You're saying you want to see her again."

A ludicrous statement. "No." Cyrus's brows shoot up. "Maybe."

The server arrives with a fresh set of highballs full of their best bourbon. "Thought you gentlemen might need a refill."

"Ah, I love that you're a mind reader, Denise." Cyrus smiles at her as she places the glasses on the table and removes the finished ones. "Thank you."

The moment she sashays away from us, I'm giving him shit. "Denise?"

He shrugs, taking a healthy sip from his fresh glass. "We come here often. I asked what her name was."

"Interesting." I grab my glass and sling it back like I'm trying to get drunk. Maybe I am.

"Stop trying to change the conversation. Let's get back to your girl."

I grimace. "She's not my girl, though that is an apt descriptor for what she is. Just a girl."

"An eighteen-year-old pussy hasn't been touched much." Cyrus smiles to himself, staring at the inside of his glass while he speaks. "You into that sort of thing?"

Am I? I never gave it much thought. "I don't think she's ever been with...anyone."

"Ever?"

"Except me." A primal sensation swirls in the depths of my gut at the thought. Pretty little untouched Sin. Corrupted by me and no one else.

"And I think you're enjoying that." Cyrus sets his half-full glass onto the table between us. "Sick fucker."

"It's not my usual kink. You know this."

Virgins are terrified. Literally. Of men like us. Of men in general. Or so I thought. Once upon a time, I was a virgin. We all are at some point. But I have now fucked a variety of women, always steering clear of anyone who gives off even a hint of innocence nowadays.

With the exception of this woman.

"Are you wanting to pursue something with her?" Cyrus asks.

"Define something."

"Serious? A relationship? Make her your...girlfriend?" His voice rises, and if he's trying to sound feminine, it's not working.

My grimace deepens with his every suggestion. "Absolutely not." It's my automatic response always.

"Then what are your plans?"

"Do I have to plan anything? Can't I just—toy with her?" My smile feels menacing. I'm sure I look like a serial killer.

"You sound like a serial killer."

"You're a mind reader." I glance up, making eye contact with the server, and I flash her my most disarming smile. I can tell I terrify her and she'd rather deal with Cyrus, but she still makes her way over to us.

"Need another refill?"

"Please. And a menu, if you have one." My smile widens and I lick my tongue across my teeth. "I'm suddenly starving."

CHAPTER TWENTY-ONE

SINCLAIR

"**I** need to ask you a huge favor."

Elise and I are in our dorm room, getting ready to start our day. I've wanted to approach this idea with her since August mentioned it in his incredibly rude way and while I know deep in my soul that I shouldn't give this man what he wants, I'm tempted. I'm more than tempted. I've already made the appointment and I'm hoping against hope Elise will go with me as moral support.

She's applying mascara to her eyelashes, her gaze finding mine in the reflection of the mirror she's currently in front of. "What do you need?"

Taking a deep breath, I blurt, "I want you to come with me to my first waxing appointment."

"Ow." Elise nearly pokes her eye out with the mascara wand and she drops it, turning to look at me. "Well, that was the last thing I expected you to say."

"What did you expect?"

"I don't know, but not that." She's grinning, despite the streak of mascara beneath her right eye. "When is your appointment?"

"Later this afternoon." I sink my teeth into my lower lip so hard, it stings. "I'm nervous."

"Oh, don't worry. It's not so bad." Elise shrugs.

"You've done it before?"

Nodding, Elise grabs a Q-tip and turns toward the mirror once more, dabbing away the stray mascara. "Plenty of times."

I'm not surprised. She's far more daring than I could ever be. "Are you completely bare or do you leave a little strip?"

"I've done the strip. I've gone totally bare. I'm bare now, though it's growing back in a little." She grimaces. "That can be itchy, just to warn you."

I don't even care about itchy. My biggest hang-up is the fact that someone is going to have their face down there. A stranger. And that's weird.

You let August shove his face down there. He had his mouth and tongue all over you and you didn't protest. As a matter of fact, you were sad when it was over.

That naggy little voice in my head can be a real bitch sometimes.

"Why are you doing this anyway?" Elise turns to look at me again, grinning. "For Tim?"

I frown. I almost ask who when she said his name. Then I remember everything that's happened between all of us—specifically Elise, Rafe and Tim—and I roll my eyes. "Stop trying to make Tim happen. It's never going to happen."

Her smile fades. She doesn't even mention my *Mean Girls* reference, which is disappointing. "Come on, Sinclair. You know I feel guilty about all of that."

"And it's fine. It really is." I mean it, though she never believes me. I'm not interested in Tim anymore. I never really was, especially once August reentered my life and proceeded to rock my world. Not that it could happen again. I'm probably waxing my entire vagina for nothing. I'm sure he's forgotten all about me. "I don't care what you three do."

Elise's gaze is full of guilt. "You're such a good friend. I don't deserve you. Anyone else would judge the shit out of me and I wouldn't blame them. I'm a total ho."

"You are not a ho." I go to her and wrap her up in a hug and she clings to me for a minute, her face pressed against my shoulder. "I envy how—free you are."

"Free?" She pulls away slightly, frowning. "Free like I spread my legs too much? Is that what you mean?"

"No, of course not." I keep my tone gentle. This girl beats herself up a lot. Makes me wonder if people judged her in the past. "I envy your sexual freedom. You're not afraid to experiment, Elise. Most everything you do, I could never."

"Well, college is the best time to let go and be free. Trust me." She's smiling again, her earlier worry forgotten. "I'll go with you to your appointment."

"You will?" I'm actually touched and surprised. I'm so used to doing most things on my own, not wanting anyone to help me. Especially since I never want my parents around or involved that much in my life. They're embarrassing. My mom talks too much and makes everything about her. When they sent me away to boarding school, it felt good to get away from them all the time. Once they came into the money, they became completely overbearing. Especially my mother.

"Sure. Maybe I could get a wax there too. We can do it together! It'll be fun." Elise grins.

Do it together? Is she serious? That doesn't sound fun.

Not at all.

• • •

I made the appointment online at The Wax Studio, which was the closest waxing salon to our campus. Since I scheduled it at three, that gave us plenty of time to walk over to the strip mall where the studio is located when we were finished with school for the day.

"Oh, this place looks cute," Elise says as we approach the building. The front of the studio is nothing but glass windows and while I'd normally agree with her that it looked cute inside, I'm too nervous about what's going to happen. It's like I'm tongue-tied and I can't speak.

Elise rushes forward and opens the door for me and I walk inside, not daring to look at the various women who are waiting in the lobby. I approach the sleek white desk and sign my name on the check-in form.

"Do you take walk-ins?" Elise asks the woman sitting behind the desk. She looks about our age and has the most perfect eyebrows I've ever seen.

"Sometimes. Depends on the schedule. What do you want done?"

"I'd love a Brazilian. Every hair down there, gone." Elise makes a whistling noise as emphasis, waving her hand toward her crotch and my face heats with embarrassment.

The receptionist doesn't bat an eyelash at Elise's response. "Have you had one before?"

"Yes."

"Then it probably shouldn't take too long." The woman smiles at Elise, her gaze shifting to me. "Did you two come here together?"

"I'm her emotional support." Elise leans over the desk and whispers loudly, "She's never done this before."

My face is now on fire. I jab her in the ribs. "Shut up."

"Oh, you'll be fine. We just need you to fill out this paperwork first before you go in." The woman hands me a clipboard and I take it from her with a murmured thank you.

The woman hands Elise a clipboard as well and we settle into the pale pink chairs, sitting next to each other. I start filling out the form, my embarrassment slowly dissipating. Maybe Elise is trying to make me feel better. Trying to get me to relax. This isn't a big deal. Women get waxed all the time. The estheticians who work here have probably seen hundreds of vaginas. Maybe even thousands if they've been at this place for a while.

Once we finish filling out the information form, we're told we have to wait.

"Want me to go back there with you if they let me?" Elise asks.

I hurriedly shake my head. "It's not necessary."

"Come on. Look at you." She waves a hand at me. "You can't stop bouncing your leg."

I immediately stop. It's something I do when I get nervous. "I'm fine."

"It's not like I'll be staring at you down there anyway." Elise laughs and I turn away from her. "Oh come on, Sinclair. Don't be such a prude."

"Fine, you can come into the room with me." I cross my arms, feeling stupid. She's right. I don't need to act like such a prude. Again, this is no big deal.

So why the hell do I feel so nervous?

My knee starts bouncing again but thankfully, Elise doesn't seem to notice.

Ten minutes later and we're being led into a private room. There's a bed/cot-looking thing in the center of the room with a folded robe sitting on top of it.

"Change into the robe, please. Make sure you're not wearing any panties." The woman smiles and leaves the room, pulling the door shut behind her.

"Did you ask for a full Brazilian?" Elise sounds shocked.

I nod. "May as well get rid of all of it."

"Well, that's not all of it." Elise taps her finger against her pursed lips as she watches me start to take off my shorts. "What about the hair on your butt?"

I pause, lifting my head to meet her gaze. "My butt?"

"Oh yes. We're furry down there too. Want me to check?" She bursts out laughing at what I know is a horrified expression on my face. "I'm kidding! But you might want to add the butt wax to your services."

Good lord, this is growing more complicated by the minute.

When I'm in the robe—still wearing my T-shirt and bra thank you very much—I'm sitting on the edge of the table when there's a knock on the door. A dark-haired woman in black scrubs enters the room seconds later, a pleasant smile on her face.

"Hi, Sinclair. Such a pretty name." Her smile grows when her gaze lands on me.

"Hi." I curl my hands in my lap, winding my fingers together.

"My name is Debbi. I see on your personal information sheet that this is your first time getting waxed."

I nod and of course, Elise starts talking.

"She's never done it before but she's in college now and may as well make it look nice and clean down there, right?" Elise glances over at me.

I send her a pathetic smile, regretting my choices.

"You're not doing it for a certain man in particular, are you?" Elise's gaze narrows and I hurriedly shake my head.

"Not at all," I lie. "This is for me."

And August, if I get lucky and run into him again. The probability of that happening is probably less than one percent but hey.

A girl can dream.

CHAPTER TWENTY-TWO

SINCLAIR

Saturday night and I'm in my room with Elise. We're getting ready to go out and do The Stroll, as they call it. It's when all of the fraternities and sororities have a sort of open house that's sponsored by the various organizations that fund them. Meaning alumni. It's a tradition Thornhill has upheld for at least thirty years and it's one of the most exciting weekends of the fall semester.

I'm standing in front of my pitiful closet, examining my pitiful clothes and I can feel Elise approach, a sound of disapproval leaving her. "You have nothing sexy to wear."

She's right. I don't. That's why my closet is feeling pathetic.

"You want to borrow something?"

I glance over at her, sizing her up. She's skinnier than I am but not by much. And she has bigger boobs. "Like what?"

"I don't know. Let's go through my closet."

We thumb through her clothing, pausing over one sexy dress after another. She owns a lot of them, and I don't know why I didn't put two and two together earlier. Elise is outgoing, loud and has no problem flaunting what she's got. She came at me acting like a demure little princess when I first met her, and I wonder if she was just mimicking my own energy back at me.

"Do you think I'm a demure little princess?" I ask her as she holds a red strapless dress to the front of me. The fabric looks tight. Unforgiving.

"Yes," she says without hesitation, waving the dress at me. "Try this on."

"No way." I shake my head. "I'll end up looking like a sausage."

"Oh my God, you will not." She shoves it at me, the hanger falling with a clatter on the floor. "Please. Do it for me."

Grumbling, I shed my T-shirt and shorts and slip the dress on, struggling to get it into place. Elise helps me, straightening the sides, adjusting the top before she steps away to study me.

"Wow. Okay, skinny queen."

Rolling my eyes, I turn to the full-length mirror on the wall, pausing when I catch my reflection. Elise wasn't lying. I definitely look like a skinny queen, like she said. The dress clings in all the right places, emphasizing my faint curves and showing off my cleavage, of which I never really thought I had any until this moment.

"You are stunning," she breathes, coming to stand just behind me.

"Are you sure I look okay?" I tug at the fabric at my hip and she slaps my hand. "Ouch."

"You look amazing. Stop picking at the dress. If you act uncomfortable, you'll look uncomfortable and no one finds that attractive." She rests her hands on my shoulders, smiling at me in the mirror. "Red is your color."

"I don't look…slutty?"

"Take that word right out of your vocabulary, please." She heads back to her closet and starts digging for her shoes. "What size do you wear?"

"Eight and a half."

"Oh perfect. I wear an eight." She pulls out a pair of strappy gold stilettos and holds them out to me. "These are an eight and a half. I've never worn them because they're too big."

"Why did you buy them, then?" I take the shoes from her, my gaze lingering on the thin, pointy heel.

"Because they didn't have my size and I was hoping I could make them work." She shrugs. "They're yours now."

"Hey thanks." I slip them on, tying the straps up around my calves, feeling stupid as I wobble over to the mirror. But oh my God, the shoes look amazing with the dress. "I have gold hoops I could wear."

"Put those fuckers on," Elise says. "And wear that bracelet and matching necklace you've always got on too."

I add my jewelry, watching myself in the mirror the entire time. Thinking of August naturally because when do I not think of him?

Realistically? I should despise him. There's a part of me that does. He's a horrible human with a bad attitude and an arrogance that is astounding. I've never met anyone like him. Maybe that's what intrigues me.

Well, that and his talented tongue and fingers.

My cheeks turn red and I press my cold hands against them, still watching myself. "I look like a joke."

"Oh stop it. Your self-esteem is the worst when it shouldn't be. I mean, look at you." Elise stops right next to me and I take in her outfit. Short black leather mini skirt and a tight black short-sleeved bodysuit that makes her boobs look ginormous. "You're gorgeous."

"So are you."

"Right." Elise nods, grinning. "We're gorgeous, we're young, we basically own this campus. We can do whatever we want and tonight, we're going to have fun and kiss whoever we want!"

I turn to look at her, shocked by what she said. "Why aren't you wanting to kiss GG? Or...Tim?"

Elise wrinkles her nose. "I'm bored with them already."

I know for a fact she was with them just last night because she told me. "But you went to their dorm room."

"Ugh, and watched them make out instead of them making out with me. I swear I think they're into each other. I'm just a prop for them to have around so they feel straight. They need to admit their feelings for each other and just get on with it." She blows out an aggravated breath, irritated.

I watch her stomp away, going to her closet so she can dig through her shoes again. She pulls out a pair of black leather knee-high boots and holds them up. "I think I'm going to wear these. I want to look like I can kick someone's ass."

"Okay." I swallow hard, shocked by her mood change. Now she seems frustrated. I wonder if she's upset at her throuple falling apart? "Maybe you should go talk to Rafe—"

"Nope. No way." She shakes her head as she pulls a pair of socks out of the top drawer of her dresser and puts them on. "The best way to get over someone is to get under someone else."

I've heard that before and never thought it applied to me. But maybe...

Maybe that's what I should do. Find some hot guy and hook up with him. I'm probably hung up on August because he's literally the only guy I've ever been with. For all I know he could be complete shit at the sex thing and I just don't know any better.

Probably not, but hey, it's possible.

Elise pulls on the boots and studies herself in the mirror, a pleased expression on her face. "Okay, the boots are the perfect touch. I love it."

"I love it too. You look great." She really does. Completely unlike the girl I met on move-in day, but I'm guessing I look nothing like that girl either. That's a good thing. We're growing. Changing. Aren't we supposed to evolve during college?

"Ready to go?" Elise asks as she shoves her phone in a tiny black purse.

"Definitely." I send one last look at myself in the mirror and then turn to face Elise with a smile. "Let's do this."

...

The streets are packed with people, and the majority of them are drunk. Meaning they're loud and obnoxious. Most of the fraternities and sororities are in the same neighborhood, making it easy for us to move from one house to the other. The problem is, we can't get into the more popular houses because they're already packed. There are actual lines of people waiting to get in and everything.

"This sucks," I tell Elise after we're turned away at yet another house. This one was a sorority and the girls at the front door were kind of snobby. "Maybe we should set our sights a little lower."

"Did you hear that one chick? I'm pretty sure she called us skanks." Elise shakes her head, a fierce expression on her face. "Like seriously. They don't even know us. They have no idea if we're skanks or not."

I feel like we're a little overdressed for the occasion, but I don't have the heart to tell Elise that. The majority of women I've seen out tonight are wearing jeans, though they're almost all wearing skimpy tops. I've seen a few dresses and a few in high heels but for the most part, I stick out the most out of anyone in the red dress. And yeah, I probably look like a skank.

I'd give anything to be wearing a pair of flip flops and sweats. The gold stilettos are killing my feet and the dress keeps riding up my thighs every time I walk, which is nonstop. I can't quit tugging on the skirt, yanking it down because I'm terrified my ass is going to hang out of it.

I should've never let Elise convince me to wear nothing underneath the dress. No bra, no panties. I've never felt so exposed in my life.

Well, there was the one time I had August Lancaster's face buried in my pussy but that doesn't count.

See how he pops up in my mind at the most inopportune times? It's annoying. I still haven't told Elise about him. She probably wouldn't believe me. Or worse, she'd force me to seek him out so we could try and hang out with him and his friends. She told me not even fifteen minutes ago she was set on leveling up, as she called it. Finding a man who has immense wealth and power—direct quote. There are a lot of men like that on this campus, and while she didn't mention August by name, I wonder if she was referring to him.

Ugh, I don't know. More like I don't want to know.

"And what do you mean, we should set our sights a little lower?" Elise asks, sounding indignant. "What's wrong with trying to get into the most popular house?"

"What's wrong is none of them are letting us in. We should go to a less popular house and see if we could get inside there," I suggest, coming to a stop so I can readjust the straps wrapped around my calves for about the hundredth time.

"No one cares about the less popular houses." Elise keeps walking and I envy her wearing the boots. They look way more comfortable. "Come on. Let's go to the Alpha Squared house."

I freeze, coming to a complete stop while Elise keeps walking. I watch her go, my throat constricting at the idea of showing up at August's frat house wearing this. He'll probably laugh at me. Or maybe he'll grab my hand and drag me into his bedroom where he'll demand I give him a blow job.

My pussy throbs at the thought.

Elise eventually comes to a stop when she glances over her shoulder and realizes I'm not right behind her. She throws her hands up in the air. "Come on!"

"Sorry." I reach for the shoe straps again, pulling on one to make it look like I'm adjusting it. "These stupid shoes keep slowing me down!"

"They're the worst," Elise agrees, waiting for me with her hands on her hips. Love how she agrees with me that they're terrible. No wonder she gave them away so easily.

The moment I'm next to her, she hooks her arm in mine,

flashing me a reassuring smile. "Don't feel so intimidated by going to the Alpha house. I'm nervous too."

"You are?" I'm shocked. Lately Elise doesn't seem fazed by anything.

"Of course. Rafe and Tim will be there. It might get weird. Especially with you being there too," she explains.

"Why would I make it weird?" I don't even think of Tim in that way. I'm too hung up on someone else, which is stupid. A complete waste of my time too.

"Tim likes you, Sinclair. He feels terrible that you know what happened between us." Elise doesn't act guilty over it though. And she shouldn't. I wasn't interested in Tim then and I'm not interested in him now either.

"I don't get it." I shake my head as we keep walking. The Alpha Alpha house sits at the end of the block, large and imposing, and I swear my knees start quaking the closer we get.

"He wants what he can't have." Elise sighs, leaning her head against my shoulder for the briefest moment. "That's probably where I blew it. I made myself too readily accessible to them."

"I think you got in over your head."

We walk in silence for a while, surrounded by all kinds of people who seem to be headed in the same direction. A group of guys walk directly behind us, making rude comments, but we ignore them.

"Do you really think that?" Elise asks me once the group walks past us, one of them making kissy noises from over his shoulder, his friends jostling him like that was the funniest shit ever. They're stupid. "That I got in over my head?"

"Maybe?" I give her arm a squeeze. "I support you no matter what, though. I'm not about to pass judgment on you."

"You should. I'm a skank, just like those girls said, while you're a sweet virginal angel."

Confessing my secret is on the tip of my tongue, but I swallow it down instead. I don't need to make that reveal at the moment. "You're too hung up on my virgin status."

"It's weird, huh."

"That you're hung up on it?"

"No, that you're a virgin." I gape at her and she bursts out laughing, nudging me in the ribs with her elbow. "I'm kidding. But I should probably warn you before we get into the house."

"Warn me about what?" I ask warily.

"Tim said I would be fine but supposedly there's some sort of contest at Alpha Squared during this weekend where every guy tries to get with a virgin. Something to do with a sacrifice and it keeps the house in good order? Those were his exact words."

I hate what she just said. Worse, I hate how it made me feel. "That sounds fake."

"I hope it is."

Me too.

CHAPTER TWENTY-THREE

AUGUST

"**T**his party is bullshit," I whisper-shout in Cyrus's ear. It's the only way he'll hear me because the music is ear-splitting loud and there are so many people in our fucking house, I'm worried we're going to get trampled to death before the night is through.

"You're telling me." Cyrus is grinning, bopping his head to the music, and I know my best friend is eating this shit up. He loves a good party. Loves the idea of getting blackout drunk and finding some hot girl that he can titty fuck for the night. And I only know this because he confessed all to me during our sophomore year after a night of debauchery on this very weekend where he titty fucked a few girls. It's his secret kink.

I personally don't find it that exciting but to each their own.

"You love it." I sound disgusted. I am disgusted. I'd rather go up to my room and lock the door so I can hide away for the rest of the evening, but I'm the president of this fucking frat and have to put in an appearance.

I check my watch, noting that it's not even ten o'clock. Fuck, it's going to be a long night.

"I do." Cyrus is still grinning, his dark hair flopping across his forehead as he continues nodding his head to the beat of the music. "Look at her."

He indicates a beautiful blonde currently gyrating on the makeshift dance floor, clad in dangerously short denim cutoffs and a white tube top that threatens to fall with every bounce. Her tits are huge. Meaning she is Cyrus's dream girl.

"She looks like your type."

"Great set on her." He nods.

"Is that all you care about? Tits?" I'm genuinely curious.

"Tits and ass and a sweet-smelling pussy."

"There is no such thing as a sweet-smelling pussy." Not quite true. I think of Sin's. It was pretty sweet and shiny and juicy as fuck. Minus the pubic hair. I wonder if she got waxed. I wonder if that pretty little kitty is bare and smooth and delicious…

"I'm gonna go dance." Cyrus is gone before I can stop him and I watch him walk right up to the blonde, his head angled toward hers as he whispers something in her ear. She nods and smiles and they start to dance. Both of them awkward and goofy-looking because I can only assume the two of them are drunk off their asses.

I wish I was drunk. I've been taking it easy since I'm running this entire party, but fuck it. I need something strong to drink.

Right now.

I move through the crowd, baring my teeth in what's supposed to be a smile and nodding at everyone because all these fuckers are calling out my name, though not a single one of them is familiar. They fucking wish we were friends. Being close to me brings people a certain cache that most will never attain. I have way too much money and power compared to anyone else on this campus. This is what happens when you're a Lancaster. And I'm not just any Lancaster. I'm the firstborn son of *the* Whittaker Lancaster. Everyone knows what a fucking prick my father is.

A powerful, wealthy prick that they all wished they knew, but a prick nonetheless.

The sitting room in the back of the house is blessedly empty. They even set up velvet ropes to keep the entryways blocked off, just for me. I step over one and head straight for the bar, pouring myself a whiskey and slamming it back in one swallow. It burns going down, setting my lungs on fire, and I exhale raggedly, fully expecting to see flames shooting out of my mouth. I pour myself another. And another. Until my head starts spinning and my vision gets a little blurry. Surefire signs that I'm on my way to getting fucked up.

I go over to where the DJ is set up and move behind his table, watching him pretend to work the turntable, but he's really just bringing up music on his laptop. He has a bird's-eye view of everything happening and I scan the crowd, searching for a distraction. Anyone would do.

Yet none of them measure up. They're either too made up or not made up enough. Too blonde. Too dark-haired. The outfits, the hairstyles, their fucking faces—they're all wrong. None of them appeal. Meaning something is really fucking wrong with me when I can't pluck a random woman out of a crowd and want to fuck her for the night. At the very least, get a blow job. A hand job?

My upper lip curls at the thought, and not in a good way.

"Have any requests?" the DJ screams at me, a big smile on his face.

I shake my head. "You're the expert. Play what you want."

"The girls love this song." He makes the switch, the heavy bass making the entire room vibrate, and he's not lying. All the women throw their hands up in the air and start shaking their asses to the beat.

I watch them, wishing my dick would find at least one of them semi-interesting when I do a double take, positive that I'm hallucinating but no. It's her.

Sin.

She's with her silly little friend who let that one guy grope her in public, and the two of them are dressed like utter tramps. Some of the girls give them side-eye as they push through the crowd, laughing once they walk past, and I can't help but feel a glimmer of pity for them. They are obviously first-year students experiencing this weekend, and it shows.

I track her with my gaze, drinking her in. She's wearing some whorish red dress that she keeps tugging on, clearly uncomfortable. I hate how it shows off her shoulders and tits and legs. How the tight fabric clings to her ass and those shoes make her look like a streetwalker. The garish gold straps that wind up her slender calves—tasteless.

The women may be looking at them with disgust, but the men are blatantly checking them out—Sin in particular. An unfamiliar feeling rises within me when one of the men approaches her and asks her to dance. She doesn't refuse him because of course she doesn't. Instead, she smiles and nods and lets him take her hand. He pulls her into the center of the room, surrounded by his bros, and they begin to dance. She moves easily to the beat, her expression faltering when he pulls her in close. He rests his hands on her hips and I want to rip them off his body. He tugs her even closer, his hips thrusting like he's trying to fuck her and that's it.

I see red.

There is no thought when I make my way through the crowd, pushing past people as if they're made of air. None of them protest or call out to me—I'm their leader after all—and the jackass dancing with my Sin is oblivious to my rage as I approach them. When she spots me, her eyes go wide, and her lips push together in the sexiest fucking pout I've ever seen in my goddamn life. The next thing I know, I'm yanking the asshole away from her. Violently.

"What the fuck, man?" the guy yells, his gaze meeting mine. He shrinks back the moment he realizes who I am. "Oh. Hey. Sorry."

"Keep your fucking hands off of her." I'm seething. Furious. I won't even look at her. It's like I can't.

"I didn't know you two were together!" He throws his hands up, and I swear to God a whimper escapes him. "I'm sorry!"

He's screaming like a little rat, the fucker. I just glare at him for a moment. The music still plays but no one is dancing. They're all watching me.

I never lose my cool. I don't try and start fights at a party and I definitely don't haul people around like I'm going to knock heads together. I'm not that type of person. Any issues I might have, I handle with dignity.

Tonight, I have lost all dignity, thanks to one silly little girl who makes me feel things I don't understand. And when I turn to finally look at her, I see that she appears as angry as I feel. Good.

This ought to be interesting.

CHAPTER TWENTY-FOUR

SINCLAIR

THE PAST

We got invited to a party and I'm trying to play it cool, but it's so hard. The seniors are holding the gathering out at the ruins, the old building that burned like over a hundred years ago or whatever. It's where they have the annual Halloween party, one of my friends told me. That's happening at the end of the month. I hope I can go. Feels like a good sign that we got invited to this party, which is just a casual night of drinking. That's how they described it anyway. We all went to Lolo's dorm room and got ready together, all of us lamenting our wardrobe choices and worried the boys would see right through us.

Which they're going to do. We're freshmen and we look like it. As we arrive, I see the older girls watching us, their expressions incredulous as we approach. One of them even yells, "What are *you* doing here?"

"We were invited," Lolo tells her, earning a few laughs for her response. Lolo is our unspoken leader. Her actual name is Lauren, but she hates it, so she insists we all call her Lolo, which she claims is a childhood nickname. I feel silly calling her Lolo but whatever. We climb the steps, entering the burned-out shell of a building that has no roof but somehow still has walls. There's a massive ice chest sitting in the room, the lid open and lots of beer cans nestled in ice inside. We all take one, including me, and I open it, the liquor inside hissing and I lean forward, taking a sip of the foam that's already spilling over.

Oh God, that tastes so gross.

Choking it down, I clutch the beer can and watch my friends talk casually, their eyes in constant motion. Looking for a boy? I'm guessing yes. That's Lolo's main goal. She wants a boyfriend and she wants him to be older because she's sick of being treated like a baby.

Direct quote.

"Oh, here comes August Lancaster!" Lolo starts hopping up and down, her excitement palpable. "He's the ultimate catch."

I almost snort out loud at her words. Is she for real? August is the freaking worst.

"He's so good-looking," says another one of my friends.

"Right? I mean look at his face. And his lips! Swoon."

The face that's always sneering? The mouth that's always saying crappy things to me? Give me a break.

"I know he put you on the spot and humiliated you in front of everyone," Lolo says to me, sticking out her lower lip in a pout. "I'm guessing you don't like him much."

"I despise him," I stress, hating that she brought up the incident I'd rather forget. "He's a complete dickface."

"Nice language. Who are we insulting now, hmm?"

I close my eyes for a moment when I hear the familiar voice coming from behind me. I don't have to look to know who it is. I can feel his presence, sense his aura. I can smell him, that familiar cologne mixed with his own unique scent. My entire body lights up at hearing him speak and I remind myself that I'm not desperate and I can't stand him.

Maybe if I chant those words enough in my mind, I'll eventually believe them.

Glancing over my shoulder, I see the recognition in August's eyes, and the disappointment that fills them. I feel the same exact way.

"It's you." His voice is flat, his gaze dimming.

I turn away and face my friends again, mortified. I refuse to say anything.

"Hi, August! Oh my God, thanks for the invite! I can't wait to party with you guys! Do you want me to get something to drink for you?" Lolo is bouncing like a puppy, putting on the—is that supposed to be charm?—for August and all I can think is how much he's going to hate her over-eagerness. It's embarrassing.

"What's your name again?" August drawls, and his friends who are crowded around him begin to laugh.

Lolo doesn't let it faze her though. "Lauren, but my friends call me Lolo."

"Lolo." August grimaces. "Sounds like a pet name."

Lolo blinks, but otherwise doesn't react. "Do you need anything? A drink? A snack?"

"You can be my snack." He sends me a look before going to Lolo, slinging his arm around her shoulders and tucking her close to his side. "What do you think, Lolo?"

He asks her the question, but the entire time he says it, he's staring straight at me.

"Okay," Lolo breathes, her eyes shining as she looks up at him like he's her every dream come true.

"Think your friend will join us?" He keeps his gaze fixed on me and my entire body reacts, goosebumps scattering across my skin like he actually touched me.

"What? Who? Which friend are you talking about?" Lolo seems nervous and I can't help but think she's in over her head.

"That one?" He inclines his head toward me. "You into threesomes, freak?"

The other boys laugh again and I fight the embarrassment that wants to sweep over me. I can feel my face is hot but no way will I back down. "I wouldn't touch your dick if you paid me to." He seems impressed. "Considering my family is extremely wealthy, that's quite the statement. I bet ol' Lolo here will touch my dick for free."

I don't say it out loud, but I'm sure he's right.

"Whatever you want." Lolo's voice shakes the slightest bit.

I send her an imploring look, one that I hope says, *have some more dignity* but I can tell it doesn't compute.

August removes his arm from her shoulders and she goes stumbling forward, nearly falling on her face. The boys continue their laughter and I grab hold of Lolo's arm, stabilizing her while I glare at August.

"Little baby girls don't interest me, *Lolo.*" He says her name like a curse and stalks off, his friends following him. The moment they're out of sight, Lolo is pulling away from me, chugging from her beer and letting out a big burp, which makes her giggle.

"I need to get drunk," she declares and the rest of the girls drink from their beer cans too. "Maybe then August Lancaster will notice me."

Hate to break it to her but I'm guessing...

He's already forgotten all about her.

CHAPTER TWENTY-FIVE

SINCLAIR

August is furious. His face is red and his eyes are blazing with anger and I've never seen him look hotter. He pulled that gross guy off of me like he weighed nothing and the way he told him to keep his fucking hands off me? I melted. Who knew I liked violence? Who knew I'd find it so freaking sexy?

But I'm also mad. Who does he think he is, interrupting us like he just did? That guy was making me uncomfortable, but I could handle it on my own. I don't need August Lancaster running to my rescue. Though he's looking at me currently like he'd rather toss me out on my ass than want to help me.

We're glaring at each other silently, but it feels like we're communicating with our eyes. His broad chest rises and falls at a rapid rate and I can feel everyone else is watching us too. We have an audience.

His gaze cuts across the crowd before it returns to me and he grabs hold of my upper arm. "You're leaving."

He wouldn't kick me out of his frat, would he? Nooo...

I can tell from the serious intent in his gaze that yes. Yes, he would kick me out. God, he's a dick.

"I am not!" I try to tug out of his grip, but he's too strong. I glance around the room, trying to spot Elise, but she's nowhere.

I know she was looking for Tim or Rafe and I'm guessing she found them.

Meaning I'm all alone and about to get escorted out of this frat party by the freaking president.

"You are." He drags me through the crowd, leading me toward the front door and my anger grows. Rising inside of me and getting bigger and bigger until I'm sure I'm about to blow.

At the last second, he doesn't take me to the front door. Instead, he turns right and leads me up the stairs, his grip never lessening and I swear he's going to leave a mark. I try and put up a fight, but he just looks at me, his narrowed gaze both intimidating and somehow sexy.

God, I hate him. He's so fucking bossy and mean. I can't stand it. I can't stand him and the way he always fucks with my good time. I knew we shouldn't have come to this stupid house. I just knew—

He pushes open a door and shoves me inside the room, which I recognize as his bedroom. I go stumbling in, nearly falling on my knees thanks to the too-high stilettos, and when I turn to face him, he's still standing by the door, his fingers curled around the handle.

"I should make you stay here and lock the door so you can't escape." His voice is more of a growl and the sound of it alone has my core clenching tight.

"Aww and leave me in your room all by myself?" I mock pout, letting my anger drive me. "I don't know if you can trust me not to go through your stuff."

"Joke's on you because I wouldn't leave shit in this room that I wouldn't want anyone to find." And with that, he slams the door, turning the lock and keeping me a prisoner.

A distressed cry leaves me and I look around the room, my breaths coming so fast my lungs ache. Who the hell does he think he is? I should have him arrested for kidnapping! He can't keep me in here against my will.

I march toward the door and try the handle but nothing happens. Laughter comes from the other side and it dawns on me that he's standing out there in the hall. Listening to me.

Pressing my mouth to the crack where the door meets the frame, I shout, "Let me out!"

His laughter gets louder.

"August!" I pound on the door with my fists hard enough that it hurts. "Open the door! Now!"

"Fuck you, Sin."

That only makes me madder. I am banging on the door over and over, tears stinging the corners of my eyes. I need to find my friend. I need to leave. I want to go back to my dorm and take off this stupid dress and these stupid shoes, crawl into bed and never leave it again. I hate it here.

I hate him.

Eventually exhausted, I stop knocking and screaming, slumping against the door and squeezing my eyes shut tight. My chest aches. My eyes do too and I'm on the verge of bawling like a baby out of pure frustration.

"Beg for it," he says.

I lift away from the door, glaring at it like he can see me. "What did you just say?"

"Beg me to open the door and I will." His voice gets closer. "Like you did the other night."

This fucker. He's sick. Demented.

"Do it, Sin, and I'll reward you."

"With what?" I slap my hand over my mouth, wishing I'd never asked.

"Whatever you want." Oh, he sounds amused. I'm sure he thinks he's got me, and you know what?

I'm going to let him think that.

"Please, August. Please unlock the door."

"You sound too polite."

He's deranged, I swear it.

"Cry for me, Sin. Let me know just how badly you want out of there."

I clear my throat, irritation flowing through my veins. God, he's insufferable. "Please, August. I'm begging you. Let me out. I'm scared."

"Scared of what?"

"Being in here alone." I am lying through my teeth. I'm too pissed off. Fear isn't even a second thought. "Help me, August. I'm scared."

"You should be scared of me." He's undoing the lock and I step away from the door, watching as it slowly sweeps open and he's standing there, as handsome as ever, a smug look on his gorgeous face. "Don't be scared, Sin. I'll take care of you."

Is he for real right now? God that was easy.

I put on my best pleading expression and rest my clutched hands against my obvious cleavage. His gaze drops to them, lingering there, and I realize he's staring at my chest. Figures. "Thank you. Thank you so much."

"You're wel—"

Before he can get the words out, I'm darting out the door, exiting his room and running down the hall toward the stairwell. He chases after me, grabbing me around the waist and picking me up so my feet are dangling. Squealing, I struggle within his hold, kicking my feet and trying to break free, but he just squeezes me closer.

"I can't trust you for shit," he mutters close to my ear, his mouth brushing the sensitive skin, making me shiver. "Who the fuck do you think you are?"

"I'm going to scream," I threaten. "Loud enough for the entire house to hear."

He slaps his hand over the lower half of my face, effectively silencing me as he drags me back into his bedroom, kicking the door shut. I'm yelling beneath his palm, trying to turn my face, but his grip is too strong. A gasp escapes me when he pushes me onto the bed and I fall backward, landing with a hard bounce. Rising up on my elbows, I watch as he stands at the foot of the bed, taking him in.

His legs are spread and his arms hang at his side, his hands clenched into fists. His breathing is ragged and he licks his lips, his gaze skimming over me, lingering on my thighs, which are completely exposed thanks to my dress rising up.

"You make me fucking insane," he mutters, taking a step toward the bed. Then another one. "I should punish you for that little stunt you just pulled."

"Fuck you, August." I spit his own words back at him, fueled by hatred and lust and some inexplicable emotion that's swirling within me. An emotion I always seem to feel whenever he's near. I have no idea what it is, but I hate it. Crave it.

Need it.

He reaches for me, each of his hands locking around my ankles as he jerks my legs open. A gasp escapes me, a trickle of fear and lust pooling in my stomach. Lower. His fingers are gentle, streaking up the inside of my calves, making goosebumps rise on my skin and his smile is knowing.

"I can smell you." His gaze lifts, locking with mine, the color of his eyes fiery pools of blue. "Your cunt."

I stare back, unable to speak. Too overcome.

"You like this, you sick little fuck." His hands shift higher, spreading my thighs wide, palms against my flesh pinning me open for his gaze. "No panties."

I'm dripping down my thighs at having him touch me, looming over me. Big and powerful and filled with the capability to snap me like a twig if he wanted. His fingers crawl up my left thigh, encountering nothing but smooth skin and the pleased growl that leaves him makes me nearly hum with pleasure.

"Bare." His gaze is fixed on my pussy, which is fully exposed, thanks to my dress riding up past my hips. "You did as I asked."

I remain quiet, closing my eyes to fight off the humiliation that wants to take over. I'm weak when it comes to him and I hate it.

Worse, I don't understand it. It doesn't feel right, to like this. To want this. With him.

"A pretty little pink pussy, just like I knew it would be." He dips his head, dropping a kiss right at the top of my slit. I nearly jerk off the bed. His lips are burning hot against my wet skin. "You dressed like a complete slut tonight."

I try to close my legs, but I can't. He's got them wide open, his torso pressing against my embarrassingly wet pussy, and he thrusts his face into mine. "Don't try and hide yourself, little whore. You were trying to catch someone's attention? Well, you got it."

He lets go of my leg and reaches in between us, his fingers curling around the top of my dress. Slowly he pulls it down, exposing my breasts, the cool air kissing my skin and making my nipples harden even more. His gaze drops and he rubs his lips together, his tongue peeking out. Reminding me of a hungry predator about to devour its prey.

I swallow hard when his gaze returns to mine, his pupils so blown out I see nothing but black. He looks crazed. I *feel* crazed. I want him to do something horrible to me—what, I don't know, and I close my eyes when shame washes over my skin at my confusing thoughts.

"Open your eyes." His fingers curl around my chin, giving my head a little shake, and I do as he says, staring into his icy blue gaze, terror making my heart pump twice as hard. I'm afraid. Shaking. Quivering with need and fear. "You need to remember who's doing this to you."

"Wh-what a-are you going t-to d-do t-to me-ee?" My words are a harsh whisper. I'm barely able to speak, I'm so scared and overwhelmed, and oh God, so stupidly *horny* for this man.

"Fuck you in the ass so your virginity stays intact? Is that what you want?" He nips at my lips and I cry out at the sting of his teeth. "Force you to suck my dick? It's what I promised the last time we were together."

I've never seen his dick and I'm dying to. I'm dying to see him completely naked, if I'm being truthful. I reach for him without thought and he grabs hold of my wrist, stopping me. Gathering up both of my wrists and raising my arms above my head, pinning me there. I say nothing, unsure of what he wants. Wondering if he even knows because he seems as baffled as I feel.

"Take off that shitty dress." He lets go of my wrists and moves away from me as if he's disgusted by my mere presence. I scramble on the bed, sitting up. "Now."

I whip the offensive dress off, tossing it onto the floor without hesitation, eager to get naked for him. I like the way I feel when his eyes roam all over me and he's doing it now, examining every inch of my exposed skin, his lips curling in a barely-there smile. I reach for the sandals, ready to take them off, but his command stops me.

"Keep the shoes on." He shakes his head, rubbing his chin with his fingers. "Fucking tacky. You look like a cheap hooker."

"You're an asshole," I tell him, not holding back.

"I think you like it." His expression hardens and I scramble backward on the bed until my butt hits the stack of pillows. "Spread your legs for me, Sin. Touch yourself. Show me how wet that pussy is."

I automatically do as he says, spreading my thighs as far as they'll go and bracing my feet on the mattress, dragging my fingers along my slit and holding them out to him. They shine with my juices and the pleased grunt that leaves him when he sees my glistening fingers has my pussy flooding even more.

"You love it when I treat you like shit." He grabs hold of my hand and bends over, drawing my fingers into his mouth and sucking them dry. A whimper leaves me when his tongue swirls around them, lapping up every bit of my juices before he pulls them out of his mouth. He takes a few steps back as if he needs the distance, standing at the foot of the bed. "Take my pants off."

I crawl across the mattress over to him and rise up on my knees, working the snap and then the zipper of his black pants, my fumbling fingers eager. He's got on black boxer briefs underneath, his cock straining against the fabric and I sit back, staring at him. Staring at it.

I've never touched a dick before. I have no idea what I'm doing and I know, I just know, he's going to make fun of me for it.

"Take it out," he demands, and I tug his underwear down, his erect cock thrusting toward me. I stare at it, unsure of what to do next. "Don't be so fucking shy, Sin. Act like the whore you came as and touch it."

I tilt my head back, glaring at him. My mouth trembles at the corners and I'm so mad, I could almost cry. I despise him. He's the worst. I should grab hold of his dick and squeeze until he's screaming in pain. I'm about to do exactly that when he does the most unexpected thing ever.

His hand cups my cheek, his touch gentle as his fingers skim over my skin, leaving me confused. He guides my head and tilts it back, our gazes clashing once again and while his still appears somewhat angry, his voice softens.

"I dream of that mouth. That cunt," he admits, his deep voice twisting my insides. "I can't stop thinking about you."

The words are familiar and I'm about to ask him if he sent that one mysterious text to me, but his mouth finds mine before I can speak. His lips are soft. Persuasive. Coaxing mine to part, his tongue sliding in, circling mine. I kiss him back, drowning in the taste of him, the commanding way he possesses me with his mouth, the low sounds of pleasure coming from deep in his chest.

He's enjoying this as much as I am. We're both completely fucked up.

And I never want it to stop.

CHAPTER TWENTY-SIX

AUGUST

This woman infuriates me. Fascinates me. Doesn't back down from a fight, begs for me to let her out of my room and then tries to run away from me. No woman I know would do that. They'd be down for whatever I suggested. Wear a butt plug to prepare them for a thorough ass fucking? Of course! Drip hot wax all over their naked flesh? I can't wait! Let me whip them with a leather strap until their skin welts? Please do!

I bet Sinclair would run from me if I tried to push a plug into her delectable ass. And she'd only let me smack her with a leather strap if she could do the same to me.

But I don't want to do any of that to her. That all feels like extra. Gimmicks to excite and I don't need any of that. Just looking at her excites me. I want to taste her. Everywhere. Run my lips all over her smooth skin. Fuck that pretty mouth of hers and come on her lips. I want to see them shiny with my cum and then I'd eat that little pussy of hers and fuck her ass with my finger until she squirted all over my face.

Fuck. I'm hard and aching just thinking about it.

I cup her face with both of my hands, climbing onto the bed and guiding her backward until she's sprawled across my mattress. I keep our mouths fused, my tongue working against hers. Stroking and circling and licking at the inside of her luscious mouth. I drift one hand down her front, running the back of my fingers across her nipple and the bit of flesh hardens even more. Tempting me.

Feeling weak, I give into temptation and pull away from her mouth, ignoring the frustrated sound that leaves her as I blaze a trail across her skin with my lips. Along her neck, her collarbone, licking across her breasts before I take one perfect pink nipple into my mouth and suck it as hard as I can. She immediately shoves her hands into my hair, clutching me close, arching against me. She responds so perfectly for me and I know we'd be so good together. Fucking her. Coming all over her...

Not yet though. She's not ready.

Pulling away from her greedy hands, I roll off the mattress and rid myself of my clothes. She sits up, pushing her dark hair away from her face, watching me with that heated golden gaze. Her nipples are hard rosy points that are begging for my mouth and I still can't get over that she waxed her pussy bare.

For me.

"I'm going to come down your throat," I tell her, my fingers wrapping around the base of my dick. She watches with complete fascination. "Think you can take it?"

She nods, licking her lips like the whore she is. Though I'm thinking she's really only a whore for me.

"Come here," I murmur. "Crawl to me."

I remain standing by the bed and she crawls across the mattress until she's right in front of me, her gaze on my dick. She's about to rise up on her knees when I speak, stopping her. "Stay just like that."

She's the prettiest thing I've ever seen, completely naked, only wearing those slutty gold sandals, her rounded ass sticking up. I take her in, her big golden-brown eyes watching me, her pouty lips parted and heavy. Like she's dying to suck me up. Stepping closer, I grab hold of my cock and brush the head against her lips. She purses them slightly, her eyes shifting up to meet mine.

Fuck, I could come just doing that. The look on her face. She's stunning.

"Open up," I croon. "Stick your tongue out."

She does as I command and licks me, her tongue tracing the flared head of my cock, her touch so light I'd almost think it wasn't happening if I didn't see it. "Suck me between your lips."

Sin pulls me into her mouth, her jaw working, her gaze returning to mine. My stomach clenches, my balls tightening up when I take her in. Looking like my every fantasy come to life as she stares up at me with her mouth full of my cock.

"Take it deeper, baby. I know you can do it."

I feed my dick to her, inch by inch, and she gags at one point, her throat working. I tell her to relax and she tries, her eyes watering when I feel the head of my cock bump the back of her throat, and goddamn, this is the hottest experience of my life.

Ever.

Slowly I pull almost all the way out of her mouth before I plunge back in. I do it over and over, keeping my pace even, trying not to overwhelm her and I'm already close. Like a kid in high school getting his first BJ, I can feel that familiar tingle at the base of my spine. In my balls. I'm going to come. She's barely sucked me.

I withdraw from her mouth completely, turning my back to her and I can feel her confusion, though she doesn't make a sound. I grab hold of my cock, cupping it, closing my eyes as I fight off the overwhelming need to blow and I hear the creak of the mattress as she moves. Feel her hand rest on my back briefly before it drops away. Like she's afraid to touch me.

"Did I—did I do something wrong?"

The moment is too vulnerable, too tender, and I fucking hate it. I turn around and grab hold of her, pushing her back onto the mattress and pinning her there yet again. "I'm going to feed my cock to you until you choke on it."

Before she can respond, I rise up on my knees, straddling her, sitting on her chest, never putting my full weight on her. Her mouth opens like she's going to yell at me and I do as I promised, shoving my cock in between her lips, shutting her up. Pushing, pushing, pushing until I can barely see my dick before I pull it back out, the veins bulging and my skin stretched tight, glistening from her saliva.

I fuck her mouth and she just lies there and takes it. Groaning. Whimpering. I could be hurting her, I don't know and I don't really care. I fuck her like I'd fuck that delicious little pussy, harder and faster until I feel it. My cock flexes and that first spurt hits her tongue. I groan, flooding her mouth with my semen, not even caring about her anymore—if I ever did. I'm too focused on the intensity of my orgasm. How it goes on and on like it's never going to stop, all thanks to this woman who lets me use and abuse her without protest.

When my orgasm is finally over, I slump on top of her, my chest in her face, my elbows resting on the pillow just above her head. I close my eyes, trying to control the wild beating of my heart. My breathing. I can't catch my breath. Can't believe I just came like that and she swallowed every fucking drop. I immediately feel like an asshole and want to make her leave. I need to be alone with my thoughts because what I just did to her?

Was seriously fucked up.

She wraps her arms around me, her hands pressing into my back, her touch gentle as she drifts her fingers up and down along my spine. A shiver moves through me at her sweet touch and when I finally lift up so I can look at her face, I see that she's smiling. Looking very pleased with herself.

"You liked that."

Grunting, I pull away from her and climb off the bed. "You should leave."

"No way." She rolls over on her side, contemplating me while looking like a fucking queen. "It's my turn."

"I don't know who the hell you think you are, demanding it be *your turn*." I reach for her, grab her by the arm and haul her up until she's standing right next to me. "Go."

She arches a brow. "Like this?"

I barely look at her. Worried if I do, I might do something stupid like fuck her senseless. "Yes," I bite out.

Sin shrugs, pulling out of my grip. "Okay."

She saunters toward the door, her hips swaying, her ass cheeks jiggling. Her body is unreal. Her ass is a perfect round shape and her legs are so fucking long. She has the body of a goddess and dismay fills me when she turns the handle and opens the door, about to step out into the hall completely naked.

Fuck that.

I lunge toward her, grabbing around her waist and holding her against me as I slam the door shut and walk us both back toward the bed. She's laughing the entire time, her pleasure at my reaction palpable and I hate myself for it.

Like a complete asshole I toss her back onto the bed, barking my demands. "Keep your feet on the floor."

She drapes her body along the edge of the bed, her feet planted before she spreads her legs. I fall to my knees in front of her— the second time I've done that and I don't go on my knees for any woman—and I spread her sticky thighs open, leaning in and breathing deep. Her pussy is musky sweet and when I dip my head and lick at her distended clit, she nearly jumps out of her skin.

"Ohmygod, stop." She tries to push me away but I don't move. "I'm too sensitive down there."

"You can take it," I mutter as I lick up all of her juices. She's soaked, my horny little Sin. Half my face is covered in her as I bury it against her pussy, licking her everywhere. Searching her, flicking at her sensitive skin with my tongue, swirling it around her entrance. The little hole that's supposed to take my cock with ease. Probably not. At least, not yet.

I tongue fuck her, holding her hips, opening my eyes to watch as she arches her back. Her eyes are closed and her lips are parted. She's fully immersed in me eating her pussy and I thrust my tongue inside her as far as I can go before I pull away and replace it with my finger.

Her greedy little hole suctions around my finger and I start to push deeper. Slowly at first, not wanting to hurt her. She takes it like the good girl she is, her back arching, sending my finger deeper and deciding she's ready, I add another one. Thrusting faster, stretching her wide like I did last time, but this time, she doesn't whimper in pain. She's thrashing her head back and forth, her groans loud and I love how she doesn't hold back. She's completely into this, into me, and I dip my head down, tonguing her clit while I fuck her with my fingers and her entire pussy seems to spasm.

"Oh God, yes," she cries just as a fresh gush of wetness floods her. Her inner walls clench around my finger in a rhythmic sensation, over and over, and I realize she's coming. Hard. To the point that her body bows forward and she gasps, a shaky moan sounding from deep in her chest. I won't let up, keeping my mouth on her, letting her ride out her orgasm on my face until she's pushing me away with her hands, her palm slapping against my nose and holding me away from her so she can roll over, her back and ass to me.

"What the fuck?" I mutter, staring at her plump backside. Her entire body shudders with the aftereffects of her orgasm and I realize I took things way too far. To the point that she can't handle it when I go down on her. It was too much.

I wipe the back of my hand across my face and breathe deep, the scent of her cunt flooding my senses. She is everywhere. All around me. I lost complete control with her and I never do that. Ever. I am in control of everything all of the time. It's my world and everyone just lives in it.

With the exception of this infuriating, captivating woman.

CHAPTER TWENTY-SEVEN

SINCLAIR

If I'm going to hell for everything I just experienced with August, then what a way to go because my God. My pussy still quivers from the tremendous orgasm I just experienced and my heart won't stop racing. I try to take deep, even breaths, but it's no use. I feel completely out of control and I don't mind. In fact, I prefer it when he takes utter control of me and tells me what to do. There's no guessing with him. Not really. I know he doesn't particularly like me and I feel the same. But there's this weird, overwhelming chemistry between us that sparks the air every time we're near each other. I'm attracted to him, which sounds so utterly weak and silly, those four words.

I'm attracted to him isn't enough to describe what happens between us when we're together like this.

"Get up." His voice is dark, full of irritation, and I yelp when I feel his palm come down hard on my ass cheek. The smack is loud in the otherwise quiet of the room and I try to roll away from him, but he reaches for me, his fingers gripping my hips. "You need to leave."

I tug out of his hold and sit up, pushing my hair out of my face so I can properly glare at him. "You're so fucking rude."

His expression doesn't falter. He just watches me with that impassive look on his face. In his eyes. All while he grabs a pair of black sweats that were draped across the back of a chair and steps into them, covering his lower half. What a disappointment. "You've served your purpose. Now it's time to go."

I gape at him, at a loss for words for a moment. "You can't just—treat women like that, you know?"

"Interesting you say that, considering this is the second encounter we've had and you seem to enjoy being with me." His gaze takes on a predatory gleam. "Something about you brings out the worst behavior in me."

"You're a fucking asshole." I've never spoken so cruelly to him before and it feels good.

No, scratch that. It feels great. Liberating even. Fourteen-year-old me would've loved the opportunity to call him exactly that. Though fourteen-year-old me would also be incredibly confused by my wanting to suck his dick.

He doesn't respond. Just watches me from where he's now perched on the edge of his massive bed while I grab the stupid red dress off the floor. I'm about to slip it on when his words halt me.

"You're not going back out in that."

I tug the dress into place, readjusting it around my boobs, hating how hard my nipples are. Enough to poke against the thin fabric like I'm still aroused which, okay fine, I still am. Just having his eyes on me is a turn-on. "I don't really have a choice."

"Hold on." His aggravated exhale makes me sigh in frustration as well. He goes to his closet and throws open the door, pulling out a random sweatshirt before he brings it over to me. "Put it on."

I stare at the hoodie like I have no comprehension of what it is. "Why are you giving me this?"

"I don't want you going out in public in that whorish dress. Who convinced you to wear it anyway?"

"It's Elise's," I admit.

He rolls his eyes. "Figures. Here." He shoves the sweatshirt practically into my chest and I grab it, shaking it out before I pull it on over my head.

It's huge, falling almost to my knees and oh God, it smells just like him, which is dangerous. If I had my choice, I would never give this sweatshirt back to him ever. I will own it for all time and I will never wash it, which is disgusting, and I'm disturbed by my thoughts but not disturbed enough to hand the hoodie back to him.

"That's better," he says as he examines me. "Can't even see the dress anymore."

"Was it really that bad?" My voice is soft. I'm having a total moment of weakness and I hate that it's happening in front of him.

"It was worse than you can possibly imagine. How unfortunate that you still have to wear the shoes." His upper lip curls in disgust.

"Have any other shoes for me to wear then?"

"Oh yes. Let me check my endless supply of women's shoes that I keep in my closet." He sends me a wry look. "Of course I don't have any shoes for you to wear. You're stuck with those gold abominations."

The straps have fallen down around my ankles and I bend over to fix them. "You weren't complaining when you asked me to keep them on earlier."

"I highly recommend you don't talk back to me." I glance up to find him glaring at me.

"What are you going to do, huh? Punish me?" I drag the last two words out, because come on. I need to examine why exactly I act the way I do when I'm with him, but now is not the time.

"No. You'd like that too much." He reaches for me, carefully grabbing hold of my arm and pulling me up until I'm standing. "Time to go."

"Let me go." His fingers press into my skin, making goosebumps rise. Making me uncomfortable.

"No." He smiles, devastatingly handsome when he does that.

"Take your hands off me before I call the cops." My tone is measured, my gaze never wavering. I mean business.

His laughter is mocking. "Please. You wouldn't have the courage."

"Don't forget I almost left your room completely naked," I point out.

The laughter dies, his expression turning fierce. "I would've killed every motherfucker who looked at you twice if you walked out there without a stitch of clothing on. And that would've been everyone because your body is unbelievable. Their blood would be on your hands."

My jaw drops at the offhanded compliment. He even seems startled that it slipped out and an unfamiliar feeling unfurls in my chest, warming me from the inside out.

It's satisfaction. Bone-deep, delicious satisfaction.

Once I'm finished fixing the stilettos, I saunter over to him, smiling. Smug with the knowledge that he thinks my body is *unbelievable*. He's admitted a few things to me that I think he hates confessing. And while most of the time I feel unsure and confused around him, right now I am practically brimming with confidence.

"I don't think we should see each other anymore," I announce.

He tilts his head down, scanning me as I stand before him in his hoodie and the stupid shoes. "Really."

His voice is flat. He doesn't believe me.

I refuse to let him break me down. I need to leave this room with the upper hand. "What we have is really—fucked up."

He snorts but otherwise says nothing.

"And it's freaking me out." I let my smile drop and hope I look frightened. That's what I'm going for at least. It's also kind of the truth because what we share between us is super intense and raw and almost...depraved? That feels like such a strong word to describe what's happening, but I don't know how else to describe it. I've gone from a virgin who's barely done anything to having him shove his cock down my throat. He threatened to fuck me in the ass so I could keep my virginity intact. Like who does that?

He crosses his arms, which causes his biceps to bulge, and my mouth waters a little bit. For a man who doesn't seem to have an athletic bone in his body beyond whatever he does sexually, he's definitely fit. Though I have no idea if he participates in any kind of sport but he seemed over it at that football game.

"If it's freaking you out, then you should probably leave."

We stare at each other for a moment, and I know what he's doing. Reverse psychology in the hopes that I'll get out of here, which is what he's wanted all along. I can go along with this.

"I will." I offer him a tiny wave and grab my bag from where it dropped on the floor. "See you around."

I exit his bedroom without a second glance, releasing the breath I didn't know I was holding only after I shut the door behind me. I run a hand over my hair, hoping I don't appear too trashed and I tug on the giant hoodie, knowing full well I look ridiculous but I don't care.

With my head held high, I walk down the stairs, though no one is paying attention to me. Somehow, the house is even more crowded than it was when I first went to August's room and I scan everyone's faces, already frustrated. It's going to be impossible to find Elise. She wouldn't hear her phone if I tried to call her, it's so loud in here.

"Sinclair! Holy shit!"

I turn at the familiar voice, pasting on the fake smile as Tim makes his way toward me. He's clutching a beer can in one hand and there's a giant grin on his face. He seems very glad to see me, while I am the complete opposite of that. "Hey, Tim."

"Elise said you were here but I didn't believe her." He pulls me in for a quick hug and I make sure and pull away from him as fast as possible. "What's up with the hoodie?"

"Oh, I had a minor—accident. Spilled something on my dress and this was the best thing to cover it up!" I am bright and cheery and eager to talk about something else. Anything else. "How are you? Where's Rafe?"

Tim makes a face. "He took off with Elise."

"Really?" I'm surprised, but then again, he's the one who approached her first. I wonder if Tim is jealous.

"Things were getting weird between all of us." He takes a step closer. "That's why I'm glad you're here tonight. I thought we could—talk."

I am not talking to him. Not when I still have remnants of August's cum on my lips. Not when the imprint of his hands and mouth and tongue still lingers on my skin.

"There's nothing to talk about, Tim." I tilt my head and try to send him meaningful glances but he doesn't seem to be picking up what I'm trying to put down. "It's better if we're just friends, don't you think?"

"I don't know what to think." He throws his hands up in the air, his frustration obvious and I almost feel sorry for him. But then I remember how he fucked my roommate with his roommate and all sympathy flies out the window. "I thought we could have something and now you're friend-zoning me."

"It could never work. You know this." Pretending I'm not completely crushing his feelings, I change the subject. "Hey, do you think you could get Elise for me? I really want to head back to our dorm."

"I'll walk you back," he suggests, and I'm shaking my head, cutting him off.

"I don't think that's a good idea."

His expression is crestfallen. "Come on, Sin. Don't be so uptight."

I don't like how he calls me Sin. And I definitely don't like him calling me uptight either.

"Go get Elise for me. Please." I try to smile, but his expression is sullen and his eyes are dark. Giving off vibes like he's looking for a fight and that's the last thing I want.

"No. I'll take you home. You don't need her." He grabs hold of my arm, like he's about to steer me out of the house, and I resist, trying to pull out of his grip, but he's surprisingly strong.

"Tim, no—" I jerk my arm extra hard, shocked when his hand falls away from me and I'm about to chew him out when I hear another familiar voice. One that fills me with dread.

"Is there a problem?"

My heart drops into my stomach and I close my eyes for a moment when I realize how close he is to us. To me. August.

Great.

CHAPTER TWENTY-EIGHT

AUGUST

She literally just exited my room like some sort of dignified queen and now here I am running to her rescue like I'm her knight in shining armor. You could never convince me fairytales were real when I was a kid. I called bullshit on all of them. And while my parents are the most romantic couple I've ever witnessed, I'd boldly claim that romance is dead in my withering, hateful soul and I'm okay with it. I don't need love. All it gets you is turmoil and stomach aches and that constant, nagging feeling that you have to protect someone. That someone depends on you and needs you more than air. That *you* need them more than air.

Just thinking about that is scary as fuck.

But here I am, helping Sin out with the loser Tim. He's sending glares that if looks could kill, I'd have a cut across my face with little bleeding. Meaning the guy is relatively harmless, but I don't think Sinclair believes that. She looks ready to run far and fast from him, even though I doubt he'd do much to her.

"We're good, prez," Tim finally says with a short nod. "Just about to walk Sinclair back to her dorm building."

"Oh." I can feel her watching me and fuck if I like it way too much. "That's funny because that's what I was just about to do too."

Tim frowns. "Really? You walk?"

"Well, no. I'm driving her." I pull my car keys out of my sweats pocket, turning to look at Sin. "Ready to go?"

She nods, her eyes flashing at me before she turns to Tim. "That's what I was trying to tell you."

"Oh. Yeah. Sorry. I guess I didn't…" Tim squints at us. "Are you two together?"

I chuckle. Sinclair full-blown laughs.

"No," I snap, my chuckle dying.

"Absolutely not," Sin agrees.

"Are you ready to go?" I offer her a baring of teeth because no, I'm not smiling at her. Not tonight and hopefully never again. "The car awaits."

"Perfect. Bye, Tim." She sashays in front of me toward the door, the hem of my hoodie swaying back and forth and maybe if I tilt my head just right, I might see her bare ass. But, no. I'm wrong.

Such a pity.

The moment we're outside she's turning on me and I steel myself, fully prepared for her to blast me for whatever false grievance she might have against my heroic act. Instead, she surprises me.

"Thank you for offering to take me back to my dorm." Her voice is small and she wraps her arms around her middle, a shiver visibly moving through her. "He was getting a little pushy."

"He was?" Pure hatred for Tim runs through my veins and my hands are clenched into fists. "Want me to take care of him?"

Her head jerks up, her eyes full of surprise at my offer and I suppose I deserve that. I'm surprised too, that I would make the offer.

"No. Please don't hurt him. It's just—he's not worth it." She's hanging on my arm, sending me a pleading look and I gaze into her eyes for a beat too long, drowning in their depths.

Fuck, she's beautiful and I despise it. There is no reason this woman has such a chokehold on me yet here I am standing in the front of the frat house on a Saturday night clad in just my sweats and a T-shirt that is—I glance down at myself—yep, inside out. Eager and ready to drive her back to her dorm room.

"Does your offer still stand?" she asks, after waiting me out to see if I'll say anything.

"What offer?"

She rolls her eyes, full of sass. "That you'll drive me back to my dorm building."

"Let's walk." When she starts to protest, I talk right over her. "It's not that far. And I'm not going to make you go alone."

"You're not?" She peers at me from beneath her thick eyelashes.

"I'm not a complete animal," I mutter as I start walking. She doesn't move and I get at least fifty feet away from her before I glance over my shoulder and say something. "Are you coming or what?"

"Yes! Oh my God." She's running in those horrible heels and somehow manages to stay upright, catching up to me with ease. "Thank you."

I say nothing in return. I don't deserve her thanks. I'm a dick who's only got one thing on his mind and that's how soon can I taste her delicious pussy again.

Wait. That's not necessarily true. I'm also thinking about what an asshole Tim is and how he can't pick up on her signals that he makes her uncomfortable. Or how many times she has to turn him down and he still doesn't get it. Is he purposely obtuse or just a complete dumbass? I still haven't figured him out. I don't think she has either.

We're quiet for most of the walk and I'm cold because I'm the idiot who only wore a T-shirt outside and it has to be fifty degrees, tops. That and the Gucci slides on my feet, which make me feel tacky because come on. They're Gucci, and I'm not a fan.

I'm a label snob. Sue me.

The walk to her dorm building goes by swiftly and she's glancing over her shoulder to study me as we head up the walkway that leads to the double door entrance of her dorm, her brows lowering. "Are you shivering?"

"It's fucking cold out here," I state the obvious.

"Do you want your hoodie back?" Her tone is reluctant and her movements slow as she starts to take it off. I practically lunge toward her, stopping her by pressing my hands on her arms and keeping them at her sides.

"No. Keep it." I like how she looks in it. Like she belongs to me.

I drop my hands and take a step back, scratching the back of my head. Uncomfortable with my thoughts because come the fuck on. Where did that come from?

"How about you come up to my dorm room and I can give it to you then."

I send her a questioning look. "I thought you didn't want to see me anymore. That I'm depraved."

"I don't," she says bluntly. "And it's what we do together that's depraved, though I do believe you're the root cause."

"Gee thanks."

"But I can return the hoodie to you so you can wear it on your walk back," she offers.

"I'll be fine."

"No, you won't. Come on." The little sinner actually has the audacity to grab my hand and drag me toward the doors, somehow digging into her purse at the same time, pulling out her key card and waving it in front of the lock pad so the doors swing open for us.

"Am I even allowed to enter this den of virginity?" I drawl as she practically drags me inside.

"It's Saturday night," she says as if that's the proper answer. "And I'm probably the only virgin in this entire building."

Doubtful but if she needs to keep telling herself that, then so be it.

She leads me over to the elevators and the doors slide open as if they were waiting for our arrival. The interior is dingy and old, the fluorescent lights flickering as we take the short ride to the third floor and when the elevator stops and the doors slide open, I practically jump out of there. I might take the stairs when I leave because that elevator has definitely seen better days.

"My room is this way." She flashes me a beguiling smile and leads me down the hall. The stench of burnt microwave popcorn fills the air and I can hear someone strumming a guitar—badly—while attempting to sing. Also badly. It's been a long time since I was a first-year student at Thornhill, but I never stayed in the dorms like this. I had my own private apartment that I shared with Cyrus and we had every amenity you could think of. We didn't have to deal with the riffraff.

Guess I'm spoiled.

"Okay, here it is." She comes to a stop in front of a door that's covered in what looks like a bunch of motivational quotes. The one right above Sinclair's head says, "Strive to be the best version of you," and I almost want to laugh. All I can envision is Sin spread across my bed, my face smashed against her pussy while I fingerfuck her. Is that her best version?

Christ, I'm sick in the head.

"Thank you for walking me." She opens the door and then wedges herself in between it, trying to take off the hoodie, but it's not working. "Come inside for a few."

"I don't think so..."

"I can't hold the door open and try and take off this hoodie—the door is too heavy. And don't worry, Elise isn't inside. She's back at the frat house with Rafe." She fully enters the room, holding the door open for me, and what am I supposed to do? Tell her to fuck off and leave?

Instead like the gentleman I am, I slowly enter her dorm room, turning to see the door slam shut with a hollow clang that rattles me straight to my bones. Reminding me that I'm in a room with her and it's just the two of us.

Alone.

"Okay. Give me just a minute." I watch her wander over to the tiny closet and tug open the door, pulling her own hoodie off a hanger and tossing it on her nearby bed before she reaches for the hem of the sweatshirt she's wearing and yanks it off. She tosses it on the bed as well and whips the dress off without warning, leaving her standing in front of me naked save for the shoes. Without a care in the world.

I snap my mouth shut, unaware it was hanging open but fuck, who could blame me. She's got the most beautiful body I've ever seen. Soft skin I haven't even begun to explore thoroughly. Things always seem to happen fast between us. One minute we're snapping at each other, the next thing we know, I'm shoving my dick in her mouth.

Guess we just get carried away.

Seconds later, she's wearing her hoodie and she's kicked off the gold stilettos. She finds a pair of blue and white cotton boxer shorts in her top dresser drawer and steps into them, covering herself up completely and I wonder if she planned that little strip show just for me.

"There we go. Oh my God, those shoes were the worst. Okay." She grabs my hoodie and turns to face me, pushing the wad of fabric into my chest and not giving me a choice but to take it. "Thank you again."

"For what?" I fully expect her to say the earth-shattering orgasm.

"For walking me to my room. And for the hoodie. I would've been frozen if I wasn't wearing it." She smiles. "Now you don't have to freeze on your walk back to the house."

"Right." I tug the hoodie on, hating how it smells like her. Fifteen minutes and she's branded my clothes like she owns them.

"It looks good on you." Her eyes are lit with interest and my entire body responds, which is a mistake. Been there, done that twice. Don't need to ever do it again. "Funny how it's so huge when I wear it but on you, it fits perfectly. You're a lot taller than me, you know."

I do know. She's stating the obvious.

"You didn't have to walk me back here. I could've done it on my own."

"And have Tim chase you down? I don't think so. Besides, if he'd done that, I would've ended him and I don't need someone's murder on my hands tonight."

"What, like you've murdered someone before?" She sounds amused.

I glare at her. "Of course not."

"You really would've done bodily harm to Tim?" Her brows shoot up.

"If he'd chased after you, yes," I bite out, hating how easy it is to be honest with her.

"That's so...sweet."

I bark out a laugh. "Don't get confused, Sin. I'm not a sweet person. I don't even fucking like you."

"Yet you'd defend me against Tim."

"It has nothing to do with you."

"Liar."

The word hangs in the air between us, like it's a living, breathing thing, and I hate it. Hate how she's watching me with that gleam in her gaze and the word somehow grows in between us, reminding me how much I hate liars and somehow, every damn time, I end up feeling like one when I'm with her.

"I'm leaving." I turn and head for the door, my steps determined, my mind awhirl with all of the stupid mistakes I made that led me to be here. Alone in Sin's dorm room. What the hell was I thinking? She's a baby. A little girl who's in over her head with me and now believes we're matched?

Please.

"You don't want a goodbye kiss?" she calls.

I spin around to face her, enraged. "Are you *mocking* me?"

"I don't know, August." She pauses, her eyes glowing. Why the hell is she extra beautiful right now anyway? She's a fucking mess, thanks to what we did in my room not even thirty minutes ago, and I swear I can still smell the scent of my cum on her skin, which has me in a feral state of mind. "Am I?"

If she wasn't mocking me before, she definitely is now. This girl—this supposed little innocent virgin who has more tricks up her sleeve than the most wizened whore currently working the streets—will be the fucking end of me.

CHAPTER TWENTY-NINE

SINCLAIR

August is halfway right. I'm mocking him but only because he pushed me. Taunting him because I find him irresistible when he's angry. More than anything, I'm trying to see how far I can go before he gives in. Because that's what I want—for him to give in to me. I want to witness him lose control on my turf and I want to see what might happen next between us. And while I meant what I said about us needing to stay away from each other because what we do together freaks me out a little, I can't resist one more try at getting to him. He's fun to provoke and for whatever reason, I seem to do it well.

"You're a menace," he murmurs, his gaze skimming over me from head to toe, heating up my already fiery skin as if he's actually touching me.

"I think that's the word I'd use to describe you." I turn my back to him, making sure my voice is extra cheery. "Time for bed."

Without warning I whip the sweatshirt off, tossing it on the floor before I pull back my covers and climb into my narrow little twin bed. I glance over at him to find he's still standing there, his fingers flexing at his sides, his gaze locked on my chest, which is completely exposed since I haven't pulled my comforter up yet.

"Is that how you normally sleep?" he asks between clenched teeth.

"Yes," I chirp, the lie coming easy.

"Even with Elise in the room with you?"

"We're both girls, you know. You've seen one set of tits you've seen them all." I smile sweetly at him, reaching for the hair tie on top of the mini fridge before I lift my arms and twist my hair into a sloppy bun. Making sure to arch my chest out so he can't miss my nakedness. "It's no big deal."

"Don't tell me you have naked slumber parties in here with her."

"In your dreams." I giggle, sounding like an idiot. He seems to be enjoying this so I keep it up, though I decide to be truthful. "Fine. I don't normally sleep topless."

"Now who's the liar." He arches an eyebrow, looking like a sexy motherfucker and ugh. This man.

"I was just kidding."

"Uh huh." He approaches my bed, his nose wrinkling in disgust as he examines it. "God, that's a small fucking bed."

"Don't think you can fit, huh?" He definitely can't fit. He's over six feet tall and broad-shouldered. His feet will definitely dangle off the edge of the mattress.

His heated gaze lifts to mine. "Are you inviting me into your bed, Sin?"

I can't say anything for a moment, overwhelmed by the desire in his gaze and the challenge in his deep voice. I get lost in his symmetrical features for a moment. His high cheekbones and the angular jaw. The square chin and soft, delicious lips.

He's too handsome for his own good.

I should be yelling at him to leave. I should've run from him weeks ago and stayed holed up in my dorm room. But it's not like I sought him out on purpose. We just...kept running into each other. To the point that it almost feels like fate.

No. That's reaching. I've never been one to believe in that sort of thing and I definitely don't believe in it when it comes to him.

I realize he's still waiting for a response and I glance around the bed, preparing myself for his rejection before I speak.

"Well, if you can't fit in my bed with me, I guess it won't work." I purse my lips into what I hope is a sexy pout, wondering who am I and what have I become since I've started this—whatever you want to call it with August.

"I can make this work." He tears the hoodie off. Then the T-shirt. Gets rid of his sweats too until he's completely naked, his erect cock pointing straight at me. My entire body floods with heat and I gasp when without any warning, he whips the covers back and climbs into bed with me.

I squeal when he grabs hold of my waist and lifts me as if I don't weigh a thing, readjusting me until I'm sprawled out on top of him, my legs draped around his hips, my pussy pressed against his stomach. I lift my head, our gazes snagging and he reaches toward me, brushing the hair out of my face, his fingers tracing my skin so lightly I could almost believe it wasn't happening at all.

"What are you doing?" I whisper.

"What do you think?" He grins and my breath catches at the sight of it. The man is too beautiful for words. If I keep staring at him, I'm worried I might faint. "We're having a naked slumber party."

"I still have shorts on," I remind him.

"We'll need to take care of that." His assured fingers dive under the covers, landing on the waistband of my boxer shorts before sliding beneath them. He caresses my ass, a single finger tracing my crack and I know my shorts are now completely soaked thanks to him. "Is Elise coming back any time soon?"

"I hope not," I whisper, dying to know what he might do to me next.

"How did we end up in this bed together again?" He appears momentarily confused. Completely adorable.

Wait a minute. August Lancaster, adorable? Impossible.

"Maybe we could just snuggle," I suggest as he slides his hands into my shorts and cups my ass cheeks.

"Naked snuggling?" He dips his head, pressing his face against my neck and breathing deep. "You smell like fucking sex."

"We haven't even done it yet," I whisper, my eyes falling shut when he starts kissing my neck. Soft, barely-there kisses that have my entire body tingling with anticipation.

"Just because we haven't done *it* doesn't mean we haven't had sex. How would you describe what we've been doing?" He's still cupping my ass cheeks, kneading and stroking them, and I can barely think with the way he's touching me.

"Hooking up?" I rest my hands on his shoulders, then slide them up his neck, shoving my fingers into his silky soft hair.

He lifts away from me, his clear blue eyes meeting mine and I realize he's frowning. Like he might be disappointed in me. "I have a different definition of hooking up then."

"What's your definition?"

"You giving me a blow job before I kick you out of my room. Or my car. Or the downstairs bathroom at the house." His smile is faint, his gaze shifting into villain mode. "I'm a selfish bastard."

"You do try to kick me out." But he's also been a giver with me, though I choose not to point that out. "You're one of the worst people I've ever met."

His chuckle is deep, making my pussy flutter. "Yet you invite me into your bed."

"It's a terrible bed. I hope you're uncomfortable," I immediately say, which makes him chuckle even more.

"The bed isn't so bad." He removes one of his hands from my boxer shorts and wraps it around the back of my head, holding me still so I have no choice but to stare at him in return. "I don't particularly like you either."

His words are like tiny stabs to my heart, cutting me deep. I lower my lids, not wanting him to see the turmoil that is surely swirling in my eyes, but his hand slides down and he squeezes the back of my neck, forcing me to look at him again.

"I didn't like you at first," he tacks on. "But now..."

He remains quiet, his fingers threading through my hair, stroking. Making me want to purr like a cat, his touch feels so good. How can he say such cruel things yet touch me like I matter? "Now, what?" I dare to ask, bracing myself for another insult. "Now I can't stop thinking about you. Like, ever. It frustrates me. You frustrate me. You don't back down from a fight and you seem to—like everything I do to you." His gaze turns turbulent, like there are a thousand storms swirling in the blue depths. "And I don't do those sorts of things to just any woman."

My heart swells and I feel giddy, which is stupid. I shouldn't believe anything he says. He's probably just using lines on me to get me to do something even more depraved than usual. Right?

There's something so sincere about the look on his face though. The sound of his voice. He almost appears pained that he admitted such a thing to me. Little ol', not important to him whatsoever, me.

"Should I feel honored?" I dare to ask.

"More like you should run screaming from this room." His lips lift in a barely-there smile and unable to help myself, I dip my head, pressing my mouth to his in the briefest kiss.

I try to pull away but his hand clamps tighter around my neck, keeping me there as he thoroughly ravages my mouth. His tongue is everywhere, searching, tangling with mine. I instinctively start rubbing against him, grinding my hips, desperate for friction. His dick pokes against my ass, insistent, teasing my crack and I grip his shoulders, moving my body over his, whimpering when he nips at my bottom lip with his teeth and gives it a tug.

"Such a horny little thing," he murmurs once he lets my lip go. "Always trying to get off."

I have no words. He's described me perfectly.

"You want to lose your virginity to me in this stupid little bed on a Saturday night? What if your roommate shows up?" He kisses along my jaw. Down the length of my neck. Setting my skin on fire with his warm, wet mouth.

"I don't care." A moan leaves me when he pinches my nipple so tight the ache spirals throughout my body, settling between my legs.

"You don't care? Really." His voice turns flat and he removes his hands from me. His mouth. Shoves at me until I have no choice but to practically fall off my bed a gasping, shivering mess.

"What are you doing?" He climbs out of my bed and starts putting on his clothes, his movements jerky, his expression dark. Almost scary.

"Leaving." He glares at me. "You don't care, right? Find somebody else to fuck you then."

August Lancaster storms out of my room, slamming the door so hard my teeth rattle in my head. I stare at the door for a moment, glancing down at myself. My skin is rosy red, my nipples aching hard points and the front of my boxer shorts are soaked. I was this close to orgasm, this close to knowing what it would be like to have August inside me and he…what? Got hurt because I said I didn't care?

I start to laugh. This man is absolutely ridiculous.

He just might have feelings for me.

CHAPTER THIRTY

SINCLAIR

Three weeks go by and I don't see August, which is probably for the best. Midterms are happening this week and the school workload has intensified. Elise and I are constantly in the library, desperate for quiet time so we can get our assignments done. Working on papers and studying for tests and oh God, the group projects I'm currently working on make me want to curl up in a ball and die.

Only at night do I think of him. When I'm alone in my little bed, remembering what it was like to share this space with August. I was sprawled across his hot body and he touched me almost reverently. How he kissed me. What he said to me. I should feel regret for what I said to trigger him into leaving, but then again, I don't. I still stand by my feelings about us staying away from each other. It's best. He's terrifying. What we do together is terrifying. And how he makes me feel?

Is the scariest thing I've ever experienced in my life.

I'm currently in the library at this very moment, trying to write an essay for my ethics class while Elise is studying for her physical anthropology test. She's trying to memorize various animals just by identifying them with a photo and her constant murmurings of "ring-tailed lemur" and "Bengal slow loris" are driving me crazy.

"I am so sick of this." Elise slams her laptop shut, echoing my mental sentiments. "If I don't know what these animals are by now, I'm hopeless."

"You've been studying a lot," I agree, wishing I could give up on my paper. "When is the test again?"

"Tomorrow morning. My brain is fried. I'm going to grab something to eat and go back to our room. You coming with?" Elise shoves her laptop in her backpack and zips it closed before she stands.

"I wish I could but I need to finish this paper." I glare at my laptop screen, hating how I'm barely halfway finished, and that's probably a generous description. More like only a third finished if I'm being real. "It's due at midnight."

"You've got time, and you always manage to bang those out." Elise offers me a little smile. "You sure you don't want to take a dinner break with me?"

Dinner breaks with Elise are my favorite. We gossip the entire time, which usually consists of her telling me what guy she's with now and sharing all the intimate details while I ask her endless questions. It never feels one-sided though. She tries to get information out of me and I always change the subject. I've never been that comfortable sharing personal details with people. I'm always afraid they're going to be used against me.

"I would love to but I want to finish this paper now so I'm not writing it at eleven-forty-five tonight." A sigh leaves me and I slump in my chair. "Wish me luck?"

"You know it." Elise smiles and offers a cheerful wave. "See ya!"

Once she's gone, I get serious, putting my AirPods in and typing away. I'm in the zone, the paper coming easily and an hour goes by. I'm nearly finished when I swear that I can feel someone watching me.

Pausing the music, I glance around but see nothing. I'm pretty deep into the library, not too far from the study rooms at the back of the building, and not that many people come here. Most everyone stays near the front, where all the action is. I like to sit in the front too, but not when I'm dealing with too much homework.

I turn the music back on and finish the paper, then save it and close my laptop. I'll grab something to eat before I head back to our dorm room, and after I take a shower, I'll look over the paper one last time before I turn it in. I'm pulling my AirPods out of my ears when I hear someone say my name.

A male someone.

Bracing myself, I glance over my shoulder to find August standing in the middle of the aisle closest to my table, his gaze searing into mine. God, he looks amazing. There's a bit of scruff on his face, like he hasn't shaved, which isn't normal but such a good look for him. His hair is swept back from his gorgeous face and his normally full lips are pulled into a straight line.

Like he's annoyed to see me.

I jerk my head, facing forward again, moving like a robot as I grab my backpack and start putting my stuff away. Internally I'm buzzing, anxious to get out of here. Away from him. I told myself I didn't need him. Didn't miss him. But seeing him right now, having him in my presence and so close, my entire body is lit from within.

And that's the wrong reaction to have.

I pull my backpack strap over my shoulder and am about to leave when I can feel him drawing closer, his hand lightly resting on my elbow. I whirl on him, my heart hammering, threatening to burst out of my chest and I see the regret flash in his eyes for the quickest moment before it's gone. Replaced with the typical gleam of disdain that always seems to be there.

"Sinclair." His voice is flat, and I wonder why he stopped me in the first place if he didn't want to talk to me. "Hello."

"August." I match his tone, not wanting him to think I'm thrilled to be in his presence. I mean, I am, but I don't want him to know that. And it's more my body is excited to be close to his. Not my mind. My mind is screaming at me to leave. Now. "Good seeing you."

I start walking and he keeps pace with me. "It's been a while."

"It has." I send him a condescending smile. "I'm sure you've been avoiding me."

He frowns. "I thought you were avoiding me."

Oh please. Like he cares. "If I was, it must've been a happy accident."

I move through the stacks, August trailing just behind me, the spicy scent of his cologne lingering in the air, making me dizzy. I'd never admit it to him, but it took me a while to wash my pillowcase after he laid his head on it. I would fall asleep to the scent of him and it was…comforting.

Which is dumb. I am a dumb, hopeless girl when it comes to this man and I sort of hate myself for it.

"I was trying to give you space," he finally says once we're walking through the front of the building. Past the help desk and the many tables that are filled with students. All of them are watching us, I can feel their eyes as we walk past, and I'm sure they're wondering who *the* August Lancaster is talking to.

"Space?" I come to a stop in front of those tables, in the mood to make a public spectacle. "If I remember, you're the one who ran away after getting thoroughly pissed at me for something stupid that I said."

His gaze hardens, as does his expression. "What you said was bullshit."

"What I said was meaningless. Or did I hurt your little feelings?" I turn on my heel and storm out of the library, heading straight for my dorm building. God, he's infuriating. I don't even know why I'm so upset at running into him in the library, but seeing him sparked something inside me. Irritation and desire. Always the desire.

The library doors clang shut and I can hear him shouting my name like a scorned boyfriend. I pick up my pace, desperate to get away from him. I'm almost into a full-blown run when he catches up with me, grabbing hold of my arm and stopping me. Twisting me around so I have no choice but to face him.

And when I do, I don't want to look at his face. He's too handsome, too intoxicating and my hormones always react. I stare at his chest instead, the charcoal gray hoodie he's wearing and how he manages to look classy and sophisticated even in the most basic of outfits. Rich men are the worst.

"You did," he says, faintly breathless, and I tilt my head back, staring into his eyes when I told myself I wouldn't look at his face. But he's too alluring, too freaking *much*.

I frown, confused. "I did what?"

"Hurt my feelings," he bites out, and I wonder how difficult that was for him, admitting that.

My brows shoot up and I decide to fuck with him. "You have feelings?"

"I know, right? It's baffling. I was confused myself. That's why I ran out of your room that night. What you said, fucked with my head. More than that, it enraged me."

"What did I even say?" I sort of remember, sort of don't. That entire night is a blur to me now because of all the things that happened.

"Your exact quote was, 'I don't care.' After I asked you if you wanted to have sex with me." His voice is stiff, his cheeks ruddy with...what? Embarrassment? Come on.

When I hear him say those words though, the memories come flooding back, reminding me of our conversation. "I meant I didn't care if Elise was coming back to my room. You asked me about that too. And I said I didn't care because in that moment, the entire building could've filed into my room and it wouldn't have mattered to me. I was that caught up in you."

I press my lips together the moment the words leave me, mortified. I should've never admitted that. I don't want to give him all the power.

His brows draw together as if he's trying to recall our conversation. "Really? You weren't referring to—"

It's his turn to press his lips together, going quiet. But I know what he was going to say, and he's right. I wasn't referring to him.

We stand in front of each other for maybe thirty seconds tops and he's shaking his head, that familiar look of disgust on his face. "This is pointless. You said we needed space and you were right. I think we might need it—permanently."

He pushes past me, his shoulder knocking into mine like he wanted that one last point of contact between us and I turn to watch him go, anger rising within me. Emboldening me. "Why do you say that? Because you're too scared of your feelings? Oh right, you don't have any."

August keeps walking, though his pace slows.

"Keep running away from your emotions, August! I'm sure it's a Lancaster trait!" I am shouting at him, as loud as can be and not caring who hears me. Not that there are a lot of people outside at the moment. Feels like it's pretty much just the two of us.

He comes to a stop in the middle of the walkway, tilting his head back to stare at the darkening sky. Resting his hands on his hips. I don't move, keeping my gaze on him, curious as to what he might do next. And he doesn't disappoint.

Turning, he strides toward me, his expression determined. "You don't know what my family is like, so don't bother trying to figure them out."

"Did I hit a nerve?" My brows shoot up in question. I've heard of his ruthless father. He sounds like a giant dick. Like father, like son.

"Yes, only because you're so fucking wrong." He grabs my hand, jerking me to him and our bodies collide. Just like that, my skin tingles, even with the layers of clothing I'm wearing and my body leans into his like the traitor she is. "My mother is the sweetest woman on this planet who is always there for us. She's still there for us. And my father has a tough exterior, but he is completely obsessed with my mother and worships the ground she walks on. Growing up, their love for each other made me uncomfortable. It fucking terrified me, because who could actually love someone that much? Be that obsessed with someone to the point that nothing else mattered as long as they had each other? That shit is scary."

He's breathing hard and so am I, his words shocking me. Is his parents' relationship toxic? Are they too reliant on each other? Is that what scares him about love and relationships? Because clearly the man is uncomfortable with the topic.

"I've never met someone who made me feel even a little bit like that. I kept the walls up because it was easier. When you grow up with all of your relatives, including your father, telling you that when you know, you fucking know, they make it sound like a curse. I didn't want to be afflicted."

"A curse? And afflicted with what?" He makes it sound like he thinks of emotions as a disease.

"Obsession. Love. It doesn't seem to matter if you're in my family. They're one and the same." He tugs me closer, thrusting his face in mine. "I can't explain it. I don't even know you, Sin, and I'm fucking *obsessed* with you. Just like I feared would happen to me, what I've been avoiding for years. They warned me my entire life this would happen and here I am, fucking gone over a girl who's barely legal and fights with me all the goddamned time. Why? Why you? You're nothing special."

"Thanks a lot." I try to jerk out of his hold, but he won't let me, his fingers tightening around my arm, his body crowding mine. My backpack slips off my shoulder, falling onto the ground with a thud and I glance to my right to see where it landed. But August grabs hold of my chin, forcing me to look at him again and what I see in his eyes is...overwhelming.

Desperation. He even seems traumatized, and I'd guess he's the sort who doesn't discuss his feelings. Like ever.

"I didn't mean it like that." An exasperated noise leaves him and he shakes his head, closing his eyes for the briefest moment before reopening them. His grip relaxes on my arm and he leans back a little, as if he's giving me space. "You're just—you're an ordinary person, so why can't I stop thinking about you?"

He sounds agonized and I should feel some satisfaction in that, but I don't. I feel as tortured as he looks, my emotions threatening to wash over me in the most overwhelming way possible and I tug out of his hold, taking a few steps back. Needing distance to clear my head.

"Obsession isn't healthy," I murmur, rubbing at the spot where his fingers burned into my skin. "What we've shared so far...isn't healthy either."

"You're right. It's not." He visibly swallows. "But it's still there. I can't deny it. Can you?"

CHAPTER THIRTY-ONE

AUGUST

I do not say such things ever. Put myself on the line for someone I barely know? Never. I keep my circle tight and it consists of my family—who I can barely tolerate sometimes—and the very few friends I have, which are almost nonexistent. I'd like to think I've lived a mostly solitary life and I have zero problems with that. I don't need anyone. I don't want anyone.

Until *she* walked into my life.

Now Sinclair is all I can think about. She pissed me off with the *I don't care* response and I took it personally like a little baby bitch. Something I never do. Taking things personally isn't part of my nature because nothing is ever personal. I am just living. Moving through life like a fucking shark who just swims and swims and never stops. Who eats when he wants. Fucks when he wants. On an endless loop, perfectly satisfied.

That's me. That's the way I prefer things until Sinclair Miller comes along and fucks it all up. Fucks with my head and my body. My dick wants no one else. Hell, I tried talking to some nameless, faceless woman at a party last weekend and felt nothing. Zero interest. She was beautiful. Flirtatious and willing to do anything I wanted. She basically said that, and I turned her down flat. Left the party and went back to the house, where I locked myself away in my bedroom and jerked off to thoughts of her. Sinclair.

Jesus. I am fucked.

"I-I need time to think," Sin admits, her voice low, her expression skittish. She looks ready to run at the first opportunity. "You're overwhelming me."

Just being in her presence and hearing her speak is overwhelming, but I can't say that. She'll run and I'd chase after her and catch her because I always do. Sling her over my shoulder and take her back to my room at the frat house—I hate that I live at the fucking frat, I need out of there—and fuck her senseless. Until she can't speak or think and she's drenched in my cum. Smelling like me because she belongs to me—

See? My thoughts are fucked up and crazy and it's all because of her. I have a problem. Is this what my father experienced with my mother? God, I should ask him. I could really use some advice right now.

But maybe I don't want to know. What if that's exactly how he felt when he met Mom? Like a lightning strike, forever changed. Forever fucking *ruined*.

That's what it feels like. I hate it.

I'm obsessed with it.

"Maybe we can take this slow," she adds.

I squint at her, trying to comprehend what she means by that. "Take what slow?"

Slow isn't part of my nature. I don't do slow for anyone. I waste zero time and I'm impatient to a fault.

"Us. Whatever this is that we're doing." She waves a hand between us, her delicate brows drawn together. She seems confused. Unsettled. But at least she doesn't look ready to bolt any longer. "You could take me on a date."

"A date? Aren't we passed that nonsense?"

Her expression turns sour. "No. No, we are not. And taking a woman on a date isn't nonsense. Have you ever done it?"

"Done what? Gone on a date?" She nods. "Well. No."

Sin rolls her eyes. "Oh my God. How old are you again?"

"Twenty-two."

"And you've never been on a date." She sounds absolutely disgusted. With me. Like that ever happens. "I'm not even going to bother asking if you've ever been in love."

"Have you been in love?" I will kill the asshole if she has. No one on this earth deserves her love. Not even me.

"No. But I've been on dates." A sigh leaves her and she slowly shakes her head. "You want to make something of this? You should ask me on a date."

"Will you go on a date with me?" The words automatically leave me and I feel like a fool. Is this what it's supposed to be like, asking a woman to go out with you? It's borderline humiliating.

Her eyes are actually sparkling. She's eating this shit up. "I would love to. Where are you taking me?"

"Where do you want to go?"

"No, it doesn't work like that, August. You have to plan the date." She is beaming, she's so pleased. "What are you thinking? We could go out on Friday?"

"It's Monday." Friday is forever from now. I can't wait that long. "How about this evening?"

"Noooo." She draws the word out, laughing. "I'm so busy this week with school. There's no way I can get together with you until Friday. Well, maybe Thursday night? That could work too."

"Thursday it is." My voice is firm. I'm not about to let her change her mind.

"Okay. Perfect. You'll have to tell me how I should dress."

For fuck's sake. "What in the hell do you mean by that?"

"Well, if you're taking me to dinner, then I need to know what kind of restaurant it is so I can figure out what I should wear. Something casual? Or something more…formal? I know how you rich guys are. You love fancy places."

You rich guys? "Isn't your family wealthy?"

"Well…yes."

"Are you close to them? Your family?"

She grimaces. "I don't want to talk about them."

That's definitely a no. "You want me to plan our date and then tell you where we're going?"

"You don't have to give away all the details but just…let me know how I should dress. I want to wear something appropriate." She clutches her hands together beneath her chin, looking younger than her eighteen years, which makes me feel like a lecherous old man. "You're really going to take me on a date."

She sounds surprised, which is…cute. And I don't think anyone or anything is cute. Not even my niece. That little monster is the complete opposite of cute. Astrid is terrifying with all her screaming and wailing and thrashing about.

"You keep talking about this date, the more you're going to convince me it's a bad idea," I warn her, though I don't mean a word of it. If this is what she wants, this is what she'll get.

"My lips are sealed." She mimes zipping her mouth shut, locking it and throwing away the key. "Text me!" She's about to walk away when she stops, turning to face me once more. "Do you have my number?"

I do. I sent her a text once and while she did respond, I could never reply back because I was worried she'd think I was an out-of-his-mind stalker. But I decide to lie. "I don't."

"What's your number?"

I rattle it off and she adds it to her phone, sending me a text. My phone buzzes and I check it.

Can't wait for our date.

She even included a smiley face emoji. I rarely use them. I think they're stupid.

When I glance up, I see her watching me carefully. "You've texted me before, you know. You're the one who said you couldn't stop thinking about me."

This entire experience is mortifying. No wonder I've never asked anyone on a date before. It's a nightmare situation. "See? I've been afflicted since pretty much day one."

"You make it sound like a bad thing." Her smile is huge and the sight of it has my heart twisted up in knots. The poor thing. It's been nonfunctioning my entire life and now it's pounding all the time and probably confused as fuck. "See you Thursday, August."

I watch her walk away until she disappears into the darkness, rubbing at my chest. Hoping that she's safe. I send her a text.

Tell me when you're in your dorm room.

Sin: *Why? Do you want to sext me?*

Hmm. That sounds interesting, but not at the moment. I decide to be honest because lying just gets me in trouble.

Me: *I want to make sure you're safe.*

Sin: *Awwww. Big bad August actually cares.*

Fuck. I do. More than I'd ever want to admit.

. . .

Two days later and I still haven't planned our date. Considering I'm a novice, I have zero idea where to start and I'm not about to ask my best friend because he'll mock my ass the entire time and ask me stupid questions like if I'm in love or some such shit. I'm not in love. But I am hopelessly obsessed and wondering if I can work Sinclair out of my system. This could be a momentary blip in my life and eventually we'll realize we're not good for each other. Or she could be the love of my life and I'll have to convince her we could make it work.

Either scenario, I'm the one doing all the heavy lifting, but it's fine. I'm fine.

I consider asking my mother where would be a good restaurant to take a date to but that'll just get her hopes up and I don't want to do that. I've shown no real interest in girls my entire existence beyond fucking around with them and I definitely would never tell her that. Mentioning the word *date* to my beautiful, romantic mother would be a huge mistake and open up all sorts of questions I don't want to answer.

I decide to ask my sister for advice instead. Risky but fuck it. Iris has taste and she'll know what to do.

Hitting the FaceTime button, I wait for her to answer. I'm taking a chance because she could be breastfeeding her little monster and that's the last thing that I want to see but I'm desperate.

Iris answers on the fourth ring and blessedly, it's only her I can see in the camera.

"August! Oh my God! Are you unwell?" The concern in her voice is obvious.

I'm immediately irritated. "What the fuck, Iris? Can't I just... call you?"

"No. You can't. There's always a reason and honestly? You look...not irritated?"

"Do I usually look irritated?" I already know the answer.

"For sure," she says without hesitation because if there's one thing I can count on, it's my sister being brutally honest. "And while you don't necessarily look happy right now, you don't seem pissed either. I take this as a good sign."

I exhale loudly enough for her to hear, needing her to know I am now, indeed irritated, but she just sits there and grins. "I, uh, I need your opinion about something."

The smile fades. "About what? Seriously, is everything okay?"

"I'm fine," I bark out, immediately feeling like an asshole. "I just need help."

"From me?" She rests her hand on her chest.

"Yes, from you. Where's a good place to take someone to dinner?"

Iris blinks slowly. "Who are you taking to dinner?"

"A woman."

"Are you going on a date, Augie?" Her eyes are huge and she's got her hand on her chest again. Or did she ever remove it? "An actual date with an actual woman you're...actually interested in?"

That's three actuals in one sentence. "I don't know if I'm interested in her."

There I go lying again. I'm beyond interested in her. I literally cannot stop thinking about her. It's fucking maddening.

"Who is it?"

"You don't know her." Lie number two.

"At least give me her name. You'd be surprised by how many people I actually do know."

Iris is far more social than me. Friendlier. She's a good time while I am most definitely not. "I don't want to tell you who it is."

"Then I don't want to help you." She crosses her arms in front of her chest. "Guess we're done with this conversation."

She is beyond exasperating. "Where's your child?"

"Napping."

"Where's Brooks?"

"At work."

"He works?"

"For his father, yes." A sigh leaves her and she tilts her head to the side, her blonde hair cascading past her shoulder. "We're living our lives over here, August. Brooks is working and I'm taking care of the baby. We don't have the luxury like you do of having fun at college and going on dates with random women."

I'm older than her by a few years and she's making me feel like an idiot. I don't like this. At all. "It's Sinclair Miller. That's who I'm going on a date with."

Her jaw drops and her eyes nearly bug out of her head. "Are you fucking serious? The girl you bullied and tortured her entire freshman year agreed to go on a *date* with you? Has she lost her mind?"

"She's forgiven me for my past sins." Has she? I have no idea. I've never apologized to her for what I did, but that was so long ago.

"Well, isn't she the bigger person." Iris squints into the camera. "You're really going out with her?"

"Yes, and it's happening tomorrow night so I need ideas, Iris. Now," I snap.

My sister laughs at me because she's got me by the literal balls and there's nothing that I can do about it. "Do you want to impress her?"

"Aren't I impressive enough?" I'm a Lancaster. I've impressed her with my dick and all the things I can do to her with my fingers and mouth. What else is there to impress her with?

"Oh, Augie. You're hopeless." Iris shakes her head. "Of course, you want to impress her. You need to take her somewhere in the city. Like the most popular restaurant there is, though you might have a hard time getting a table if your date is tomorrow? Hmm, and it's on a Thursday—that might be your only saving grace."

"It was her first night available." I swallow whatever else I might say that makes me sound eager and ridiculous. "And I can get a table at any restaurant in Manhattan. All I have to say is my name when I make the call."

"True. Well, you should pull out all the stops. Like, fly her in on the helicopter." Our father recently acquired one. That's a good idea. "Take her to the most buzzed about, expensive restaurant in the city and put on the charm. Can you do that? Put on charm? You're never charming to me, but I'm thinking you might have it in you. Daddy is charming and you're a lot like him."

"I can be charming." Maybe. I don't have to work hard at trying to charm anyone because everyone I encounter pretty much bows at my feet. I put in zero effort and always have their respect. "You need to give me a list of the best restaurants. I don't have a clue."

"You have Google," she points out.

"Yes, but that's not the same as you knowing what's out there. I trust your opinion, Iris, though maybe you don't get out as much as you'd like." I'm starting to sweat. She might've been a bad choice, but what are my options? I suppose I could ask Rowan or Willow. But Willow doesn't even live here anymore. She's too busy chasing after her football playing fiancé, and Rowan is in high school doing stupid high school things. Why would I ask him for advice?

"I'll compile you a list. Brooks and I do have a social life, despite what you think. We go out often because Mom always wants to watch the baby for us." Iris taps her pursed lips with her index finger. "Let me think on this and I'll text you a few restaurant names."

"I need the names now."

"I know, I know," she mutters, rolling her eyes. "Always so impatient."

"Hurry." I end the call before I do something stupid like thank her. If I'm polite and grateful she'll definitely think something is wrong with me. Though maybe there's no point in playing it cool. Something is definitely wrong with me.

And her name is Sinclair Miller.

CHAPTER THIRTY-TWO

SINCLAIR

I've been a jumble of nerves since my encounter with August in the library. His brutally honest confessions left me on edge and I still can't believe he's taking me on a date. Like he's what… serious about me?

No way.

Maybe?

Probably not.

He finally reached out Wednesday afternoon and told me to wear something sexy but classy. That was his only guidance. I freaked the hell out because of course I did. I am almost nineteen years old and the last time I wore something that I thought was sexy, he continuously insulted me and made me feel like I dressed like a cheap hooker.

I'm not good with sexy, clearly. Classy I can do. I spent enough time around the other girls at Lancaster Prep that I know classy when I see it. My mother would be no help, because she's as tacky as they come. God love her.

She would probably love it if she knew I was going on a date with August Lancaster. Not that I'm about to tell her though. She barely contacts me now that I'm gone. I bet she's relieved she doesn't have to see me on a daily basis anymore.

My parents are the worst.

It's Thursday and I just finished my last class so I'm in my dorm room, staring at the boring options in my closet. Elise is sprawled across her bed, hugging her pillow and watching me with pity in her eyes.

"You should wear that red dress again," she suggests.

"Absolutely not. He hated it."

"Hated it so much that he basically tore it off your body." Oh she sounds pleased, and she is. I finally had to confess all to her about August, and she is practically green with envy over my situation. "I have some options."

Her options won't work. I already know it. "I guess I could go to the mall."

Elise sits up. "I could go with you."

There's a knock at our door and I go to open it, curious. One of our RAs is standing there with a massive box clutched in her hands. It's so big, I can't even see her face until she peers around it. "Oh hey. Exactly the person I was looking for. You have a delivery."

She holds the box out to me and I take it from her. "Wow. Thanks. I wonder what this is."

"I have no idea but it says Bergdorf Goodman on it so it must be something expensive." The RA waves at me and takes off down the hall.

I let the door slam behind me and go to my bed, setting the massive white box on top of it. It does say Bergdorf Goodman on it. I used to go shopping there with my mom when I was in high school and my parents had just run into their fortune. Not that I got anything for myself. More like I tagged along and watched her spend a bunch of money.

"Who's it from?" Elise asks.

"I don't know." But I have my suspicions.

"Open it up and find out."

Carefully I open the box, pulling the lid off the top to see an envelope with my name on it lying on a bed of white tissue. I open the envelope to find a thick white card inside it.

Wear this tonight.

A

"It's from August." I glance over at Elise who is watching me carefully. "He said I can wear whatever's in here on our date."

"Oh my God, well let's see what it is!" Elise practically squeals.

I push away the layers of tissue to discover a pale blue box inside, Prada written on top of it. I take off the lid to discover even more tissue. I pull the garment out, holding my breath as I examine it.

The sheath dress is sleeveless, with a deep V neckline in the front, and it's constructed entirely of beige sequins. It's sheer, almost see-through and I take the dress to the full-length mirror, holding it up in front of me.

"It's beautiful," Elise breathes as she comes to stand behind me.

"You can probably see through it." What in the world do I wear underneath this?

"Sexy but classy." She's smiling. "He has good taste."

"He has a lot of money," I correct.

"Just because someone has money doesn't mean they have taste."

True. Dang it.

"There's more in the box," Elise reminds me.

August thought of everything. There's not only the dress, but he also included a pair of the sheerest black tights I've ever seen, a pair of black Prada peep toe heels with delicate straps that wrap around the ankle, and a black Prada bag covered completely in crystals, but no undergarments. Which has me stressed the most.

What do I wear beneath this thing?

My phone buzzes with a notification and I check it to see I have a text from him.

August: *I see my gift arrived.*

Me: *Everything is beautiful, thank you! But what do I wear underneath it?*

August: *Wear only what's in the box, Sin.*

My skin warms. I can hear him say those words and they seem to vibrate just beneath my skin.

Me: *But there isn't a bra or panties. And the dress is so sheer!*

August: *Trust me. I spoke to a sales associate. She has exquisite taste and told me you'll look stunning.*

Trust him. I can't trust him. He's horrible most of the time. I think he enjoys making me squirm. Humiliating me. And there's a small part of me that enjoys it too.

Me: *If you say so.*

"I'm supposed to wear this without any underwear." I drop the sequined dress onto my bed. "I'll look like a slut."

"Oh, you will not." Elise grabs the dress and holds it up practically to her face. "It's not that sheer. It'll probably give the illusion that you're naked underneath it."

"And I'm supposed to wear the black tights beneath it? That'll look stupid." He's setting me up, I swear.

"It won't. You're going to look like a goddess. He'll swallow his tongue the moment he sees you."

"He better not. I happen to like his tongue a lot," I retort, making Elise laugh.

I start laughing too. This is the most surreal experience of my life and I should just go with it, but it's hard. Especially when I don't necessarily trust the man who's going to take me on a date tonight.

There's another knock on the door and I answer it to find our RA standing there with yet another box. "For you."

I tear into it the moment she's gone, a gasp leaving me when I pull out a heavy faux fur coat in the most beautiful golden-brown color. "It's so soft."

"You're going to look like a mafia wife with that coat," Elise says with a smile as I shrug it on and admire myself in the mirror. "I love it."

Another text from August comes through as I'm shrugging out of the coat.

August: *It's going to be cold tonight. Thought I would send something to keep you warm.*

Me: *Thank you. It's beautiful.*

He doesn't respond but it's fine. My heart is giddy. If he's trying to impress me?

It's working.

· · ·

A hired car and driver arrive promptly at six to pick me up. Once I'm in the car—I folded myself in carefully, terrified I'd rip the dress or my tights—I'm a bundle of nerves, curious as to where we're going. Even more curious as to August's whereabouts. He's definitely not in this car and the driver isn't talking. I decide to send August a text.

Me: *Where are you?*

He responds quickly.

August: *Waiting for you.*

Me: *That's nice, but where?*

August: *You'll find out soon.*

Ugh, I hate surprises. I'm not a spontaneous person and I don't like not knowing what's going on. Leaves me on edge and I hate being on edge.

We end up at a small airport about fifteen minutes away from campus. The driver pulls up practically on the tarmac and I see a helicopter sitting beside us with the doors wide open. The driver gets out of the car, but someone else opens my door. The driver can't move that fast. When I glance up, I see it's August standing there, his gaze roving over me almost hungrily. He's wearing black dress pants and a white button-down that's open at the collar, showing off the strong column of his neck and oh my God, he looks gorgeous.

"There you are," he practically growls, impatient as always. "You took forever."

"The driver was kind of slow," I tell him as I take his hand and let him pull me out of the car. The moment I'm standing upright, I'm smoothing down the front of my dress, unbearably self-conscious. I am wearing everything just as he asked, the dark nylons showing underneath the beige sequined dress.

I was so worried how my outfit was supposed to come together cohesively that I went on the internet and looked up the dress to find I'm wearing it exactly how it's shown on the Prada website, which is reassuring. I also discovered the dress cost over six thousand dollars and while yes, I come from a wealthy family, no one I know spends approximately ten grand or more on their date's outfit. Like we barely know each other and he's dropping that much money on me?

Not going to lie, I sort of love it.

"Jesus, you're beautiful." He says it like a curse. Like he can't stand the thought that he finds me attractive and all I can do is smile at him. His obvious pain over his conflicting emotions gives me strength. It's the karma he deserves for being such an asshole to me when I was an awkward freshman.

"Thank you." I practically preen as he continues to take me in. I feel like a princess. No man has ever treated me like this. I'm already impressed and the date has hardly started. "I love the bag."

I hold up the tiny bag that's completely covered with jet black crystals. I can barely fit my phone in there and a lipstick. That's it.

"You're a fan of Prada?"

"I've never owned anything Prada," I admit. I've never worn a lot of designer brands because it makes me think of my mother, who will go out in public decked in Fendi or whatever brand she's currently obsessed with from head to toe. She makes sure everyone knows she's wealthy, thanks to the obvious designer logos all over her clothing.

"The dress is stunning on you." His expression, his gaze are both gravely serious. He can't tear his eyes off me. "Are you ready to go?"

"Where are we going?" My skin is already warm from his compliments, but the moment he rests his hand on the small of my back, I'm practically on fire for him.

"You'll see." He smiles and I'm breathless for a moment, overcome with how handsome he truly is. His hair is neat and his face is smooth. His entire demeanor reeks of class and wealth, and I hope I can match his energy. "We're taking my father's helicopter to our destination."

"Oh." I swallow hard. "Wow."

I've never been in a helicopter before. And what's that like, having a helicopter to use whenever you want? The Lancasters are insanely rich and have been for generations. My parents, on the other hand, are new money and so obvious with it.

All hopes of being able to match his classy energy fly right out the window.

August leads me over to the helicopter and helps me inside, his hand resting on my ass momentarily as he gives me a boost. I settle into one of the seats and he takes the other one, handing over a headset for me to wear before he puts on his own. Within minutes, we're in the air, the pilot pointing out landmarks as we fly through the darkness.

I feel like Cinderella and August is my Prince Charming. Sweeping me off my feet and spoiling me. There isn't any sign of the August I'm used to dealing with. He doesn't seem exasperated with me at all. In fact, he seems rather muted, and while I appreciate everything that he's already done for me tonight, I can't help but wonder if he's purposely trying to be a gentleman to…what? Impress me?

He got me to go on this date by being his usual rude self. He doesn't need to change.

I can tell we're getting closer to the city because the lights get brighter and there are more of them. Soon enough we're flying directly over New York City and within minutes, we're landing on a helipad on top of a skyscraper. We exit the helicopter, the wind whipping my hair across my face, making me squeal. August takes my hand and leads me away from the helicopter, the two of us practically running, and only when we're inside and waiting for the elevator to come, do I catch my breath.

"That was fun," I tell him with a faint smile.

"Really? You enjoyed the helicopter ride?" He sends me a sideways glance, his gaze dipping to my chest. Lingering there.

"It was my first time in one," I admit.

A smirk appears, the sight of it reassuring me. "You've been experiencing lots of firsts."

The elevator dings and the doors slide open. He leads me inside and I turn to look at him, only speaking once the doors close. "So have you."

He frowns. "Like what?"

"Going on a date." My smile grows. "With me."

Another one of those growls leaves him and he grabs hold of me, his hands on my hips, his body pressed close. He's so hot, practically scorching my skin when he curls his fingers around my chin and tips my face up. We stare at each other for a moment, lost in each other's eyes, my brain filled with all sorts of dirty thoughts. How long will we be in this elevator anyway and what exactly could we do in here?

"You must know I don't date just anyone." He makes a face of utter disgust and I almost laugh. "I don't date at all."

"I know."

"I'm making an exception for you." He skims his thumb across my chin, drifting it upward until he's pressing it into the corner of my mouth. His voice lowers to a deep rumble. "God, your mouth is the stuff of fantasies."

I ignore the compliment—is it a compliment? Whatever, it doesn't matter. "Why am I the exception?"

The elevator lands with a soft thud and the doors slide open. He doesn't answer my question, which frustrates me. He takes my hand once more and leads me out of the elevator and across the expansive lobby of the building, heading for the front doors. I tip my head back to examine the light fixtures hanging above us, impressed with their beauty. Everything in this building is stunning. Perfect. A little too sterile for my tastes, but I can still appreciate it.

We walk outside into the brisk late October air and August ushers me into the back seat of a waiting car, climbing in after me, the driver shutting the door. Once we're inside I glance over at August, dying to know his answer.

"You never acknowledged my question."

He adjusts his shirt sleeve, toying with the cufflink. "What question?"

Oh that bored tone of his should make me mad but like the fool that I am, I find it sexy. "I asked you why I was the exception."

"Exception to what?"

It's my turn to growl. God, he's frustrating. "You never dated anyone—until me. I am the exception. You just said that and I want to know why. What made you change your mind?"

His gaze sinks into mine, both of us quiet, the air in the car charged with that familiar energy that always seems to grow between us when we're together. I lean into him, my body swaying as if I have no control, and his gaze finally drops, landing on my chest, sliding lower. My entire body reacts, gooseflesh rising as if he physically touched me and he leans back into his seat with a ragged exhale. The spell broken, just like that.

"That's why," he murmurs and he doesn't say anything else. Doesn't need to explain it because I feel the same exact way.

CHAPTER THIRTY-THREE

AUGUST

Iris recommended a French restaurant. Address is on the Upper East Side and her friends have been raving about this place. Supposedly even our parents went there and loved it. Considering I don't necessarily crave French food and was reluctant to make the reservation, Iris sent me a bunch of photos of the place and I liked the vibe.

The bar was massive, with floor-to-ceiling backlit shelves that were crowded with an endless array of liquor bottles. I knew if all else failed, I could get fucking drunk and that would make the evening easier to deal with. Not that I was filled with doubt. From the moment I set eyes on Sinclair in the dress that's see-through yet somehow not, I can't stop looking at her. My fingers tingle with the need to touch her and I've been sporting a semi since we climbed into the helicopter together.

Needless to say, I won't need liquor to get through the night. If anything, I should refrain. What if I get too buzzed and try to touch her inappropriately in public? She'd probably slap me and I'd probably deserve it.

"It's beautiful in here," Sin whispers to me once we're seated at our table. She's looking around the restaurant with wide, all-seeing eyes, the glow from the lit candle sitting in the middle of our table lighting up her face, making her somehow even prettier than she already is.

It pains me to watch her for too long. I start thinking—romantic thoughts. How I want to whisk her away and lock her up in a massive house for the rest of our lives so no one else can see just how achingly beautiful she is.

I push the unhinged thought out of my brain because it's pointless. I can't lock her away and keep her to myself. No matter how much I want to.

"My sister recommended it," I tell her, deciding to be truthful. I'm tired of lying to her. She always finds out anyway and luckily, she hasn't told me to go to hell yet so I must be doing something right.

"Iris?" When I nod, she smiles. "I remember her. She was always so much fun."

"That's one way to describe her," I say wryly.

"How is she? Is she still with Brooks?"

"Yes. They have a child."

"Oh my God, really?" Her enthusiasm at the mention of the beast is shocking. "How old? Girl or boy?"

"Girl. And I don't know how old she is. She can't walk yet."

"Aww! Oh, I'm sure she's adorable. What's her name?"

"Astrid. It's a family name. Some great aunt from long ago," I explain.

"I love it," Sinclair breathes and I believe her. She sounds sincere and I'm slightly baffled. Why would she care? Though I suppose people are different than me and care about things that I think are trivial. Not that my sister or my niece don't matter to me, they do, but why would they matter to Sin?

We make small talk while the server pours us each a glass of water, the two of us going quiet when she recites the nightly specials. Once I order a bourbon and Sin says she'll stick with water, the server leaves us alone. To make idle conversation while surrounded by many others doing the same thing.

This is why I was never interested in going on a date with someone. Making mundane conversation and pretending to be interested in what the other person is saying sounds dreadful. I take a drink of my water, keeping my gaze fixed on Sin. She smooths the front of her dress down again before pushing the hair off her shoulder, exposing the elegant length of her neck. My body responds as per usual and I know the physical chemistry between us hasn't waned whatsoever. As a matter of fact, it feels even more intense than the last time I saw her. Is that because it's been far too long since I've had my hands on her body?

"I didn't realize you were such close friends with Cyrus Thornhill. His family owns the university, right?" Sin's voice breaks through my thoughts, bringing me back to the present.

"He's my best friend, and yes. His great-great-great grandfather founded it." My gaze narrows as I contemplate her. "How do you know we're friends?"

"Oh. Tim told me." She waves a dismissive hand, her cheeks turning pink while my vision turns red.

Fucking Tim. Such an idiot. Why is she still talking to him again?

"Are you and Tim—close?" I say the last word with utter disgust. If she says yes, I might flip the table and storm out of here.

But only if I can take her with me and fuck her in the back seat of the car.

"Oh no." She laughs, the sound uncomfortable. "I mean, he wishes we were. And he's nice but..."

She goes silent and I clutch my fisted hands in my lap, desperate to bang them on the table like a heathen. "But what?" I finally ask.

"I'm not interested in him like that. He's just a friend." She shrugs one shoulder, the light catching on the sequins that cover her dress, making it sparkle.

One would think a dress covered in sequins would be flashy and obvious but not these sequins, and not this dress. Prada designs are subtle. Understated. I appreciate the elegant cut, and the hint of sexiness with the semi-sheer fabric. My gaze drops to the front of her dress and I wish I could see her nipples through it. I swear I almost can, but not quite.

I will have those nipples in my mouth at some point this evening. I lick my lips in anticipation.

"What are you thinking about?" Sin asks me and I freeze, feeling caught.

Clearing my throat, I adjust the front of my pants, thankful for the table hiding my erection. "You don't want to know."

"I definitely want to know." She's smiling, her eyes sparkling like they did the night I asked her on this godforsaken date. Do we really have to go through with this ritual when all we want to do is fuck each other's brains out? Seems like such a waste of time.

"I was thinking about how I can almost make out your nipples beneath the dress." I grab my glass of water, bringing it close to my lips. "And how I want to have those nipples in my mouth later."

Her face turns about thirty shades of pink at my words and she dips her head, her eyelids lowering. Ah, so modest when I know she's a filthy girl who gets dripping wet every time I play with her ass.

"I don't know if that's proper after-dinner behavior during our first official date," she murmurs.

Is she fucking for real right now? "Are you saying you've turned into a chaste little angel who refuses to play in the back seat of the car on the way home?"

Her lids lift, her gaze locking with mine. "We're not taking the helicopter back?"

I shake my head. I had specific plans for the long car ride home and now she's making me reconsider everything. "Unfortunately, no."

The server reappears with my drink, setting it in front of me. "Would you care to order any appetizers?"

I'm about to say no, but Sin responds first.

"I'd love to try the truffle frites." She's leaning across the table, speaking to me. Asking for permission I suppose, which—not gonna lie—I love.

"We'll take the truffle frites," I tell the server.

"And the fried artichokes," Sin whispers.

"Those too." The server smiles at me and I scowl at her back.

"I'll get those orders in," the server says before she scurries away.

"You were mean to her," Sin accuses.

I lean against the red leather booth seat, wondering if Sin would notice if I slowly but surely start sliding closer to her. "How?"

"You scowled."

"I scowl at everyone. Including you."

"She probably thinks you're mean."

"I am mean." Why bother hiding it? "She's fine. I'll never see her again after tonight."

"You really just don't give a damn, do you?" Sinclair sounds shocked. Amazed by my behavior.

"I don't. Why should I? Who is she to me? No one important." I shrug.

"But she's a human being. She matters to someone. You should at the very least treat her with respect," Sin points out.

I take a huge swallow of my bourbon, savoring the burn as it slides down my throat. I might need to get drunk after all, if my date is going to come at me every chance she gets. "I'll consider what you're saying."

Sinclair beams. "Perfect."

"Only if you'll sit closer to me," I tack on.

Her smile falls the slightest bit. "Why do you want me to sit closer to you?"

Why wouldn't I, is the question. I want to feel her thigh pressed into mine. Smell her skin and her hair. Watch her breathe, for Christ's sake. Is there any harm in that?

Most likely. I sound like a lunatic in my thoughts and I might, in fact, be crazy, but only because of her.

"It'll be easier when we share the frites." I smile at her, trying not to scowl or grimace or whatever other facial expression I do that makes me look, as she said, mean.

The table isn't so large that I wouldn't be able to share a dish with her but she scoots closer to me without protest, careful not to put any strain on the skirt of her dress. I'm glad I double-checked the dress code here with Iris because everyone else is dressed similarly and I wouldn't want to make Sinclair uncomfortable or embarrassed.

I wipe my hand across my mouth, disgusted with my thoughts. Who am I again? Why do I care about her? As she loves to remind me, we don't even know each other. Physically we're compatible but whatever happens between us tonight feels like a test. One I will most likely fail.

Epically.

CHAPTER THIRTY-FOUR

SINCLAIR

The food is delicious. August ordered an Aperol spritz for me and the server brought it without question, not bothering to card me. It was the perfect drink to accompany the truffle frites and fried artichokes, which were both amazing. The alcohol also calmed my nerves and steadied my shaky breaths. It's like I can't breathe when he looks at me. As if he's trying to see through my clothes, my skin, into the very heart of me. Not that August cares about my heart.

Does he?

But now I'm three spritzes in and feeling as loose as a freaking goose while I nosh on yet another piece of their delicious table bread, praying it soaks up all the alcohol I've consumed.

I glance over at August to find him already watching me, his thigh pressed intimately against mine. Like he needs to keep it there so we're in constant contact. It's hot. He's hot. It's baffling to me how I've become the exception. *Me*. The girl he used to bully and taunt and humiliate. I still don't get how this happened.

"Tell me about your family." He slouches against the back of the red leather booth, the epitome of a relaxed, confident man who's just finished a meal and is now looking at his date as if she has somehow also become a continuation of his meal that he can't wait to devour. My entire body tingles in anticipation until his question truly sinks in.

Talking about my family is the last thing I want to do.

"I'd rather not." I rest my hands in my lap and try to put on a demure act, but the gleam in his eyes tells me he's not buying it. "It's a boring story."

"I don't think anything you say can possibly be what you call a boring story."

He should not say those sorts of things while looking at me that way. Ugh. He's infuriating—with a hint of sweet. "You'd hate them."

"Who?"

"My parents." I mock shiver like I'm disgusted. "They're…kind of awful."

"As awful as I am?" He arches a brow, as sexy as ever.

"You're awful in a different way." In a, *I want to rub myself all over his body*, sort of way. Not that I'd say that out loud. "My father had a startup business that took off and they made a bunch of money in a short amount of time. Then he sold it and made even more money and now they just spend it on the tackiest stuff ever and do all the things that they think they should be doing, but really? They just look like they're trying too hard and it's embarrassing."

"What kind of startup?"

Oh, he would ask that. And that makes this conversation even more embarrassing.

"Um, it involved…athletic gear." I press my lips together, not wanting to go any further, but I can tell from the look on August's face he wants to know more.

"Athletic gear? I'm not into sports by any means, but what exactly are you referring to?"

"Well, it's not actually gear. It was an—anti-itch cream. For the—" I gesture toward his lap. "—area."

Realization dawns all over his gorgeous face. "Wait a minute. You're not talking about Jock Rot, are you?"

I cover my face with my hands, hating that my parents made their fortune on something called Jock Rot. "Maybe?"

"Maybe." He snickers, reaching toward me and slowly peeling one of my hands away from my face. My cheeks are as hot as an oven, I'm so embarrassed. "Your dad is the guy who invented Jock Rot. I can't believe it."

Ignoring his snarky tone, I give him the condensed version of how Jock Rot came to be. "I have a much older brother who played a lot of sports and was always sweaty. And while there are plenty of products on the market, my dad wanted to make something specific for younger athletes, like middle school and high school. He wanted to give it a funny name that would appeal to them, and one day he overheard my brother say to one of his friends that he thought he had jock rot. And my father thought that would be the perfect name to call it."

August nods, absorbing my explanation. "You'd think they'd call it something else because it sounds like the cream is what's giving them the rot."

"But see, the name is what gained the product all the attention. Teenage boys loved saying it, and they were the market he wanted to appeal to. My dad was right when he said he wanted to give it a funny name. It totally worked.

"The company that bought my parents' business said exactly that. It got famous on social media because of the name but the moment the corporation that bought Jock Rot acquired it, they changed the name almost immediately and sales tanked. My father thinks it's hilarious," I explain.

"Your father is probably correct." August frowns. "Why would they change it?"

"Because the big box stores refused to have something on their shelves called Jock Rot. It sounds and looks awful."

August is smiling. Laughing and shaking his head. "How much did dear old Dad get for selling his jock rot?"

"Fifty million or something like that?"

He whistles low, shaking his head. "That's a lot of money for some crotch anti-itch cream."

Just hearing him say that out loud is embarrassing. "Do you see why I don't want to talk about my family?"

"I don't know. Isn't your dad proud of the fact that he made that much money?"

"I suppose, but the way they manage their wealth is so over the top. They're very..." I try to think of a nice word to describe how they are, but nothing comes to mind.

"Nouveau riche?" he offers.

"Yes. That's it." A sigh leaves me. "They're just so obvious. My mom wears every expensive label she can find and is always waving her hands around so people can see how many diamond rings she's wearing on her fingers. Her wrists. Around her neck. They joined a country club and spend all of their time there. Bought a hideous mansion that's just obscene and he drives a bright red Porsche."

"I own a Porsche."

"You're twenty-two. He's like, fifty-five and acting like he's in college again. I'm surprised he's not here with me trying to get into the frat parties." I mock shudder at the thought.

"Sometimes people can act...vulgar when they come into money," August observes.

"Something you've probably never dealt with considering you were born into it?" I don't fault him for that. He can't help who his parents are or what family he was born to. I'm sure plenty of people think he's lucky to have that much wealth. Money solves a lot of problems, but it also creates new ones.

Like how my father can't keep it in his pants and my mother chooses to look the other way because no way is she leaving him now. She's earned this. She's told me that more than once.

"I have my own problems I deal with." That's all he says, Mr. Mysterious. And while I'd love to pry more, I remain quiet, staring at my mostly empty dinner plate, my head swimming thanks to the spritzes. And August's cologne. The press of his hard thigh against mine and how his hand just settled on my leg, warm and heavy. Like a brand on my skin, sizzling into my flesh and marking his territory.

"I feel like I just trauma dumped on you," I admit, hiding the hiccup that rises up. No more spritzes for me.

"I don't mind." He sounds like he means it and when he squeezes my thigh, I sort of want to melt into the booth seat. "I have a confession."

I'm frowning, my entire body growing tense. I really hope he doesn't drop a bomb on me. "What is it?"

"I thought this date would be boring. That the most exciting thing that could happen was me staring at your pretty face all night." He gives me another thigh squeeze, his fingers sliding up higher, and I swear he's so close to my pussy I'm tempted to spread my legs and allow him access. "But it hasn't been boring. At all."

"I'm glad I can entertain you." My voice has an edge of sarcasm, like I can't help myself.

"I am too." He lifts his gaze to mine. "Want to get the hell out of here so I can fuck you in the back seat of the town car?"

I blink at him, my mouth falling open. "August…"

"Yeah, yeah. I know what you said about first date etiquette or whatever the fuck." He removes his hand from my leg and I immediately miss his touch. "We could make out instead. I could feel you up. Finger you. You could give me a hand job. Or is that moving too fast for a first date?"

My mouth is dry at the images his words conjure up. "Did you pay the check yet?"

"Already taken care of." The smug look on his face is practically criminal. He's so pleased with himself. "Ready to go?"

All I can do is nod my response.

• • •

We sit in the back of the car for at least the first fifteen minutes of our drive in complete silence. He's focused on his phone, texting someone, I don't know who and I'm too afraid to ask. I read over my notifications, but I've got nothing. A few social media things. A text from Elise reminding me that she's going home for the weekend. Meaning I'll be in my dorm for the next three days, all alone.

Glancing up, I check on August to find he's not staring at his phone anymore. No, he's staring at me with a lazy expression on his face. His eyes are hooded and he's sprawled across his side of the back seat, taking up every inch of available space. Devastatingly handsome as per usual and I'm fairly certain he undid a couple of the buttons of his shirt, offering me a better view of his glorious chest.

"You should probably stop looking at me like that," he warns, his voice low. "Unless you want me to attack you."

Any other man would use the term "attack you" and I'd freak out. With August? I'm ready for it. Dying for it even.

"I don't know." I sink my teeth into my lower lip, wondering where I come up with these moves. Pretty sure he brings it out of me. "You don't want to ruin the dress, do you?"

"I could not give a fuck." He starts moving toward me across the seat.

"August." My voice sharpens. "The dress was over six thousand dollars!"

"So?" He reaches for me, his hands landing on my hips, tugging me closer to him. "Worth every fucking dollar to see you wearing it tonight."

"It wasn't too much?"

"The cost? No. I already told you." His fingers curl into the dress fabric.

"No. I mean…how it looked on me?" I'm whispering, worried over his answer. It felt like too much. Like I was putting on some sort of show for an audience of one—August. "Did I pass the test?"

He frowns, his grip easing on my waist. "Did you believe I was putting you through some sort of test?"

"I wasn't sure." I shrug, wishing I never said anything in the first place. "You can be a little intimidating, August."

His gaze roves over my face as if he's trying to memorize every little feature and my entire body grows warm. "It never seemed to bother you before. You've had zero problems standing up to me."

"Things have changed between us. After everything you admitted and I made you ask me on a date." I'm gnawing on my lower lip again, feeling like a fool. "Do you regret it? You spent a lot of money on me tonight. Do you want the bag back?"

I thrust the bag at him, and he literally tosses it over his shoulder like it's trash. "Keep the bag. Keep the dress and the shoes but these?" He runs his hand under my dress, fingers skimming over the nylon tights I'm wearing. "I'm afraid I'm going to destroy these."

His words are a warning and I hold my breath as his hand slides up. Over my hip, shifting to my front, his fingers curling into the waistband of my tights. He tugs with all his might, ripping the thin fabric to shreds with a few jerks and I gasp, my core clenching when he exposes me completely.

"Fucking nuisance," he mutters as he tears the stockings off my body, removing them completely. He shoves my dress up until it's bunched at my waist. All of those beautiful sequins bent and misshapen, but I can't worry about that now. I'm breathing hard, my chest aching, my heart hammering, my skin tingling. The spot between my legs throbs incessantly and when he spreads my legs, he stares at my pussy, licking his lips like he's already imagining how I taste. "Still bare for me?"

I nod, pressing my lips together, trying to calm the quaking that's slowly taking over my body. I've kept up on the waxing in the hopes that a moment like this might happen again and here we are.

"You have the prettiest pussy I've ever seen," he murmurs, rising up so he's sitting beside me again, his fingers sliding in between my thighs. "Pink and smooth and so fucking wet."

I can't speak. Too overwhelmed with how close he is. He dips his head, his soft lips finding mine, his rough fingers thrusting inside of me at the same time and I cry out, his hungry mouth swallowing the sound. It's such a juxtaposition, his tender mouth and delicate tongue and those long, rough fingers pushing inside my welcoming body.

His mouth leaves mine, lips drifting downward to kiss my jaw. My neck. His fingers still busily stroking my pussy, the wet sounds of my flesh filling the confines of the car. He's fully dressed, my lower half completely exposed and it feels dirty, what we're doing in the back of the car. The partition is up, the driver unaware of what we're doing, but I bet he has an idea. I should be mortified. I should push August away but I can't. More than anything...

I don't want to.

"Is this proper first date etiquette, Sin?" He drifts his mouth along the length of my neck, fingers pinching at my clit and making me squeal.

"N-no." I shake my head. "Probably not."

"Want me to stop?" His gaze lifts, those intense blue eyes meeting mine just as his fingers go completely still, cupping my pussy like he owns it.

I shake my head over and over, my entire body trembling with anticipation. "NO!"

He smiles at my shout, leaning in to kiss me once more as his fingers work their magic on my sensitive flesh. Without thought I reach for him, my hand landing on the bulge beneath his pants, stroking once. Fumbling, really. It's awkward in the back seat of the car but he makes it seem like it's easy, his skilled fingers circling over my clit again and again. Tighter and tighter. I suck in a breath, my fingers finding the button of his pants and undoing it so I can shove my hand beneath the fabric and cup his incredibly hard dick.

He ends the kiss, his eyes opening and he pauses, watching me carefully. I don't remove my hand from his cock. I even try and slip my fingers beneath his boxer briefs so I can touch his bare flesh and he laughs, the bastard. "Greedy little whore."

There's a fresh flood of wetness between my legs when he says it and I suppose I should feel ashamed at how I respond to the insult, but I don't. I like it when he calls me that. When he seems so pleased with my responses and the naughty things I might do. It's empowering, his approval. Makes me want to earn more of it. To always please him and give him what he wants.

Give myself to him completely.

He removes his fingers from my slick flesh. He stops touching me completely and I open my eyes, fighting the disappointment washing over me. "What are you doing?"

His back is to me as he reaches for the bag he tossed, opening it to peer inside. Within seconds, he's got my lipstick and he holds it out to me. "Last time I saw one of these, you were throwing it at me."

I recall the moment with fondness. "You were such a jerk."

"I told you that lipstick belonged to our housemother." He twirls the tube of lipstick in between his fingers.

"I find that very hard to believe," I sigh, gasping when he presses the lipstick against my swollen clit. "What are you doing?"

"Hmm, toying with you." His gaze is fixated on my spread legs as he circles my clit with the lipstick. The tube is shaped almost like a bullet, with a narrow lid and he runs it along my slick flesh, pausing at my entrance before he slowly pushes it inside. "Fucking you with the lipstick."

Oh God. The words. His voice. The lipstick inside my body. It's not big enough to give me the friction I crave, but it's still incredibly hot, what he's doing. He pushes it in and pulls it out, his rhythm slow. As if he has all the time in the world to play with me. I'm whimpering, lifting my hips, wanting more but he's not focused on me. Well, more like he's only focused on what he's doing to my pussy.

Eventually he pulls the tube all the way out, pressing it against my clit once again, circling. Teasing. Playing with me, as he just said.

"You are always so fucking responsive." His heavy gaze lifts to mine and I go breathless at all the heat I see swirling in the blue depths. "I call you a greedy whore, you're gushing all over me. I fuck you with a lipstick, and you're moaning like you're about to come."

"I am—about to come," I admit, my voice barely above a whisper.

He tosses the lipstick away and reaches for me, placing both of his hands on my hips. He pulls me forward until I'm on his lap, my sopping wet pussy nudged against his stiff cock. "Rub against me, baby. Get off on me."

"Wh-what?" My head is spinning, the scent of my pussy filling the confines of the car. Did he really just ask me to rub against him until I come?

His hands are on my ass, tilting my body forward, his mouth brushing against mine as he speaks. "Use me. Get me wet, Sin. Let me feel your cunt spasm when you come all over me."

I could come just from his words, they're so hot. I toss my head back, gripping his shoulders as I begin to do exactly what he told me to do. Grinding against his rigid erection, riding him like a cowgirl and lifting my hips up and down. Mashing my pussy against his thick cock. The fabric of his boxer briefs adds a little friction and oh God, it feels so *good*. So freaking liberating. I almost scream when he grips my left breast in his hand, his fingers working my nipple while I press against the base of his erection. Within seconds, I've lost all control. I grip his shoulders extra tight, a high, keening cry leaving me as the orgasm hovers just on the edge, threatening to sweep over me completely.

"Come on, baby," he murmurs and those words, his lips brushing against mine, his fingers pinching my nipple until it hurts—the combination of it all sends me straight into orgasmic bliss.

I'm coming, crying out his name, my stomach heaving, my entire body a shuddering mess. My clit throbs so hard I worry I'm going to pass out and when it's finally over, I collapse against him. My head is spinning and my heart threatens to burst out of my chest, it's beating so hard.

I think I might've died.

But then I feel August's lips brush against my temple, reminding me that I am very much alive. I play dead slumped against him until he presses me against the seat, giving me no choice but to open my eyes. Oh, he seems pleased with himself, from the look of satisfaction that I see on his gorgeous face.

His lips brush mine, his tongue sneaking out for a lick. "Was that proper first date behavior?"

"No." I am smiling, and I close my eyes again. Like I'm afraid to look at him.

"Open your eyes, Sin." I do as he says and he's right there. All I can see. Like he's become my entire world and nothing else matters. "I have zero patience. I enjoyed our dinner, but I'm not going to take you on five dates before I can finally fuck you. It feels like I've been waiting for this moment for months. My entire fucking life."

I gape at him, shocked at those last words he uttered. Does he mean what he says? About the impatient part, most definitely.

"I don't like playing games either. Tell me now if you want to continue this."

"Continue what?" I ask, in a daze.

"This." He swallows. "Us."

CHAPTER THIRTY-FIVE

AUGUST

It feels like everything hinges on what this eighteen-year-old angel-faced beauty is about to say and I'm pissed at myself for falling so hard for her. But it's like I can't control my emotions. Something I have been in control of my entire life is wiped away by one woman. I didn't think this sort of thing was possible.

But here I am. More than eager to finger or eat her pussy as many times as I possibly can without getting anything in return just to witness her coming. Because the girl comes hard, every single time, and it is a sight to behold.

Her smile is small, her face flushed and covered with a light sheen of sweat. She's the prettiest thing I've ever seen. "I want to continue this." She hesitates. "Us."

My chest grows tight and I wonder if that's my heart. Look at what she does to me with just a few spoken words. I'm all twisted up over this girl and I fucking revel in it.

"I want you to come home with me." My voice is low, my intentions clear.

Sinclair frowns. "To the frat?"

I slowly shake my head. "To my apartment I have in the city."

"You have an apartment in the city?" I think my girl is in shock. She looks delightfully confused.

"I have homes all over the world. Well, my family does." The apartment I'm referring to is mine. Once I came into my inheritance, I made the purchase from my cousins Grant and Finn. They run a huge real estate brokerage and got me an excellent deal.

"I should probably go back to campus—"

"Do you have classes tomorrow?" I already know the answer. She shakes her head.

"Then you're coming home with me." The matter is settled and I lean back against the seat, dragging her with me until she's curled up in my lap. Her soft curves sink into my body and my skin sizzles everywhere we make contact.

I need to get her out of this car and into my bed immediately.

"My head is spinning," she mumbles.

I puff out my chest, proud. I must've given her an earth-shaking orgasm. "We'll be home soon."

I say home like it's our home and maybe someday it could be.

Jesus, I have truly lost it. But for once, I'm not fighting it. I'm going to soak this up and...enjoy it.

"My stomach hurts." She shifts against me. "I don't feel so good."

I glance down at her, noting the sudden yellow tinge to her skin, and I sit up, hitting the button that lowers the partition between us and the driver. "Pull over."

He meets my gaze in the rearview mirror. "We're in the middle of traffic."

"Unlock the doors then. She's going to be sick."

The click of the doors being unlocked sounds and within seconds, I'm ushering Sinclair out of the vehicle, pulling her through the congested traffic, panic making my heart race. We're just about to hit the sidewalk when she bends over and pukes in the gutter, making these horrible noises that sound like she's dying.

My panic increases and instead of leaving her alone like I would do for anyone else who's throwing their guts up in the middle of the city, I remain by her side. Gather her hair up in one hand and hold it away from her face while I rub her back with the other. Murmuring reassuring words to her while she gags and spits and nearly hits my shoes with her vomit.

It's disgusting. It's downright horrific but something keeps me by her side. I want to take care of her and make sure she's okay. This has never happened to me before.

Ever.

"Oh my God." Her voice shakes and she sounds absolutely miserable. "I can't believe I just did that."

"It was the spritzes." I'm rubbing circles on her lower back, wishing I had something to wipe her mouth with. A piece of gum. Anything to help.

"And all that rich food." She clutches her stomach, her entire body shuddering, and I worry she's going to throw up again. "I need some water."

She rises to her full height and my hands drop away from her as she turns to look at me. Her eyes are bloodshot, and her face is streaked with tears. She looks traumatized. "You must think I'm so gross."

"I don't." My voice is soft and rings with sincerity. I mean it. I'm not disgusted by her whatsoever and normally I would be. "It's not like you meant to puke your guts out on the street."

"Oh shit." She looks around, brushing her hair away from her face before she glances down at herself, the relief on her face obvious. "At least I didn't throw up on the dress."

"Fuck the dress." I grab her hand and tug her close. But not too close because she kind of smells. "Are you all right?"

Sin nods, tipping her head back to look at me. Her eyes shine with not just unshed tears but also gratefulness. "Thank you for taking care of me."

Something tugs at my chest when she says that, and how she looks at me. I squeeze her hand. "I didn't take that good of care of you."

"You held my hair back." Her smile is small. "That was so...
nice."

She sounds amazed that I would do something so simple. And
rather logical if you ask me. Why wouldn't I hold her hair away
from her face? She was retching and puking on the side of the
damn street. I'm not that heartless.

What the fuck? I *am* that heartless. I've always been that
heartless.

"Come on." I tug on her hand and lead her back to the car.
"Let's get out of here."

. . .

We arrive at my apartment about thirty minutes later. I was
able to clean up Sinclair pretty well in the back of the car, but
when we arrive at my place, she's immediately asking where the
bathroom is so she can take a shower.

"I feel disgusting." She dips her head, scanning the front of her
dress yet again. "I'm worried I ruined the dress."

She's too fucking hung up on the dress. For someone who
comes from money, she worries about it constantly. "I'll have it
dry cleaned."

"I can do—"

I interrupt her. "I said I'll take care of it." She flinches at my
sharp tone and I take a deep breath, reminding myself she's in a
delicate state and needs to be handled with extra care. "Let me
show you the bathroom."

We move through the apartment, me turning on the lights
here and there, hoping for some sort of response from Sinclair
but she says nothing. Considering she's most likely not feeling
well, I remind myself I shouldn't be surprised. But I am a little
disappointed. I've never cared about impressing someone before.

Until Sinclair.

"Here are some towels." I grab a stack of thick cream-colored towels out of the cabinet, setting them on top of the marble counter. Sin just stands there, rubbing her hands up and down her exposed arms as if she caught a chill, staring off into space. "Do you need help with the shower?"

"I can manage it," she mumbles, not looking at me.

I find that hard to believe, so I stalk toward the shower and turn it on, checking the temperature and only stepping away when I deem it warm enough. When I glance over my shoulder to check on her, she's still standing in the same exact spot.

"Take off the dress," I snap, making her startle.

She automatically does as I say, shrugging out of the dress and letting it fall to the ground in a heap of sequins. She kicks it away from her feet, standing there naked in the middle of the bathroom, only wearing the shoes. Reminding me of when she was naked, save for those hideous gold stilettos.

"Sin." I approach her carefully, my movements slow. She barely looks at me. "Are you all right?"

"I'm mortified." She ducks her head, and fuck, she sounds so sad. "I basically demanded you take me on a date and I end up ruining everything."

"You didn't ruin anything." I reach for her, curling my fingers around her upper arms, holding her gently. "Look at me."

She barely lifts her gaze to mine, her humiliation obvious, but she doesn't say a word.

"Do you think I'm angry with you?"

"No. Maybe. I don't know." She shrugs, looking away. "You're intimidating, August. Sometimes you make me nervous."

Remaining quiet, I lean in closer to her, pressing my lips to her forehead, wanting to ease her distress. I remain there, breathing her in for a moment, running my fingers up and down the back of her arms. Steam from the shower slowly filters throughout the room, fogging up the massive mirror, and I start to sweat.

From the hot water. From my fragile feelings for this girl. Comforting people is not my forte. I have no idea how to handle a situation like this, so all I can do is wing it.

"I'm not." I keep my voice low, my gaze level on hers once they lock. "Let's get you in the shower."

She gives a barely-there nod acknowledging my suggestion and I help her out of her shoes and into the shower, tempted to join her but no. I can't push myself on her when she's feeling so raw. Instead, I leave her alone and try my best to accommodate her every need once she's finished. Like leaving the towels close to the shower so she can easily grab them. I set out a brand-new toothbrush and tube of toothpaste I find in a drawer. I even find a bottle of fragrant body lotion in the drawer and set it on the counter, hoping she likes the scent.

After I leave one of my T-shirts for her to wear on the counter, I exit the bathroom, closing the door behind me. Exhaling loudly and running my hands through my hair a few times as I pace the length of my bedroom.

I've never been in a situation like this before and I feel…inept. Helpless. I want to make sure I'm taking care of her needs, but I have zero clue if I know how to do that. I can't read her mind and I've certainly never cared enough about another human— woman—to want to take care of them in every way I can. I hated how sad she seemed. How defeated. Am I responsible for her feeling that way?

God, maybe I can't be fixed. I'm a complete asshole and I'm just going to have to deal with it. Live with it.

Which means Sinclair is going to have to live with it too. Will she want to? Or will she tell me to go straight to hell?

I'd deserve the hell comment. I really would.

Irritation flows through my veins and I let go of my hair, resting my hands on my hips as I study the closed bathroom door. I'm tempted to bust into the room and beg her forgiveness for being such a prick. But I don't.

Instead, I collapse on the edge of the bed and hang my head, resting my arms on my knees and studying the pristine carpet. This apartment is untouched. No one uses it except the house cleaning company who comes in once a week and does a quick tidy up. It's cold in here. Soulless.

Like me.

CHAPTER THIRTY-SIX

SINCLAIR

The shower is just what I need to cleanse my body and my wayward thoughts. Throwing up is one of my least favorite things to do in the world, and knowing that I did it in front of August while he held my hair away from my face and murmured soft, soothing words in my ear is something I might never be able to live down. Not that I think he'd give me any grief over it. Or maybe he would? I'm not sure. When it comes to August, I'm always unsure. But in this particular instance...

I'm the one beating myself up over the most humiliating moment of my life. Could it get any worse? Well, I could've puked *on* him. He probably would've freaked out. Been absolutely disgusted with me, pushed me onto public transit and told me to find my own way home.

Instead, he brought me back to his luxurious apartment and now I'm standing in his equally luxurious shower.

The water pressure is perfect, as is the temperature, and I stand under the nozzle for far too long. Until my skin grows wrinkly and I start to feel like a drowned rat. I turn the water off and open the door to find two thick, fluffy towels sitting on the edge of the counter. I grab one and wrap it around my head, trying to squeeze the excess water out before I grab the other towel and begin to dry off my body.

I sag with relief when I spot the toothbrush and toothpaste waiting for me by the sink. I brush my teeth for far longer than necessary, desperate to get the lingering nasty taste out of my mouth. Once I'm done, I grab the bottle of body lotion and flip the cap, breathing deep its delicious floral scent and lather up my skin with it. Careful not to think about who this bottle of body lotion belongs to and why it's here.

That's none of my business.

I brush my hair and then slip on the black T-shirt August left for me to wear, disappointed to find it doesn't smell like him at all. Truthfully? I'm addicted to his scent. His warmth. The words he said to me earlier still ring in my head and I can't believe we're at this point in our—relationship? Do we actually have one?

According to him, I think we do. Or at the very least, we're on the cusp of one.

I'm a little freaked out at the thought of facing him. He's just on the other side of the closed door, waiting for me, and I hope he's not disappointed. What if the car is still waiting downstairs and he sends me on my way? He might. Talk about a horrible night.

Taking a deep breath for courage, I open the door and head into the bedroom, stopping short when I see August lying on the bed. Asleep.

His eyes are closed, his thick lashes making me envious. His pinkish-red lips that are slightly parted give him sleeping, sweet baby boy vibes, which is the very last thing he could ever be. Is this what he looked like when he was a little kid, fast asleep and dreaming in his bed?

My heart warms at the thought.

Abandoning my earlier hang-ups, I carefully crawl onto the bed, keeping my gaze locked on his beautiful face. I shift closer, my movements slow, afraid I might jostle the mattress and ruin the moment. I only stop when my face is in his. I can feel his breath coming from his still parted lips and I lick my own, amazed at how much better I feel after taking that shower.

My body responds to being so close to him, everything on high alert. I want him. I want him, I want him, I want him and I think I could have him. For how long, I don't know but I sort of don't care. I just need to be careful and not completely fall for him. To do so would be detrimental to my mental health.

Falling in love with August Lancaster only for him to reject me would be soul-crushing. Life ending. He has far too much power over my emotions.

Slowly, I bend my head until I'm close enough to brush his lips with mine and his hand comes up automatically, fingers curling around the back of my head and holding me there.

"Thank Christ you brushed your teeth," he murmurs against my lips, nipping at my lower lip.

I'm shocked. I thought he was asleep. "You're awake."

"I felt you crawling on the bed—that's what woke me up." His lips brush against mine with every word he speaks, making tingles cascade all over my skin. "Feeling better I assume?"

"Yes." I part my lips on a sigh when he kisses me far too briefly. "Thank you for the T-shirt."

"Looks better on you anyway."

My skin warms at his compliment. "You haven't even opened your eyes to look at me."

"I don't need to." He kisses me again, his lips parted on mine, as if he's trying to breathe me in. "You make everything look better."

My stomach erupts like a bazillion butterflies took flight inside me, their wings flapping and tickling, making me shiver. He shouldn't be allowed to say something like that. It's too sweet, too... romantic. And he's not the type. He'd be the first to admit it too.

Tilting my head, I try to deepen the kiss, but he rears his head back, ending our sort-of kissing.

"We're not doing this tonight." His voice is firm.

I fall back on my haunches, the disappointed sound leaving me loud enough to make him finally crack his eyes open. "You're serious."

"You're not feeling well enough. I'm not going to have this night tainted with your upset stomach or whatever the fuck," he practically growls.

I can't help but smile because him saying that proves he wants this moment to be special for me. He wants it to be good because he cares and oh my God, if that doesn't make my heart want to sing, I don't know what else could make me feel that way.

"I feel lots better—"

He cuts me off. "No. Some other time. Now, come on." He rolls off the bed and stands, stripping off his clothing until he's standing in front of me in just his navy boxer briefs, his semi-erect cock pushing against the front of them. "Time for bed."

Fighting disappointment, I slip under the covers and he joins me, pulling the sumptuous comforter over us. He rolls toward me, his heavy arm settling across my waist as he pulls me into him. "Your hair is wet."

"I couldn't find a hair dryer." I rest my hand on his chest, right over his thundering heart.

"I don't believe there is one since I rarely use a hair dryer." He pauses. "Did you like the lotion?"

"It smells nice." If he tells me it belongs to his ex, I'm going to lose it.

"I don't know where it came from."

I breathe a secret sigh of relief.

"I don't spend much time at this apartment. I only just bought the place," he explains. "Once I graduate, I imagine I'll move in."

"You want to live here?"

"As of right now, yes. I'm not quite sure what I want to do after I graduate. The future is wide open and filled with endless possibilities." He sounds like he's repeating something someone else told him.

"I don't know what I want to do either," I admit, resting my head on his hot chest. I bet his skin could dry my hair. "I'm just winging it."

"I thought you were focused on getting good grades and didn't want any distractions."

I frown. Did I tell him that? Sounds like something I'd say. "I mean, I am focused on getting good grades and not wanting any distractions. I want to make something of myself once I graduate and not depend on my family's money."

"Aren't you depending on it right now by going to college? I assume Daddy Jock Rot is paying for it."

God, I really hate that he brought up Jock Rot. "Well, yes. I'm not going to turn down my parents when they offer to pay for my education."

I got into Thornhill because my father made a huge contribution to the alumni fund, despite him not being a graduate. My grades were solid at Lancaster Prep. I was one of the valedictorians because I threw myself into my studies my freshman year, thanks to being harassed by the very man that I'm in bed with. And after getting straight A's my first year there, I kept it up. I liked being a top student and the attention I got from it. It's the only positive reinforcement I received when I was at Lancaster and my parents were thrilled.

Dad said he greased a few palms—direct quote—at Thornhill and I didn't stop him. Whatever it took to get me in, I was there for it. I'd like to think my grades alone made it happen, and I'm sure they contributed somewhat, but even I know...

When they say money talks, it's not a lie. My father's contribution helped pave the way for my entry into Thornhill. August got in because he's a Lancaster. Ivy League schools care about who their star students are, and while I'm sure they don't want the Jock Rot name attached to the school, they'll definitely take that Jock Rot money.

Ugh. I hate even thinking the term jock rot. It's so gross.

"I appreciate your honesty."

I glance up at his face when I note the admiration filling his voice, though his words also sound faintly sarcastic. Knowing

August, they are, but no. The look on his face is also filled with admiration. He means what he says. "Thank you."

"Most women would tell me they don't care about money." His expression turns hard. "They're full of shit."

"They'll tell you that because you have infinite loads of money and they want to look like they're not after it," I point out.

His gaze locks with mine and he reaches out, brushing a few damp strands of hair away from my face. "You don't seem to care about my wealth."

"I can't even begin to fathom how much it affects your life."

He doesn't speak for a while and neither do I. We just watch each other, our bodies molded together, the beat of our hearts in tandem. I feel completely attuned to him and while it's a tad overwhelming, this...*feeling* growing between us also feels natural.

Right.

"You surprise me," he finally murmurs.

"In a bad way or a good way?" I ask warily.

He smiles and my heart pangs at how genuine it looks. "My feelings are positive. I was referring to how you seem completely unaffected by my wealth and power."

"When you talk like that, all I want to do is roll my eyes." I do so just for his benefit, which makes his smile grow.

"See? That right there. I don't intimidate you at all." He runs a hand over my hair, resting it on the side of my head. "I find that—appealing."

"You made it your goal to intimidate me for a solid year," I remind him, my voice a raspy whisper. "All these years later, I finally grew into myself and stood up to you."

That's not exactly true. I did stand up to him back then—more than a few times.

"And look where it got you." He chuckles, his fingers sifting through my hair. "In my bed."

"Fourteen-year-old me would have a hard time believing it."

"I barely remember bullying you." His smile fades, his gaze turning deathly serious. "But I do remember enough to know that I was a dick."

"You were."

"I made your life miserable and I don't know why. Probably because you reacted so strongly."

"Maybe you sensed my devasting beauty beneath the braces and the zits and you knew it would be detrimental to you." I'm trying to tease him, but I end up sounding ridiculous. I'm sure that's not it.

But his expression remains serious, his gaze never wavering. "I probably did. And you are fucking detrimental to me. At least I'll die with a smile on my face."

When he kisses me, he steals my breath. My thoughts. All I can do is feel. The sensuous way his mouth moves against mine, coaxing my lips apart, his tongue sliding in for the barest lick around mine. He's gone before I can respond, pulling his mouth away from my still-seeking lips and he tucks me firmly against him, my head lodged in that warm space between his neck and shoulder.

"Go to sleep," he murmurs and like the obedient girl I am, I shut my eyes and fall into deep slumber within seconds. I'm exhausted, yet I feel...safe.

Safe in his arms.

In his bed.

Life has definitely taken a turn.

CHAPTER THIRTY-SEVEN

SINCLAIR

I wake up to the sound of voices.

Female voices.

My eyes pop open and I realize I'm alone in the massive bed. I have no idea when August left, but his side of the mattress is cool so it's been a while.

Sitting up, I shove my tangled hair away from my face and look around the room before rubbing the sleep from my eyes. I hear the voices again, a little louder this time, and I recognize August's deep baritone. The distinct sound of a feminine laugh.

My stomach twists, and that's not from hunger. There's a woman in his apartment, possibly two and he abandoned me in his bed to go...what? Entertain them? What time is it anyway?

Spotting my phone on the nightstand, I reach for it and see that it's past ten in the morning. I have texts from Elise, all of them growing more insistent.

Elise: *How was your date with Lancaster?*

Elise: *Did he fuck your brains out? Please say yes, even if you have to lie.*

Elise: *I bet he's got a giant dick.*

Elise: *Sorry. I didn't mean to piss you off, talking about your man's dick.*

Elise: *Sinclair! Where are you?*

Elise: *Please respond before I call the cops.*

Elise: *SINCLAIR MILLER YOU BETTER ANSWER ME OR I'M GOING TO THINK AUGUST MURDERED YOU AND LEFT YOU FOR DEAD IN THE MIDDLE OF MANHATTAN.*

I hurriedly tap out a response to her, not wanting her to panic any more or worse, actually call the police.

Me: *I'm fine. I spent the night at his apartment and I just woke up. Drank too much last night and threw up on the side of the street. I'll give you all the deets later.*

Another giggle from the mystery woman sounds and I clutch the phone so tight, my fingers turn white. Who is that? How dare he flirt and talk to someone when I'm still in his bed? God he's the absolute worst.

I knew the way he acted last night was too good to be true.

Huffing out a loud exhale, I throw back the covers and jump out of bed, not caring if my hair is a mess or that I'm in one of his T-shirts. Maybe that'll make a point—I'll look freshly fucked and whoever this woman is will know it. Possibly be devastated by my appearance.

Good. I'm borderline devastated too.

I march across the cavernous bedroom and open the door, striding toward the voices, realizing they're all in the kitchen. I'm fuming, my breaths coming fast, my entire body going hot at what I'm about to see. August having a grand old time with other women. The asshole.

I clench my hands into fists and strut into the kitchen, hoping I look like I've had the most spectacular night of nonstop sexual escapades, even though that's a lie. The illusion will have to be good enough.

But the moment I spot who's talking to August, my heart bottoms out and I wish I'd never walked into this room looking like this.

"Well, good morning." The amused voice belongs to his freaking sister, Iris, who's watching me with dancing eyes. "Sinclair, right?"

I want to shrink into myself and disappear because I know, I just know, the older, absolutely stunning woman standing beside Iris is their mother.

"Yes. Um, hi, Iris." I duck my head, hoping she doesn't notice the way my face flames with embarrassment.

"Sinclair." August sounds surprised and I'm terrified to look at him. I probably wasn't supposed to make my appearance known. Did he leave me a note somewhere? He definitely didn't send me a text asking me to stay in the bedroom. "How are you feeling this morning?"

I chance a look at him to see he doesn't seem bothered by my appearance at all. "Much better, thank you."

His smile is faint. "Good. I was just telling my mother and sister what happened to you last night."

"Sounds awful." Iris is relishing this moment. I can tell from the devious expression on her face.

"You poor dear. I can't imagine how terrible that must've been." Their mother approaches me and I freeze, my lips parting but nothing comes out. "It's nice to meet you, Sinclair. I'm August's mother."

"Uh." A gargled noise leaves me and I try to swallow it down. "It's nice to meet you, too, Mrs. Lancaster."

"Please, call me Summer." She pulls me in for a hug and I return the gesture, surprised at how warm and kind she is. Though I suppose she has to be a saint to tolerate her husband. The rumors about Whit Lancaster abound. If I think August is intimidating, I'm sure his father is ten times worse. "It's wonderful to see you here. August never brings a girl around."

"Because you do stuff like this," August says once his mother lets me go. "I should've known you'd check my location and show up here unannounced."

"Iris and I were in the neighborhood to go shopping." His mother lifts her chin, looking as dignified as she sounds. "I saw you were at your apartment and we had to stop by."

"Oh yes, we did." Iris sounds like she's going to start laughing at any second while August just scowls at her.

I take the pair in, noting how they're dressed to perfection with not a hair out of place and I'm a wicked mess with bedhead and clad only in August's T-shirt. This is not the first impression I wanted to make on his family. Hell, I never even thought about impressing his family because I didn't believe I'd ever get the chance to meet them. It wasn't on my radar.

"Well, you two should go on with your shopping then." His tone is polite, but I hear the faint ferocity in August's voice. He wants them gone. Is it because he's embarrassed that they caught us together? I can't blame him. He seems to keep his private life extremely private, even from his family.

"I suppose we should." Iris and her mother share a look before they turn toward me, a united force while I stand there gaping at them like an idiot. "It was lovely meeting you, Sinclair. Hopefully August brings you over for dinner soon."

"I hope my brother redeemed himself in your eyes," Iris says, her focus only on me, though I know she can hear August growling at what she said. "What he did to you back in high school was just...appalling."

Summer Lancaster glances over at her daughter with a frown. "What did he do? Oh God, do I even want to know?"

"I'll tell you in the car." Iris pats her mother's arm and they approach August, wrapping him up in hugs that he ducks out of, the faint disgust on his face obvious. "Bye, Augie!"

His mother kisses his cheek and they exit the kitchen, leaving behind a cloud of expensive perfume. I stare at August from across the room, shifting my feet, not speaking until I hear the door click and I know the women are gone.

"Um." That's all I can manage to say.

He crosses his arms, leaning against the edge of the counter, his amusement at my bumbling making me fumble more. "What did you think of my mother and sister?"

"They're beautiful" is all I can come up with.

"They're a pain in my ass." He shakes his head, but his tone is full of affection. "I should turn off my location for my mom. I'm sure she told Iris I was here after checking where I was at. And I'm positive my sister had a suspicion you would be with me."

"Wait—you're saying they came over here to meet—*me*?" I squeak, resting my hand against my chest.

"I don't let just any woman into my inner sanctum. I told you this." He pushes away from the counter and drops his arms to his sides, making his way toward me. "I've never had anyone here before. I don't like sharing my space with a woman for too long. They start to get…ideas when I do. Not that I ever have."

"What do you mean, ideas?" If he's completely playing me, I'm going to be pissed. Seriously. Though why would I think that? I'm here. He's sharing his private space with me and introduced me to his mother and sister. This means something, doesn't it?

It just might mean everything.

"That I'm serious with them. If I let a woman spend more than a few hours with me, the next thing I know she's picking out our wedding china and making lists of our future children's names." He shrugs. "I'd rather not deal."

"What if I told you I have a list of baby names that I like."

His brows shoot up. "Are those names you came up with while imagining that I'm the father?"

"Well…no." Ugh, he got me there.

"Then I'm not fazed by it. Maybe you'll share the list with me someday."

I rest my hands on my hips, feeling sassy. Which means I'm also feeling a lot better compared to last night. "You really want to see my favorite baby names list?"

"I might like some of the names. Who knows?" His gaze narrows as he contemplates me. "You should change into something more decent."

"This is all I have." I throw my arms up in the air. "And I'm not about to put that dress back on."

He tugs on his lower lip, his gaze roving over me, sparking my skin everywhere it touches. "I'll buy you something."

"Wait a minute—" I rush after him when he turns and exits the kitchen. "I don't need new clothes."

"You do right now." He barely glances at me from over his shoulder. "Don't bother arguing with me, Sin. Let me do this."

"But—"

He whirls on me, grabbing hold of my arms and giving me the slightest shake. "I think you enjoy fighting with me."

I clamp my lips shut because...he's right.

I do.

"I'm going to order you some clothes. What are you?" His gaze drifts down the length of me once more. "A size 4?"

Oh, isn't he generous. He should know considering he bought that dress for me. "I'm more like a size 6."

"Hmm." His hand drops to my butt and he palms one ass cheek, like he's checking it for size. "I like that you're not stick thin."

"You really shouldn't—"

He speaks right over me.

"Makes it easier when I throw you around in bed." He dips his head, his mouth inches from mine. "I know you can take it."

August lets go of me and walks away, tapping at his phone before he brings it up to his ear. I don't hear who he's talking to or what he's saying. I'm too rattled by what he just said to me.

And all the promise I could hear in his voice.

CHAPTER THIRTY-EIGHT

AUGUST

I spend the entire day with Sinclair and I don't get sick of her. Once I get her properly attired, we go out and grab brunch. I convince her to drink one mimosa because everyone knows the best way to cure a hangover is more alcohol and she was a little tipsy when we left the restaurant, which I enjoyed. She had a big smile on her face as we wandered around the city and she was extra flirtatious. Not argumentative like she was before I got her fed.

Though maybe it was the food that healed her. She did admit that she often gets hangry if she doesn't eat for long periods of time.

We're now at another restaurant for dinner. This one isn't too far from my apartment, and it's a quaint Italian restaurant that's owned by a big family. The only reason I know this is because I've been here before and the entire family works at the restaurant. They greet me with interest, curious about the woman I've got with me, but I say nothing.

"No alcohol for me tonight," Sin says once the server walks away after setting a bread basket and two waters on the table. "I can't believe you're taking me to another restaurant with rich food."

"You'll be fine." I snap open the menu, though I already know what I want. This restaurant has the best chicken Marsala I've ever had but maybe something else will catch my eye. "Do you like pasta?"

"Spaghetti. Chicken alfredo."

I make a face. "The two most common Italian dishes you could find."

"Lasagna."

"Make that the three most common."

She rolls her eyes. "I guess I'm trying to tell you I don't go out for Italian food much."

"Do you go out for food at all?"

"Not very often." She shrugs. "I was stuck at Lancaster Prep for most of my high school life."

"You didn't ever go into the town nearby and eat?"

"Not really." She drops her gaze. "I didn't have a ton of friends there. Only a few close ones. I wasn't popular."

I feel guilty as hell because I'm the root cause of her high school trauma. Once I went through my old yearbooks and saw her freshman year photo, it was a painful reminder of her appearance back then, and the memories came back. Though I did give a lot of people shit back then.

I was such a motherfucker. God, I can barely tolerate the memories and hate myself for being so awful toward her.

Taunting a bunch of nerdy girls back in my high school days was like a hobby for me. I was a giant prick who flat-out didn't give a damn about another person's feelings. For the most part, I would say that describes me at this very moment as well.

Which means I can't stand the fact that I treated Sinclair so poorly. That I made her despise me like I did. I can't believe she still doesn't hate me because she should. I was a dick. I deserve her hatred.

Instead, she's sitting across from me, watching me with those shiny golden-brown eyes, the faintest smile curving her lush lips.

She's got on a navy sweater and a pair of jeans that fit her perfectly, showcasing her round ass that I would like to get my hands on later. Preferably in bed.

Preferably naked.

We order when the server returns, Sinclair choosing a grilled chicken dish with a side of pasta while I choose the Marsala. I also order a bottle of red wine, much to Sin's dismay, but I only pour a small amount in her glass, which she sips on as we eat our salads and she consumes endless slices of table bread. The lighting in the restaurant is dim and there's piano music softly tinkling in the background and fuck if she isn't the most beautiful thing I've ever seen. I want to take her back to the apartment and fuck her on the bed. The sofa. The kitchen counter. The shower. Wherever she'll let me, I want to take her. Make her mine. For real.

Halfway through eating our entrees, she receives a phone call, one that has her grimacing when she sees the name flashing on her screen. The insane jealousy I feel over anyone else she may have in her life rears its ugly head and I take a moment to get it under control before I speak.

"Who is it?" My voice is even while my insides are in chaos. I hate thinking of her talking to anyone else, which is stupid. She talks to other people because she's a normal human and not a hermit. I can't just whisk her away and keep her from her friends and family. She'd hate me for it. Or maybe she wouldn't mind as long as I kept her naked and in bed while giving her endless orgasms. That sounds like a dream.

"My mother." A sigh leaves her and she stares at her phone until the call ends and it goes to voice mail. "I don't want to talk to her."

Relief fills me. If it had been Tim, I might've thrown her phone across the restaurant. "Why not?"

"Well, first of all, it's because I'm with you." Her smile is small, coy and she won't quite look me in the eye, which I'm thinking is on purpose. It's obvious that her mother calling disturbs her. "And second...I just don't want to."

"You don't get along." I don't ask it as a question. Sin has problems with her family and it makes me grateful that I like my parents and tolerate my siblings. If anyone has a problem in our immediate family, it's me. Everyone else is relatively normal—save for my father who is a raging lunatic but knows how to control himself and play nice with others.

I inherited his traits and am learning how to play nice, but fuck it's difficult sometimes.

"She's only calling to see what I'm doing on a Friday night. I've never seen a mother so worried about her daughter's social life before." Her expression turns sour. "If I were to tell her I'm out with you, she'd flip out."

"Because I'm a Lancaster?"

Sin nods.

"Then tell her."

She lifts her head, blinking at me, her shock at my encouragement apparent. "If I tell her I'm—*dating* you, she won't leave me alone until she gets to meet you."

"Then let's meet Mom and Dad. Mr. and Mrs. Jock Rot." I grin, fucking *grin* at her, and she grins back.

"I hate how you always bring up the Jock Rot thing."

"You should've never told me." That's why I bring it up. I want to get under her skin. What would she say if I told her she's burrowed herself so deeply under my skin I'm afraid I'll never be able to let her go?

"I didn't," she reminds me. "You figured it out on your own."

I tap the side of my head. "I'm just that smart, I guess."

"I guess so."

We keep grinning at each other like idiots and I lean forward, stretching my hand across the table so I can take hold of hers. "Let's get the hell out of here."

More blinking. I think she enjoys pretending to be shocked at what I say. Or maybe I do actually surprise her. "You want to leave? Now?"

I lower my voice. "I want to get you alone."

A slight shiver moves through her, but I notice. I notice everything about her. I'm fixated on her. And I'm tired of playing around. Tired of waiting. The need to fuck her, claim her, burns inside me. Insistently.

"What do you want to do to me when we're alone?" Her eyes have gone wide and I feel like I've created a monster. She's part seduction, part innocence and God, the depraved things I could tell her would probably burn her ears and make her want to run far, far away from me.

"How about instead of telling you, I show you instead." I grasp her fingers in mine and give them a gentle squeeze before letting her go. "Let's leave."

"You didn't finish your—"

"Fuck the meal, Sinclair. I'll pay on the way out and we're going back to my apartment. Now." There I go again, acting like an impatient prick, but I can't help myself. We don't need to stall this moment any longer.

She nods, ducking her head for only a moment before she returns her gaze to mine. "Okay."

Satisfaction makes my chest tight and I take a deep breath, relieved. Damn, I love a submissive woman.

CHAPTER THIRTY-NINE

SINCLAIR

August hustles me out of the restaurant at breakneck speed and we hurry down the sidewalk together toward his apartment building, neither of us speaking. It's cold outside and I can see my breath every time I part my lips. Late October and the weather has already turned.

Not that I care about the weather. Though I suppose I'm thinking about it or else my thoughts stray to what we're about to do, August and me. Have sex. Intercourse. For the first time ever. That I've taken my bully as my lover is still mind-blowing. I can only imagine what fourteen-year-old Sinclair would say to me.

She'd tell me I've lost my marbles. I probably have. But the connection August and I share is so strong and feels so right. It's hard to explain or describe. It's just there, always brewing between us. Growing and growing throughout the evening at the restaurant until I saw the flicker of impatience in his eyes. He was over what he'd probably call a play date. He's ready to get to the good stuff and while I'm eager, I'm also incredibly nervous.

What if it hurts? What if he can't even get inside me? I had a friend in high school who had that problem. She'd freeze up so badly every time her boyfriend tried to enter her, he literally couldn't push his way inside of her. She was clamped up so tightly, he'd try and try, but it was like trying to bust down a steel door. They couldn't make it work because sex was basically impossible and eventually, he broke up with her.

What a jerk. So insensitive. And that worries me because August is the least sensitive person I know. Will he end things with me if the sex is bad? So far, our experiences together haven't been bad at all, at least to me. But what do I know? I don't have a lot of experience when it comes to this sort of thing. He hasn't left yet. He actually says he's obsessed with me and that's…well I don't know how to feel about it.

I love it, but is he being real with me? Maybe he's just obsessed with what he can't have. Tonight, he's going to get it and he might leave me after. If he does, what an asshole.

Ugh, that part is scary because we all know August is an asshole. I'm the one who's putting everything on the line for this guy. To get dumped by him will break me. I'm in too deep. No matter how much I tried to warn myself, here I am. Completely into him. On my way to falling for him.

I'm hopeless.

The moment we enter the lobby of his building, he grabs my hand and heads for the elevator. The doors slide open as soon as he hits the up button and he drags me inside, turning toward me when the doors slide closed with a soft swoosh.

He's on me in an instant, his hands cupping my cheeks and his mouth finding mine in a hungry kiss. I respond in kind, parting for his probing tongue, winding mine around his. He pushes me against the elevator wall, his body flush with mine and I can feel him. Hard and thick and insistent.

The elevator comes to a stop and the doors slide open. He's off me just as quickly, smoothing his hair away from his forehead as he strolls out of the elevator. I follow after him on wobbly feet, overcome with a thousand emotions his mouth and hands seem to elicit within me every time we collide. Why was I nervous about this moment again? The second he places his hands on my body all rational thought leaves me. And currently, I'm thinking too much. Thinking too hard.

It's pointless. I need to just go with the flow. Nature will take its proper course and I am, after all, in good hands.

Spectacular hands, truly.

He reaches the door as I'm still walking down the corridor and he opens it, his impatience radiating toward me. I make my way to him, walking past where he stands and entering the apartment with my head held high and he lets the door shut behind him, his hands landing on my waist, keeping me still in the foyer.

I'm trembling when I feel his mouth brush the side of my neck, goosebumps erupting all over my skin. His hands slide forward, settling on my stomach, and I rest my hands over his, closing my eyes and tilting my head back to give him better access.

"Do you know how beautiful you are?" he murmurs against my skin.

No, I want to tell him. I have no clue. I always thought I was average. Many years ago, I thought I was hideous, thanks to him. And I sort of was at fourteen. That he thinks I'm beautiful now feels like some sort of redemption for what I had to suffer through all those years ago.

"All I could think about through dinner was this." His hands shift, settling on the waistband of the jeans he bought for me. He undoes the button and tugs the zipper down impatiently, his hand slipping inside. Cupping me with his large, hot hand. "I'm fucking obsessed with your cunt."

His words make me wet and I whimper when he pushes his fingers against my pussy. I can't speak but what would I say anyway? Gee, thanks for being obsessed with my vagina? That sounds silly.

"I told myself I would be patient and take it slow but I can't." His fingers shift to slip inside my panties, brushing against my bare, damp flesh, and he groans close to my ear, the low, rough sound doing something to me. Giving me power.

I make him feel that way. Respond that way. I could have August Lancaster on his knees for me and that is astonishing to realize. That he wants me.

That he cares. This man cares about hardly anyone.

We remain in the foyer, our harsh breaths filling the space, his fingers slicking through my pussy noisily. "You're so wet. Drenched for me."

I may have power over him, but he has just as much power over me. His words, the way he touches me makes me weak and I lock my knees so I don't melt into the floor. When he removes his hand from my panties, I almost want to cry, I miss his touch so badly. He reaches for me, and I go willingly, a surprised gasp leaving me when he hauls me into his arms and carries me to his bedroom.

He says nothing and neither do I. Words are unnecessary when this incessant need throbs between us, overwhelming us both. I wrap my arms around his neck and bury my face against his throat, clinging to him. Breathing deep his spicy scent, it floods my senses, making me dizzy. I shriek like a scared little girl when he disentangles me from him and I fall onto the mattress with a bounce.

Pushing my hair out of my face, I look up to find he's watching me with those intense blue eyes while taking off his clothes. He sheds his sweater and the T-shirt he was wearing underneath it, exposing his glorious chest. I eat him up with my gaze, my core clenching when he reaches for the fly of his jeans and undoes it, shedding them and his boxer briefs in seconds. Until he's standing in front of me completely naked and beautiful.

My gaze drops to his dick and I lick my lips like the greedy girl I am, though a tinge of fear streaks through me. He's…big. At least, he looks big to me. Maybe he's average-sized, I don't know but I'm nervous all over again now that I see him naked.

"You look terrified."

I meet his gaze, swallowing hard. "You're…"

"I'll fit." He grips the base of his cock and gives it a short stroke. A pearly drop of pre-cum appears at the tip and I remember what he tasted like. How pleased he was with me after I gave him my first blow job ever. "Don't be scared, Sin. I'm going to make it good for you."

He's on the bed with me, stretching his long frame out beside me, his mouth finding mine in a carnal kiss. Our tongues tangle, our teeth clash, and I scoot closer to him, wanting more. Needing more. His hands rove all over me, slipping beneath my sweater, easily finding my breast. He didn't buy me a bra when he purchased my clothes this morning and I'm sure he did that on purpose.

Well, I'm not complaining now because he has easy access. His fingers stroke and knead, his thumb circling around one nipple, then the other. Back and forth, teasing me, working me into a frenzy that leaves me breathless. And when he takes off my sweater and ducks his head to draw a nipple into his mouth, I buck against him, the strong pull of his lips tugging on something deep inside me, drawing me deeper into mindless pleasure.

He runs his mouth all over my chest. Licking and sucking and biting my skin like he can't get enough of me. I thrust my fingers into his hair and hold him to me, always afraid he might end all of this and send me on my way. I can hardly bear the thought of him calling it off between us, it destroys me so badly.

August destroys me. Slowly but surely with his mouth and tongue and fingers. His hot words whispered into my skin, that blazing intensity in his eyes. When he lifts his head to stare at me, I stare back, helpless. I can hardly breathe thanks to the way he's watching me. Like he's trying to figure out how exactly he got here with me. In his bed.

Is he as shaken with the intensity that simmers between us as I am? I'm on edge, on the verge of orgasm already and we've only just begun.

But it feels like we've been working toward this moment since the day we encountered each other all these years later. When I was so angry and he was intrigued. My anger and ambivalence drew him to me and that was the last thing I wanted.

Or so I thought.

He removes my jeans and panties until I'm as naked as he is, and when his fingers dip between my thighs and begin to stroke, I let my legs fall open. My breaths come faster when he increases his pace, matching his movements and when he pinches my clit between two fingers and tugs? I sink my teeth into my bottom lip to keep from crying out.

"Not going to let you come yet," he murmurs, pressing slow circles against my clit with his thumb. "You like that, Sin?"

I nod furiously, lost to the sensation that races through me. The circles become tighter and tighter, faster and faster, and a wave slips over me, pulling me under. Straight toward bliss.

August removes his thumb from my clit and I want to sob. My entire body is strung tight; I was so focused on that one spot where so much pleasure radiated outward. I open my eyes to find him kneeling on the mattress between my spread legs, his cock standing straight out from his body. His skin is covered with the lightest sheen of sweat and I realize I'm sweating too. It's too much and not enough all at once and I drape my arm over my eyes, unable to look at him for too long.

He hovers above me in an instant, carefully removing my arm from my face and when I spot the gentle glow in his eyes, some of the tension leaves my body as I sink into the mattress.

"You want me to eat that pretty little pussy of yours?" His fingers slide up my thigh, drifting across the top of my pussy.

I nod, arching my hips. Seeking his touch.

"Say it." He removes his hand like the sadist he is. "Beg for it, baby. You know I love it when you cry."

This fucker. I'm immediately incensed, hating how my stomach tightens at his words. The fresh flood of wetness between my thighs. He knows just what to do and say to make me wetter. Hotter.

"Please, August." I lift my hips again, spreading my legs as wide as they can go. "I need you."

"How bad, hmm? Tell me what you want me to do to you, Sin." He shifts so he's lying on his stomach, coming face to pussy, and I wonder if it hurts his dick, to lie there like that.

"I want you to—lick me." He does exactly that, making me hiss in a breath. "I want you to suck my clit." He does that too, wrapping his lips around the distended bundle of nerves and sucking hard. "Fuck me with your fingers."

He slides one finger inside me and begins to pump. In and out, his pace slows, curling his finger when he slides it deep and hitting something within that has me seeing stars. He adds another finger and increases his pace, fucking me with his fingers just like I asked while his mouth is still on my clit. His tongue lashes at my skin and I brace my feet onto the mattress, my seeking hips lifting as if they have a mind of their own.

Without warning the orgasm slams into me and I can't breathe. I can't see either. I'm lost to the sensation of wave after wave sweeping over my skin, rippling my belly and my core. My inner walls clench around his fingers, my clit throbbing and he continues his assault upon my flesh until I'm a gasping, trembling mess. I try to push him away, my skin too sensitive but he won't stop. His lips are insistent, sucking on my clit while he continues to fuck me with his fingers and oh God, another orgasm rips through me. This one smaller but just as intense.

"Fuck, you're drenched," he mutters against my skin before he pulls away, wiping the back of his hand across his mouth. The lower half of his face shines with my juices and I watch helplessly as he reaches for the nightstand and opens the drawer, pulling out a condom. "Not taking any chances, Sin. You on birth control?"

I shake my head, feeling like a fool.

"That's what I thought. You need to get on something." He tears open the wrapper and discards it over his shoulder, rolling the condom on with intense concentration. "I want to fuck you raw."

Oh God. I want him to fuck me raw too.

He positions himself so he's between my legs again, his fingers curled around the base of his cock, his other hand braced on the mattress. His cheeks are red and his skin shines with sweat and I've never seen him more beautiful. This big, gorgeous man is about to push his away inside me and I'm fucking giddy at the thought. Ready for it.

Desperate for it. For him.

CHAPTER FORTY

AUGUST

I avoid virgins like the plague, but here I am, about to slip inside one for the first time since...forever and I'm so fucking worried I'm going to hurt her, it's ridiculous. If I think about it too much, I'm going to deflate my erection and ruin the entire moment so I concentrate on her. Those little tells of Sin's that let me know she's enjoying this. I brush the head of my cock against her soaked folds, paying attention to the sharp intake of her breath. The way she arches naturally. Seeking me. Needing my entry into her welcoming body.

Going slow, I slip just the head into her pussy, pausing. Gauging. I stare at her expressive face, note the way her eyelashes flutter and her lips part on a breath. I push farther, still keeping my focus on her. She winces when I slip deeper. Sucks in a breath when I'm fully seated inside her, tensing up. I hesitate, waiting for the tension to slowly dissipate from her body, but her body stiffens further.

"Breathe, Sin." She does as I ask automatically, her body going soft beneath mine and I start to croon pretty words to relax her. "Your pussy feels so fucking good, baby. Relax. I'm going to make you come so hard. Look at you. God, you're beautiful."

She is. And so fucking tight. Her cunt has my cock in a stranglehold and I know all it would take is two short pumps and I'd be coming way too early.

I squeeze my eyes shut tight and think about mundane things. School. Tests. Frat shit that I need to take care of, which has me thinking of Tim and how much he'd want to be in my place. That only enrages me.

"Hold on," I grit through my teeth, overcome with the need to rut. To fuck and make her mine, though there's a small part of me that's worried I could hurt her and that's the last thing I want to do.

But fuck, being in this moment is sending me straight over the edge. This is the final part of my claiming. Once I fuck this woman, she is mine and there is nothing she can do about it. Nothing sweet little Timmy can do about it either. And why the hell am I thinking about him again? Maybe because imagining any other man even looking at Sin makes me feral.

I push into her, my hips flush against hers and she whimpers, sucking in a harsh breath like I hurt her. "Oh—God."

Pausing, I stare down at her pretty face, noting the way her brows are knit together as if she's trying to ward off the pain. "Are you okay?"

She nods, keeping her eyes closed, her lips twisting into a grim smile. "Just—let me get used to you for a minute."

I remain still, my entire body shaking with the need to move. "Sin."

Her eyes crack open and I dip my head, kissing her. Keeping it soft and sweet and as persuasive as possible. I lick at her mouth, tangling my tongue with hers and she moans, her body relaxing beneath mine. I start to move, slowly at first, and she shifts beneath me, her movements tentative, as if she's trying to figure it all out.

"Wrap your legs around my hips," I demand, and she does it, pressing her soft skin into mine. I increase my pace, thrusting inside her steadily, wishing I could fuck her harder. I'm on edge, filled with the need to come, to fill her with my semen like some sort of rabid dog and I hate the fucking condom. I hate it so damn much.

Like an inept fool I lose all restraint and fuck her hard, slamming into her body again and again while she takes it like the goddess that I knew she could be. I readjust myself, rising above her, grabbing hold of her hips so I have some leverage as I move inside her. My balls slap against her ass and I'm grunting with every thrust. Groaning at how fucking good this feels. The connection. The easy way our bodies move with each other. We're so attuned it's like we've been doing this our entire lives and when my orgasm creeps up on me, my balls drawing tight and the base of my spine tingling, I don't fight it.

I revel in it, moaning when I begin to come. I shudder and shake, her name falling from my lips as I slam into her once. Twice. Holding myself there while the orgasm washes over me. I drain myself into the fucking condom until I fall on top of her, utterly spent.

The room is quiet save for our harsh mingled breathing, and I press my face into the mattress, my eyes closed as I try and calm the racing of my heart. She's breathing just as hard, our skin sticking to each other, her hands sliding up and down my back, soothing me.

Normally I'd bolt after a moment like this. I wouldn't stand for her touching me like that. Like she fucking cares. Now I want this woman to care. To show that I matter to her, that she cares about my pleasure as much as I care about hers.

And God help me, I care far too much. I'm in so deep, I don't know how I'm ever going to climb out.

"Are you okay?" she whispers.

I almost want to laugh at her question. No, dearest Sin, I am not. I am fucked in the head when it comes to you and I don't know what to do about it.

But I don't say any of that. I'd sound like a fool if I did.

"Aren't I the one who should be asking you that?" I lift my head, staring into her eyes, my stomach twisting when I see her smile.

Damn it, what is wrong with me?

"You just—didn't move and I wanted to make sure you were still alive." She stretches beneath me, her body rubbing against mine, my dick stiffening despite the fact that I experienced a ball-draining orgasm not even a minute ago.

"Are you all right?" I reach for her, brushing the damp strands of hair away from her forehead, my gaze roving over her face. Looking for a sign that she might be in pain or worse? It was a bad experience for her and she wants me to move.

She nods, a dreamy expression on her face. "I'm great."

Great seems like a small word for what we just shared. "I need to get rid of this condom."

With reluctance, I pull out of her and roll off the bed, heading for the connecting bathroom where I dispose of the condom and take the quickest piss. I'm eager to get back into bed with her and do it again but I don't want to push. She might be aching and sore and I don't want to make it worse.

The moment I slide back under the covers, she's shifting closer, draping her languid body over mine, throwing her leg across my front. Her pussy is nestled against my thigh and I can feel her. Wet and hot and just begging me to fuck her again. That's how I interpret it, at least.

"I'm tired," she breathes into my neck, dropping a soft kiss there. I lie beneath her stiff as a fucking board, afraid to move for fear she'll roll over on her side. Swallowing, I try to come up with the proper words I'd like to say to her but it's like my brain can't string a sentence together.

"Me too," I manage to say, though it's a lie.

"Tell that to your dick." She grabs me, her fingers curling around my balls and cupping them and that's it.

I roll over so I'm on top of her again, my face in hers, my erect cock nudging at her entrance. Eager to get back inside so we can do it again. "Fine. I lied."

She mock pouts. "You know I don't like it when you do that."

"I didn't know if you were...sore." I wince, hating how my greed for her threatens to consume me. I'd fuck her all night if she let me. I'd never leave this pussy again. I'd just live with her and we could fuck like rabbits for the rest of our lives.

"I am a little sore," she admits, wiggling her body and driving me crazy. God, she's hot. Sexy as hell and all mine. "But I want to do it again."

"Right now?" I'm hesitant, which is completely unlike me, but I've changed for this woman. I don't want to hurt her. I want to protect her. Make sure she's okay.

"Mmm hmm." She stretches, her arms going around my neck and tugging. I dip my head, our mouths meeting, and she whispers, "Maybe this time I could be on top?"

I kiss her, teasing her tongue with mine before I pull away. "Whatever you want, Sin, I'll let you do it. All you gotta do is ask."

CHAPTER FORTY-ONE

SINCLAIR

I am in heaven. On cloud nine. All the cliché sayings that I've heard my entire life about happiness, I am feeling because oh my God, what August and I just shared over the last couple of days was the most momentous experience of my life.

Spending time with him at his apartment, getting lost in his arms, his bed for hours at a time…I didn't want to leave. I would've happily quit school just to have the chance to spend the rest of my days in that apartment with August. Forget the world. We only need each other and the occasional meal and shower.

But reality intruded and reminded us both we needed to return to campus. We headed back early Sunday morning, August dropping me off at my dorm building, kissing me in the back seat of the hired car so thoroughly I had to finally make my escape or else we probably would've ended up doing it in the dorm parking lot.

I float into my dorm building, taking the stairs instead of the elevator, practically running down the corridor to my and Elise's room. When I throw open the door, our room is blessedly empty, and I throw myself onto my bed, clutching my pillow to my chest and sighing blissfully.

My body is exhausted but in the best way and my brain isn't quite firing on all cylinders, but I don't care. I am happy after being thoroughly fucked for the last forty-eight hours or so. I didn't know it could be like this. Feel like this. I now understand how Elise acted when she came back to our room after her encounter with Rafe, her golden god. Though of course, she lied to me about the losing her virginity part, but I can forgive her for that.

I can forgive everyone for lots of things as long as I know August is in my life.

My phone rings and I don't even bother checking it, my gut telling me it's August. He can't even be apart from me for a minute. He's already calling me and I feel exactly the same way.

"There you are! I've been trying to call you all weekend."

My stomach drops at the sound of my mother's voice and I regret not checking who the call was from. "Oh. Hey. Sorry. I've been busy."

"Uh huh. Having the time of your life, I'm sure." There's an edge to her voice that's always present when we talk lately and I sometimes can't help but think she's jealous of me being away at college while she's stuck in her mundane life. I don't think she's happy. How can she be, when she has to deal with my unfaithful father?

"I suppose," I hedge, reminding myself I don't want to tell her about August.

"Have you finally met someone?"

A sigh leaves me. "Why does my being busy always have to involve a man? School is keeping me busy too, you know."

"Because you're just like me." She laughs, and the sound grates. I've never thought I was like her. "You've blossomed into a beautiful young woman and I know all the men must be coming around. I remember what it was like when I was in college. I can only hope you're having the same experience."

"Were you a ho?" The question leaves me before I can second-guess myself and I sort of regret it.

But then again, she goes completely silent, so I sort of *don't* regret it either.

"A ho? Are you asking me if I slept around when I was in college? The answer would be yes." She giggles and I grimace. This is information I don't need to know about. "And then I met your father and fell hopelessly in love with the man. Now he's stuck with me."

I never want August to feel stuck with me. That sounds awful. "Did you know he was the one you wanted to spend the rest of your life with right away?"

I don't know if I feel that strongly for August. I definitely care about him but is this just a phase for us? Will he move on after he's had his fill? I want to protect myself from falling deeper because what if it's not reciprocated? I'll be devastated if that happens.

"No, of course not. I don't believe in love at first sight and you shouldn't either." She goes quiet for a moment. "So you have met someone."

"Sort of." I'm desperate to keep his name to myself. "It's nothing serious."

Those three words leave a bad taste in my mouth and I regret saying them. I don't mean it. What August and I share is… overwhelming. In a good way. In a serious way.

"This is the period in your life where you should have fun," Mom says, her voice soft. "You don't need to settle down yet. You're only eighteen. You have your entire life to fall in love. Considering this is your first year in college, you should be partying and having the best time ever."

She is surprisingly logical and that's not like her.

"I've definitely been having fun." I launch into a story about going to a party with Elise and Mom eats it up, asking all sorts of questions and laughing along with me. But it feels wrong, talking about a stupid party when I should be telling her about August and how much he means to me instead.

I'm conflicted. There's that bigger part of me that doesn't dare mention him, but then there's that tiny, falling in love with August part that wants to spill her guts and tell Mom everything.

My heart seizes in my chest at the thought. Falling in love with August? Is that what's happening between us? Hard to believe. Why would I love him?

Why would you not love him, whispers that secret voice buried deep in my brain.

"I sort of am dating someone though," I admit after my party story.

"Oooh, what's his name? And please tell me it's just a fling," Mom encourages.

"His name is—August Lancaster."

Dead silence greets me and I grip my phone tight, my stomach churning. I wait for her response, mentally preparing myself for the blast.

"Are you serious?" she screeches and I close my eyes, hating how excited she sounds. It's not because she knows August and adores him. It's that she knows his family name and how much wealth they have. I know how she operates. "You're dating a Lancaster?"

"It's not a big deal—"

"It's a huge deal, Sinclair! The Lancasters are one of the wealthiest families in this country. They have so much money it's ridiculous. Isn't August Lancaster Whit's son?"

That she even knows Whit's name fills me with dread. "Um… yes."

"My God, Sinclair! This is—this is big news! Your father will be beside himself."

"Why?" I'm clueless. Is it because they'll feel special hanging out with Lancasters? I don't want to let my parents anywhere near any Lancaster, especially August.

"He's trying to find people that are on his level." Mom makes this sound like such a logical response and I hate to tell her, but Dad is nowhere near the Lancasters' level. I don't even think I am, yet I just spent days with August.

"Is it serious?" she asks when I haven't said anything. "With August?"

"I don't know." That's the truth. I'm confused and don't know how I feel about him. About us. Do I want it to be serious? My mom is right—I'm going to be nineteen soon. Do I really want to tie myself down with someone at this point in my life? There's still so much to do. Like finish school. Figure out what I want to do with my life.

And is it stupid to get involved in a relationship with August when he's going to graduate soon? He'll be gone and I'll still be here. On campus and missing him while he's off living his life and forgetting about me.

My heart pangs just imagining it.

"You should try and figure it out soon, sweetheart. He's a catch." Mom giggles again and that's it. I can't stomach this conversation any longer.

"I need to go. I have to get to the library before it closes." The lie falls from my lips easily and I don't even feel bad. I'm desperate to get off this call.

"Of course, of course! I'll let you go, but Sinclair? Keep me posted about what's happening between you and that August Lancaster. Your father is going to want every single detail." Mom sounds downright giddy.

Like I would give my parents every single detail about my "relationship"—I'm sure there are some parts of my relationship with August dear old Dad does not want to know.

"Bye, Mom." I end the call before she can say anything else and flop back on my mattress, staring up at the ceiling. This is how Elise finds me when she enters our room minutes later. I don't even look at her but I can sense her coming to a stop, watching me.

"Are you okay?"

A sigh leaves me, and I keep my gaze fixed on the ceiling. "I think I'm in over my head."

"With what? School? I am positively drowning in homework." Elise settles heavily on the edge of her bed and I finally turn to look at her, our gazes meeting. Hers is full of sympathy. "I spent the entire weekend with my family and going out with my old friends instead of doing schoolwork and now I'm going to pay the price."

"You had a good weekend then?"

"Oh yeah, it was so much fun. I even met up with my old boyfriend." Her smile is small. "He's learned some new moves."

"You had sex with him?"

Elise nods. "It was nothing. Just casual."

"Oh." I glance up at the ceiling, wondering how I'm going to bring up what happened between me and August.

"Did you have a good weekend? Oh my God, how was your date with August? Did you have fun? Did he hold you captive all weekend and fuck your brains out?"

"Basically." I glance over at Elise to find she's gaping at me in shock. "Yes. I stayed at his apartment all weekend in the city."

"He actually held you captive?" Elise squeaks.

"I stayed because I wanted to." I sit up, gathering my hair in my hands and holding it off my neck. "He didn't need to hold me captive."

"I bet." Elise's smile is sly. "So…how was it?"

"Good."

She arches a brow. "Good? That's all you can say? Come on now. Don't hold out on me. I need all the details."

I don't want to give her all the details. What happened between me and August is private. Just for me. Just for us.

"He knows what he's doing." Just from the look on her face I can tell that's not good enough. She wants more. "He's also got a giant dick."

Elise grins. "I knew he would! I bet it's magical."

Honestly, I have no one else to compare it to, so for all I know August is average. But I don't know… "It was pretty magical."

"I'm sure." She shakes her head. "I can't believe you two are a thing, but I think it's awesome, Sinclair. And what a story! From being your bully in high school to him being your first. Are you guys like, official now?"

I sort of hate that she brought that up. From August being my bully to being the first guy I had sex with. Is that normal? It doesn't feel normal. From the first interaction with August all those years ago, nothing has been typical.

When I realize Elise is watching me expectantly, waiting for my answer, I clear my throat and shrug. "I'm not sure."

She's frowning. "You didn't discuss it?"

"Are we supposed to?" I sink my teeth into my lower lip, feeling inept. She's had way more experience than me, but has she ever had a steady relationship? "I've never had a boyfriend before."

"Not even in middle school?"

I shake my head. "I showed you the pictures of me from middle school. I was a hideous troll."

Elise bursts out laughing. "You were not. You were just going through an—awkward stage."

"Awkward enough that I didn't have a boyfriend throughout the entirety of middle school and high school." Panic floods me and I remind myself there's no reason to feel this way. Whatever happens between August and me, I'll be fine.

Even if he dumps me. I should prepare myself for that. The possibility is there. Look at his track record—he doesn't do relationships. What makes me so special?

Nothing, that's what.

"You'll be fine. Just follow your instincts."

She makes it sound so easy. "I have zero instincts when it comes to this kind of stuff. You've seen him—he's such a polarizing presence. Larger than life while I'm just...me." I sound insecure. I am insecure when it comes to this man. I can't help it.

"You're not just you." Elise comes over to sit on my bed, grabbing my shoulders and giving me a gentle shake. "You're Sinclair fucking Miller and you just spent the entire weekend with August Lancaster. It's obvious he likes you. He might even be falling for you. That's a big deal."

"You really think so?" Voicing my insecurities makes them feel that much more real and it's scary. "I don't—"

"Nope." Elise gives me a little shake again. "Stop all the negative talk. This man likes you, Sinclair. How many times do you have to hear it? Has he said those words?"

"Kind of." I shrug and she lets go of me, thank God. I was starting to feel like a bobblehead every time she shook me. "It's hard for me to believe that someone who hated me all those years ago now wants to spend all of his time with me."

"Maybe he never hated you. Maybe he was attracted to you and didn't know how to express himself," Elise points out.

I burst out laughing. "No way. He despised me."

"Okay, maybe he never really thought about you one way or the other then. I think all the hate came from you."

She's right. I hated him. I walked into that frat house not too long ago prepared to see him and hate him all over again. Instead, I flirted with him. The chemistry was hard to deny and it's only grown since then. He's all I think about and I'm pretty sure he feels the same way. Maybe we can make this work.

Maybe we already are.

CHAPTER FORTY-TWO

AUGUST

"I'm in a—predicament." I stop talking, trying to come up with the right words to say but unfortunately, my best friend is watching me with that constant amused look on his face and considering my mood, I don't want him to make fun of me. I need serious help.

Well, that sounds drastic. More like I need advice. Guidance. And that's not something I ask for easily.

"What sort of predicament?" Cyrus sounds genuinely concerned. The smile even falls off his face. Probably because I rarely ask for help.

We're in the sitting room at the frat house. What the others call my lair. I like how that sounds. Like I'm the king and this is where I take my court or speak with my trusted advisors, such as Cyrus. I want to tell him what's going on, but where do I begin? He knows some of the details, but not all of them and I'm afraid I'm going to shock him.

My mind goes to Sinclair as it usually does. I haven't seen her for two days and my soul feels like it's slowly slipping out of my body and evaporating into thin air. Fucking dramatic I know, but it's true. We've texted briefly but no plans have been made. No demands either because since I had sex with her—earth-shattering, mind-blowing, rock-my-world sex for a solid weekend while we were holed up in my apartment—I'm cautious. I want to see her again. Immediately.

This isn't like me.

"You've been quiet lately, August. And it's concerning," Cyrus adds, his voice grave.

I send him a questioning look. "Concerning?"

"You're never quiet. You've always got something to say, and you've been quiet since you came back Sunday, which is out of character. You're worrying me. Is something wrong? Please don't tell me your father is dying."

"What the fuck, Cyrus?" Why would he go straight to the most drastic conclusion? "My father is fine. He's perfectly healthy. My entire family is."

"Don't tell me Iris and Brooks are getting divorced."

"They're not even married." I frown. Are they? If they are, they didn't invite me to the wedding and that's fucked.

"Then what is it? Are you failing a class? Did you gamble away your trust fund? Have you met a woman and fallen hopelessly in love with her?"

How did he know?

"I think—it might be the last one."

Cyrus's jaw drops and he gapes at me for an uncomfortably long time. To the point that I'm glaring at him and about to curse him out but he comes to his senses before I have to. "That's the last thing I thought you'd say."

"You really think I'm stupid enough to gamble away my entire trust fund?" I shake my head, disappointed.

"I don't know! I'd guess you'd do that before you fell in love with someone."

"It's not love." I have no idea what it is, but the thought of her makes my chest ache, which is...odd. Is she avoiding me on purpose? She's complained about school and I know things get busy this time of the year. We're already in October and the semester will be over soon. What happens to us when winter break hits? I'll go to my apartment in the city and spend time with my family during the actual holiday, and what will Sinclair do? Go home to her wretched parents?

Wretched probably isn't strong enough, but it's close. They sound awful. There's a small part of me that wants to avoid them completely but then there's a bigger, braggart part of me that wants to invite them to the family home for dinner. Just to dazzle them. They don't give Sinclair enough credit. She's smart. Beautiful. Classy. They must've done something right to raise her so well, but from the way she talks, Sinclair makes them out to be horrid beasts.

I'm in the mood to slay a couple of horrid beasts. It would give me immense pleasure to show them what their daughter could potentially have.

Clearly, I've lost my mind.

"Then what is it? And *who* is it?" Cyrus asks, interrupting my thoughts.

"I can't stop thinking about her." I hesitate before I admit who. "Sinclair. Fuck, she haunts me."

"Haunts you? The girl you used to bully in high school? That makes sense. She's probably put some sort of spell on you to fuck you over for what you did to her in the past."

I've never thought she could possibly do something like that. "Please. That sounds ridiculous."

"How ridiculous, hmm? She comes into your life out of nowhere and has you completely obsessed. Now you think you're falling in love with her, and that's not normal, August. Not for you, at least. I think you're being tricked."

"Tricked? Are you saying some little eighteen-year-old girl could make me fall for her like she's some sort of witch? Please. That's preposterous."

"Is it? Has this ever happened to you before?"

"No."

"Did you fuck her?"

Such a crude way to put what happened between me and Sin. Yes, I love talking about fucking her, but when someone else says it? It sounds…meaningless. And what Sin and I have shared isn't meaningless. Not even close.

"We had sex, yes."

"How was it? Must've been better than the last one you hooked up with. You couldn't even remember her name." Cyrus shakes his head.

"Because she didn't matter."

"But Sinclair does."

I stare off into the distance, watching as the front door swings open and in walks my least favorite person in the world, Tim. I haven't even given him a thought but now here he is, and I sort of want to talk to him. About Sinclair.

"Yes," I bite out. "She matters to me. It's the family curse."

"Family curse?"

"When a Lancaster falls for someone, that's it. That's their person. For life. I've avoided getting to know women in fear of having that happen to me. My parents are obsessed with each other and while it's reassuring to know they love each other so deeply, as I got older, it—scared me. Their kind of love."

Cyrus actually has the nerve to chuckle. "Scared you? That's not typical, August. Nothing scares you."

"Falling in love with someone does." I'm not ready. I'm too young. Sin is far too young. What if there's someone else out there better for me? Better for her? Am I settling? Is she?

Unfathomable. I wouldn't settle for anything less than what I deserve and damn it, I deserve Sinclair.

"But you just said it's not love, what you feel for Sinclair."

My gaze stays on Tim and his goofy friend, Rafe. They're laughing and talking and high-fiving each other and I can't stand it.

"It's not. Yet."

Cyrus is laughing, the dick. "If she is a witch, you're done for, dude. You've completely fallen under that spell she's cast on you."

"It's not such a bad place to be." I rise to my feet, my focus on the two idiots standing in the foyer. "I'll be right back."

I make my way over to Tim and Rafe, who catch on quickly that I'm making my approach. They both go quiet, watching me with bug eyes and open mouths. Like they're little kids who are about to get in trouble. Tim is the braver of the two when it comes to me and he snaps his lips shut, putting on a friendly face.

"Hey, prez. How are you?"

I hate the nickname. It's disrespectful. "I'm well. How are you two imbeciles?"

Neither of them responds to my insult. It's like they didn't even hear it.

"We're good." Tim keeps nodding like he can't stop and Rafe mumbles a response I can't decipher.

"Can I speak to you privately for a moment, Tim?" I glance over at Rafe, who looks ready to bolt. "You understand, don't you?"

"Yep. See you." Rafe is gone, leaving Tim and I alone and I lead him back to my lair, Cyrus nowhere in sight. Perfect.

Turning to face Tim, I cross my arms. "Are you still speaking to Sinclair?"

Tim frowns, squinting up at me because I'm taller than him. "We have a class together. I sit next to her. Yeah, I still talk to her."

"Well then, you need to stop." I put on my most intimidating expression. "Keep away from her."

Tim's cheeks turn ruddy and I can tell he's trying to contain his anger. "Seriously? How can I avoid her when we share a class?"

"Don't sit next to her, don't talk to her. It's that easy, Tim."

"Are you two together?"

"We're going to be."

"So it's not official yet."

Why isn't he readily agreeing with me that he'll do as I say? "It's going to be."

"I'm assuming you haven't discussed this with Sinclair?" Tim asks.

I drop my arms to my sides, frustrated. "It's none of your fucking business."

Tim has the audacity to laugh, the fucker. "Since you two aren't actually together, I consider her open game, but I appreciate the warning. See you later."

He walks away and I let him go, fuming. The balls on this guy. Who the hell does he think he is?

Open game? Tim believes *my* Sinclair is open game to *him*? Absolutely fucking not. I stride through the house, throwing open the front door and making my way outside, ignoring everyone. I'm headed straight for Sinclair's dorm room before Tim can beat me. The little motherfucker. He wants to play with fire?

I'm going to light him with kerosene and watch him burn.

CHAPTER FORTY-THREE

SINCLAIR

I'm sitting on my bed in my dorm room alone, scrolling through social media, when there's a loud, incessant pounding on my door, startling me so badly I drop my phone on the floor.

Bending over, I grab it, irritated when the pounding starts back up again. I'm trying to decompress after taking a huge test that I've been studying for the last two days straight and I really don't need this hassle right now.

I stomp over to the door and throw it open, startled when I see it's August turning to face me, an agonized expression on his beautiful face. He doesn't say anything at first. Just stares at me for a beat before he looks beyond my shoulder. Like he thinks someone else is in the room with me.

Hmm.

I lean against the edge of the door, waiting for him to say or do something first. His gaze lands on my face once more, lingering for only a second before letting it roam all over me, lingering on all the parts he likes best. My skin warms in response.

"I've missed you" is the first thing he says and my heart flutters at the sincerity in his voice. This man means it.

"Hi. I've missed you too." I tilt my head to the side, noting the way his fingers flex. How they grip into a fist over and over, as if he's trying to gain some control over himself and failing miserably. "Everything okay?"

"No. No, it's not okay." He pushes past me and enters my dorm room without asking, turning to face me once I shut the door. "How can you act so—normal?"

I frown. "What do you mean?"

He doesn't move. It's like he doesn't trust himself. "Being in your presence, all I can think about is…touching you."

My stomach flutters again. So does the spot between my legs. "Then touch me, August."

He doesn't move. "You make it sound so simple."

"Isn't it?"

"I get my hands on you, and I don't know what might happen."

The promise in his deep voice lights up everything inside me and I lock my knees to keep my legs from shaking in anticipation. "I'm not scared."

My words are like a dare because he charges toward me, his hands landing on my waist, gripping me tight. Without hesitation he tugs me into him, our bodies colliding and I glance up to find his head descending, his mouth landing on mine in the sweetest, most delicious kiss I've ever experienced.

"God, I've missed you," he repeats, murmuring against my lips, his tongue darting out for a lick. "So fucking much."

"It's only been two days," I remind him, distracted by the path his hands are taking up my sides. The assured stroke of his tongue.

"Two days too long." He delivers a tongue-filled kiss, making me groan. Making me whimper. When it's finally over, I stare at his face in a daze, overcome. "Tell me you missed me."

"I already did." Rising up on tiptoes, I brush my lips against his, pulling away before he can kiss me senseless. "I missed you, August."

The relief in his eyes is a little shocking. Was he that worried?

"How did your test go?"

I appreciate him asking. "I did all right."

"I'm sure you did great." He glances around the room, his gaze immediately returning to mine. "Where's your roommate?"

"She's in class." And she won't be back for a while. Tonight is when she goes to hot yoga.

His gaze shifts to my narrow bed, lingering there. "Should we get naked and cuddle?"

"I doubt any cuddling will be involved." I laugh, but I can see from his expression that he's deeply serious. "We don't need to get naked."

"We don't?" He appears shocked.

"Not yet." My smile is small and I reach out, hooking my finger around the belt loop of his jeans, pulling him even closer. "Come on."

I let him go and turn away from him, tossing back the comforter before I climb into my tiny bed. August toes off his shoes before he joins me, his hands landing on my waist, readjusting me so I'm lying sprawled across his big, hot body. His hands settle on my ass, tugging me even closer to him and I can tell he already has an erection.

"This bed is fucking ridiculous," he declares as he tries to get more comfortable, jostling me as I lie on top of him.

"I can't help it that you're a giant."

His brows lift and I swear he looks pleased at my description. "You think I'm a giant?"

I ignore his question. "How tall are you anyway?"

"Six-two. Not that tall." He shrugs one broad shoulder.

"You're tall." I scoot up so I can press my face against his neck and I breathe deep, inhaling his spicy cologne. "And you smell good."

"What does that have to do with me hating your bed?" He removes one of his hands from my butt, tangling his fingers in my hair. "You sure you don't want to get naked?"

"Only when you answer a few questions." I pull back from his neck, noting the deep frown on his face. His brows are drawn together and that scowl would intimidate just about anyone. Save for me. "What are you doing here?"

"I told you. I missed you."

"You could've texted me first."

"Maybe I wanted to surprise you."

"You don't seem like the impulsive type." He's methodical. He likes to plan things and make sure everything is executed properly. Just the way he wants it.

"When it comes to you, all normalcy leaves me. I've become a different person." His expression tells me he finds that... confusing.

Poor August. His life goes a little sideways thanks to me and he doesn't know what to do about it. And while I would never admit this out loud, there's something buried inside me that finds this reaction from him...

Satisfying. He made my life hell for months. He became my biggest enemy and what's so wild is, he had no clue. I wasn't memorable enough. That's how callous he was. A part of him is still that way. Callous and rude and demanding. A complete and utter snob.

But from the look currently on his face and the way his hands wander all over my body like he can't get enough of me—the man is obsessed. With *me*.

I'm giddy over it.

All of my earlier insecurities evaporate just like that. This man looks tortured over me and I love it. The feeling is mutual. I've been trying to focus on school because I needed to but he always infiltrated my thoughts, and I felt unsure. When would I see him again? Would he want to see me again?

Apparently, the answer is a resounding yes.

"You look baffled." I pat his chest, my hand resting over his wildly beating heart and again—it's downright thrilling that I'm the one who can make him feel that way. React so strongly. The poor, clueless man.

He catches my hand before I can remove it, pressing his palm over mine and keeping it pinned there. "You want honesty or do you want me to lie?"

"That's a crazy question, August." He knows I don't like liars.

"Then I'll give you honesty. I've never allowed a woman to bury herself so deeply inside me before. We haven't known each other long so I know this is just...I'm going to sound like a lunatic when I make this confession." He goes quiet, leaving me hanging, and when he still doesn't say anything, I'm overcome with the need to push him.

"What are you trying to tell me?"

"My family firmly believes that once they find their someone, that's it. It's an all-consuming, overwhelming obsession that can never be stopped. My parents have it. Their love for each other has never waned, even after all of these years. My father became fixated on my mother when they were only fourteen, and I always thought that was—terrifying."

From the look on his face, he's telling the truth. There's a glimmer in his gaze that I've never seen before.

"Big, momentous love scared me, especially when your entire family talks about finding the one and then that's it. Your life is over. I didn't want to be tied down at fourteen. That's fucking ridiculous. I still don't want to be tied down. I'm only twenty-two. I've barely started living my life and now you come along and I can't think about anything else. Feel anything else. It's just you. All the fucking time. Right here." He taps the side of his forehead, the despair on his face apparent. "It's been a struggle I've been dealing with ever since I first saw you at that party. You've consumed me, Sin. I think about you every second of the day. I worry about you, and I don't worry about anyone. Not a single soul. Maybe my parents. I definitely worry about my parents because someday, they won't be here anymore and I can't even fathom it so...yeah."

He goes silent again and I stare into his beautiful blue eyes, loving how vulnerable he's being. How open and honest and incredibly raw. It doesn't even bother me that he said he's not ready to be tied down. I don't want to be tied down either. But... August Lancaster has consumed me too. Ever since I crossed his path all those years ago. I hated him. But I was also secretly... obsessed with him? Yes, I totally was. Maybe we had some sort of connection and neither of us even realized it. Could that be possible? He didn't even know me or care about me back then. He forgot I even existed. Or at least that's what he claims.

I should be offended I was that forgettable to him, but I can't deny the connection between us. The chemistry. The power in knowing that this influential, wealthy man has fallen for me.

Me.

"I've done a lot of shit in my life that's fucked up, and I never apologize for it. Saying sorry doesn't come easy for me because I'm rarely sorry about anything. I do what I do and move on. Did I hurt your feelings? Sorry. Did I forget your name the second after I fucked you? Definitely."

While I know he's not talking about me, his words do hurt a little.

"I forgot all about you after making your life a living hell and, Sin, that fucking digs deep. It makes me feel like a terrible human."

"You are a terrible human," I remind him.

He grimaces. "Having you in my life will be that constant reminder. That I treated you so terribly and dismissed you from my memory is just—heartless."

I touch his cheek, letting my fingers drift across his stubble-covered skin and he leans into my palm, his eyes closing briefly. When he opens them, I see the sincerity glittering there and it takes my breath away.

"I'm sorry for how I treated you back then, and I know that what I did was unforgivable but, Sinclair, I'm begging you to forgive me." His voice is rough and he clears his throat. "Please."

CHAPTER FORTY-FOUR

AUGUST

She drops her hand from my face the moment I finish speaking and I take it as a bad sign. I've never been more nervous in my life. As a matter of fact, I don't get nervous. Ever. Until the moment I found this girl. This woman who's become such an important part of my life. I don't understand my feelings for her, but I'm trying. Instead of running away from it, running away from her, I'm coming to her and laying myself bare.

Vulnerability doesn't come easy for most men, but especially Lancaster men. I'm not what anyone would describe as a sensitive person. Quite frankly, I'm an unfeeling bastard and have always been okay being perceived as such. Until it came to her.

Sinclair.

I never understood the saying *pins and needles* until now. My skin prickles and stings the longer she takes to answer and my head swims. The possibility that she could say no never crossed my mind, but she might. I need her like I need air, but does she need me? Does she want me, or is my past treatment of her too big to ignore?

She hasn't kicked me out of her bed yet so I take that as a good sign.

When she takes a deep breath, I can feel her chest rise against mine. I'm attuned to her every little movement. The way she breathes. How often she blinks. Her tongue peeks out, the tip touching the center of her upper lip, and I can't take it anymore. I'm about to say something most likely risky as fuck that could possibly ruin everything but she speaks first.

Thank God.

"I forgive you," she murmurs, her lids lifting and revealing her shiny golden gaze. She even smiles, her body shifting. Rising until her mouth is level with mine. "I forgave you a while ago, I just hadn't said it out loud yet."

"Thank you." I crush her to me, burying my face against her fragrant neck, my eyes closed so tightly it hurts. "Thank you."

She wraps her arms around me, her hands sliding into the hair at the back of my head and when I lift my head to look at her, our mouths meet. Melt into each other in a sweet kiss that I try to keep that way, but it's so fucking hard. She tastes delicious and when our tongues meet, that's it. A groan sounds deep in my chest, the kiss going from sweetly sexy to filthy in an instant. I want to consume her and I do, thrusting my tongue in her mouth, searching. My hands wandering, gathering the hem of her T-shirt, desperate to touch her bare skin. She's warm and smooth and she helps me get rid of her shirt, tossing it over her head so it lands on the floor.

My hands on her hips, I shift her into position so she's sitting on top of me and I'm lying on my back on the mattress, opening my eyes to find her already watching me. My gaze drops to her chest, her perfect tits encased in pale pink lace, and I can see her nipples straining against the thin fabric. My mouth waters and I run my hands along her waist, cupping her breasts, rubbing my thumbs across her nipples. She arches into my hands, her head falling back, exposing the length of her neck, and I lift up. Licking a path along her throat, nibbling the spot where her neck meets her shoulder and making her hiss in a breath.

Reaching around her, I mess with the clasp until I've got the bra undone and she shrugs out of it, tossing it onto the floor so it lands on top of her T-shirt. Within seconds, my mouth is on her skin, licking and sucking one nipple, then the other. She holds me to her, whimpering when I pull extra hard with my mouth and I wonder if she knows how much I want to devour her. I can't get enough.

My need for her is so strong I'm willingly doing this in her twin bed in her dorm room for the love of God. I don't fuck girls in dorm rooms. Not even random ones. For Sinclair? I'll make the exception.

"You sure your roommate isn't coming back soon?" I lift away from her nipple, glancing up at her. Her cheeks are pink and her eyes are hazy. She looks overcome with lust, and God, I'd love to take a photo of her right now and capture this moment, this feeling forever. But reaching for my phone will ruin the moment.

I'm not about to risk it.

She tugs at my shirt and I lift up, removing it quickly. She's wearing thin pants and she's pressing her hot pussy against my erection, driving me out of my mind. I want to get rid of our clothes and fuck her senseless, but I also want to prolong the moment. Drag it out. Make it last because it feels like we're running on limited time. Is that because her roommate could return at any moment or is it because I'm worried about something else? Like the possibility that I might lose her?

I don't know. And I don't want to think about it either.

I fuse my mouth to hers to drown out my thoughts, my hands on her hips so I can shift her against my cock. She grinds against me, driving me out of my mind with lust and I worry I won't be able to keep this up much longer. I'm gonna blow like a fucking kid who has zero control but that makes sense. When it comes to Sin, I'm a wreck.

When I'm about to slip my hands into her panties, there's a knock on the door. It's subtle. Quiet. Nothing like the way I banged on her door not even thirty minutes ago. We both pause mid-kiss, breathing into each other, silent as we wait for whoever it is on the other side of the door to leave.

There's another knock and I release an aggravated exhale, ready to tell whoever it is to get the fuck out of here, but Sinclair rests her hand over my mouth, silencing me.

"They'll go away," she whispers, her wide-eyed gaze meeting mine and I nod, refraining from calling out. Enjoying the way that she's touching me too much to ruin the moment.

"Sinclair? Are you in there?"

Fuck me, I'd recognize that voice anywhere. It's Tim. I knew that prick was headed over to see her. That's why I didn't hesitate and got here before he did. Thank Christ.

The panicked look on Sinclair's face tells me she recognizes his voice too and she doesn't know how to handle it. Gently I remove her hand from my face, dropping a kiss on her palm before I whisper, "Let me take care of this."

She nods, not saying a word, and I remind myself as I remove her from my lap and climb off the bed that I need to remain in control. I can't go all rage-bro and unleash on him. Despite the fact that I think he's a dipshit and I hate that he believes he has a chance with Sinclair, he is also a fraternity brother and there are rules. Especially since I'm the frat president.

God, I wish I'd never taken on the responsibility but what's done is done. I need to act like a dignified leader when I open this damn door.

Slowly, I turn the lock and crack open the door, peeking around it to find Tim standing there with a hopeful look on his face. All that hope dies the second he spots me and I open the door farther, letting him see that I'm shirtless. My hair is a mess and I'd guarantee I look like I've been fucking around with Sin.

"Hey, Tim." My voice is easy because it feels good to win. "What's up?"

"Uh." He shoves his hands in his pockets and shuffles his feet. "I was looking for Sinclair."

"She can't talk right now." I smile, wondering if he can see my dick straining against the front of my jeans. I'm sure he can if he looks. "She's a little—preoccupied. And not properly dressed."

"Yeah. Okay. I get it." Tim pulls his hands out of his pockets and lets his arms hang at his sides, utterly defeated. "I guess you win."

"I guess I do." I grin at him like the fucking maniac I am and let the door shut, enjoying the way it slams with a finality I feel down to my soul. That little fucker better stay away from what's mine.

I turn to find Sin sitting in her bed with the comforter pulled up to her chin, her eyes huge. "What did you say to him?"

"I told him to get the fuck out of here." I grin for real this time and undo the front of my jeans, getting rid of them in seconds. I rejoin her in the bed and pull her to me, flipping her over so she's beneath me. "Now where were we?"

She arches against me, her lids falling to half-mast, looking every inch the sexy siren that she is. "Please don't tell me you forgot."

"Like I could," I mutter.

Just before I attack her.

CHAPTER FORTY-FIVE

SINCLAIR

Somehow August gets rid of my sweatpants and panties in mere seconds, leaving me naked beneath him. He's still got on his boxer briefs, his dick straining against the front, and he nudges it against me every chance he gets, driving me out of my mind as he kisses me. Devours me.

We're hungry for each other and I blame the serious conversation we just had. How he apologized and admitted his wrongdoing, which I don't think is something that comes easily for him. But he did it for me.

August does a lot of things for me, I'm realizing. Like telling Tim to leave. I am so tired of dealing with a hopeful Tim, and it's difficult for me to be mean toward him. He didn't do anything wrong, but he's so persistent. He doesn't give up. I can't help it that I don't like him in that way.

Maybe now finally, Tim will get the hint.

I lose myself in August's hands. His mouth. The press of his cock against my drenched pussy. I want the boxer briefs off, desperate to feel skin on skin contact, and when I reach for the waistband, he pauses in his movements, pulling his mouth from mine to look at me.

"I didn't bring a condom."

Disappointment floods me. "I don't have any."

"Would your roommate have some?" He glances over at Elise's bed.

"Maybe?" I shove at him a little and he rolls over on his side so I can get off the bed. I glance around, pushing my hair out of my face and trying to figure out where she'd keep them. She doesn't have a nightstand since we use the mini fridge for one instead and I don't want to go through her drawers. That's such an invasion of privacy. "I don't know."

I turn to look at August, admiring the view for a moment despite the fact I'm standing in the middle of my room completely naked. He's got the comforter bunched around his waist and I stare at the glory that is his sculpted chest. "Do you work out?" I blurt like an idiot, only faintly mortified thanks to the genuine smile that stretches across his face.

"Well…yeah. I don't play any sports but I do go to the gym with Cyrus."

"Is he your best friend?"

"One of my only friends." The grin fades. "Why are we talking about Cyrus? Get your ass over here."

He flips the comforter back and pats the mattress.

Hesitating, I remain standing in the middle of my room, both dying to go to him and reluctant to make this step. It feels like a commitment, and it also feels vaguely dangerous. He wants to have sex with me and I want to have sex with him, but we don't have condoms and I'm not on any sort of birth control. This is risky.

There's a small part of me that wants to turn him away but the bigger, greedier part of me wants to return to the bed with him and see what happens.

The greedy side wins and I climb into bed with him, letting him tuck me beneath him, his mouth finding mine yet again. The way he kisses me is like a drug, pulling me under, making me lose all cohesive thought and I drown in him for a moment, only rising back to the surface when his fingers slide between my thighs, gently stroking me.

"Fucking so wet like always," he mutters against my lips, a pleased grunt sounding from him when he slips two fingers inside me with ease. "And so tight. I'm dying to fuck your delicious little cunt, Sin." His words make me shiver. I love it when he uses the word cunt, which means I'm screwed up. I'm sure of it.

"Then do it." My voice trembles the slightest bit at my invitation and I hope I don't regret this choice.

He pulls away slightly to look into my eyes, his expression deadly serious. "Are you sure?"

I nod, trying to hide the fear that wants to sweep over me. I'm worried once we do it like this, we won't be able to stop. It'll feel too good, too right.

"I'll pull out before I come." He positions me beneath him, tugging me into place as he rises up on one hand, palm braced against my pillow as the other wraps around the base of his cock and he guides himself inside me. "Oh, fucking hell, you feel so good like this."

Slowly he pushes in further and I close my eyes, bracing for it. Still stiff and a little sore from what we did over the weekend. My body accommodates him easily and when he's buried to the hilt inside me, I release the breath I didn't know I was holding, sending him even deeper.

"It's going to be hard, keeping myself under control." He says this like a warning to me and himself as he grits his teeth. "You're so hot and tight."

I readjust myself, wrapping my legs around his hips and sending him even deeper and that's what does it. He begins to pump inside me, a steady in and out that has me moaning every time he nearly pulls out. The drag of his cock within my body, the pause before he plunges back inside is delicious. I rock against him, arching my hips, moving with him in a perfect rhythm that has the two of us breathing hard. Sweating. The slap of our bodies connecting fills the room and I hang on to him, moaning when he dips his head and puts his mouth on mine.

I lose all track of time when he kisses me like this. Fucks me like this. When he slips his hand between our bodies and touches my clit, I gasp, not realizing I was close until that very minute. He strokes and teases my clit, pressing little circles against it until I'm a whimpering, moaning mess, overcome with the orgasm that sweeps over me. He drives into me faster and faster, his fingers still working their magic and another gasp leaves me when his hand falls away from me and he pulls out with a groan.

The first splatter of semen hits my stomach and I open my eyes to find him jerking his cock with his fist, his eyes closed, every muscle in his body standing out in definition as he strains with his orgasm. More semen splashes onto my stomach and I watch him in complete fascination, my own body heaving with the aftereffects of what he did to me.

When he's finished, he finally opens his eyes, blinking me into focus. I lie there like a content cat, stretching my body, the sensation of his semen running across my skin, but I don't mind.

I kind of like it.

"I made a mess." He stares at my stomach before lifting his gaze to mine. "I told you once that you made a mess and tried to kick you out of my room."

"I remember." I touch the warm, thick cum, tracing lazy circles across my skin with it. "You're the worst."

"You still think so?" He arches a brow.

I nod. "I know so."

"Insulting me will result in you getting punished, you know." His tone is a warning that has my pussy clenching in anticipation.

I miss mean August. How twisted is that? But I do. I like it when he's sweet and gentle with me but I absolutely love it when he's awful toward me.

Does that mean I'm fucked up? Maybe so.

"What's my punishment?"

"I should spank your ass." He hesitates, and when I stare into his eyes, I see a devilish gleam form there. "And finger it."

Lifting my hips, I try to buck him off me and he goes willingly, rolling off the bed and glancing around the room. "You have a towel in here?"

I point at the pile of towels that are sitting in the plastic laundry basket on the other side of my desk. "I just did laundry."

He grabs one and comes back to the bed, standing beside it. He drops the towel on my stomach. "Clean yourself up."

His demanding tone has me moving fast, wiping at the remaining semen on my stomach before I toss the towel on the floor.

"Roll over," he commands and I do as he says, rearranging myself so I flop onto my stomach, wagging my ass at him, eager for him to do as he promised.

August climbs onto the bed, settling his back against the wall that my bed rests against. "I don't punish girls who want it this bad." His smile is smug as he drags his fingers back and forth across my ass cheeks, tickling me and making me giggle. "Seriously, Sin. You're way too happy about this."

"I want it." I lift my hips, my butt rising, and he slips his hand lower, his fingers sliding with ease into my soaking wet pussy. A groan leaves me when he teasingly pushes in and out, my inner walls trying to grasp around his fingers and keep him there. "Please, August."

"Well, since you asked so nicely." He removes his fingers from inside my pussy and drifts them up, barely grazing my puckered hole. I suck in a breath at the sensation, spreading my thighs wider so he can have better access.

He teases my crack with one finger, up and down. Slow and easy and making me shiver. I close my eyes and melt into the mattress, savoring the sensations of his touch, tensing up immediately when he tries to press his finger inside.

"Relax," he croons, his finger going still. "Come on, baby. You can take this."

Breathing deep, I will my muscles to relax, trying to calm my still racing heart. He works his finger farther, until he's knuckle deep and I cry out at the sting of pain.

"Keep still," he demands, keeping his finger inside me as he somehow maneuvers himself so he's lying between my spread thighs, his mouth landing right on my pussy.

I cry out for a different reason, his tongue sweeping all over my sensitive flesh, making me quiver. He misses no spots, licking me thoroughly as he slips his finger deeper inside and starts to move it. I press my face into the mattress, a tiny spiral of shame streaking through me at what he's doing. How good it feels.

How much I like it.

He can't get to my clit but it doesn't matter. I'm coming in minutes because of the forbidden thing he's doing to me. He won't let up either, his face pressed against me the entire time, his finger still buried in my asshole, tongue fucking me until I'm practically crying, begging him to stop.

Eventually he crawls off the bed, standing in the middle of my dorm room stark naked and with his cock erect and ready to go again. "I'm a fucking disaster. I need to wash my hands."

I start giggling all over again, rolling over onto my back so I can stare at the ceiling. "The bathroom is down the hall."

"What the fuck—I hate dorm buildings." He slips on his jeans and strides out of my room without a care in the world. I can't imagine what some of the people in my dorm building are thinking as a shirtless August Lancaster moves down the hallway with no access to the bathroom that he so desperately wants. And he doesn't have a key.

I'm throwing my clothes back on and slip on some shoes, not bothering with my bra or panties when the door swings open and—oh God—Elise enters the room. She immediately comes to a stop when she sees me, throwing her backpack on the floor and sniffing the air.

"It smells like sex in here," she declares, her narrowed gaze landing on me. "And you look like you just got laid."

My face heats up and I shrug. "I need to go."

There's a rapid-fire knock on the door and since my roommate is closest, she goes and answers it. August walks in, still shirtless, doing a double take when he spots a gaping Elise standing in front of him. "Oh shit. When did you get back?"

"Were you banging Sinclair just now?" she asks, resting her hands on her hips.

My face has to be flaming red.

"As a matter of fact, I was." He sends me a smirk that makes my insatiable pussy flutter. I have a serious problem. Maybe I'm a sex addict?

More like an August addict.

Elise can't speak. I don't think she expected him to answer truthfully.

"We're leaving." He swivels his gaze onto me. "Come on, Sin. Let's go back to my place."

Sending Elise a helpless look, I grab my phone and August takes my hand, dragging me out of my room. Well, that's not entirely true.

I leave willingly because of course I do.

CHAPTER FORTY-SIX

SINCLAIR

It's November and we're about three weeks into our nonstop sex fest when August drops a bomb.

"I want you to come home with me." His tone is casual, as is his body language, but I see the flicker of something unfamiliar in his gaze just before he jerks it away from me.

It looked like nerves. As in he's nervous.

Well, that's just great. I'm now anxious too.

We're in bed in his room at the frat house. I sort of hate coming here, but it's guaranteed privacy since he has his own room and we can't hook up all over campus all the time, though we have. In one of the study rooms at the library. In an unused classroom in the science building. August is rather creative and when he wants me, he wants me. He won't take no for an answer, not that I tell him no much.

Have I uttered the words no to him lately? I don't believe so. He tells me where to meet him and I do it. Tells me to take off my clothes and they're flying off my body. Demands I get on birth control so he won't get me pregnant and I willingly go to the on-campus clinic. The last thing I want is a baby. Right now, all I want to do is practice making them. With August. All the time.

"Did you hear what I said?" His deep voice bleeds through my sex-filled thoughts and I blink at him, confused at first.

Then I remember what he said.

I want you to come home with me.

Oh shit. This sounds serious.

"Come home?" I sound like an idiot, repeating his words, but I need more clarity. "As in to your apartment in New York?"

That's what I'm hoping he's referring to.

He slowly shakes his head. "I want you to spend time with my parents. Meet my father."

I swallow hard, unable to find words. This is—momentous. Important. I know enough now about the Lancaster family to know they believe in instant true love, just like August explained to me. If he wants to take me to meet his parents? I think this means he's...what?

Falling in love with me?

Noooo.

The tiny voice inside my brain screeches, *hell yes, bitch! Open your eyes!*

That tiny voice can go to hell.

"Um...when?" My voice is shaky and I hate myself for being so obvious.

"This weekend."

I sit up in bed so I can look into his eyes. It may be dark but I can still see him. "August. It's Thursday."

"So?"

"Thursday night," I stress, scratching my bare shoulder. Yes, I'm naked and yes, we just had sex and it was amazing as per usual. "When do you want to leave?"

"Tomorrow morning. You don't have class and neither do I and we can beat traffic if we leave early enough," he explains, sounding completely logical.

Me on the other hand? I am feeling completely irrational at the thought of leaving tomorrow to go meet his freaking parents. "You haven't given me enough time to prepare."

"What is there to prepare for? Pack some clothes and whatever essentials you need to bring and we'll leave."

"How are we getting there?"

"My car."

"You have a car here?" I had no idea.

"Not recently. But I just received my new car Monday night." He smiles. I swear his teeth shine in the darkness. "Had it delivered and everything. I upgraded to a new Porsche."

Oh God. My dad would love to get his hands on that, I'm sure. "You didn't tell me about this."

"I wanted it to be a surprise."

"Your car? Or going to your parents for me to meet them?"

"Both." He sits up, grabbing hold of me so I have no choice but to sit in his lap. "They're going to love you."

"Maybe," I hedge, nerves eating me up inside. What if they don't? What if they don't approve? I am the daughter of the inventor of Jock Rot. That's not prestigious at all. And these Lancasters tend to pair up with people who are on the same level, and I am not even close to their level.

"They are. My mother already does." He says it with such finality I can't help but get caught up in believing him. He slips his arms around my waist and tugs me closer so that I'm sitting directly on top of his now erect dick. "Why do you look worried?"

"I am...me." I tap my fingers against my bare chest and his gaze drops to the spot, lingering on my naked breasts. "And you are—" I tap the center of his chest. "You."

"What the fuck is that supposed to mean?"

He sounds offended and that's cute. It really is. Unfortunately, he doesn't get it.

"My dad invented jock anti-itch cream. Your parents—"

"Fell in love despite the fact that my mother's mother had an affair with my father's...father." He grimaces. "It's a complicated story."

My jaw drops. "You made that up."

"No. I didn't." He dips his head, his mouth on my neck, leaving a trail of hot kisses across my skin. "My dead grandmother despised my mother. Hated her guts because she represented the woman her husband had an affair with. My family is fucked up. Just like yours."

I close my eyes, sucking in a breath when his hand settles on my breast and gives it a gentle squeeze. "But they're rich."

"So are yours."

"Old money is better than new money." I'm shaking at the way he thumbs my nipple, toying with it.

"Old money is—different than new. It's not necessarily better." He removes his hand from my breast to cup my chin, forcing me to look up at him. "Come home with me. I'm dying for them to get to know you."

"Why? Is this some sort of trick?"

An irritated noise leaves him and he gives my face the slightest shake. "What do I have to do to make you believe me when I say that I'm serious about this. About you."

I blink at him, overcome. My throat is thick with emotion and I don't know why. It's not like he's declared his undying love for me, but this is close. August isn't great with emotion and neither am I so that makes us quite the pair. But for whatever reason, it works. I care about him.

I'm falling in love with him, and it's scary.

"I want you to meet my mother." He leans in and kisses me, his lips still on mine when he continues to speak. "My father. My brother and my sister and that bumbling idiot she might be married to. Oh and their monster baby."

"I know Iris. And I did meet your mother." Far too briefly and just remembering how we met is still embarrassing.

"That's right." He kisses me again. "I want you to get closer to my mother and sister. And the monster baby and my father. He's the biggest monster out of all of us, but I know he'll love you."

I am flat-out terrified at him calling his father a monster. "What if he doesn't like me?"

August kisses me again, his tongue darting out for the lightest lick. Right at the center of my mouth. "If he doesn't like you, then fuck him. That's what he said about his mother. He'll understand."

I very much doubt that but I don't bother arguing with him. "Okay."

He pulls away slightly so he can stare into my eyes and when our gazes meet, his is filled with so much happiness my heart threatens to burst out of my chest. "You'll come home with me?"

I nod, surprised at how enthused he sounds. August isn't enthused with much of anything unless it involves the two of us naked and wrapped around each other like connected pretzels. "Yes. It'll be—fun."

"It will be." He kisses me yet again. "You've told your parents about me, right?"

I freeze and he senses it, leaning back to look into my eyes yet again. "Um..."

"Sin." His voice is firm and I keep my head bent, ashamed. "Tell them about me."

"I told my mom. Sort of." And that feels like a long time ago. She kept harassing me after I did mention August's name, constantly asking if things had become serious between us, but I either ignored her texts or avoided her questions. Eventually she stopped asking and I haven't brought him up since.

"What about your dad?"

I shake my head, fighting the humiliation that wants to spill all over me. Once my father finds out I'm dating a Lancaster, he'll become insufferable. For all I know, he could drive August away completely.

I don't want to risk it.

"We should invite them to dinner."

I jerk my gaze up to his. "What? No. No way. That sounds like a nightmare."

"We have to get this moment over with eventually, don't you think? Our families coming together and getting to know one another."

"Your parents don't want to know mine. They aren't the same kind of people," I protest, but August is shaking his head.

"You don't know that. They might get along great."

Oh look at the always negative August, being upbeat and positive about something once in his life—and I cannot get on board. "My father will be like a bull in a China shop. He'll say something embarrassing, or worse, he'll try and show off and end up sounding like a complete jackass."

"My father is a jackass too. They'll probably get along perfectly."

His mouth is on mine before I can protest, his tongue doing a thorough sweep that has me losing all cohesive thought. "It's happening, Sin. Whether you like it or not, we need everyone to meet."

"Why?" I sound near hysterics and I swallow down my fear. Take a deep breath and remind myself that nothing can go wrong as long as I have August by my side. Right?

"Because I have serious intentions when it comes to you. Us." He drags his mouth across my cheek, settling right at my ear so he can whisper, "I think about making you my wife."

"What?" My voice is a thin whisper, and I'm not even sure he heard me.

"We make a great team, you and me. Can't you envision it? I can."

My heart sinks. A great team. Well-matched. I don't hear anything about love or affection or any of that sort of thing. He's not what I would call a romantic—unless eating my ass is romantic then yes. He's an incurable romantic in that sense.

I wonder if I'm fooling myself. Getting caught up in the fantasy of it all. Being with August on campus is one thing. He's pretty low-key and doesn't necessarily flaunt his wealth and privilege.

Being with him outside of school is different. He's powerful. His name alone opens doors for him that are permanently closed for most other people. As his girlfriend—and even potential wife—that would send me into a completely different stratosphere than I've ever been involved with before in my life. I am woefully unprepared for anything that might come my way.

Plus, him not saying he's falling in love with me or that he cares about me is telling. August likes me, I don't doubt that. Obsessed with me? Yes, I can even agree to that. But is he in love with me or is this a proper business merger to him?

I'm not sure.

CHAPTER FORTY-SEVEN

AUGUST

I am driving home in my new Porsche 911 Carrera with the red interior and turbo engine that roars like a beast every time I barely touch the gas pedal. The windows are down and the air is cold, making Sinclair squeal and shiver and complain as she bats her hair away from her face. All I can do is laugh at her grumbling, feeling good, feeling fucking *free* for the first time in my entire life.

It's because of her.

I'm not nervous about Sin formally meeting my parents. When I called to tell my mother that I was bringing Sinclair home for the weekend and could she reach out to Sin's parents for me and have them over for dinner Friday night, Mom didn't even hesitate. She's as excited to spend more time with Sin as I am. Maybe even more so.

The moment I reached out to Iris and asked her to come home for the weekend, she didn't even hesitate to say yes. Iris lives for family drama and is usually the one causing it all, so I'm sure she'll enjoy being a spectator for once in her life. My younger brother Vaughn is at Lancaster Prep and has zero interest in meeting Sinclair, which is fine. I understand what that's like. That period in life when you'd rather be with your friends and spending all of your time with them. The absolute drag of having to go home for the weekend when you know your friends are going to have a better time than you since they're all together. Considering he'll be home for Thanksgiving break, I'll just bring Sin back again for the holiday and he can meet her then.

I'm that confident about this decision. This woman is going to become mine. Permanently.

Forever.

By the time we arrive at my family home, it's obvious Sinclair is nervous. She's not talking much. Just fidgeting in her seat, constantly running her fingers through her windblown hair and chewing on her lower lip. She's going to make herself bleed if she keeps it up and finally, I can't stand it any longer.

Resting my hand on her slender thigh, I give it a squeeze. "It's going to be okay. They're all going to love you."

She sends me a grateful look. "Thank you. I just worry about my parents."

"They'll be fine."

"Will they, though? You haven't met them. You don't know what they're like." She starts gnawing on her lower lip again and when I pull up in front of the house, I throw the car in park and turn toward her, removing my hand from her leg so I can cup it around her chin.

"Your parents aren't you." I lean in to kiss her, forcing her to stop eating her damn lower lip. "Stop being so hard on yourself. And your lip."

She smiles, returning my kiss, and I let go of her chin, turning to glance up at the house my parents live in. I grew up here somewhat—my earliest memories are of the apartment we lived in that Mom and Dad still have, but I spent a lot of years in this massive house. And while some crazy shit has happened here—like the death of my grandmother when she fell down the stairs in a tragic accident—it's a house full of great family memories that even my grumpy ass can appreciate.

As I'm staring at the set of stairs that leads to the front door, my mother comes running down them, a giant smile on her beautiful face. I climb out of the car and she tackle-hugs me, squeezing me tight and rising up on tiptoe to murmur in my ear, "I'm so glad you're home."

I hug her in return before I pull away to check on Sinclair, who's already exiting the Porsche, that nervous look back on her pretty face. "Sin. Come here."

She approaches us, a shy smile on her face when she makes eye contact with my mother. "Hi, Mrs. Lancaster. Thank you for inviting me here this weekend."

"Please, I already told you. Call me Summer." My mother wraps Sinclair in a hug, patting her back before pulling away. "And we're so glad you're here. Let's go inside."

A servant grabs our bags while Mom leads us up the stairs and into the house. There are fresh flower arrangements on every available surface, the furniture gleaming with candles burning everywhere. My father exits his study, coming to a stop when he sees me and a smile stretches across his face as he approaches.

"Son." He pulls me into his arms for a quick hug. "Glad to see you come home for once willingly."

I grimace. He chuckles. Always giving me endless shit.

"Dad, this is Sinclair." I step aside so he can see her and I don't even hesitate when I add, "My girlfriend."

Sin's eyes go wide but otherwise she doesn't react to my statement. Her smile is polite and she dips her head. "Nice to meet you, Mr. Lancaster."

"Nice to meet you, too. And call me Whit."

They shake hands, Dad sending me a quick look of approval.

We make small talk as we move through the house, Mom pointing out the various rooms to a curious Sinclair. When Mom offers to show Sinclair the guest bedroom, they both go, leaving me alone with my father.

"She's an attractive girl," is the first thing he says once they're gone.

We enter his study, me sitting in one of the large leather chairs while dear old Dad makes us each a drink.

"I'm going to marry her," I declare, knowing he's the only one I can say something like that to and he won't overreact.

Mom? She'd have the wedding planner on speed dial and would be asking us for dates.

Iris? She'd let everyone know we were engaged before I could even slip the ring on Sin's finger.

My father? He barely reacts as he hands me a glass of brown liquid that I know just from the scent that it's bourbon.

"Does she know this?" he asks once he settles in the chair across from mine, taking a sip of his drink.

"Not yet." I take a sip as well, wincing at the strong taste. It goes down easy though. Nice and smooth. "But she will."

"She's young. Your mother told me she's only eighteen."

"She'll turn nineteen in January." Sinclair is incredibly young. When I was eighteen, I was a fucking wreck who wanted zero responsibilities. And here I am, ready to spring marriage on her. I'm rushing things but damn. Every family member who said it happens fast was right. I know she's the one for me.

The only one.

"A baby," my father murmurs, staring into his glass. "We were babies too, your mother and I."

"I know."

"And look at us." He lifts his head, his gaze hazy. Making me think he's consumed with memories. "We've been married a long time and we're still happy."

"Are you?" When he frowns, I continue. "You're truly happy with Mom? Nothing bad has happened between the two of you? You're not sick of each other?"

That's always the fear for me. Commitment is a lifelong thing. There's not much divorce throughout my family. I could never imagine wanting to be with someone forever until recently.

"Plenty bad has happened over the years. You can't form a life with someone and not have the occasional tragedy occur. Deaths in the family. Scandal. Drama. It's all part of life, son. Your mother and I have arguments. We get irritated with each other. I hate how damn cheerful she is in the morning and the woman doesn't even drink coffee. And I drive her crazy with how I'm an asshole all the time for no real reason."

Sounds familiar.

"We've dealt with familial issues. Sometimes we don't always agree on things, but we know how to compromise. Our love for each other is too strong to just give up," he explains. "Life isn't perfect but it's ours and what we share is enough. More than enough. I'm a lucky man."

The reverence in his tone for my mother is sincere. When I was younger their love overwhelmed me. All the stories and family lore made it seem like they were completely obsessed and I'm guessing they were and still are. I didn't like the idea of being so caught up in someone that you can't think about anything else.

And now here I am, living it. Caught up in Sinclair to the point that I know she's going to be my wife. Maybe not right away, but eventually. I can be patient.

Somewhat.

"Can I give you some advice?" Dad asks after a few quiet minutes.

"Sure." Will it be something I want to hear or what he thinks I should hear?

"Don't rush it. She's going nowhere, but if you push her too hard, she might run away and then you'll have to chase her." He frowns, lost in his memories, no doubt. "There's nothing worse than having the love of your life hide from you because she's—scared. Don't let that happen to you and this girl. Don't scare her."

"I would never," I scoff, offended.

The look my father sends my way is a very obvious *come on*. "You're just like me, August. And we can be...intimidating."

"So don't intimidate her. Got it." I nod once, already bored. My Sin gets off on me intimidating her. It's her favorite thing. I won't scare her. This is a woman who stands up to me every single time.

We'll be fine.

CHAPTER FORTY-EIGHT

SINCLAIR

The Lancaster house is huge and opulent. The rooms are ginormous. They even have a ballroom, and that's where many of the family weddings and receptions have been held. When August's mother drops that little factoid, I immediately envision my wedding with August in this very room. Me in a beautiful white dress and August in a black tux. Hundreds of people in attendance with pink and white flowers everywhere and a string quartet playing. I can see it.

Silly but true.

Originally, we were supposed to have dinner with my parents tonight, but they couldn't make it, so the big family dinner will be tomorrow, which is unfortunate. I liked the idea of getting it over with and being able to breathe easier for the rest of the weekend.

I guess that's not what's in store for me.

We go out for dinner tonight, August's parents taking us to a restaurant not too far from their home. Iris and Brooks come with us, baby Astrid as well, and I can't stop cooing at her in the restaurant. Lucky for me, I'm sitting next to Iris and she's holding Astrid for most of the meal so I help her distract the baby whenever I can.

"I think she likes you," Iris muses when Astrid reaches out and grabs onto a strand of my hair, tugging it hard.

"Ow, little princess. That hurts." I gently pry her fingers from my hair and move away from her. This results in Astrid making a pouty face just before she scrunches it up and lets out a loud wail.

"Maybe she doesn't like me so much after all," I murmur, watching as Iris hands off the baby to Brooks, who takes her in his arms and starts tickling her belly. She immediately starts laughing, her distress forgotten though there are still fat tears clinging to the corners of her eyes.

"She's getting into a bratty stage, I fear," Iris tells me as she reaches for her glass of white wine and sips from it. "And the only person who can console her completely is her daddy."

The love shining in Iris's eyes as she watches Brooks with their daughter tells me she's beyond happy with her little family and that warms my heart.

"She's not a brat. She's sweet," I murmur, smiling.

"Augie calls her a monster." Iris shakes her head. "If anyone is a monster, it's my brother."

I don't know if I'd call him a monster, but if she'd said that a couple of months ago, I would've readily agreed with her.

Funny how things change.

"He's not so bad," I finally say, earning a pointed look from his sister.

"He made your life a living hell."

I didn't need the reminder but there it is. Do his parents know about our past? If they do, what do they think about it? It's a little embarrassing, that our original connection was when he used to bully me.

"Iris, can I ask you a question?" Iris turns to face me once more, nodding. "Did you know Brooks was the one for you the minute you met him?"

"Oh no. Not at all. I loathed Brooksie when we first met. He just immediately rubbed me the wrong way. But the more I got to know him, the more enthralled I became with him and the next thing I knew, we were sneaking off together and hooking up constantly. Oh, we had the best time back then. We were so horny every minute of every day and we couldn't get enough of each other." She rests her fingers over her mouth like she needs to shut herself up. "I probably shouldn't have said that to you."

"No, I don't mind." It reminds me of my situation with August. I loathed him too, for years. Until eventually we became horny for each other as well. "August has mentioned there's a family curse when it comes to love."

"He told you about that? And called it a curse?" Iris begins to laugh. "Oh, that's hilarious. I wouldn't call it a curse. It's just a basic fact. Lancasters find their person right away. Usually when we're young. I sometimes think that's why he bullied you."

I frown. "You think he bullied me why? Because he was... interested in me?"

That's laughable. I was desperately unattractive and awkward and an ugly duckling who hadn't quite bloomed into a swan. I find what Iris is saying hard to believe.

"Yes. Definitely." Iris looks smug. Like she's been dying to tell me this. "Think about it. He wouldn't leave you alone. He was constantly giving you shit for the entire year. Who does that? Why would he do it? Because he was secretly obsessed with you, which is another Lancaster male trait. They hide their feelings and pretend they hate you when that's the furthest thing from the truth."

"That sounds ridiculous." I'm scoffing. Shaking my head. She can't be for real right now. "He hated me. Told me I was ugly and stupid."

"God, see? He's a monster! Are you sure you want to be with him?" Iris rests her fingers on her lips once more, shaking her head. "I'm sorry. I really shouldn't say that but I can't help it. I love my brother but please—just make sure his intentions are true."

Unease slips down my spine as I absorb what she said. "Do you think he's trying to what...trick me?"

"I don't know. I should've never said anything about this." She shrugs, obviously uncomfortable. "He would never do that to you. He seems like he's completely in love with you."

I almost scoff at that. The words have never been spoken out loud by him and I just find it's too soon for love. Right? Does August even have a heart big enough to love someone? He treats me well. We have sex constantly. But is that all it is? We're horny for each other, as Iris described herself and Brooks.

"I don't know if it's love," I start, and Iris is shaking her head, a panicked look on her face.

"I regret saying what I said to you, Sinclair. My brother wouldn't do anything like that to you. He pays attention to no one. Is dismissive of almost everyone. He's falling for you. I'm sure of it."

Her words ring hollow and I'm sure that has to do with my sudden lack of self-esteem thanks to our conversation. But I put on a brave smile and nod like I agree with her, grateful when she changes the subject and starts talking about Astrid teething. I half listen to her, my gaze going to August who is sitting on the other side of the table, engrossed in a conversation with his father.

He brought me here for a reason, I remind myself. To spend time with his family. For my family to come here as well and meet. That has to mean something. I can't let what Iris said linger in my brain. She didn't mean to sound so negative, and besides, she doesn't know what my relationship is like with August.

No one really does. Just us.

For the rest of the dinner, I'm quiet. August notices, sending me questioning looks from across the table but all I can do is offer him a tiny smile in return, though it doesn't feel real. He can tell too. Or at the very least, sense my mood. The distress radiates from Iris like palpable waves and I feel sorry for her. She didn't mean to upset me and I know she didn't purposely try to hurt me either. Iris is a nice person. All of the Lancasters I've met are lovely people.

Save for the very one who I'm involved with. Maybe I'm in over my head. Maybe I've already drowned and can't be saved.

. . .

I'm in the guest bedroom stripping out of my clothes when there's an urgent knock on the door. The handle rattles and I hear a muffled curse. I stand in the middle of the bedroom, clad in only my bra and panties, my mouth dropping open when the door swings wide and reveals an impatient August, who strides into the room as if he owns the place. Which I suppose he does in a sense, but still.

"August, what are you do—" He doesn't let me get the rest of my question out, talking right over me.

"What's wrong with you?" He grabs hold of my arms, his touch gentle, his gaze searching, wandering all over my face. Looking for a sign. Or an answer. "Tell me, Sin. Something is bothering you."

I start to shake my head. "Noth—"

"Bullshit," he interrupts, bending his knees so he can be at eye level with me. His gaze is imploring and the confusion I see swirling there has my stomach twisting. "What did my sister say to you? I'm going to murder her, I swear."

"You can't murder her. Then Astrid won't have a mother," I protest.

"That little monster can probably raise herself," he mutters, though there's no malice in his tone. He adores that baby despite the fact that he calls her a monster. I saw the way he held her earlier and when she batted his face with her chubby hand. "Tell me, Sin. What happened? Something is bothering you."

There are a multitude of things that happened this afternoon and evening that have led me to feel the way I do. I can't list them all and I don't want to. I hate feeling uneasy around him, but it's also a familiar emotion. He's had me on edge since the day I met him. "Iris warned me that I should make sure your intentions toward me are…true."

The murderous gleam that appears in August's eyes is terrifying. "I'm going to kill her."

"No, you're not. She was immediately apologetic and has been worried sick since she said it. And she only mentioned that because of our past."

He lets go of me and starts pacing the length of the room, his anger radiating off of him in thick waves. "She had no business telling you that. What the fuck was she thinking? I've never messed with her relationship, even though I believe she can do much better than that bumbling idiot."

"She felt bad," I remind him. "But I suppose what she said is a little warranted. Our situation is—unique. You can't deny it."

He whirls on me, despair etched into his features. "I can't change the past, no matter how badly I want to. I hate that I did that to you. Fucking hate it. And it feels like it's always going to be thrown in my face no matter what I do."

"I don't throw it in your face." Not lately at least.

"No, but others will, like Iris. And she'll probably continue doing it too. Damn it." He wraps his hands around the back of his neck and tilts his head back, staring at the ceiling. He exhales roughly. "I hate that she said something to upset you and ruin the entire weekend. I shouldn't have brought you here."

I go still, shock freezing me in place. Did he mean what he just said?

He drops his hands and turns toward me, his brows drawn together. "More like I shouldn't have asked her to come this weekend. A small part of me wanted to earn her approval and look what it got me? Nothing but trouble."

I don't respond to him at first, still stuck on what he said. That he shouldn't have brought me here. Does he mean it? Is our relationship doomed because of our past?

"I have to ask you, August." I hesitate for only a moment, my voice trembling. "Are your intentions true? For me?"

His eyes go ice cold, his expression shuttering closed. "If you don't realize what I feel for you by now, then what's the point of this? Of us?"

My heart sinks, regret making it heavy. I regret what I said and now I know how Iris felt after she opened her mouth. "You never say how you feel about me, August. You talk about being obsessed and that you can't get enough of me, but that's it."

He stares at me, disbelief all over his face. "That's it? What you're telling me is that what I do and say isn't enough for you?"

"No, I—"

"I'm sorry I disappoint you. I'm new to being in a relationship and I don't know how to navigate it. You know this. And now you're implying what I do and what I say isn't good enough. If that's the case, Sinclair, then why are you here? Why are you with me?"

I gape at him, unable to form words, the panic rising inside and gripping me in a chokehold. I try to speak, yet nothing comes out but a distressed noise that has him shaking his head and snorting in disbelief.

"Guess I'll just have to prove it to you in a more obvious way then," he states just before he turns and rushes out of my room, slamming the door behind him.

The moment he's gone, I collapse on top of the bed and close my eyes, wrapping my arms around my middle. I'm shaking, my mind running a million miles a minute and I don't know what to do. Should I chase after him? Should I leave? My mind replays his words over and over again.

Guess I'll just have to prove it to you in a more obvious way then.

What does that mean? It almost sounds positive but am I too hopeful? Or was it an insult? If he didn't want me here, he would've had no problem escorting me out of the house himself. Yet he didn't.

Maybe there is hope for us.

CHAPTER FORTY-NINE

SINCLAIR

I wake up to the sound of birds chirping outside and when I open my eyes to stare at the gigantic glittering chandelier hanging above me, I wonder if I've landed in the middle of a fairytale.

But no. My life is anything but a fairytale at the moment thanks to me upsetting the man I'm falling in love with. My stupid words sent him out of the room like he couldn't get away from me fast enough. He probably hates me.

Oh God, I hope he didn't murder his sister like he said he would.

I practically fall out of the bed, I'm trying to get out of it so quickly. I toss on some clothes, brush my hair and teeth and then make my way downstairs, coming to a stop at the base of the stairs when I realize I don't know where to go.

Luckily, I follow the scent of bacon and baked goods until I find a massive dining room where only Whit Lancaster is sitting at the table, sipping from a cup of coffee while he looks over his iPad. He's wearing glasses and I wonder for a moment if August will need glasses someday. And how devastatingly handsome his father is—August looks just like him. Meaning I know how August will look when he's older and he's going to be such a DILF.

Ugh, that I even had that thought about his freaking dad is wrong, I'm sure.

The elder Lancaster lifts his gaze as if he sensed my presence, taking off his glasses and setting them on the table. "Good morning, Sinclair."

"Good morning." I glance around the cavernous room, noticing the covered dishes on the sideboard along with a platter of fresh fruit and a basket with what looks like croissants. My stomach growls at the sight of it all. "Where is everyone?"

"Iris and her mother took the baby to do a little shopping downtown. Brooks is most likely still sleeping and I don't know where August is. I assume you were with him last night." The little smile on Whit Lancaster's face is faintly teasing and I wish I didn't feel so fragile.

I'm this close to telling him the truth—that I have no idea where his son is and I'm worried our relationship is over—but I keep my mouth shut.

"Are you hungry? Breakfast is still available if you want it." He waves a hand toward the sideboard and I dash over to it immediately, serving myself fresh fruit, a croissant and a pile of scrambled eggs with a couple of pieces of bacon. Do they really serve up food like this every day here? If so, a girl could get used to this sort of treatment.

"Thank you," I tell him once I'm seated and about to dig in. After being so upset last night and barely getting any sleep, I'm surprised I'm so hungry.

"You're welcome." I can feel his eyes on me as I eat and I grow self-conscious. Lifting my head, I find that he is most definitely watching me and he doesn't even look embarrassed getting caught.

"How are you?"

"I should ask how you're doing." Whit tilts his head to the side, his gaze narrowing. "You seem...unsettled."

I practically choke on a wad of croissant and I swallow it down, reaching for the glass of orange juice I poured myself and gulping from it.

"Perhaps I'm the one who leaves you unsettled." He leans back in his chair, his gaze still on me. "If that's so, please let me apologize. I'm just curious."

"It's not you," I manage to say, clearing my throat. "Last night was…rough."

"Please tell me you didn't argue with August."

"He was upset with me," I admit. "I might've said some things that I shouldn't have and he stormed out of my room."

"Ahh."

That's all he says. *Ahh*. The quiet in the room becomes oppressive and I drop my head, focusing on finishing my breakfast so I can get out of this room and away from this intimidating man. It's only when I'm finishing up the last of my eggs that he finally speaks.

"My son is very much like…me. And I don't know if that's a good thing or a bad thing," Whit says.

I lift my head to find him still leaning back in his chair, his body language nonchalant. As if he hadn't a care in the world. And I suppose he doesn't. This problem isn't his. It's ours and I feel like what August and I have is messy. Hopeless.

"The origins of my relationship with my wife weren't the best," he admits.

Now I'm the one who's curious. "What do you mean?"

"I hated her." He doesn't even hesitate with his answer, his tone vehement. "She hated me. But we were drawn together despite all the bad blood between us. Her mother had an affair with my father and broke up my parents' marriage. Not that their marriage was solid. My mother was a complete sociopath, God rest her soul."

I'm blinking, absorbing his words, realizing they sound faintly familiar. Not the sociopathic mother part, but the hating part.

"Why did you hate her? Because of her mother?"

"Yes, and everything she represented to me back then. Summer showed up at Lancaster Prep the first day of senior year and I did everything I could to make her life a living hell. It worked too—mostly. But no matter how far I took it, I never broke her and that impressed me. Her strength impressed me, as well as her beauty. God, I sound like an asshole." He shakes his head, his smile faint.

"You sound like your son," I admit, realizing that they are far more similar than I thought.

"Lancaster men aren't good with their feelings. We're like a five-year-old boy at recess who chases that one girl. Pulls her hair when she's not looking. Always calling her names and pushing her away. That's how we show our love at first." Whit slowly shakes his head. "I'm guessing my son did something like that to you."

"He bullied me throughout my freshman year at Lancaster Prep and now claims he doesn't remember." The disgust in my voice is out in full force.

"We're idiots." Whit sits up and leans across the table, resting his arms on the edge of it. "He's an idiot. You can go ahead and say it. August is an idiot."

"He is."

"Then say it."

"August is an idiot," I repeat, immediately feeling terrible for insulting this man's son, even if it was at his request. "But I think I'm in love with him."

His expression softens just the slightest. "You think?"

I shrug, feeling silly. "I'm not sure. I've never been in love before."

"Neither has he. You two can figure it out together." His gaze turns hawklike. "There's a saying in our family that once you know, you know. And I'm positive you'll work it out. August doesn't give up easily. Once he's locked in, he's in for life."

That statement is both reassuring and...

Terrifying.

• • •

After breakfast I wander around the house but can't find August anywhere. Anxious, I go back to my room and put on a pair of leggings and a sweatshirt, plus my running shoes and head outside for a walk. The air is cold and crisp, the sky a pure, clear blue and it feels good to get some fresh air and wander around the impressive neighborhood the Lancasters live in. The estates are walled off so you can't see the homes or their yards that well. Only through the wrought-iron gates can I stop and take a peek, and every home I can see is absolutely gorgeous, with perfectly manicured lawns and fancy cars sitting in the driveways. My parents will die when they see this place.

Speaking of my parents, I remember that I have a missed call from my mom earlier this morning and I pull out my phone, calling her back.

"There you are!" is how she greets me. "Are you there? At the Lancaster house?"

"I am." I turn around and start heading back in the direction I came. "You're still on for tonight?"

A small part of me wants them to back out, but there's no way Mom would ever do that. "We definitely are. We'll be there promptly at six."

"Even with Dad?" I'm teasing because we both know my father is perpetually late.

"Even with your dad. I told him he can't be late for this. We have Lancasters to impress." Mom sounds positively giddy at that little fact. She is beyond thrilled this dinner is happening tonight. "He's excited to meet them."

"Please don't let him be too overbearing," I practically groan, coming to a stop when I see August's car coming down the street. The ridiculous engine roars and the car slows as he turns it toward the gate, waiting for the doors to swing open before he pulls inside.

Where was he? What has he been doing?

"You know I can't control that man! He's going to do and say what he wants." She heaves an exaggerated sigh. "I'll text you when we're on our way. Everything going well over there?"

"Um…" Not really. "Sure. It's been great."

"I have a feeling you two are going to end up getting serious," Mom singsongs. "Oh what a story this will be someday! My daughter and how she ended up with the young man from one of the country's wealthiest families."

"There's nothing to tell yet, Mom."

"Oh, I bet by the end of tonight you could have a ring on your finger! I wouldn't doubt it at all."

"You're rushing things. Please, don't expect that." I start to sweat just at the thought of it. A ring on my finger? Engaged? Absolutely not. We've only known each other for a couple of months! But his father's words flit through my brain.

When you know, you know.

If that's something the Lancaster men live by, then maybe Mom isn't too far off with her prediction. And again, that's absolutely terrifying. A ring? Marriage? I'm not ready for that. At least I don't think I am, especially since August and I are a little rocky at the moment.

Ugh. This is so dumb. We just need to talk to each other and work it out.

I get off the phone with my mom and make my way over to the Lancaster estate. I enter the code August's mom gave me yesterday and the iron door next to the gate unlocks. I jog along the driveway, anxious to see him, but by the time I get to the front of the house, I see the Porsche parked there but no August in sight.

Fighting disappointment, I enter the house. It's quiet, like no one is here and I head up the stairs to my bedroom, wishing he was around instead of me having to seek him out. The longer we go without talking, the more awkward this is going to be and

I don't want my parents to figure out that things might not be so good between us. The last thing I want is for my mom to ask me a bunch of questions and try to pry into my private life.

Sighing, I move down the hallway toward my room, coming to a stop in front of the closed door with a frown. I don't remember closing it…

I slowly open the door, peeking my head around it and gasping in shock when I see what's waiting for me.

CHAPTER FIFTY

SINCLAIR

The entire room is filled with white roses. They're literally everywhere. Vases of them on top of the dressers, the nightstands, the little desk below the window that looks out over the backyard. There are pink rose petals strewn across my bed and when I look down, I realize there's a path of red rose petals that leads from the door to my bed. Their pungent scent fills the space and I take a deep breath, savoring it.

I was gone for maybe thirty minutes tops and August arrived back at the house not even ten minutes ago, maybe a little longer. When did he have time to do this? Because clearly this was put together by August.

Hopefully.

I move through the room, guilt filling me over my running shoes crushing the delicate petals and I come to a stop, taking off my shoes and tossing them aside. I scan the room, looking for a note, a clue, a sign that August actually did this but I see nothing.

"Do you like it?"

Screeching, I nearly jump out of my skin at the sound of that familiar deep voice coming from behind me. I turn to find August standing in the open doorway of the connecting bathroom, leaning against the doorsill. He's got a nonchalant air about him, his hands shoved into his jeans pockets, a casual expression on his face. As if he hadn't a care in the world.

In this moment, he reminds me of his father. His stance, the even expression. He looks like he doesn't care but I wonder if I said a certain something, would he spring into action? Not that I know what to say...

"You did this?" I glance over at the bed before returning my gaze to his. "You went to a lot of effort."

"I told you I would," he drawls, still not moving.

"Are you trying to prove something to me?" I swallow hard, my body trembling. It's risky, asking him that question. I'm not trying to be rude. I just want to know where I stand with him. Where we stand with each other.

"Didn't I essentially tell you that last night?" He pushes away from the doorframe, taking a few steps toward me before he stops. "You're either being purposely clueless or you don't want to be with me. Tell me what it is, Sin. Put me out of my misery."

A shuddery breath leaves me. "I need to hear the words, August."

He frowns, his brows drawing together like they always do. "Hear what words?"

"That you care, that you hate me, that you like me okay. That you're in love with me and want a future with me and you can't live without me. That you want me gone, banished from your life like I never existed. Whatever it is, however you're feeling, I need to hear it. The words. I need them." I press my lips together, afraid I took things too far. I don't like feeling unsure. On edge. And I've experienced that feeling ever since August and I reconnected a couple of months ago.

I want to know how he feels, and I want to be brave enough to tell him how I feel too. This conversation needs to happen if we're going to move forward.

"You need words?" When I barely nod my answer, he goes on. "I can give you all the pretty words you need, my Sin. I care about you. I used to hate you and then eventually, I liked you okay. I'm fairly certain I'm in love with you and I want and see a future with you, and I know for a goddamn fact I can't live without you. I could never want you gone, banished from my life because life wouldn't be worth living without you in it. If you never existed? Then I'd never know." He rests his hand against his heart, clutching his fingers into a fist. "But there would be a hole in my heart because you weren't here. Don't you realize that you're mine?"

I blink, all of those earlier uncertain emotions that swirled in my brain disappearing at his declarations. He's right. He's so right. I feel the same exact way. "You're in love with me?"

He actually rolls his eyes, the infuriating man. "That's the one thing you're sticking on? Sinclair, I told you I can't live without you. That's a pretty fucking bold statement."

"Do you even know what love is? How it's supposed to feel?" My throat aches with my words. How raw and exposed I am in this moment. "Because I don't. I've never been in love before."

"Are you confused? Overwhelmed? Scared?"

I nod, locking my knees when he takes a few steps closer. I can smell him now. His delicious spicy cologne wrapping all around me. The warmth of his body radiates, drawing me in and now I'm the one taking a step. Then another. "All of those things. Is that normal? I'm worried it's not."

"I don't know," he murmurs. "But I feel the same exact way. We can figure this out together as we go. I just know one thing."

He goes quiet and my body sways toward his. When he grabs hold of me and hauls me into his arms, I breathe a sigh of relief, circling my arms around his neck. Clinging to him, waiting to hear what he might say next.

"You were never not mine, Sinclair Miller. You belong to me. You always have. Even when you hated me. You were mine." He dips his head, his mouth landing on mine in a soft yet passionate kiss. His tongue is everywhere, searching my mouth, and I end it before we take it too far.

Though it doesn't take much for us to go too far. I can feel his erection press against my stomach and my thighs are trembling.

"I love you too," I tell him, my voice shaky. "I just needed to hear the words. Any words. I didn't know how you felt."

"This wasn't a big enough indicator?" He waves a hand at the rose-filled room, his gaze locking with mine. "Bringing you to my home so you can meet my family? You couldn't tell how I felt?"

"I just…" My voice drifts. "I think I need words along with actions. And you've always confused me, August. Sometimes you say too much but most of the time, you say nothing at all."

"I'll remember that." He kisses me again like he can't get enough of me, walking me backward until my calves are bumping against the edge of the mattress. "Now let me show you."

I press my hand on his chest, my palm resting upon the thundering beat of his heart. "We don't have time."

He's scowling. Oh this man is rarely denied anything he wants and that's what I just did. "What do you mean, we don't have time? I can fuck you and make that pretty little cunt come in less than five."

My body shakes at his words and I mentally tell myself to calm down. "My parents will be here soon."

"What time?"

"I don't know but…tonight's dinner is important."

"And this moment where we confess our feelings isn't?" He arches a brow, practically daring me to deny it.

Which I can't.

"This moment is important too," I agree, my voice soft. "I'm just—nervous."

"With me?" He sounds incredulous and I suppose I don't blame him. We've done some crazy stuff. Filthy dirty things that make me blush when I think about those moments for any length of time.

"No, of course not. I'm nervous about tonight's dinner, and what my parents might say or do. They're kind of embarrassing."

"If you're worried about what they do and how it might reflect on you, please don't." His mouth is on mine again, lingering. Lips parted as he breathes me in. "They could show up naked and grunting like savages and I wouldn't give a shit. I only care about you."

"What about your parents though? I'm worried what they'll think of them." I tilt my head back when he shifts away from my mouth and rains kisses along the edge of my jaw. Down my neck. His lips are damp and warm and when he pauses to lick the spot just behind my ear, I know I'm going to let him do whatever he wants to me.

"They'll have an opinion about you and they'll form their own opinions about your parents. You are not one and the same." His hand slides up my side, lingering at my waist before he shifts higher, cupping my breast. "Stop talking, Sin. You're making me impatient with all of your protesting."

Our mouths collide and I melt into him, letting him take over. Doing my best to forget about my worries and just live in this moment. With him. He guides me onto the bed and I land in the center of it, rose petals fluttering all around me with my bounce. Their fragrant scent is everywhere, almost overwhelming and he removes a petal from his lips before he positions himself above me, his mouth back on mine.

We kiss and kiss for what feels like hours, his hands wandering, settling on my waist, like he wants to keep things chaste between us. Or maybe he doesn't want to rush it. Is instead savoring me and the thought leaves me warm and gooey inside.

I circle my leg around his hips, hooking and drawing him in and his pelvis presses against mine, his hard dick right where I want it. We have too much clothing on and I'm the one who grows impatient first, which is always his role. I'm tugging on his sweater, grunting in frustration when it doesn't budge. I move my hands to the front of his jeans, shaky fingers trying to undo the front and he wraps his hand around my wrist, stopping me.

"Why are you in such a rush?"

"I told you we don't have much time." I try to tug out of his grip but he won't let me.

"Your parents aren't going to be here for hours." He runs his tongue along my jaw. "Patience, my pretty Sin. No need to rush things."

His deep voice has me melting and I sink into the mattress, welcoming his weight on top of me. His hands roam, sliding my sweatshirt up and off. Tugging at my leggings impatiently, making me giggle. I have no bra on and no panties and he seems pleased to find me bare and naked beneath my clothing, his gaze glowing with reverence.

"You're fucking stunning." His large hands cup my breasts, testing their weight, his thumbs teasing my nipples. "And all mine."

The pride in his voice bleeds into the words and my body grows warm. I am his.

"You've always been mine. Since that first day I saw you at Lancaster Prep, when you were scared and awkward and fumbling around, something tugged deep inside of me. I *saw* you. Despite how awful I treated you, I knew it, but I was in denial." He lifts his head, his beautiful blue eyes meeting mine. "You belonged to me."

I'm breathless at his words. The gleam in his gaze. There's a part of me that believes he's just saying all of this to make me feel better. But there's also that other tiny part buried inside of me that says he's right.

I knew it too. We belonged to each other.

Ducking his head, he leaves a trail of wet kisses across my chest, sucking a nipple into his mouth while I yank impatiently at the neck of his sweater. Eventually he pulls away, getting rid of the sweater in seconds, and when I feel the press of his warm, hard skin against mine, I moan. Soon his jeans are gone too and we're a tangle of limbs and hands and fingers. Mouths and tongues and teeth. I can't get enough of him and he acts the same way, his hands and mouth greedy. His fingers slip between my thighs and stroke me, the wet sounds filling the room.

"Always so ready for me," he murmurs against my lips. "My greedy little Sin."

"You make me greedy." I tilt my head back and arch my hips, sucking in a breath when he trails his mouth down the length of my body.

"I hope the door is fucking locked," he mutters against my stomach at one point and I can't help but laugh.

"Probably not." What would happen if someone walked in at this very moment?

I can't even worry about it. I'm too caught up.

Within seconds, he slides inside me, filling me up, and I hold him close for a moment, both of us still. The connection is real. Binding. And when he lifts away, I open my eyes to find he's watching me, his fingers carefully brushing the stray hairs away from my face.

"You need the words?" he asks.

I nod. "I do."

"You belong to me." He leans in, his mouth settling on mine. "And no one else."

So possessive, I think as he begins to move. But he's not wrong. I am his.

And he's mine.

CHAPTER FIFTY-ONE

AUGUST

Women can be such…challenging creatures.

Take Sinclair, for one. I've been showing her how I feel for at least a month. Probably longer. And she was clueless. Afraid I was what? Using her? After I invite her to my parents' home so we can all spend time together? I don't do that just for fun. Hardly any of my friends have been here. And I sure as shit have never invited another woman here. Only her.

And it will only ever be her.

I suppose as individuals, we all have different love languages. It pains me to even make that mental statement because it sounds silly as fuck. But considering Iris has talked about love languages for years and mine is definitely in the acts of service realm, apparently, Sinclair's is words of affirmation. She needed the words, so I gave them to her.

As I pounded inside of her only a few hours ago, I told her how much I needed her greedy little pussy. How I owned that cunt and it was mine. She ate it up, creaming all over my cock, coming so hard I wondered if I rendered her unconscious for a moment.

Christ, I sound like I'm bragging even in my thoughts but it's true. She was a puddle by the time we were through. Wrecked and beautiful. I added to the wreck by scooping up the cum between her legs and smearing it all over her stomach, making a mark.

My mark.

I'm a sick fuck and so is she, but we're in this together. I feel like she's my match. I adore her. I do.

I love her.

I'm downstairs in the family room with Iris and Brooks, who's bouncing his precious little monster on his knee while she coos at her father. My mother and Sinclair aren't in the room yet, and my father is at the bar, making us all a cocktail.

"I need to talk to you," Iris declares out of nowhere, her focus on me.

"Go ahead and talk." I settle into the overstuffed chair, ready for her to grovel.

A sigh leaves her and she glances around the room—specifically at our father—before she returns her gaze to mine. "Not in here. Somewhere more private maybe?"

"We can discuss whatever it is in front of Brooks and Dad. I have nothing to hide." I arch a brow like the dick older brother that I am.

She clutches her hands into fists on her lap. Ah, Iris. Doesn't she realize I've got her all figured out and I know how to get under her skin? "Fine. I'm sorry for what I said to Sinclair last night."

"What exactly did you say to her?" I believe what Sinclair told me, but I want to see what Iris says.

"I told her to be careful because come on, Augie. You're not the best when it comes to women." Iris shakes her head, reaching out to pet her little monster's head. That downy blonde hair looks soft to the touch, I can't deny it. "Though I figured you were serious if you brought her here."

"When have I ever brought anyone here?"

"Never."

"Exactly. So why would you say that to Sinclair about my so-called intentions? I'd think they were pretty obvious since I brought her home this weekend with me. I never do that," I say again.

"You're right. You're right, but sometimes we need to…I don't know. Hear you say it?"

She sounds like Sinclair. I've always been told actions speak louder than words so here I am doing the actions all over the place. Guess they need the words too.

"I'll give you that." I incline my head toward her. "Please don't say anything bad about me to her parents tonight."

"I would never." Iris rests her hand against her chest. "I did a little research on them. Did you know her dad invented Jock Rot?"

Dad chokes on his drink, setting it on the bar in front of him with a hard thud. "What did you just say?"

"Jock Rot, Dad. You never heard of it?"

"No." Dad shakes his head. "Not at all."

"Wow, really? I used that stuff before back when I was playing football with Rhett." Brooks shakes his head, seemingly impressed. "It works."

"Ew." Iris shakes her head. "The name is horrible."

"I suppose I should let him tell the story, and I'm sure he will, but according to Sin, once he sold it, the business that took over changed the name and sales tanked," I explain.

"But the selling point was the name. Teenage boys all over the country loved that shit because it was called Jock Rot, which sounds gross, but it cured it," Brooks says, his voice dripping with disappointment. "Why would they change such a cool name?"

"Retailers wouldn't carry it on the shelves if it was called Jock Rot. That's why," I tell him.

"What the fuck is jock rot anyway?" Dad asks, sounding impatient.

Brooks launches into a long explanation as to what exactly Jock Rot is and Iris and I make faces at each other from across the room as Brooks describes the symptoms. So gross.

"That's disgusting," Dad says when Brooks is finished. "I'm glad my wife wasn't in here to hear all of that."

"Sorry, sir." Brooks ducks his head, his face turning red. Poor guy always puts his foot in his mouth around us and…seriously, what the fuck? Am I actually starting to feel sorry for him? That's something I never do.

"You're fine, Brooks." Dad sighs, shaking his head. "When are her parents supposed to arrive? And where's your mother? She's taking forever."

Iris jumps to her feet. "I'll go look for her."

"I believe they're supposed to get here around six." I check my watch to find that it's only just past six. "Sinclair mentioned they could be late sometimes."

"I hate lateness. It's so fucking rude," Dad mutters as he pours himself another drink. He didn't even pass around the ones he made for us and I stand, going to the bar and grabbing my drink. "Have you met them?"

"No." I slowly shake my head, taking a sip of the bourbon Dad poured for me. "She's told me stories though. They have that typical new money attitude."

"Ah, Christ. They're probably going to be salivating over us all night, right? I sound like a dick, but those types? That's what they usually do." Dad shakes his head.

"Don't be a prick, Dad." I can say this to him because he knows that sometimes, he acts like a massive dickhead. We can't help it. It's part of our DNA. "Just...try not to let them bother you. I need you on your best behavior. I don't want to upset Sinclair."

My father watches me for a moment, amusement dancing in his eyes that are so much like mine. "Well look at you. Caring about someone else for a change."

I know I can be a selfish bastard but it sucks when your father calls you out for it. "I'm trying to be a better person."

"You're not a bad person, son. You've just been wrapped up in your own bullshit your entire life. I get it. I was the same way. Then you find someone who wrecks your plans and changes your entire outlook." He sends me a measured look. "And now you're forever changed."

"Wrecks your plans? I never knew you were a Swiftie, dear father of mine." Iris appears out of nowhere, standing right beside me. When I send her a questioning look, she explains. "Those are lyrics from one of her songs. Well, kind of. Close enough."

"I am not a Swiftie." Dad appears positively offended. "And I thought you went in search of your mother and Sinclair."

"I couldn't find either of them." Iris shrugs, unbothered. "I'm sure they'll make an appearance soon."

Nerves eat at my gut, which is not normal. I could not give a shit about impressing people but with Sinclair's parents? For whatever reason, I want them to like me. I want their approval and that goes against everything I normally care about.

Maybe Sinclair did wreck my plans—for the better.

CHAPTER FIFTY-TWO

SINCLAIR

There's a knock on my door and I assume it's August coming to fetch me. I've taken far too long to get ready and make sure I look the part of August Lancaster's girlfriend—it's hard for me to believe that he actually thinks of me as his girlfriend—because I'm nervous. And anxious—terribly anxious. I don't want my parents to act tacky, AKA like their usual selves, and ruin the evening. I'm desperate to make a good impression.

This is the most nerve-wracking night of my life, and I've lived through some harrowing moments since I first met August. He's put me through it. I've put myself through it too because despite it all, I'm forever drawn to him. To finally have the confirmation that he feels the same way is a relief. An absolute thrill. He cares about me. He said he was in love with me.

What is this life?

Opening the door, I'm about to say something, but I snap my lips shut when I see who it is.

August's mom.

"Hi, Sinclair." Her smile is gentle, as is her entire demeanor. Her calm vibe seems to permeate the room every time she enters it. She has this soothing effect on her entire family and I like that about her. Probably because I find she calms me too. "I was hoping you were still in here."

"Hi." I stand there clutching the door handle feeling awkward. I really need to learn how to relax. My worry over tonight could make everything worse. "Am I running late? Are my parents here?" I assumed Mom would text me the second they pulled through the gates. But maybe not.

"No, not yet. May I come in?"

"Of course." I open the door wider, taking Summer Lancaster in as she enters the room. She's effortlessly elegant in her simple black dress, her dark hair cascading down her back in soft waves. You'd never believe she's the mom of three and that her youngest child is in high school. I can only hope I look that good when I'm a mom.

I shut the door and turn to watch as she settles into the pale blue velvet chair in front of the small desk in the room. She aims a friendly smile in my direction and I automatically smile in return. "You're nervous."

There's no point in denying it. "I am." I even wring my hands together, letting it all hang out since she called me on it. "Tonight feels like a big deal."

"I can't lie—it is a big deal. August doesn't bring just anyone home. My son…he's always been such a private person, rarely allowing someone into his life. He likes to think he doesn't need anyone, which reminds me of his father." Her gaze settles on my face and it feels like she's trying to examine me, see through my skin and bones, into my brain. "You must be a special person in order for August to bring you here for the weekend and introduce you to all of us."

Swallowing hard, I scramble to come up with the right thing to say. "I care about August. A lot."

"I can tell. And he cares about you too. I like watching the two of you together." Her smile fades the slightest bit. "I know how… difficult August can be sometimes. He's very much like his father, and when I first met Whit, our interactions were unconventional, to say the least. Neither of them are good at expressing their feelings."

The biggest understatement of the year. "August has mentioned to me before that he's a lot like his father."

A sigh leaves Summer and she shakes her head. "I'd hoped my firstborn wouldn't be like that, because I always believed Whit's behavior stemmed from being raised by two neglectful parents. I did everything in my power to ensure that our children never felt like we didn't care, and August still ended up acting just like his father. I suppose genetics are difficult to change."

"I suppose so," I agree, unsure of what else I can say.

"I just wanted you to know that it takes a special person to handle these Lancaster men, and I appreciate you—caring about my son." Summer sniffs and even dabs at the corners of her eyes, like she might be crying? "I've worried about him and how closed off he can be for years. And now he's found you and I don't have to worry any longer." She laughs before I can respond, sniffing loudly. "I didn't mean to become so emotional."

"It's okay." I smile at her and she smiles back.

"You're a nice girl, Sinclair. And don't worry about tonight." She stands, smoothing out the skirt of her dress. "Everything is going to be just fine."

. . .

We enter the room together, Summer going to her husband who's currently standing behind the bar and making everyone drinks. I scan the room, my gaze landing on August who's sitting on the couch with baby Astrid in his arms.

Something tugs at me deep, watching him smile down at his niece, who reaches for his nose and tries to grasp it in her little fingers. Iris is sitting next to them and bursts out laughing, making some comment about how her baby is getting back at Uncle Augie, but he ignores her. Instead, he pries the baby's fingers from his nose and she wraps her fingers around one of his, making a cooing noise at her uncle.

My heart melts at the scene. He calls her a monster and a beast, but I see the genuine affection he has for her. I'm about to make my way over to him when my phone buzzes in my hand. I check it to see a text from my mom.

We're here!!!!

Oh God.

"Sin." August's voice makes me look up from the phone. "Come hold the monster with me."

"You really need to stop calling her that," his sister chastises with a scowl. "Look at her. She's a precious little baby!"

"Who's an absolute beast. Did you see the way she grabbed my nose?" He makes a tsking noise but I can tell he's joking. "She's a Lancaster through and through."

"Hey. I had something to do with making her," Brooks protests from where he's standing by the bar.

"Don't remind me," August mutters, his gaze only for me as I make my way to the couch, sitting on the other side of him. "Want to hold her?"

Before I can answer he's dumping the baby in my arms and I wrap them around the squirming baby tight, worried she could slip right out of my hold and wouldn't that be awful? I'm also concerned she might take one look at me and start bawling.

But she doesn't do any of that. Astrid stares at me, waving her arm up and down and I take in her dainty features, those bright blue eyes that remind me of August's. I touch her button nose, which makes her smile.

"She likes you," August murmurs and I lift my head to find him watching me carefully. "And she doesn't like just anybody."

"Oh, come on." I dip my head, smiling down at Astrid who offers me a toothless grin. "She's a sweetheart. I'm sure she loves everyone."

"No. She's picky and rude, just like her uncle," Iris informs me. "You must have a magic touch."

"She does," August readily agrees, making me laugh while his sister groans.

"I do not need to hear about your weird sexual fetishes, Augie," Iris warns, her voice a little too loud.

"Why do you always have to take it there." August sounds exasperated but I ignore their little argument, focusing on the baby in my arms. She shifts her weight around, wiggling in my embrace, and I give her a gentle poke in her stomach.

Astrid is adorable. Someday, I'd love to have a baby. Maybe even a couple of them, but that's a long way off.

Like...a loooooooong way.

I hear the doorbell ring and my heart drops into my stomach, nerves eating at it like tiny nibbling fish. The moment I've been waiting for and dreading all at once. Iris swoops in and plucks Astrid from my arms and I shoot to my feet, shaking out my now sweaty hands. "They're here."

August stands, slipping his arm around my shoulders and pulling me in so he can softly kiss my forehead. "Relax. It's going to be all right."

"Your mom said the same thing."

He frowns down at me. "When did you talk to her?"

"Earlier. Before we came downstairs." I square my shoulders, his arm falling away as I put on a brave face. "Please pray to baby Jesus that my parents won't say or do something that causes all of us to get kicked out of the house, okay?"

"That won't happen." He takes my hand, and I get the feeling he's trying to present as a united front. Which I appreciate more than he'll ever know. I need him by my side to get through this night. "Love your dress, Sin. You look good enough to eat."

My face goes hot. The dress is a deep green with a simple design, with long sleeves and a short skirt that I paired with knee-length black leather boots. "Thank you."

"I'll be taking it off later tonight." He nuzzles the side of my face with his nose, and I dip my head closer to his. "Though you can keep the boots on."

"Stop." My protest is weak and I rest my hand on the solid wall that is his chest. "My parents will be here any second."

"I'm trying to distract you." He pulls away slightly, concern all over his face. "You're worried."

"They're a menace. The two of them." I drop my hand from his chest, but he grabs it, lacing our fingers together.

"They can't be that bad…can they?"

My parents enter the room before I can respond, escorted by one of the servants who works at the house. My mom is bug-eyed as she takes everything in, her head tilted back and I swear I can see her calculating the value of everything in her brain and she's stumped because she can't count that high.

I knew she'd react this way. My dad heads straight for the bar, enthusiastically shaking Whit's hand and practically screaming that he's so glad to meet him. I can't even look in their direction. Can only imagine Whit's reaction to my father and when I glance over at my mom, she's got a big smile on her face, her gaze landing on me standing beside August, our hands still linked.

I squeeze his hand and let it go as she stops directly in front of me, an actual squeal leaving her.

"Sinclair! My God, aren't you a sight? Look at you! I love the boots! Are they made by Frye?" She yanks me into her arms, hugging me fiercely, her mouth at my ear as she murmurs, "This house is *huge*."

"Hi, Mom. My boots are Steve Madden and half the price." I return the hug, disentangling myself from her so I can stand at August's side once more. "Looks like you made it here okay."

"Oh, we did. The drive was a little long but the scenery was nice. Your father drove too fast though. He had to bring the Porsche. Wanted to make sure the Lancasters are duly impressed." Mom swivels her attention to August, her smile wide. "You must be August Lancaster. I'm Jennifer."

He shakes my mother's hand, a polite smile on his face. "It's nice to meet you."

"Oh my, you are handsome." Mom rests her hand against her chest, blatantly taking him in. "When Sinclair told me she was dating you, I found it hard to believe, especially after I did a little googling. What would a man like you see in my daughter?"

I blink at her, stunned she would say such a thing. "Mom. I'm standing right here."

She laughs, the sound extra loud in the hushed quiet of the room. Even Dad has subdued but maybe that's because he's downing the drink Whit just made for him. "You know what I mean, honey. Let's be real. He's a Lancaster."

I know what she's implying, even though she doesn't say it out loud. The Lancaster family is filthy rich and of a class of their own. What would August see in me?

Everything revolves around money for her. For my dad too, though Mom is worse. She won't stop shopping. Won't stop feeding that empty spot inside her that only seems to grow more and more as each year passes. Dad has affairs and buys expensive cars. Mom shops constantly and converts every room she can into a closet.

"Your daughter isn't with me because of my family's money." August's voice is calm, but I can hear the slight edge to it. The man is pissed. "She didn't even like me at first."

"Oh come on, Sinclair! You didn't like him? Look at him!" Mom waves a hand in August's direction. "What's not to like."

I try to smile at her but it's impossible. I don't bother responding to her either. What's the point? She doesn't recall the fact that he bullied me in high school and I don't want to remind her. She might start insulting me even more and that's the last thing I want to deal with.

"Your house is beautiful." Mom glances over at Summer, who stops to stand with us. "Thank you for inviting us for dinner."

"We thought it was only proper to have you over as well as your lovely daughter." Summer sends me a sweet smile. "We're just glad to have you all together tonight. Sinclair obviously makes my son very happy."

"Well, isn't that nice? I suppose I trained her well." Mom snort laughs and I want to die. "Are you going to make my daughter an honest woman or what?" Mom asks August, who doesn't react at all to her bold question while I'm already wishing I could curl up into a tiny ball and disappear.

"Mom. I'm only eighteen," I remind her through clenched teeth.

"You're an adult. You can get married. Probably would be smart on your part to do it right away." And with that statement, she wanders away from us, her gaze greedily scanning the room. Summer follows after her, engaging her in conversation, and I'm grateful that August's mom is trying. If she was smart, she'd give up now because my mom…

Is a hopeless cause.

I share a look with August, who seems completely unaffected by that humiliating conversation.

"I'm so sorry. Please forgive her," I whisper and he grabs my hand, giving it a quick squeeze before he brings our linked hands up to his mouth. He presses a soft kiss to my knuckles before letting it go.

"Don't worry about her. It's fine. She's fine."

But she's not fine. She's like this for the next thirty minutes as August's father makes us all drinks and a servant brings out a couple of trays covered in a variety of appetizers. Mom downs the vodka sodas Whit keeps making her and shovels the appetizers in her mouth, talking nonstop to Summer, while Whit asks my father questions about the infamous Jock Rot. Dad goes into intricate detail about the rise and fall of his business, Whit sneering with faint disgust when he describes the symptoms of jock rot, not that I can blame him. It's disgusting, but my father talks about it with absolute glee. It's become such a part of his life that he doesn't recognize how gross it is to anyone else.

All I can do is sit in misery with August, who's observing everything with that narrowed gaze of his. The one that tells me he's judging everything they're doing and saying, not that I'm surprised. Iris and Brooks are wrapped up in the baby, trying to get her to calm down when she starts to fuss. Mom doesn't even acknowledge them, only when they leave the room does she say something.

"Who's the baby?"

"That's my niece," August answers, his voice smooth. "My sister's daughter."

"Oh right. I saw you had a sister." That's all she says, ditching us, including Summer, so she can wander around the room again, examining every detail. "How much was this?" Mom pats the back of an overstuffed chair and I wither at how vulgar she's acting, asking about the price of the furniture. I want to die every time she opens her mouth and I don't know how many times August has squeezed my hand in reassurance, but it's a lot.

By the time we've moved into the formal dining room for dinner, I ask for an alcoholic beverage—any kind of beverage, as long as it has liquor in it, because I know it's going to be a long night.

"You probably shouldn't have a drink," Mom tells me from where she's seated directly across from me. I can barely see her thanks to the abundant flower arrangement sitting on the table between us. "You're only eighteen."

Like I don't remember how old I am. "I'm not going anywhere so I'll be fine." I smile up at the server who's taking our drink requests. "Thank you."

He moves on and Mom leans over the table, her gaze fiery when it lands on me. "Sinclair, what in the world is wrong with you?"

I glance around to make sure no one is paying us any attention before I answer her. "Nothing. What's your problem?"

Oh God, I sound like I'm fifteen and fighting with my mom about the length of my skirt or whatever. Why do I always revert to that version of me when we argue?

"What's my problem? First of all, you're not twenty-one, meaning it's illegal for you to drink. Second, you are defying my wishes, and since you seem to have forgotten, I am your *mother*." She lifts her chin, trying to stare down her nose at me and failing miserably. "And you shall do what I say."

I roll my eyes. "You're being—"

"Do we have a problem here?"

I go still at the tone of August's voice, taking a deep breath before I turn to look at him. "It's fine."

"It doesn't sound fine," he practically snaps, glancing over at my mother. "Why are you yelling at Sinclair again?"

"I'm her mother. I can yell at her if I want to." Mom sounds indignant. And she's treating me like a child when I'm an adult who doesn't even live with her anymore.

"You're in a stranger's house, sitting at their table and about to eat dinner. If I were you, I'd tone it down a little," August says to her.

The look on my mother's face has me wanting to slide under the table. I'd sort of forgotten that look, but it all comes back to me now. Whenever I'd talk back to her—which wasn't often—she'd fume. Her lips would thin and her nostrils would flare and it's happening right now. She's fuming mad at my—what do I call him? My boyfriend? My lover? Oh, that one would send her straight off the rails.

"And who are you to tell me how to treat my child?" Mom throws at him.

He stares at her for a moment, the entire table going quiet, and I hold my breath, dreading his answer. Almost looking forward to it too because I've never seen anyone talk to my mother like this before.

I kind of like it.

"Who am I? I am the man who's going to marry your daughter one day, so watch how you speak to her." He glares at her. "Got it?"

Oh God.

CHAPTER FIFTY-THREE

AUGUST

This woman—the mother of the woman I have fallen in love with—is an absolute nightmare. Who the hell does she think she is, speaking to Sinclair like she just did in front of my family? We're practically strangers and she's letting it all hang out, so to speak.

Sin warned me and I thought she was exaggerating, but apparently, she wasn't at all. Her mother is awful. Her father though? He's latched on to my dad and Brooks and they're having a grand time talking about football and cars. I'd rather be in on their conversation than have to deal with Jennifer Miller, but I'm doing this for Sinclair. She needs someone to stand up for her.

And that someone is me.

"Just because you have more money than me doesn't mean you can tell me how to talk to my child. I've been her mother for eighteen years and you've only just waltzed into her life," Jennifer retorts, crossing her arms in front of her. Reminding me of a spoiled kid who isn't getting their way. "Goodness, Sinclair. Are you really going to let him treat me this way? I am your mother. You should show more respect toward your elders, young man."

Getting chastised by this ridiculous woman isn't what I planned for this evening. Someone needs to put her in her place. "And listening to you insult the woman I love isn't showing much respect to your daughter, don't you think? You are a guest in my home. You have no business talking to Sinclair like that."

I can feel the worry come off of Sinclair in waves. I think she might even be shaking, but I can't look at her. To see the worry on her face might make me go quiet on her behalf but goddamn someone needs to shut this woman up.

Sin's mother stares at me, her gaze narrowing. I get the sense she's trying to size me up and doesn't like what she sees, which is fine. The feeling is mutual. "You're one of those bossy types, aren't you?"

She doesn't know the half of it. "I am merely pointing out that you should speak more respectfully to your daughter in a public setting."

"We're in your private home—"

"With people you don't know." I smile, but it's more of a baring of teeth. "You want to make a good impression, don't you?"

The woman goes silent and I finally glance over at Sinclair, who's watching me with gratefulness shimmering in her glassy eyes. I hate that she's been so worried about this moment and I should've listened to her. Her worry was warranted and her mother is a nightmare.

My gaze shifts to my own mother, who's a saint for putting up with my dad and me. With all of us. She's chosen to engage with the other side of the table and I envy her. Iris is telling a story about Astrid, and Mom is eating it up. Dad is still chatting with Sin's father and Brooks, and for once, my father doesn't seem annoyed with Iris's husband. This feels like a breakthrough. One I can't even focus on because I'm dealing with something else.

"Are you going to just sit there and not say a word?" Jennifer asks Sinclair, who remains silent. "You're going to let him insult me in his home? Shouldn't he be the one treating his guests with respect?"

"Mom." Sinclair sends her a pleading look. "Please. Just…stop talking and listen for once."

"Listen for once? I've been listening all my life and finally it's my time to shine. I'm tired of sitting back and letting everyone else get the attention. Your father. Your brother. You." Jennifer sneers. "Why doesn't anyone give me any credit? That's all I want. I've been the backbone of this family ever since I married your father and I have nothing to show for it."

"Nothing but two children and a husband and a pretty wonderful life if you ask me," Sinclair says, making me proud. "If you don't like how your life is, you have the power to change it, you know."

"But you don't know what it's like. Your father—"

"Enough." I slap my hand on the edge of the table, making everything shake. Everyone goes silent, turning their attention on me, and I just can't give a shit. "I'm tired of listening to you whining. If you can't stop making a spectacle of yourself, I'm going to ask you to leave."

Her expression switches to indignant in a second and she rises to her feet, tossing her cloth napkin on top of her plate. "You don't need to ask me to leave. I'm going on my own. Come on, Ron. Sinclair. Let's go."

I glance over at her husband, who's frowning at her. "What's the problem, Jen?"

"This man." She waves a hand at me. "Is rude. And disrespectful. He's kicking me out."

"You just said you were leaving on your own terms," I remind her, which makes her even angrier.

"Fine! We're leaving! Now!"

She starts to march out of the dining room but neither

her husband nor her daughter are following. Pausing in the doorway, she turns, leveling her gaze on her daughter. "Sinclair. Let's go."

"I-I'm not going with you. I'm staying here." Sin shakes her head, her gaze going to mine and I offer her a reassuring smile.

An aggravated noise leaves Jennifer and she glares at her husband. "Ron! Come on. I'm not staying in this house for another second."

"Thank you for having us," Ron Miller tells my father, his movements slow. Almost reluctant as he stands, offering an apologetic smile to my parents. "I'm sorry about this. Hopefully we can meet up again another time."

"I'm disappointed in you, Sinclair," her mother states before she trounces out of the dining room, her husband following after her. Not even a minute later the front door slams, and then the entire room goes quiet.

"Well, shit. Despite all the jock rot talk, I liked him," Dad declares, taking a sip from his glass. "And that was the last thing I expected. What did you do to get her all worked up, August?"

"Yes, tell us, Augie," Iris adds, watching me with a particular gleam in her eyes. She's always loved it when I get in trouble.

"He stood up for me against my mom." Sin sends me a grateful look before she continues on. "She's talked down to me practically my entire life and I sort of got used to it, you know? I don't think she likes that I defied her."

"You don't have to worry about her. I've got your back," I tell Sinclair, my voice quiet. I reach for her hand, interlocking our fingers. "She had no business speaking to you that way. I don't care if she's your mother. She can't treat you like that."

Tears shine in Sinclair's eyes and they make my heart ache. My entire body ache. I hate seeing her in pain. I never thought I could care so much about another person and here I am, wanting to slay all of Sinclair's dragons and make sure she's protected from everyone. "Thank you."

I scoot closer to her, my voice lowering, my words just for her. "Don't you realize I'd do anything for you? You're the most important person to me."

She nods, a tear sliding down her cheek, and I reach for it, pressing my thumb against it and absorbing the moisture. "No one has ever done that for me before."

"I will always defend you." My voice is fierce, my heart racing. I'm angry on her behalf and I have no one to take it out on. "Don't ever doubt me, Sin."

Leaning in, she presses her mouth to mine, whispering against my lips, "I won't."

CHAPTER FIFTY-FOUR

SINCLAIR

My mother texted me throughout dinner, slinging insults at first and then turning it around, begging me to leave the Lancaster house. She offered to come back and pick me up. That the Lancasters are mean, awful people and I have no business being there. That August Lancaster will only bring me down.

I ignored all of her texts, not responding to a single one. There's no point in arguing with her. She believes she's right and she'll die on that hill.

August eventually took my phone away from me and I enjoyed the rest of the night stress-free, pushing all thoughts of my mother out of my mind. I'm glad that everyone seemed to like my dad, which isn't always the case. Maybe he's changed. Maybe my mom has too. I don't know what to think about them, especially her.

"You want me to give you my opinion?" Iris finally asks me after the dinner plates have been cleared and we're waiting for dessert.

"Yes," I say at the same time August says "No."

Iris ignores her brother. "I think she's jealous of you. Your mom. She sees you and how happy you are. How we're all accepting you as part of our family, and it makes her feel left out. Maybe she's unhappy with her life, I don't know, but I get the sense that her behavior toward you is all driven by envy."

Her words linger in my thoughts for the rest of the evening. If anyone would've told me my mom was jealous of my life, I would've laughed. She's the one with the big house and all the money to spend. Why would she be jealous of anything I have? She has far more than me.

But I'm younger. I'm just starting my life while she's fully settled in hers and I think she's been dissatisfied for a while. Not that I'm excusing my father's behavior, but maybe there's a reason he's cheating on her. Maybe it has something to do with her too, and not just him. I have a hard time forgiving him for his infidelity, but marriage is a two-way street. It's hard work.

I've come to the conclusion that I don't want to be like her. Jealous and unhappy. Nagging everyone and asking inappropriate questions. If she's truly unsatisfied, she needs to leave my father. But she won't.

I know she won't.

We return to the sitting room after dessert, but I'm so tired I can barely keep my eyes open and when August catches me yawning yet again, he finally has to say something to me.

"You should go to bed. You seem exhausted."

I offer him a sleepy smile. "It was a rough night. I knew it would be."

"You did." He pats my shoulder, a chaste move on his part. "It's late. Go get some sleep."

I say my goodbyes to everyone and exit the room, walking slowly up the staircase, taking in the opulence that is the Lancaster house.

It's nothing like my mom and dad's house. Does Mom feel like she can't measure up? No one can when compared to this family. She might be hard on me, but why is she also so hard on herself?

I don't get it.

Parental trauma is real and I suffer from it. Maybe that's what drew me to August in the first place? Oh God, that's just too deep for me to contemplate at the moment.

By the time I'm in my room and taking off my clothes, there's an urgent knock on my door, followed by the door handle rattling. I can't help but smile. I'd know that knock anywhere.

Rushing to the door, I turn the lock and open it, August crowds me, pushing his way inside and shutting the door behind him, switching that lock back into place before he reaches for me. I go willingly, crashing into his arms, gasping when his hands land on my butt, slipping beneath my sheer panties and gripping my bare flesh. His mouth is on mine in an instant, his kiss almost frantic, lips moving and tongue searching like he's trying to dig deep.

"Are you mad at me?" he murmurs against my mouth as he walks me backward, heading toward the bed.

"Why would I be mad at you?" I'm seriously confused. He's done nothing but stand by my side all evening and he thinks I'm angry?

"I talked some shit to your mom, Sin. She might've made you mad, but I was mean to her and that's your mother." He lifts away from me, his lazy gaze meeting mine. "I'll go down in flames defending my mother. I wouldn't stand for anyone insulting her."

"That's because your mother is a wonderful person who believes in you. Unlike mine." I hook my arms around his neck, sliding my fingers into his silky soft hair. "I don't want to talk about her."

"You sure about that?" His eyes fall to half-mast and I know he likes the way I'm stroking his hair.

"Positive." My voice is firm, my thoughts settled. "Though I do have one thing to say."

"What is it?"

Rising up on my tiptoes, I level my mouth at his ear and murmur, "Thank you. What you did for me tonight, what you said—it meant a lot."

He turns, his mouth aligning with mine. "And I meant every word I said. She can't treat you like that anymore, Sin. Not with me by your side."

I melt against him, loving that he's still fully clothed while I'm just in my panties. He grabs hold of the back of my thighs and lifts me up, and I wrap my legs around his hips, fusing my mouth with his as he carries me...not to the bed, where I thought he was going, but to the door, pressing me to it, pinning me there with his body.

"August—" I start to protest but he cuts me off with his lips and I moan when his tongue licks at mine. His hands are on my waist, and he's grinding his erection against the throbbing spot between my thighs, and I know my panties must already be soaked.

"You don't belong to them anymore," he whispers against my neck after he ends our kiss. "You belong to me."

He's referring to my parents, and he's right. I'm not theirs any longer—I'm August's. And while I should be against the archaic thought of women being men's property, I know August doesn't fully mean that. He believes in me. Readily supports me, and I love that about him.

I love him.

"I thought about being nice and fucking you slow on the bed." He lifts away from my neck, his dark gaze meeting mine as he unbuckles his belt and kicks off his shoes before he sheds his pants and boxer briefs. "But I decided I'd rather fuck you hard and fast against the door. Do you have a problem with that?"

His words, the look on his face and the sound of his voice have my entire body turning to jelly. "No." I slowly shake my head. "It's what I want, August. I want you."

He wastes zero time, impatient as always, tearing at my panties. Frustrated, he jerks them to the side and slides into my welcoming body, filling me to the hilt. I groan, thumping the back of my head against the door and he immediately slides his hand beneath my head, protecting me.

My heart soars. This man who tries to act like he doesn't care about anyone else but himself cares about me with his whole heart. He's protective and strong and my defender. He stands by my side and reassures me that everything is going to be all right as long as I've got him. He loves me.

And I love him too.

I cling to him as he fucks me steadily, his hips moving, his cock going deep until I swear it hits my soul. I am breathless, unable to think. All I can do is feel. Our bodies moving together, his hand cupping my breast, his cheek pressed to mine as he pants dirty things into my ear.

"This fucking cunt is mine and goddamn, Sin. You grip me so tight. I'm going to come. I'm going to fill that pussy with my cum and I'm going to wreck you just like you wrecked me."

I go still at his words, resting my hand on his chest. He pauses, lifting his head from mine, so he can look into my eyes. "I wrecked you?"

August nods, removing his hand from my breast so he can cup the side of my face. "For the better. You came into my life and disrupted it completely but I needed that. I needed you."

I smile, my chest tight, my eyes glassy with unshed tears. I see the faint panic on his face and I know he didn't expect me to become emotional in a moment like this, but what we're saying, what we're doing, everything we've experienced today feels monumental.

Life-changing.

"I love you, August," I whisper, shocked that I could be so overcome with emotion for someone else. This has to be love. What else could it be? "I appreciate what you did for me tonight. How you stood up for me."

"I always stand up for what's mine. And that's what you are, Sinclair. All mine." He goes still and ducks his head almost like he's embarrassed. "I let you down before but I vow to never do that again."

"You've never let me down. Not since we've been together like this." He lifts his head, his gaze meeting mine and I cup my hand around the back of his head, tugging down. Our mouths meet in a soft, sweet kiss. "I forgive you, August." For what, I'm not exactly sure but it feels like he needs this from me. "But you'll have to make it up to me for the rest of your life."

"I will." He starts to move again, steadily thrusting inside me, ratcheting up that familiar feeling, my orgasm imminent. "I swear to God, Sin. I'll do my best to make sure you'll never want for anything."

"All I want is you," I say, gasping when the orgasm sweeps over my body.

"You've got me, baby," he whispers against my cheek. "You've got me."

EPILOGUE

AUGUST

M<small>AY</small>

As I watch my girlfriend, the love of my life, talk animatedly with her best friend Elise, all I can think is, I am a lucky man. That Sinclair is mine.

All mine.

She catches me staring, doing a double take, that slow, delectable smile appearing on her face and I want to lean over the massive table and kiss it off her but that would cause a scene and we're right in the middle of my post-graduation dinner with my family and Cyrus and his family so there's no point.

I'll just kiss her later tonight. All night long if I'm so inclined. All over her body.

Sounds like the best plan I've had in a while.

Sin blows a kiss at me, making Elise laugh, and I can't stand it any longer.

"What are you two talking about?"

Their laughter dies, matching mischievous smiles on their faces.

"You'll never believe it," Sinclair says.

"Try me."

They share a look and Elise is the one who announces, "Rafe and Tim are together. Romantically. Like they're a couple."

I go silent, taking in what she said. Running it through my brain over and over again until all I can manage to say is, "What the actual fuck?"

They burst out laughing, in on the joke that I'm not privy to and while a part of me is aggravated, I'm also glad to see Sinclair having so much fun with her friend. These two are troublemakers together. Elise is what my mother would've called a bad influence when we were younger, but there's something so damn likable about her, I don't worry about it when they spend time together. Sin is the rational one and Elise needs to be reined in on occasion, which makes them a well-balanced pair.

"It's true," Sin says with a nod, her lips curled into the cutest smile. One I want to kiss off. I think I'm obsessed with her mouth. As a matter of fact, I'd like to stuff it full with my dick. A graduation present for myself, so to speak. "Elise has always suspected they had a thing for each other."

I know all about the throuple situation Elise had with Rafe and Tim—I was shocked as shit when Sinclair told me—but I had no idea the guys were into each other.

"When we'd hook up, sometimes they forgot about me," Elise says. "I knew then, but they were in total denial."

"Interesting." I stroke my chin, thinking of the many times I believed I had legitimate beef with Tim and it turns out he was into Rafe all along. Life is a wild ride. "I hope they're happy together."

Sin's mouth drops open. "You don't mean it."

I shrug. "I do. Why would I wish them ill will?"

"Because you hate Tim," Sinclair reminds me.

"Not if he isn't a threat. And he hasn't been for a while." If ever. "What can I say? I'm a changed man."

"Uh huh." She slowly shakes her head, her eyes glowing and I have a feeling she's dying to get her hands on me too. Stupid dinner party has to go and ruin everything.

We're in the city, at a restaurant not too far from my apartment. My parents are in for the weekend, staying at their penthouse not too far from my building and of course, Iris and Brooks are with us, too. Their sweet little monster is spending the evening with Brooks' mother so my sister is drinking copious amounts of alcohol and running her hands all over Brooks every chance she gets, which I'm trying to ignore. Vaughn is also with us tonight. He brought his little high school girlfriend and they're wrapped up in their own conversation, ignoring all of us. She's an adorable blonde whose name is…fuck.

I don't know.

Cyrus's parents are sitting close to mine and Cyrus is next to me, downing one scotch after another, getting shit-faced and feeling melancholy. Nostalgic.

"Remember the time we broke into the library our freshman year and wrapped the entire front desk in toilet paper?" Cyrus asks me, slurring his words.

"What? I've never heard this story." Sinclair rests her chin on top of her curled fist, her elbow propped on the table. "Tell me more, Cyrus."

They get along, my best friend and the woman I love, thank Christ. The problem though? He constantly fills her head with stories about our sordid pasts, always making me look like an epic tool. Sinclair eats these stories *up*. Like she's doing right now, listening to Cyrus go on, her gaze never straying from him while he regales her with exaggerated tales about our frat.

"We were getting hazed and the seniors in our frat were fucking bastards. I can't believe all the shit they made us do." Cyrus rests his fisted hand against his mouth, burping into it. "We were much easier on our pledges."

"We were not," I remind him, shaking my head. "I am a nightmare. So are you."

We keep up the steady conversation, Cyrus and I sharing story after story while Sinclair and Elise seem to eat them up. Elise keeps sending sultry looks in Cyrus's direction and his drunken ass keeps sending flirtatious winks and smirks back. By the time we're leaving the restaurant and walking back to my apartment arm in arm, Sin and I discuss their potential.

"Do you think they'll hook up tonight?"

"They did leave together," I remind her.

"Oh God. I'm sure they're going to do it." Sinclair sighs. "Elise isn't interested in a steady relationship with anyone."

"Perfect. Cyrus is very much a fuck 'em and leave 'em kind of guy," I tell her. "Maybe they could have a summer fling."

"Or a one-night stand. That's my prediction."

"I'm sure we'll hear all about it. At the very least, Elise will text you all the dirty details."

We're quiet for a moment, walking along the sidewalk, my thoughts skipping ahead to getting Sin in my bed and naked the moment we walk through the door.

"You were like Cyrus too, once upon a time," Sin points out, leaning her head against my shoulder for a brief moment before she tilts her head back to catch me already staring at her pretty face. "You're not a nightmare anymore, you know."

"You don't think so?" I lift my brows, shocked it stuck out to her, me saying that.

She slowly shakes her head. "You've mellowed out these last six months."

Six months ago, I would've been offended. Mellowed out? Sounds like an absolute insult. I prided myself on my assholish ways. Now, though?

"I suppose I have." I steer her toward my apartment building, nodding when the doorman wishes us a good evening and holds the door open for us. We enter the lobby and I lead Sinclair toward the elevator. Within a minute, we're in my apartment and I've got my hands on her waist, trying to figure out how to take off her pale pink sundress.

"August." She slides her way out of my hold, flashing a smile over her shoulder before she starts running down the hall that leads to my bedroom. "I refuse to let you fuck me against the door again."

So I've got a thing for fucking Sin against a door. What's wrong with that?

"Hey, I'm the one who just graduated. Don't I deserve a special present?" I remind her as I pause in the doorway, watching as she undoes one tie on her shoulder, then the other, letting the straps fall down, as well as the front of her dress, exposing her chest and her perfect tits. Her nipples are hard and my mouth waters just thinking about sucking on them.

"Oh I know. Didn't you see your special message?" She bats her eyelashes at me, tilting her head to the side and I glance over at my dresser. The mirror that hangs above it has a message written in dark red lipstick.

CONGRATULATIONS, AUGUST.

I'M SO PROUD OF YOU! I LOVE YOU.

XO,
SIN

My heart expands to about three sizes bigger than normal. It's silly, that I feel this emotional over her message, but it feels like a full circle moment. "I love it."

"I thought you might." Her smile is coy. "Now tell me what you want. Whatever it is, I'll do it."

I think of all the many things I want to do to this woman, with this woman. But only one lingers at the forefront of my mind.

"How about a blow job?"

"Well, that was easy. Deal." She gets rid of her dress, standing in front of me naked and damn it, I never even realized she wasn't wearing panties tonight.

"Perfect." I'm undoing the buttons on my shirt, shrugging out of it and letting it fall onto the floor. "I was staring at your mouth all through dinner, thinking about stuffing it with my dick."

She laughs, the sound rippling through me, leaving me feeling satisfied. "So romantic, August."

"That's me. An incurable romantic." I lunge for her, making her squeal, both of us tumbling onto the mattress until I've got her pinned beneath me, my face in hers. "I love you, Sin."

The laughter dies on her lips and she lifts up, her mouth practically on mine as she murmurs, "I love you too, August."

I kiss her as if everything depended on it, grateful. Life has become much sweeter with Sin in my life.

By my side.

Forever.

EPILOGUE PART 2

AUGUST

THE PAST

It's the Friday before winter break and everyone on campus is antsy. Anxious to leave Lancaster Prep and return home to celebrate the holidays with their families. Go on glamorous vacations to exotic places and spend all of Mommy and Daddy's money over the next two weeks.

Meh.

We're going home, Iris and I. Another boring holiday season at the Lancaster household. Quite frankly, I'm getting too old for this shit. Spending the holidays with my cousins who are all younger than me and giant pains in my ass sounds like my own personal nightmare. I'd rather go on one of those vacations I see so many other people do. Maybe skiing in Switzerland. Christmas in Paris. New Year's in London. Anywhere but my parent's house.

But alas, I'm stuck doing the family thing.

It's early in the morning as I make my way across campus. Class hasn't even started yet and I'm headed to the dining hall, too keyed up to sleep in like I'd planned. I enter the dining hall to find no one is in there save for one, singular person.

That pretty little freshman who I love to give endless shit to. I don't even know her name, but there's something about her I can't resist. Maybe it's her light brown eyes. The way they happen to somehow glare at me yet also eat me up every time she looks my way. I can feel her hatred for me every time we're close to each other, but there's something else there too. Simmering just beneath the surface.

Heat. Attraction. Chemistry. Whatever you want to call it, it's hard to ignore, though I do my best. I push past the unfamiliar feelings swirling within me as best I can because come on. She's a baby. Only fourteen years old. I touch her and my ass can go to jail.

No thanks.

She's not for me. Despite how every time I see her, I feel like I got struck by a lightning bolt, which is irritating as fuck. Reminds me of what my father has warned me about over the years.

Once you find the woman you're meant to be with, you'll know, son. It'll hit you like a lightning bolt. You'll be struck dumb and you won't be able to see or think about anyone else. Just her.

Unfortunately, that's how I feel about this...little freshman who hasn't quite grown into her body yet. She's all arms and legs and those atrocious braces on her teeth. She tries to put on makeup but it's either too much or not enough. I swear every time I see her walking, I worry she's going to trip over her own feet, her movements are so damn awkward.

The moment her gaze finds mine, I see the disgust appear on her face. Accompanied by a fair dose of interest. Without thought I approach her, only stopping when I'm standing directly in front of her, my gaze scanning her from head to toe.

Still the same girl with the long arms and legs. The flat chest and not a single womanly curve on her body. She'll be a beauty someday though. I can guarantee it.

"You're up early," I tell her, my voice sharp. I lose all patience when I deal with her, mostly with myself, though I always take it out on her.

"Couldn't sleep." She shrugs. "I'm excited to go home."

I blink at her, unable to form words which is so fucking annoying.

"And nervous," she adds, her lips curving upward. Revealing that the braces are gone. Blinding me with that beautiful smile.

Shit. I can't acknowledge that I noticed the change. To do so would be to admit that I pay attention and with my reputation, I'm not supposed to notice anyone.

They're all supposed to pay attention to me, not the other way around.

"Why are you nervous?" I ask, too intrigued not to question her.

"I don't get along with my parents that well. My mom can be…a lot." She shrugs, and I can tell she doesn't want to talk about them. "What are you doing over the holidays?"

I peer at her, concerned. "Have you lost your mind?"

She rears back a little. "Why do you ask?"

"You're willingly making conversation with me."

"Oh." Her smile returns and I look away, unable to take the sight of it. "I guess I'm feeling the holiday spirit."

"Isn't that generous of you." I hesitate for only a moment. "I'm skiing in Saint Moritz."

The lie drops from my lips easily and I don't know why I say it. Am I trying to impress her? Why do I give a shit what she thinks about me?

"Fancy." She has the audacity to roll her eyes and turns away, her back to me as she calls, "Merry Christmas, August."

"Merry Christmas…" My voice drifts. "What's your name again?"

She glances over her shoulder, a mischievous gleam in her eyes that makes my body react. Which is fucking out of hand because again, she's only fourteen. I'm not interested in her. Not like that.

Not yet, anyway.

"Wouldn't you like to know," she singsongs as she walks away, her skirt swaying. It's shorter than what's considered proper dress code, showing off those long, slender legs and I have an unbidden thought.

Of this girl, only she's older. Beautiful. Fucking stunning, truthfully. Flirtatious and with a smart mouth. I love it when someone doesn't back down from me, which isn't often. I imagine this girl will be feisty when she gets older. Not afraid to speak her mind. She'd give as good as she got.

Maybe, hopefully we'll run into each other again someday. Years from now. And if we do?

She'd better watch out.

EXCLUSIVE

BONUS

CONTENT

SINCLAIR

Chasing after a toddler is…exhausting.

"Where did Astrid go?" August calls from the kitchen. We're at his sister's house, keeping watch while she goes out for the afternoon with her husband. "She was literally with me ten seconds ago."

"You can't look away from her," I yell at him, scanning the living room as I walk through it. "She moves that fast."

A loud giggle sounds, and we both go silent, trying to gauge where it's coming from. I turn in a slow circle, searching, searching. Until I find an Astrid-shaped bump behind the floor-length curtains. I creep toward her, trying my best not to make a sound until I'm directly in front of her. I whip the curtain back with a flourish, making August's niece collapse in a fit of giggles, and I bend down, tickling her stomach before I swoop her up into my arms.

"Hide-and-seek!" she proclaims, clapping her hands together.

"Your father should've never taught you that game."

I turn to find August standing in front of us, his hands on his hips and his glare directed at Astrid, who's wiggling in my arms, still clapping her hands and laughing. She loves nothing more than infuriating her uncle.

"Maybe Iris was the one who taught her hide-and-seek," I point out. He loves to blame Astrid's every bad habit on Brooks. *It's the Crosby in her*, he'll say over and over. Like the Lancasters are perfect.

Which he knows they aren't. He just loves blaming poor Brooks for...everything.

"My sister would never," he says with a scoff as he whisks Astrid from my arms and turns her upside down, making her squeal with delight. "You like this, don't you, you little monster?"

"Do it again!" she screams into his face when he flips her back up. She slaps his cheeks with her hands. "Do it! Do it!"

Her wish is his command, making me smile. Making me melt inside. He will do anything for this little girl who has a piece of his heart. He might grumble about her most of the time, but it's a facade. He adores Astrid. And she adores him. They're very similar. I can only imagine the torment he put his mother through when he was this age. Summer has alluded to it here and there when we're all together. How much Astrid is like Whit. A true Lancaster through and through.

That's what makes it extra funny when August blames all of Astrid's supposed faults on her father.

"Someone needs a nap," he tells me, hanging Astrid upside down again, his grip tight on her ankles as he starts to wave her back and forth, her hair dragging on the floor.

"Getting her worked up isn't the way to do this, you know," I tell him, shaking my head. "We need to calm her down."

"You heard the woman. Time to calm down, my little beast." He's got her right side up, his arm wrapped tight around her squirmy body, and she presses her hand on his cheek again, staring into his eyes. "Want Auntie Sinclair to read you a story?"

"Yes!" Astrid shouts, turning her head in my direction, bouncing in August's arms. "Yes, yes!"

I take Astrid and lead her back to her room, where she picks out a book from the many she has on a shelf. I let her run around the plush, pale-pink rug for a few minutes, getting her zoomies out, because the girl is full of constant energy. If I could bottle it up and sell it? I'd be rich.

Within ten minutes we're cuddled up together in her bed, her soft body snug against mine, her fingers tapping at the illustrations on the pages while I read. Her body relaxes the longer I read to her, and I'm glad she chose a book that's longer than her usual picks. It's about two swans who live in Hyde Park in London, and the illustrations are beautiful. The story, sweet. Almost romantic. The swans are in love and never want to leave each other's side.

By the time I'm finished, her cheeks are pink and her eyes are closed. When I shift out of the twin bed, she opens them briefly, her hand going to her mouth as she slips her thumb between her lips. Her eyes close once more, and I know she's done.

Whew.

"She was extra high-energy today," August says to me when I reenter the living room.

I go to where he's sitting on the couch, snuggling up to his side much like Astrid did to me only moments ago. He slips his arm around my shoulders, hauling me in closer. "You didn't help matters."

"It takes a lot to entertain that monster." His voice is soft, his fingers drifting up and down my arm. "You don't mind babysitting her, do you?"

"No, I love it. I used to babysit all the time when I was twelve. Thirteen. I like kids." I rest my head against his chest, the steady thrum of his heart calming me. "Plus, I like helping out Iris and Brooks."

He snorts. "They could hire a team of babysitters. Nannies."

"They like taking care of her on their own," I murmur, resting on my hand on the center of his chest, contemplating if I should tell him something or not.

"She's having another one." August steals my secret from my thoughts, and I lift up, my mouth dropping open when I see the nonchalant expression on his face. He shrugs. "She told me last night."

"She told me yesterday morning." I received the text from her out of nowhere, written in all caps and with a bunch of exclamation points at the end.

I'M GONNA HAVE A BABYYYYY!!!!!!!!!!!!!!

August frowns. "She told you before she told me?"

"I'm a girl. And I'm not her big brother." It's my turn to shrug. "I won't judge."

He appears offended. "I would never judge."

"I'm sure when she texted you, you responded with something like, 'Great. Another beast for us to wrangle.'" I'm half teasing, half being truthful.

His expression shifts to contrite. "I did say something to that effect, yes."

"A baby is a blessing." I pat his chest. "The family is growing."

"It is." His gaze locks with mine, his blue eyes igniting with heat. "Do you want children?"

It's a question he's never asked me before, because come on. We're young. But we are in love, and though I've never said it out loud, I do imagine the two of us together. In the future. Living in a big house in the country, with lots of kids running around.

And what I mean by "lots" is four, tops.

"Because I do. Want children," he says when I haven't answered him, his voice sounding a tinge...nervous? Hmm. August Lancaster is never nervous.

"I do too," I admit, leaning in to press my mouth against his in a brief kiss. "But not for a long time."

A sigh of relief leaves him, and he wraps his hand around the back of my head, bringing our mouths together once more. "Thank God. On both answers. I'm not ready, but I do want them."

"I haven't even graduated college yet," I remind him, tingles spreading over my skin when he kisses me yet again, his tongue diving in for a quick lick. "And I want to be married first."

"My traditional little Sin," he murmurs, our mouths connecting. The kiss turning heated. Our hands start to wander...

"Please tell me you two aren't doing it every time we ask you to watch Astrid."

We jump apart at the sound of Iris's voice, guilt sweeping over me, my face going hot at getting caught. When I dare to look in Iris's direction, I see she's smiling, Brooks looming behind her, his hand on her waist in an almost protective manner. Iris did mention her husband hovered around her constantly when she was pregnant with Astrid, always wanting to make sure she was all right. She made it sound like a complaint, but deep down I think she liked it.

"We weren't even close to doing it," August mutters, his disgust obvious. "Lighten up, Iris."

"So grumpy," his sister murmurs, shaking her head. "How was she?"

"Horrible," August says.

"A perfect angel," I say at the same time.

Iris laughs. So does Brooks. And so do I. Even August smiles and my heart flutters, threatening to soar straight out of my chest. I am a lucky, lucky woman, having this man in my life. And his family.

Life seriously can't get much better than this.

ACKNOWLEDGMENTS

It is the end of an era for me - I'm 90% positive this is it for Lancaster Prep. I know a few of you are going to be upset with me and wonder about certain characters, but I just feel this is the book to end it with. We started with Whit Lancaster and we're ending with his son August. Perfect bookends on either side of the series. While I'm a little sad to be finished with this family, I'm also excited to do different things and write different characters. I owe the Lancasters for the rejuvenation of my writing career, which was something I never expected. But *A Million Kisses In Your Lifetime* changed my career and my life and if I could give a million kisses to Crew and Wren, I so would.

But what a way to end it, am I right? I had the BEST freakin' time writing this book. Specifically August. He is the worst but he's also different from his daddy. I mean, he couldn't be that mean considering who his parents are and they raised him right! Well, they tried...

There's a bit of humor in this book and some of the things August said and thought made me laugh. Just like with his father, I felt like I had zero control over him. He just did and said whatever he wanted. I adore this asshole just as much as Sinclair does and I think they are the perfect match.

I also must thank YOU for continuing to support me by reading my words. I've been writing and publishing as Monica since January 2013 and I'm just so grateful I can still do this. I appreciate you continuing on this journey with me more than you'll ever know. A big thank you to my agent Georgana for the input. You always help me make my books better. To my editor Becky for making my words shine and to Sarah my proofreader who keeps my timelines straight because God knows, I can't. It's my biggest weakness, ha.

p.s. - If you enjoyed *You Were Never Not Mine*, it would mean everything to me if you left a review on the retailer site you bought it from, or on Goodreads. Thank you so much!

*Don't miss the exciting new books
Entangled has to offer.*

Follow us!

f @EntangledPublishing

◎ @Entangled_Publishing

♪ @EntangledPub

AMARA
an imprint of Entangled Publishing LLC